Anonymous

Scarsdale

Life on the Lancashire and Yorkshire Border; Vol. 3

Anonymous

Scarsdale

Life on the Lancashire and Yorkshire Border; Vol. 3

ISBN/EAN: 9783337056506

Printed in Europe, USA, Canada, Australia, Japan

Cover: Foto ©Andreas Hilbeck / pixelio.de

More available books at **www.hansebooks.com**

SCARSDALE;

LIFE ON THE LANCASHIRE AND YORKSHIRE BORDER,

THIRTY YEARS AGO.

IN THREE VOLUMES.

VOL. III.

LONDON:

SMITH, ELDER AND CO., 65, CORNHILL.

M.DCCC.LX.

CONTENTS

OF THE THIRD VOLUME.

SCARSDALE.

CHAPTER I.

THE TRADITIONS OF THE PORTRAIT GALLERY.— THE TEMPTER BAFFLED.

"Ah! le charmant caprice! Te voilà ma belle Rose de Lancastre dans le costume de François I., et vraiment! c'est notre tourelle du château de Blois! Ah! le joli caprice—tu portes un faucon au poing—tu as l'air de suivre avec tes beaux yeux la chasse au haut du ciel. Oh, si j'étais jeune encore, fort, et dispos pour suivre la chasse aux bords de la Loire, avec la duchesse—la sœur angélique—et la belle Rose de Lancastre!"

These exclamations escaped the Duc de Chatellerault, as, leaning on the arm of the duchess and on his cane, he stood, somewhat bent forwards, in the centre of a group opposite the portrait of Lady Mabel. The group also comprised Sir Guy Scarsdale and his daughter, Lord Pendleborough, and M. Malvoisin, who had joined, as we shall see, the party at Scarsdale Hall. The whole conversation which ensued was in French, but we shall only slightly indicate in our translation what was the form of expression used.

" That is the portrait of an ancestress, duke, not of my daughter," said Sir Guy Scarsdale. " She was at the court of Mary of Scots when Mary became Reine-Dauphine, having accompanied her father, John Erskine of Dun, one of the commission sent by the Scotch Parliament to represent them at the marriage with the Dauphin of France."

" Ah! she was then the friend of ' the four Marys of Scotland,' who formed the *entourage* of ' La belle Reine-Dauphine.' She was the intimate of Ronsard and of Du Bellay. Was she long a familiar in that court—the most elegant and joyous, but it must also be confessed, une des plus relâchées de toute l'Europe ? "

"No, duke; she was present with her father, Erskine of Dun, at all the festivities of the marriage of the beautiful but unfortunate Mary, and met at Blois Sir Juan Scarsdale, her future husband, then a chivalrous knight in the lists of the court tournaments, and afterwards a brave companion of Raleigh."

" The portrait of Sir Juan hangs on the opposite

side, duchess;" said Mabel, wishing, vainly, to draw the attention of the duke from her ancestress.

"La belle dame au faucon was then Protestant even in the regency of Marie de Guise!"

"Eleven years had elapsed since Wishart had been burned by Cardinal Beaton, and two years since Knox, released from the work of a *forçat* in the galleys of France, had returned from his grievous exile. In that time he had made many converts under the more tolerant policy of Mary of Lorraine, and among them was Mabel Erskine of Dun, our ancestress."

"But there is something strange—even supernatural—in the fascination of this portrait. I perceive," said the duke, examining the painting with care, "that it is an exquisite work of ancient art; mais je suis tout bouleversé, for I have seen the original to-day. This charming Rose of Lancaster, if she would assume the costume of François I., could not be distinguished from the lady de la tourelle de Blois."

"Take care, duke," said Mabel. "If you have any dread of ghosts, the Lady Mabel haunts this house, and appears in any great crisis of our fortunes to warn us of our foes."

"Ah! you have touched my most rooted superstition! A spectre which haunts my château in La

Vendée warns us when we wander from the traditions of our family. I have seen it several times myself. Une vieille dame, très maigre mais très distinguée, vêtue de brocart antique, passes the foot of my bed, and looks at me for a moment avec des sourcils froncés et un visage sévère."

" Have you a portrait of this lady also?" asked Mabel.

" No—we have only the story of a lady of our house, who laboured with a marvellous devotion during a long life, to restore the then ruined fortunes of our family."

" Our Lady Mabel had a similar character," said Sir Guy Scarsdale. " When her husband Sir Juan was absent with Raleigh she governed her household, educated her son, and greatly increased our wealth, both by her vigorous management of our estates, and by an alliance which she contracted for her son, which brought new possessions into our family. We say at Scarsdale, ' *Let the Lady sleep.*' By this we mean that she is disturbed only by the menace of misfortune to our house. If any one, willingly or unwillingly, would mar the fortunes of our race, she comes. Or if we act unworthily of our name, she comes. That, at least, is the Scarsdale tradition."

" Ah, then I am not so much surprised that the magic of this portrait moved me so much. The resemblance to mademoiselle is perfect, and the spirit of her ancestress must inspire the lady who has inherited her wonderful beauty."

"But Miss Scarsdale wishes, duke, to show you the portrait of Sir Juan," said the duchess, seconding Mabel's efforts.

"A la bonne heure, sœur angélique! It is not every day that one meets a sorceress as potent, to fascinate with her mysterious and supernatural influences. This tradition has nothing in it surprising to me. For, notwithstanding my constitutional superstition, and the visits which notre vieille dame de Chatellerault has had the complaisance to make me after midnight from time to time, quand je marchais rapidement vers la ruine de notre maison, I am a little rationalist—or, if you will, encyclopedist —and I say, Sir Guy, that if you had no tradition about the Lady Mabel, you ought to invent one for so remarkable an ancestress."

"Now turn to Sir Juan, duke," said Sir Guy. "He was almost a lifelong companion of Raleigh, but refused to accompany him in his expedition to Guiana. Yet he visited Raleigh daily in the Tower, attended him to the Privy Council, and stood at his side when he perished on the scaffold."

"Ah! ah! Then the brave English admiral was worthy of his lady, avec ses yeux beaux pleins de mystère.   But is he not also very like Raleigh—or is the resemblance in the beard, the costume, the cap with the plume, and the general contour of the features?"

"The likeness has often been commented on," said Sir Guy Scarsdale.

"So you call this room the cabinet of the Lady Mabel? Your tradition says, '*Let the Lady sleep.*' But she returns to warn you of danger, to deter you from fatal paths, to terrify your secret enemies.   Ah, c'est merveilleux.   But have you a souterrain?   At my château in La Vendée we have a tradition of a subterranean gallery.   I—rationalist and curious—I explored it.   I had it opened, and penetrated even where it passed under the bed of a little river.   La porte de sortie was found in a thicket in a wood, buried under a deep mound of débris.   There were strong grilles de fer in the gallery, and one of oak bound with iron, and clenched with massive studs."

"There is a similar tradition about almost all old houses which have been fortified," said Sir Guy. "Doubtless to many of the keeps and piels of the English and Scotch border such 'souterrains' were attached.   The remains of our ancient keep are probably the foundation of a similar tradition here. But Mr. Holte tells me that an old collier assured him on his death-bed that he had discovered the mouth of a passage in a cove in Scarsdale Wood, and had cleansed it from the fallen shale which it pierced until he encountered a strong oaken door well bolted with iron studs, and apparently barred on the inner side. Mr. Holte had the cove searched, and found the mouth of a passage, but the shale had again fallen so as to block it up. He did not think it worth while to have it cleared."

"Monsieur l'intendant was not encyclopedist enough. He was wrong. These secrets ought always to be unravelled, for smugglers, robbers, and conspirators of any kind may discover them, and, if you are ignorant, you cease to be safe in your own house. I urge you, Sir Guy, to have more curiosity and perseverance than your intendant has shown."

"I cannot but agree with the duke," said Malvoisin. "A knowledge of these secret passages in old houses has sometimes given facilities to crime, and much more frequently afforded an opportunity to work on superstitious apprehensions."

"In one of my manor houses," said Lord Pendleborough, "there are secret closets, with passages in the walls. One of them is called '*The priest's hole.*' It is about the size of a monastic cell, and is lighted by a narrow slit, in an obscure corner of the building; the two others are quite dark, but ventilated by flues, which issue at gratings under the eaves."

" All these signs of past perils met by secret precautions have an interest deepened by mystery," said
Mabel.

" Ah! la belle rationaliste!" said the duke. " For
myself, I have never trembled but in the presence of
that ancient lady of Chatellerault.   Philosophy is
a breastplate of steel; but when a reproach of conscience steals, in the silence and gloom of midnight,
in a supernatural form, upon an interval of awakened
consciousness, I, who am a noble of France, with the
blood of a race of heroes in my veins, I suffer a
horror as of death—a mortal agony of fear."

They passed out of the cabinet into the long
gallery, in which hung a series of family pictures.
The duke had an insatiable curiosity in all objects of
art, archæology, and antiquities illustrative of manners and domestic history.   His collections had been
one of the drains upon his exhausted revenues.   He
therefore proceeded slowly down the gallery, examining each portrait, both as a work of art and as illustrative of the dress and manners of the period, and as
a clue to the family and county history.

The duke was about forty-five years old, though
he looked much older, with elegant features, and
especially a symmetrical brow, delicate nose and lips,
and large eyebrows, which hung over the caverns of
his sunken eyes.   The face, however, was pale and

wasted, though lighted with a continually varying expression, as well as by the flashes of his expressive eyes from their hollow sockets—now scintillating with humour, now gleaming with an almost fierce penetration, and not seldom with a glare of impatience. His attenuated frame was bent. He leaned on the duchess and on his cane—and still walked with pain.

The duchess was tall, with a remarkably regular Grecian profile, and rounded lips and chin—the whole outline being one to charm a sculptor. The forehead was exquisitely smooth, but not broad, and the raven-black hair, parted with simplicity in the front, was gathered at the back of the head, except two long, jet-black ringlets, which fell on the full, well-rounded neck and shoulders. The eyes were tranquil, soft, and gentle; and the skin transparent, but pale. She watched the duke with the tenderness of a daughter.

After passing several other portraits, the duke's attention was arrested by a remarkable picture containing two figures. One had a great forehead shaded by grizzled hair; and shaggy eyebrows, over thoughtful eyes, while a white beard did not wholly conceal firmly compressed lips. The other was the likeness of an ingenuous and energetic youth, whose large eyes beamed full of love and confidence upon the old man's face. On the table between them lay a few books, with some geometrical and chemical instruments, and plans showing that one of their pursuits was strategy and fortification.

"This portrait," said the duke, " is in the style of one of the best Dutch masters, and doubtless some interesting family tradition accompanies it."

"That is the portrait of Sir Hugh Scarsdale—every way a remarkable man," said Sir Guy. "He was the personal friend of Hampden, Pym, and Vane, and resolutely supported the popular party in their parliamentary contests with Charles the First."

"But he has more the air of a profound, solitary thinker," said the duke, "than of a soldier or of a statesman."

"The portrait was taken after he had retired from public life—wearied, perhaps disgusted with its contests. He belonged neither to the Puritan nor to the Presbyterian party. Yet he armed his dependants, and, aided by his personal friends, led a considerable force to the battle of Edge-hill. After this he was one of the most active opponents of Lord Strange in the north of England, where the king's party was the most powerful, having been organized there by Prince Rupert."

"Ah!" said the duke, "those compressed lips and those shaggy eyebrows ought to have told me that the maps and plans were those of battles which he had fought."

"One plan is that of the battle of Marston Moor. Sir Hugh, driven from his own estates, had joined Sir Thomas Fairfax and Cromwell at York, suffered in the confusion of the Parliamentary cavalry when routed by the vigour of Lucas at Marston Moor, but rallied his retainers so as to flank the movements of Cromwell, whose forces turned the fortunes of the day. The other plan shows the battle of Naseby, in which Sir Hugh commanded the Life Guard of Sir Thomas Fairfax, and encountered Prince Rupert, in the 'one charge more and we recover the day,' which the king had personally but fruitlessly directed."

"That stirs my blood!" said the duke. "But how came such a gallant soldier and discerning statesman to wear the beard of a hermit, and turn philosopher?"

"When the king had been seized by Joyce, and had become the prisoner of the Puritans," answered Sir Guy, "our ancestor retired to his estates. He took no further share either in the civil or military contests of the time. He even refused to command the Parliamentary forces in Lancashire. After the king's death, he kept within his demesne, and devoted himself to scientific pursuits, and the education of his son."

" That explains the picture, which truly embodies the whole history. But that great forehead, those deep thoughtful eyes, that ascetic look of research, and that white beard must have given your ancestor the reputation of an alchemist or wizard," said Malvoisin.

" Tradition adds," said Sir Guy, " that our keep was then perfect, and that Sir Hugh carried on his investigations as to the transmutation of metals in a chamber of the tower. At night, therefore, the light of his furnaces gleamed in a long level ray far over the country, and was an object of much superstitious dread."

" But what were the fortunes of the son ? " said the duchess. " Trained by so learned and brave a father, and with such expressive features, it is impossible not to feel an interest in his fate."

" This is Sir Ralph's own portrait as a man," said Sir Guy. " After the Lady Mary married the Prince of Orange, Sir Ralph, having succeeded his father, lived chiefly at the court, or in the camp of the stadtholder, partaking in the counsels of that group of able Englishmen by whom the Prince was attended, and accompanying him in all the perils of the war of resistance to the ambition of Louis XIV."

" A career to train a great general or a minister of state," said the duke.

" Sir Ralph became one of the commanders of the Royal Guard after the Revolution of 1688; but he had no relish for the intrigues of the Catholic and Protestant parties, and soon returned to his estates, only to emerge for a time from the life of a country gentleman, to join William in his expedition to Ireland."

" What is this inscription which I perceive on the frame of the picture?" asked the duke.

" The portrait was presented to our family by the neighbouring Catholic gentry for service done to them by Sir Ralph. The inscription refers to the following circumstances. Warrants had been issued against many Lancashire gentlemen for a conspiracy to aid King James in a descent upon England. Sir Ralph rode from mansion to mansion, and in private interviews with the suspected satisfied himself, that Sir John Trenchard was acting on the information of villains, who had never been trusted by the Catholic party. From the voluntary statements of the gentry, he learned the exact nature of their connection with the court of St. Germains. Armed with this information, he went to Hampton Court with such despatch, that one of his horses died on the way. The king heard all that he pleaded impassively. Then, when Sir Ralph ceased, his majesty opened a bureau, and put into his hands intercepted letters, in the writing of his friends, which proved their correspondence with James, though they fell short of implicating them in the plot of an immediate invasion. The statements of Sir Ralph and the information derived from the letters tallied so completely, that William permitted such gentlemen as had escaped arrest to keep out of the way unsought for, until the storm had blown over, provided they were willing to give their parole as gentlemen, to attempt nothing against his authority within the realm or elsewhere."

"Duchess, this story resembles very much one of our own traditions of the wars of the Fronde, always bearing in mind that we were more truculent and vindictive to our heretics than this King William with his phlegm from the marshes of Holland."

"Sir Ralph seemed to understand the king's humour, for when he asked William not to consider him undutiful or unloyal, if he attended such of his neighbours as were under arrest on their trial, his majesty laconically answered, 'No Scarsdale can be disloyal, and their sense of honour is a safe guide.' Accordingly, Sir Ralph, amidst the cheers of the people, who were deeply incensed against the ministry, rode into Manchester with the prisoners when they were brought to trial, and attended them in court. His personal influence chiefly prevented the witnesses against them from being torn to pieces by the

mob. The knavery of the informers was exposed:—
they were prosecuted by the government: and the
affair was brought before the House of Commons:
the Jacobites had an apparent triumph ; but the secret
clemency of the king created for him friends in a
county where the Catholic gentry were more numerous and powerful than in any other part of England.
This was the occasion on which the Catholic gentry of
Lancashire placed Sir Ralph's portrait in the family
gallery."

" This hero of Protestantism, this asthmatic prince
of marshes and dykes, avec son sang-froid de reptile,
who, coughing and spitting, resisted the chivalry of
France under Louis XIV. !—did he reward his
faithful soldier and adviser only by giving him
the command of his Royal Guards, and the honour
of a seat in his council of war in Ireland?" said
the duke.

" Sir Ralph had prayed the king at Hampton
Court to put his devotion to his person to any proof.
His majesty answered this by summoning my ancestor
in 1695 to Holland, where he gave him the command
of a brigade at the siege of Namur. After the
capitulation, he was employed in the Low Countries
in frequent missions, until the peace of Ryswick. For
these missions, his knowledge of persons in authority,
of the country, and of the conduct of the war,

peculiarly fitted him.   In them he trained his son as his secretary and aid-de-camp."

"Though not a great commander himself, this asthmatic Dutchman, crowned King of Great Britain and Ireland, well knew how to choose his generals and ambassadors, and to inspire them with a supreme devotion. Strange that such a man, with an iron will, could break to pieces all the enterprises of the princes of the Catholic faith," said the duke.

They passed down the gallery, step by step, from portrait to portrait. The duke seemed to have an inexhaustible curiosity about the family history, inter-woven as it was with traditions of war, policy, man-ners, customs, and local incidents. From the copious stores of his own curious reading, the duke uttered caustic remarks on events, characters, and habits. Always the venomous fang of his satire, fastened on any dastardly or treacherous action. Through the mist of epicurean selfishness, and the cloud of disbelief in human virtue, gleamed the chivalry of the noble of France to whom life and fortune were a feather's weight in the scale with honour. However, corrupt had been the habits of the duke, he was a man of the most polished manners, elegant accomplishments, and curious erudition ; and, slave though he had been to the conventionalities by which fashion had gilded vice, the *Dame de Chatellerault* could appeal to a fibre still capable of thrilling, not merely to honour, but to duty, and even to self-sacrifice.

The coruscations which broke from the spirit of so remarkable a man, interested, in spite of themselves, the whole group. The duchess who, as Vavasour had told the duke, had a divine instinct to discern the good, had trusted herself, with unhesitating confidence, to the chivalrous honour of her lord. She seemed to have acquired no little interest in his erudition, accomplishments, wit; and even smiled at his venomous sarcasms and dénigrant habit of imputing selfish motives to seemingly virtuous actions. Her vow, her vow to Heaven! was ever present in her mind. This, this was the test of her truth and sanctity! To be true to that vow. To cherish the duke, despite of himself,—to be his ministering angel, to devote her life, her happiness, everything but her soul to the fulfilment of her marriage vow,—this was the one all-absorbing thought which possessed her being with an over-mastering intensity. This spake in all her acts. In her tender solicitude, calm patient vigilance, forethought for the smallest wants of the duke, and a winning gentleness which caused him always to address her in the tone of an indulgent father, most sympathetic to a beloved daughter.

All this was apparent to Sir Guy Scarsdale, to Mabel, and to Lord Pendleborough, and with the narrative contained in the letters which had been received from Malvoisin, enabled them to comprehend the unconfessed, but magical influence which the duchess unconsciously exercised over the duke. Her attitude was not simply the presence of an exalted purity such as the duke had remembered that Vavasour had described, as that of an angel in the house, gazing with a compassionate tenderness on all his ways. Even the supernatural presence of one so clothed in light might not have been so effectual, as the willing sacrifice of an entire life, in obedience to a vow of love, of honour, and of obedience. The spectral presence of the *Dame of Chatellerault* could make no such appeal to the conscience of the duke as the youth, the beauty, the grace, the gentleness, the perfect purity which, consciously, made this mighty sacrifice.

The duke's party had arrived only the night before this visit to the gallery, and Malvoisin had as yet had no opportunity to relate to Sir Guy Scarsdale the incidents of the voyage.

At length the duke, turning to Sir Guy and Miss Scarsdale, said,—

"A thousand thanks, my dear Sir Guy, and ma belle Rose de Lancastre, I have never been so carried away by the legends of a brave and honourable family. We began with the Lady Mabel; I hope that the last words of that unfortunate James the

Fifth of Scotland, after the fatal defeat of Solway
Moss, will be found true in the best sense in your
house: 'Cette histoire cessera comme elle a com-
mencé. La couronne est venue par une femme, et
par une femme elle s'en ira.' The Rose of Lancaster,
who inherits the beauty and genius of her ancestress,
will also enlarge the fortunes of her family, though
she may change its name and destiny."

Then bowing very low to Sir Guy and his
daughter, and to Lord Pendleborough, the duke led
away the duchess to his private apartments, leaving
Mabel agitated and confused. She had not recovered her equanimity, when Lord Pendleborough
approached to propose a walk in the garden court
until luncheon, for the morning was now far spent.
Her presence of mind had not returned, and assent-
ing, she hastened to search for Miss Wilmslow as a
companion, and to regain her calmness in a short
period of retirement in her own room. Had, then,
the duke penetrated Lord Pendleborough's secret;
or had he only, with subtlety, endeavoured to pene-
trate it by an allusion to her future fortunes which
jarred so strangely through her whole being? Miss
Wilmslow was already out on horseback with Lord
Salmesbury—Mabel hurried back to seek M. Malvoisin—he was closeted with her father. The time to
luncheon was but brief—why should she shrink from

a few turns in the garden court with Lord Pendleborough? Because of the possible interpretation of
the duke's parting speech? That was rather a reason
for unhesitatingly accepting the invitation! So armed
—having bathed her temples with eau-de-Cologne—
Mabel descended to the hall, and found Lord Pendleborough awaiting her there.

"The vision of that beautiful saint, the duchess,
watching her lord with a devoted tenderness is most
touching," said Lord Pendleborough.

"Despite the disgust which I have had of his
reckless life in Paris, and of the horror with which
his conduct in contracting this marriage had inspired
me, I cannot but think M. Malvoisin and the duchess
do him more justice than you have done, Lord
Pendleborough."

"The manly, tolerant nature of Sir Guy also
yields to Malvoisin's prognostications. The duke is
clearly oscillating between the good and evil in his
nature; but to which pole his destiny will be attracted,
I dare not conceive."

"Your bearing to the duke is austere, Lord
Pendleborough," said Mabel.

"Not consciously so; but I confess I have in my
mind the terrible scenes which preceded and accompanied his marriage—certain horrible proposals which
he dared to make to Vavasour, but which his English

nature repelled—and a message to me, vague, but shocking even in its mystery, of which Vavasour was the bearer."

" That was perhaps the oscillation towards evil, followed by his almost mortal sickness—the self-sacrificing devotion of the duchess—Malvoisin's visits and counsels—the voyage—new scenes—and the insensible influence of the duchess on his life."

" So, I confess, I interpret the oscillation towards what is good, which speaks in the patience and tenderness with which he treats his duchess."

" Such a man must be an enigma even to himself —so full of complex emotions, warring impulses, and swaying between such opposite tendencies. But I am also much struck with the interest which the duchess has in the graces of his courtly manners, elegant erudition, polished humour, and the constant flashes of fancy which irradiate his conversation," said Mabel.

" Malvoisin watches the whole phenomenon, like a physician. He is a great confessor in all moral maladies, for he has a profound sympathy with men, even in their errors, and a strange wisdom in pointing out the path leading from the abyss."

Then their conversation ran on for half an hour longer, ere the bell rang to warn them that luncheon was ready. Lord Pendleborough clearly wished to

accustom Mabel to his society, with a sense of security
that he would not recur to the intention which he had
avowed in the Ings of Hacking Hall, until he had
earned a right to renew his suit.

Meanwhile, Malvoisin had sought an interview
with Sir Guy Scarsdale in his library. There he
sketched rapidly the effect of the voyage and change
of scene on the duke. "He had proved a good sailor,
though previously little exposed to the discomforts of
the sea. He had insisted on ministering to the
duchess during her sufferings from sea-sickness—
almost banished her maid—and personally attended
to her wants. When the duchess recovered, he had
set himself to study the management of the yacht,
and to learn to take observations. Then they went
on shore at Scilly, and visited the islands. At
Pembroke, the docks, arsenal, ships of war, and forti-
fications all formed subjects of deep interest. At
Liverpool, in like manner, the forests of masts, the
great packet ships, the vast stores warehoused near
the docks, and the means of enlarging this great
haven afforded by either shore of the Mersey, the
pool of Wallasey, and the whole reach of the estuary.
The duchess had taken a calm delight in accompanying the duke, whose curiosity seemed insatiable, and
whose vigour increased from day to day. So far
for the external and physical phenomena. Occa-

sionally, when the duchess was absent, and he was alone with Malvoisin, the gloom of a profound melancholy overshadowed him.

"'I have committed a crime, and I would bear the punishment, grinding my teeth, and clenching my hands, as I best might,' he would say. 'But to involve in the consequences of my crime this angelic nature! That is what I did not count upon. You, Malvoisin, and that farouche Lord Pendleborough, have lent me your pure vision to gaze upon the spotless purity of that virgin soul.'

"'Wait a while, duke,' I have replied. 'Already you have some relief in the distractions of your voyage. You cherish your duchess with a paternal care. In the homes of England you will find much to help you in your strait.'

"'If the duchess were, in truth, my daughter, I should know what to do. Tenderly as I begin to feel that I could repay her gentleness, I would make her the wife of some honest English lord, like that reserved Pendleborough!'

"'Meanwhile, duke, she has charmed away from you much restlessness, and you find a repose when she reads to you your favourite Italian poets. It is a pleasant task to you to comment to her on all the historical allusions in Dante—to relate to her strange histories of the ducal houses, and of the painters, poets, architects, men of letters, reformers, and patriots of your long-loved Italy.'

"' Ah, Malvoisin, you have a wonderful power to charm away the worser part, and to awaken from its trance the better being within me. What you say is true—when that sweet voice makes music to me of the divine Dante, I forget everything in the wish to breathe his poetic ardour into the sacred calm of her life.'

"' Let this better being prevail, duke. Pursue these delicious associations. In poetry, in letters, in the arts, in science even, in which you take so much delight, I can conceive that the duchess may find a pleasure equal to your own.'

"' So it is while the devil returns not to the house which you have swept and garnished. But he will return, and seven other devils with him. Then a reign of passion, of rage, of frivolity, reckless waste in luxury, slavish idolatry of fashion, sensual excess, will make riot again in all the chambers of the house !'

" I have not found it wise to struggle with this mood of self-reproach," continued Malvoisin, address-ing Sir Guy Scarsdale ; " for in that frenzy he forms the most extravagant plans. One thing, however, is fixed in his mind. He has determined on an inter-view with Lord Pendleborough. As far as I can

fathom his motives, his desire for this interview
arises from a suspicion that Vavasour and I may
be right in assuring him, that he has entirely mistaken Lord Pendleborough's character in trying it
by a foreign standard, and especially by those with
which the duke is most familiar. Having arrived
at the conviction that the duchess is a saintly exception to all his experience, I fancy that he desires
to test the truth and manly integrity of Pendleborough."

At the luncheon table the party reassembled, and
as they rose to leave the room, the duke, with his
usual ease and grace, placed his hand within Lord
Pendleborough's arm, and gradually drew him away
from the rest, discussing various indifferent topics.
They wandered for some time up and down the
portrait gallery; and, at length, entered the Lady
Mabel cabinet, when the duke gently shut the door,
and threw himself into an easy chair. Gradually,
he had drawn the conversation to his own life
since his marriage. To the revelation to him of the
character of the duchess. He described his own
illness, and her tender solicitude—the strange agony
of remorse with which he had been plagued—the perplexity into which he had been plunged—and the
devious paths by which he had endeavoured to
escape from his embarrassment. He alluded only

briefly to Vavasour's visit, but described the total collapse from which he had been rescued by Malvoisin. The incidents of his voyage, and the sources from which he had derived consolation, and some renewal of health, especially his hours with the duchess — her beautiful reading of his favourite Italian authors—and his own paternal instruction were rapidly sketched. This preface over, he continued,—

" A new danger now begins to threaten me. Two months ago, I could not have conceived it to be possible ; but you, Pendleborough, who so nobly interested yourself in the destiny of the duchess, you, at least, will participate my own astonishment, when I confess to you that I encounter the great but unforeseen danger of becoming the lover of my wife."

Lord Pendleborough remained calm and cold, while he replied, without betraying any sign of surprise or emotion,—

" Under ordinary circumstances, the danger of such a passion would be small ; but, doubtless, as a man of honour, duke, you feel that such an emotion would be only a perplexity to you."

" You give expression, my dear Pendleborough, only to the smallest part of the doubt which afflicts me. The tender devotion of the duchess ought not to be a mere sacrifice. I cannot accept it from her simply as a religious act. From day to day—nay, from hour to hour, the sœur angélique de la charité chretienne fades away from me. She might be truly my wife, if I, indeed, could become worthy of her. But for that I must again be young and pure—sans un triste souvenir des orgies d'une vie passée parmi la tourbe de Comus."

" The devotion of the duchess will know no limit," said Lord Pendleborough, "except that assigned to it by the sense of religious duty, from which it springs; for she feels that you are a noble of France, to whom a thousand deaths were preferable to a breach of his plighted word. And I, too, know, that no such thought could cross your grace's mind."

"Cela va sans dire. A plighted word is like a gage of battle, to be defended to the death. But, I fear, Pendleborough, that you scarcely understand me. If I foresee the danger of a tormenting love for the duchess, I would also save her from a life devoted to a man whom she can only love, as a daughter may love a father over whose character she mourns, but a man also who in his despair may plunge again into the life of Paris, to assuage the remorseful suffering of an agonizing position."

" Certainly your *ménage* in Paris, duke, would be one of inextricable perplexity, even if you were not tormented by the despair to which you point, as the possible consequence of your marriage."

"But consider, for a moment, if you can, the frightful situation of the duchess, when these delicious hours of poetry and friendship in an English family are exchanged for the corrupt and frivolous society in which I live."

"The duchess will remember only her vow. She will remain an angel in your house, bright and pure. She may pine—nay perish—she will regret that her death will be the reproach which she cannot hide."

"I have discussed often and often with Malvoisin, whether there is not some means by which so shocking a catastrophe may be escaped."

"Malvoisin is both a penetrating and a sympathizing counsellor, duke."

"You know that, before my marriage, I had wasted all my estates in the luxury of my establishment at Paris—in my collections of paintings, of antiquities, and in every department of art. One cannot cherish fashion, art, science, letters, luxury, pleasure, equipages, play, and splendid fêtes to the governing circle of France, without a vast outlay. The territories of my ancestors were, therefore, all mortgaged, some of my collections were even sold, and remained in my cabinets and galleries at an annual rent from their former reckless possessor."

"You never concealed the state of your fortunes, in any particular, from the family of the duchess; but I was not aware, until lately, duke, of the absolute ruin into which they had fallen."

"My marriage with the duchess was a temptation of the devil, who suggested to her parents, that they should propose to me to place their daughter at the head of the *beau monde* of Paris, as Duchess of Chatellerault."

"Of that I am a witness," said Lord Pendleborough. "For both the marquis and marchioness were eager for the marriage, and expected their daughter to acquiesce, as girls taken from convents do, when quite guileless and ignorant of the world. They are usually dazzled by a coronet, and a position of the highest fashion and distinction. The father and mother had no doubt that they made a good bargain for their daughter, in purchasing your Grace's title and domination in Parisian society, with the fortune given to their daughter by her uncle."

"A thousand times thanks for the exact justice of your statement of the motives of the parents of the duchess. For myself, you will readily conceive that my experience of women had not prepared me to find in my bride a saint, formed after the purest legends of the Church, with a divine instinct, piercing into the recesses of all spirits, and reading, with angelic eyes, the terrible secrets of our consciences."

"But I remember, duke, that you at once consented to put your estates in trust, to repay the whole of your future duchess's fortune to her at your death. For that purpose, the mortgages were to be paid off by her dotation, and you assigned her a considerable separate income during your life."

" But for the repose de cette vieille dame de Chatellerault, when I was, quite recently, ill in La Vendée, I directed my notaries at Paris to sell some of my curiosities of art, and to redeem others pledged to my creditors. When these preliminaries are completed, my notaries will place the whole of my collections of art in trust, beyond the greed of creditors, or the risks of my own lavish life, to repay to the duchess the interest of her fortune."

" That is done like one of the purest race of the ancient nobles of France ; but, you have already said, duke, that this was not the sacrifice made by Mademoiselle de Clisson, for that future on which you dare not look."

" Alas ! no, Pendleborough. I gaze at this terrible future, as one is fascinated by the depth of an abyss, through the gloom of which one catches an agonizing glimpse of some victim who falls to a certain and swift perdition."

" Have you also discussed this future, duke, with
Malvoisin ? "

" Certainly ! And he replied with the calm dignity of a high and sympathetic intelligence to the
heights of which I cannot climb. All the wayward and strange suggestions of my despair were
laid bare before him, for I suffered the torments
and the temptations of hell, and one thought alone,
suggested by Malvoisin to my mind, saved me
from death by my own hands. He said to me,
that if I desired a catastrophe, truly tragical and
without remedy, that might be brought about by
swallowing the little bottle of prussic acid of which
I had spoken to him, and bequeathing to the duchess
the agonizing and indelible conviction, that her
heavenly apparition had driven me to an eternal
perdition."

" Malvoisin is a man of such lofty genius and rare
virtue, that such a warning from him, duke, doubtless came to you with the force of truth."

" I have renounced this suggestion of despair.
But my agony continues. The good counsels of
Malvoisin—the distractions of my journey—have
partially restored my strength. But, I repeat to you,
Pendleborough, I encounter the great danger and
temptation of loving my wife. Before, then, this love
becomes a supreme passion, I ask, whether there are

no means by which this marriage may be dissolved, without wrong to the duchess?"

"The duchess is acquainted with the utter ruin into which your fortunes had fallen before your marriage, and if your project were to restore to her both her liberty and her fortune, I have no doubt she would consider it impossible to reconcile with her vow your utter destitution."

"That is exactly what Malvoisin has suggested to me; and this elevation of conscience and feeling, though it afflicts me, increases the danger which I experience, of a growing love for this angelic nature. But, there is another method, at which I have not hinted to Malvoisin. The mind of the duchess is in perfect harmony with English manners and opinions. Had she been free to choose for herself, as your beautiful English ladies are, she would doubtless have found some gentleman, distinguished by birth and wealth, noble, brave, and pure, to whom she could have given her heart with her hand."

Lord Pendleborough turned to the duke's face, and found his keen and cavernous eyes gleaming with a strange and eager fire, as though they would search the innermost recesses of his heart. To this intense gaze, his own austerely placid expression was an answer.

"In yourself, Pendleborough, she has found a

brother, who has known how to receive the homage of the most beautiful women of the courts of Europe without apparent emotion. I wish to assume the position of an English father to my wife. I desire to give her the liberty of an English lady, to choose among all the rich nobility of your country a man worthy of her, to whom she can trust her future happiness, and then I will dissolve this marriage! The fortune of the duchess shall be her dotation, and I will retain during my life a third of the revenues of my estates, to satisfy the duchess and her husband that they are not made happy at my expense."

Whilst the duke spoke, Lord Pendleborough received the intense flashes of his eager eyes impassively. The duke talked with an unnatural deliberation, broken by slight pauses, in which his jaws seemed fixed by a passing spasm ; and a purple spot, which had appeared in each cheek, became livid. When he ceased, he drew in his breath involuntarily, almost like a hiss. After a short pause, Lord Pendleborough replied,—

" Your project, duke, is founded on a series of fatal misconceptions. The duchess could not possibly, with her perfect simplicity and sanctity, accept the position of being the daughter of her husband, in order that she might be courted and won by a suitor for a happier marriage. Nor would any Englishman, whom the duchess could honour by her affection if she were really free to choose, try to win the love of a wedded wife, which she could only give by infidelity to her vow."

"Well, then, there is one last resort, before I become the victim of a fatal love. Would the duchess accept a divorce, with the restoration of her fortune; and, for the satisfaction of her conscience, would she leave me, during my short life, the third of the revenues of my estates of which I have spoken?"

The intensity of the duke's gaze now resembled the glare of a wild animal, rushing upon its prey. The eyes became suffused with red, the eyebrows were involuntarily contracted, a great vein filled on the forehead, and the teeth were set. No part of this phenomenon escaped Lord Pendleborough, whose impassive calm seemed quite unruffled.

"No noble of France makes propositions to a man whom he addresses as the brother of his wife, which he would not fulfil to the letter."

"To the most insignificant particular!" said the duke.

"Your conversation has also prepared me for some deliberate result of your conferences with Malvoisin, and I regard this as a well-weighed decision, the alternative of which is, that your affection for the duchess may cease to be paternal."

" That is the spectre which haunts the future with a menace of misery and ruin."

" I have no right to anticipate the decision of the duchess, if the whole question were calmly placed before her. That which seems to me paramount in her mind is the religious obligation of her vow. She will bring every question to this test. Her happiness means peace with heaven and her own conscience! There is one way, duke, to reconcile both her vow and your possible affection. I have no right to offer counsels to a man of your race, who has had twenty years more experience of life than I. But, duke, may not your duchess be a ministering spirit, with power to lead your subtle and keen genius into a new path, towards an altar at which you shall both renew the vows of your marriage, with a deeper sense of their obligation ? "

The duke had listened in the same eager, intense attitude. When Lord Pendleborough ceased, he sank back in his chair exhausted, closing his eyes, and a slight tremor quivered through the muscles of his face, now become deadly pale.

Lord Pendleborough opened the casement of the room, and when he had done so, there was a silence, in which he watched the duke.

During this long pause, his attention was arrested by the creaking of the floor, apparently behind the panels of the room, and by a rustling sound, as though some one had brushed the woodwork with a robe. The duke was recovering, and he turned to listen, lifting his finger expressively. After a pause, he said,—

"I fear there is a secret gallery behind the wainscot near to us, and that some one has had an opportunity of listening to our conversation."

By and by the duke revived sufficiently to walk with Lord Pendleborough into the gallery, and thence to his private apartments, where he wished to repose. The ladies were all abroad on horseback, or in carriages. Lord Pendleborough, therefore, left the duke in the care of his valet.

CHAPTER II.

"LET THE LADY SLEEP."—THE PHANTOM.—A CONFERENCE.

THE Duc de Chatellerault appeared much exhausted by the attack of faintness which had succeeded the crisis of his interview with Lord Pendleborough. His valet, however, was full of resources. He approached the duke noiselessly as he lay on a couch in his private apartment, loosened his cravat, gave him after an interval a dose of ether, applied smelling salts to his nostrils, put a warm bottle to his feet and wrapped them in a blanket, and then bathed his temples and forehead gently for half an hour with cold water and eau-de-Cologne. The duke sighed deeply from time to time. By and by the skilful attendant brought a cup of hot tea, with which he had mingled a tea-spoonful of Cognac, and persuaded his master to swallow it. The duke slowly revived.

" Alphonse, thy skill and care do me much good."

" If Monsieur le Duc would put himself in bed for

a few hours, I hope that this little faintness would be altogether at an end before dinner."

" You are right, Alphonse, it is not well to expose one's infirmities in the open day."

So saying the duke rose languidly, and taking his valet's arm, with the help also of his cane, moved slowly into the next room, where he was soon undressed and in bed. After a while he dismissed his attendant, directing him to come to dress him half an hour before dinner time.

The room was panelled with dark oak in deep mouldings. Opposite the foot of the bed was the fireplace, in which, as it was an autumnal afternoon, flashed intermittingly a low fire kindled on the hearth. The room was elsewhere darkened, for the thoughtful attendant had closed the shutters, and drawn the thick curtains over them. The duke lay wakefully, half propped up by his pillows.

Above the chimneypiece was a large full-length portrait of a courtier with moustaches, in a suit of velvet, with a frill of point lace descending from the neck as a collar, deeply indented so as to form a sort of *baldequin*. At the wrists cuffs of point lace in like manner lay flat upon the sleeve, with similar deep indentures pointing to the shoulder. The dress sword worn at the side, with a buckle of silver, showed that this was a court costume. The duke's eye examined it with the curiosity of an antiquarian, while he ruminated on his interview with Lord Pendleborough.

" The last arrow is gone from my quiver," he soliloquized. " These English are past conception perplexing. I am no match for their imperturbable self-possession. This Pendleborough baffled me when I would, before my marriage, surprise him into a revelation that he had been the secret counsellor of the duchess. Truly, to this day, I know not whence her knowledge of the mode of appealing to my honour was derived. Then, to-day, what am I the wiser? I have penetrated by an adroit thrust the little secret that lies hid under the corset of my fair rose of Lancaster. Her *fierté* cannot altogether hide emotion. My allusion to the dying speech of Jacques V. d'Ecosse was a Parthian dart which disturbed even my beautiful friend. Can it be possible that Pendleborough was armed against the attractions of Mademoiselle de Clisson, even during her touching confidences in the valley of the Allier by a previous engagement, or by a secret but yet unavowed attachment to this charming heiress of Scarsdale? Malvoisin is impenetrable when he pleases. Profound as a well of truth, there is a clear crystal at the bottom. But let me adopt this hypothesis. I have proved the duchess to be a saint, with a tender, gentle woman's nature, full of the love of a daughter for her unworthy lord. Well, I am sure that Malvoisin is a man of genius, learning, and truth. A great physician for the body and the soul. He is earnest and pure. So far, so good; that is firm ground. Then let me trust appearances in Pendleborough. He has been a fearless hunter and traveller, of a haughty, reserved bearing, indifferent to the homage of fashion. Has he then really been preserved from the vanities and corruptions of our courts by a farouche, virgin Saxon nature, by the counsels of this brave Sir Guy Scarsdale, and by a growing love for his daughter? That would explain everything plausibly, if one might believe it possible to find such a group of human creatures. Certainly I have subjected Pendleborough to an almost satanic temptation, in what happened on the Allier, in my message by Vavasour, and in our interview to-day. He has to all appearances been constant in a calm, imperturbable resistance, never offensive in manner, but consistent with an utter repugnance to my suggestions, the extent of which revulsion may be concealed by his desire to keep on terms with me as a friend of the duchess. I could not even surprise him into one expression of disgust or hatred. Shall I renew this experiment, or shall I be satisfied?"

The duke mused thoughtfully; some letters at the

back of the fireplace caught his eye—they were letters of old English character cast in the iron in the reredos below the Scarsdale escutcheon, but so placed above the light on the hearth as to be illuminated by it. The duke, slowly deciphering them, read :—

Let the Lady sleep.

A superstitious qualm seemed to thrill through him. He closed his eyes. These had been the private rooms of the Lady Mabel. This had been her bed. "Is there anything really in these superstitions? Is that ancient Dame de Chatellerault really a phantom, or an illusion, called up by an awakened conscience? I never quail, except before that severe presence visiting me in silence and in darkness, to rebuke me with the frown above her piercing eyes. Yet here I am a serpent among the flowers: dragging the trail of my polluted being through this paradise, whispering the suggestions of evil into pure natures—fascinating, by my subtle gaze, innocence to flutter within my reach—plotting, it may be, ruin to the happiness of this English soldier's home, but baffled, tormented. O conscience! conscience! am I not then wholly lost? Is it possible to follow that suggestion of Pendleborough, and to find reconciliation at the altar of faith—peace in penitence, and happiness in a new vow?"

Thus musing, the firelight gradually faded from the duke's sight, his head drooped forwards, and he fell into a gentle slumber. All was quite still in the chamber, so that even the flicker of the flame on the hearth could be heard, as it shed a fitful light upon the interior of the bedstead, which was reflected on to the portrait, framed in the oak panel over the fireplace.

What was that noise? A sharp, sudden sound, as of a grating hinge, and the rustle of a woman's dress. The duke was startled! He raised his head, suddenly glancing with his inquiring eyes at the legend—

Let the Lady sleep.

opposite the foot of his bed. But ah! a new illusion! The courtier in the velvet suit and point-lace is gone! His place is occupied by the figure of the Lady Mabel, in the hunting dress, but not leaning from the spiral of the tourelle of Blois, but erect, in an attitude of warning, gazing upon him with contracted brows, and hand clenched on her riding whip. The duke sprang at once from his couch, and rushed with vehemence to the foot of his bed, but, encountering the footboard, was compelled to withdraw his eyes for a moment, as he surmounted that obstacle. When he raised them again, the vision, illusion, or whatever the apparition was, had disappeared. There was the oaken panel on which was painted the knight in the velvet dress with point lace and dress sword.

The duke, in spite of himself, almost staggered back, so great was the shock which he experienced. The same mortal quiver passed through his frame— the same pang in the region of the heart, as when he had seen the Dame de Chatellerault. Yet the speculative sceptical nature of the duke had something to suggest. The vision seemed like an actual being, standing in a recess where now was the oaken panel. The duke drew over his shoulders his *roquelaure*, and set himself to examine patiently the panel with the aid of a wax candle, which he had lighted. Though careful and prolonged, his investigation led to nothing but disappointment. Wearied, he returned to his couch, musing, sceptically. But, by and by, fatigue triumphed, and he slept until roused by his valet.

The duke dressed in silence. So absorbed was he that he appeared not to hear the inquiries of Alphonse as to his health. His attendant, accustomed to these fits of abstraction, forbore to trouble his master. By and by, the duke crept into the adjoining cabinet, and found another warm cup of tea awaiting him. He had scarcely sat down to drink this, when the duchess entered, in a riding habit, fresh from the keen autumn air.

"I pray your pardon, duke, for I have had a very interesting ride with my beautiful friend, Mademoiselle Scarsdale."

"Nay, Marie, ma sœur angélique, this horse-exercise is most favourable to thy health. Tell me, then, dear duchess, what thou hast done?"

"First, we called at the parsonage of M. le Curé, vicar of the parish, where we found a sweet and holy daughter, white and beautiful as a *fleur-de-lys*."

"Vraiment, another charming friend, as I hope!"

"Assurément, duc, we left our horses there, to walk by a road which pierced a wood in a deep ravine, until we reached a little lake in the middle of an amphitheatre of rocks and trees, where there was a hamlet of poor weavers, who suffer much from want. We visited their cottages, where my two dear friends distributed their alms, read from the Holy Scripture to the sick, and ministered to them a sweet and sympathetic comfort."

"Then, my dear Marie, all the angels are not sœurs angéliques of the true Catholic faith?"

"Fi donc, duc, je ne te dirai plus si tu me reponds par des mots encyclopédistiques. But, I fancy, that you have an air of chagrin and fatigue, duc?"

" Du tout—du tout, this beautiful English colour on thy lips and cheeks, and the joy which sparkles in thy eyes revives me from some sad souvenirs. But, Marie, it is time to dress for dinner, my child."

The duke kissed the hand of the duchess, with a tenderness, which mingled the homage of the courtier with the love of a father. She left the cabinet for her own chamber, gaily kissing her hand to him. He sank back into his chair, moody and distracted.

" Why do angels of light visit such as I am? What have I in harmony with the purity of such a being, except the mere dress of external refinement, cloaking the mystery of iniquity within? Do they come, these angelic visitants, to torture us with self-reproach? To disclose by the glory of their celestial presence the cavernous secrets of our con- sciences? To shed the light of eternity upon the memory of evil before our time? Or is it true, that notwithstanding the groans which rise from all creation, there is mercy, pardon, redemption, for all, revealed to us in the life of that perfect, sinless, but suffering Man, in whom was the fulness of the God- head, bodily? That suggestion of Pendleborough's seems the flower of the seed sown by Malvoisin, and if there be mercy and redemption, surely no angel of pardon was ever fairer, purer, or more holy than Marie!"

So soliloquized the duke, lying almost prostrate in an easy chair in the private cabinet, awaiting the return of the duchess.

Before the duchess returned, Sir Guy Scarsdale entered the cabinet.

"Duke," said Sir Guy, "I came this afternoon to make a little explanation to you, but regretted not to find you here. We are in the midst of a serious manufacturing crisis, arising from the displacement of the hand by the power-loom. We have had a machine-breaking outbreak, caused by the instigation of some men, the victims of socialistic principles, and joined by desperate ruffians, who hope to profit by the confusion. But there is extreme suffering among the hand-loom weavers, and I find it necessary to obtain general contributions to a relief fund, and to organize a scheme of distribution."

"Ah! then you will have a profound and experienced helper in Malvoisin," said the duke.

"I have availed myself of his counsels; and his secretary, Deloisir, has been engaged with some worthy assistance, in examining the condition of several hamlets scattered through the valleys of our forests."

"But, my dear Sir Guy, though I am not an economist, that interests me very much."

"I came to explain to you, duke, the fact that I find it necessary, in preparation for a public meeting to be held at Bacup to-morrow, to assemble here some of the principal capitalist manufacturers to-night, and to apologize to you, if the drift of our conversation should be very local and technical."

"But, though I am no economist, Sir Guy, I am epicurean; and I am so, I fancy in the ancient sense, for all philosophy and facts on which philosophy is built, if analyzed and arranged by such a mind as that of Malvoisin, delight me."

"For the rest, duke, the gentlemen whom I have invited are types of the highest and most intellectual class of our manufacturers. At our public meeting to-morrow, men risen from the ranks, illiterate, of a coarse mould, contracted ideas, and selfish habits, will form perhaps the bulk of the assemblage. To-night we dine with some of the *élite* of our commercial friends."

"I thank you a thousand times for the uncommon pleasure which I shall derive from the society of these instructed and experienced men, and for the great courtesy of your explanations, however unnecessary."

"Permit me, then, to introduce my neighbours to

you separately, so that, by some few prefatory remarks, I may enable you, duke, to understand the
drift of our conversation."

"That may be, if you are also pleased to be my
interpreter, Sir Guy; for though I understand
English perfectly, my sense of the ridiculous is too
strong to permit me to exhibit the graces of a foreign
pronunciation and idiom, to the admiration of the
hereditary foes of *la belle* France."

So bowing with a sarcastic air, the duke greeted
Sir Guy as he left the cabinet.

When the duke and duchess entered the panelled
drawing-room, with the rich, geometrically-figured
ceiling, which we have before described, they found,
besides the party previously in the house, Mr. Holte
and six other gentlemen assembled. Before dinner
was announced, Sir Guy presented to the duke,
first, a tall man, with a bent figure, troubled with
an asthmatic cough. He had prominent features, in
a rather rude mould.

"Duke, my friend Mr. Roger Sutcliffe permits
me, as you are a stranger in Lancashire, to inform
you that, though he visits me to-night, as exten-
sively embarked in the hand-loom weaving of the
district, he is also a calico printer, in our forest
of Rossendale, and a banker in some of our principal towns. Moreover, he is so well known in our

valleys, by supporting the missionary chapels of the Independents, that we hope much from his acquaintance with the wants of our poor."

After the duke had, with Sir Guy's help, and that of M. Malvoisin, exchanged some phrases of courtesy with Mr. Sutcliffe, a man with a broad, high forehead, and plain but expressive features, was introduced.

"Mr. James Cliderhow (to whom we are indebted for the introduction of some of the most delicate chemical processes in bleaching and printing, and for a determination to raise, at whatever personal cost, the style of our industrial art) wishes, duke, to have the honour of your acquaintance. We may, I hope, visit the Cowslip Printworks ere long."

The duke was soon involved in a most interesting conversation with Mr. Cliderhow and M. Malvoisin, on the patterns of French brocades, china, and chintzes, which was interrupted by the introduction of a third gentleman by Sir Guy.

"There is nothing, duke, that my friend Mr. William Nuttall is more proud of, than the fact that—though he is now one of the most successful, and, I may say, hospitable and generous men in this district—he and his brother entered it with packs of Scotch and Irish goods upon their backs, which they sold at all the homesteads of our moors. You will, in nothing, give Mr. William Nuttall more pleasure, than if you will consent to visit his villages, farms, and works, and to partake of his most generous welcome as a host."

The duke was at once immersed in a conversation with a tall, rubicund man, with a strong Scotch accent, and with the most genial and hearty manners.

This conversation was becoming more and more animated, when Sir Guy brought another man of a similar mould.

"My friend Mr. James Walmersley has quite a typical energy, and all the amenity of John Bull in his best mood. We shall learn much from him about all this district, for he has three stations in it, as centres for his handloom weavers; and I have heard of his leaving the Manchester Exchange in the evening, after the receipt of critical foreign news, and riding through all Rossendale and Pendle, to buy up the stocks of cloth during a winter's night."

The duke had scarcely time to open a conversation with Mr. Walmersley, ere, as dinner was announced, Sir Guy brought two other gentlemen to the duke. One was a tall, gaunt, hardy man, of wiry frame and cheerful mien.

"There is barely time, duke, to name to you my friend Mr. John Balderstone, a man of wonderful energy, as you may imagine, when I tell you that he walked, a short time ago, 210 miles out of Scotland, in three successive days; a most acute, persevering geologist; and in business excelled by no one in shrewdness, patient perseverance, and thrift. The simplicity of his habits is unchanged by the accession of great wealth."

The other manufacturer was a firmly-set man of middle height, with a bluff, open, English face of great good-humour, but also giving evidence of an iron nerve and vigour.

"Lastly, duke, my friend Mr. John Habergham, whom, if he had been bred a soldier, I should select for any task of enduring courage and constancy, for he has built up the fortunes of his family with a sagacity and resolution which has never quailed before any obstacle."

The party then moved into the dining-hall, Sir Guy leading the duchess, and the duke Miss Scarsdale.

They were scarcely seated, when the duke opened the conversation with his beautiful hostess.

"The duchess tells me, my fair friend, that you have had a charming ride."

"The duchess was so much touched by the misery of our poor weavers, and interested in their welfare, that we returned very late."

" You left the hall, did you not, immediately after luncheon ? "

" Yes, within half an hour."

The duke was lost for awhile in reflection, so profound that it gave Lord Pendleborough, who had placed himself on the other side of Mabel, an opportunity to draw her into conversation on the state of the suffering weavers. By and by, the duke seemed to be aroused from his reverie. He led the conversation to the visit to the portrait gallery, to the curious costumes of different periods, the quaint head-dresses, ruffles, collars, modes of arranging the hair, the use of powder exhibited in the ladies' portraits.

" Sometimes an old mansion has a 'garderobe,' where the costumes of the court, of fêtes, and marriages, of successive generations, are preserved as they were once worn by the great ladies and gentlemen of the ancestry."

" We have a remarkable one here, duke ; and my father wishes me, on my birthday, to appear in a splendid brocade worn by our ancestress, the Lady Mabel, at the court of Elizabeth."

" Vraiment, but I shall be much more curious to see you, mademoiselle, in that picturesque riding-habit, de la chasse au faucon, in which your beautiful ancestress is attired for her portrait of the tourelle of the château of Blois."

" But I am sorry to say that Mrs. Holte, who has for thirty years had charge of the wardrobe, has always assured my father that such a dress has never been found. As it was a foreign dress, worn at the French court before her marriage, that may account for its absence."

" Mais non ; for Sir Juan, who desired to revive the remembrance of his first sight of his beautiful and noble wife, would certainly have preserved, with care, the costume in which she was dressed. How, also, could the portrait be painted in England without that rich and picturesque costume ? "

" Nevertheless, duke, both my father and I have searched the wardrobe in vain for this hunting-dress."

" Mais c'est étonnant," said the duke, and fell again into silence, musing thoughtfully on the apparition in his sleeping apartment. After an interval, in which Lord Pendleborough renewed his conversation with Mabel, drifting this time into an account of Colonel Vavasour's health, of which he had received a painful report from Oliver Holte, the duke again resumed the conversation. Now he remarked on the costumes of the men—from the slashed sleeves, picturesque hats and feathers of the Cavaliers—the breastplates, leathern sleeves, and armplates of the Parliamentary leaders—to the plum-coloured coats and flowing wigs of Anne and the first Georges.

"There is a remarkable portrait in my chamber. The point-lace on the neck and shoulders, and on the arms, led me at first to conceive that it was the likeness of a lady in a robe of black velvet. But the upper lip wears moustaches, and I perceive a sword at the side of this courtier."

"It is the portrait of the brother of my ancestress the Lady Mabel, the last Erskine of Dun, who attached himself to the fortunes of his queen, Mary of Scots, with a chivalrous ardour. When the unfortunate queen became a prisoner of state at Fotheringay, he found refuge in this house from the vengeance of the triumphant Protestant party in Scotland, and from the jealous vigilance of the English queen."

"Ah, then, your beautiful ancestress the Lady Mabel hung the portrait of her brother at the foot of her bed?"

"Our traditions say that the Lady Mabel was devotedly attached to this brother, who had conceived a romantic passion for his sovereign. She is said to have hidden him from all pursuit in some secret chamber in this house, and fed him with her own hand."

"Mysterious galleries and secret chambers are to be expected in a house as old as this. But have any of these chambers been recently discovered?"

"Our steward, Mr. Holte, is a matter-of-fact, business-like man, but such discoveries are neither his forte nor that of Mrs. Holte. Their very accomplished son, my father's physician and secretary, has been little at home since he was a boy. I cannot get from an old servant, Seth Diggle, any clue. Nor from a minute examination of such plans of the house as my father possesses, can I divine where such passages exist."

" But the walls are very thick, and it is probable that the secret corridors are constructed within the walls. As for chambers intended for concealment, they were contrived in the enormous stacks of chimneys, by directing the flues from the stacks into the adjacent walls."

" If the tradition have any foundation, the chamber in which Erskine was hid must have been some place of this kind."

" And probably the cell communicated with some cabinet of the Lady Mabel, in which, with door closed and blinds drawn down, she could afford air and ease to her unfortunate brother, and could encourage him by conversation."

The duke again relapsed into silence, and Lord Pendleborough took this opportunity to explain to Mabel, that as soon as Malvoisin could complete some inquiries in which he was engaged as to the weaving population, he would, if the duke's health permitted it, accompany Lord Pendleborough in a visit to his Irish estates.

The ladies left the gentlemen for the drawing-room in a short time, and Sir Guy, placing the duke on his right hand, gradually led the conversation to the topics for the discussion of which he had assembled some of the most influential capitalists of the hand-loom weaving district.

Sir Guy himself introduced the conversation by a prefatory explanation to the duke, that throughout the whole of East Lancashire great distress prevailed among the hand-loom weaving population, owing to the combined effects of the introduction of the power-loom, and of a stagnation in trade. The want of work, the increasing pressure of a privation of almost the commonest necessaries of life, and the erroneous teaching of the agents of the trades' unions that the power-loom was the sole and permanent source of these evils, had prepared the population for some act of despair. They had been in a state in which a spark only was necessary to an explosion. A few desperate men, who were on the council of the Union, had been formed into a secret committee—at first without any very definite design, beyond the protection of any weavers who might be goaded by want to breaches of the peace. Once constituted, however, and in possession of funds for secret purposes, this committee associated with itself, without further reference to the Union, a dozen outlaws, like Floi-by-Neet and Ascroft, armed a gang of about thirty men, and confided the direction of this gang to six, whose astuteness, habits of poaching, stealthy evasion of the law as "moultre" gatherers, or whose desperate position in relation to the master-manufacturers or the police, placed all their instincts on the side of the unavowed and ill-defined designs of this inner council of the secret gang.

The existence of such a body had given a purpose and direction to some partial disturbances, in which the weavers of Harwood and Accrington had plundered the bread-shops, being goaded to this riot by the starving condition of their families. The subsequent excitement, caused by the operations of the military and police, had enabled the secret council to organize a simultaneous outbreak from Pendle Forest, Oswaldtwistle, Harwood, Church, Accrington, and Rossendale, which, as we have seen, had swept like a sudden storm through the valleys, destroying the power-looms, until checked by the defence of the Eagle Mill in Scarsdale Clough, and the complete dispersion of the rioters by Sir Guy Scarsdale's skilful arrangements. The utter failure of the secret gang, headed by Silas Whitaker, to reorganize the outbreak at the Sunday meeting in the Hamilton quarries, and the capture of almost the whole of the members of the gang in Rochdale and at High Collor, were then related to the duke.

Sir Guy spoke in English, and the duke, though at first reclining in his chair fatigued and melancholy, gradually took more and more interest in the narrative, marking his attention by slight ejaculations and interlocutory remarks in French.

"My friends, who have done me the honour to be my guests to-night," continued Sir Guy, "have an immense stake in the prosperity of this district, and I have had one or two interviews with most of them separately.   We are agreed, duke, that the state of trade renders it undesirable to increase the stock of cloth in the market, but that the substitution of the power-loom for the hand-loom is inevitable, when trade revives.   We have to get over a very anxious period of transition.   We propose to meet this by raising a large relief fund.   This we intend to use, in the employment of the weavers in such improvements as would not be undertaken by our local authorities, or proprietors, or capitalists, without the aid of such labour as this fund will enable us to offer.   We propose to make a general proposal to undertake the widening or levelling of township roads, the enclosure of common lands, the embankment of reservoirs, on the following terms.   The work must be approved by our central committee, as one which would not be done now, or for some years to come, without the aid of very cheap labour. Then, we intend to contract for its execution by piece-work; and lastly, to defray from the fund two-thirds of the cost of all public, and one-half the cost of any private works. I am much indebted to M. Malvoisin's extensive observation for the suggestion of this plan, which I am glad to say has obtained the hearty approbation of my guests, and we are met to-night to concert the best mode of securing a general, if not universal, support to this scheme from the manufacturers of the district.

"I ought also to add, that we propose to aid the sick clubs and benefit societies of the district, by contributing one-third of what they may find it necessary to disburse to those suffering from the consequences of prolonged privation. If we find these funds to be prudently administered, and that distress threatens to exhaust the resources of the societies, we intend to increase our contributions to one-half the amount of aid awarded in each case."

"These," said the duke, " are some of the results of the triumphant struggle of public and private liberty in England between the central power, on the one hand, and the privileges of the aristocracy and local freedom of association and self-government, on the other.   M. de Richelieu effectually stripped the French *noblesse* of authority, and so of all interest in local administration.   The Parliament and the municipal councils have become only instruments to register the decrees or orders of the Minister of the Interior.   The kings of France have exhausted every resource of their astute policy, and even lavished their revenues, under Louis XIV., to corrupt the independence of the nobles, and to transform them into titled servants in courtly liveries, bedizened with ribbons and orders, but degraded from all influence under the monarchy—a real nobility only as far as they continued, as faithful and brave soldiers, to sustain the honour of France; otherwise—I blush while I say it—the lacqueys of the king.   In France, then, the government would effect all that you voluntarily undertake."

Sir Guy translated these remarks to his guests, and the duke nodded his assent, as his host proceeded.   Malvoisin added in English,—

" The duke will also see that one reason why the idea of property is more sacred in England than in any other country, is that the passion of personal freedom of action, and of an absolute independence of all State control not unavoidable for the preservation of the internal or external peace, is that which is here paramount.   An Englishman cannot, therefore, conceive that property acquired by industry or skill, or derived from past accumulations, could be administered by the State without a total sacrifice .of public and private liberty. When the passion for equality is greater than that for entire personal freedom, such a conception more easily takes root —though it be only to wither."

" But this pernicious weed," said the duke, " may flourish long enough to sow the seeds of disastrous revolutions and terrible catastrophes."

" The passion for personal freedom is, however, here connected with the absolute independence of the municipality and the parish," continued Malvoisin; " therewith habits of local government and the consequent acquiescence of the people in the administration of an independent local authority. Hence a subordination of ranks, and a natural submission to the local influence of wealth, station, and beneficial but limited powers, are associated with the idea of personal freedom. For these reasons, I have no fear that socialism will ever have the slightest chance of undermining the institution of property in the possession of individuals in England; nor of interfering, to the extent which it has done in France, with the power of bequest. This will continue in England to be regulated rather by opinion and custom than by law."

"What, then," inquired Mr. Cliderhow, who was the most cultivated of the guests, "do you conceive to be our chief dangers in England? I apprehend that we should be agreed that it is necessary for us to provide for the rapid growth of our population by a free commerce in food and the raw staple of manufactures; you would also doubtless encourage us to become the free port of the world, as respects navigation and all international intercourse; while we maintain the police of the seas by our navy, you would advise us to abandon all exaggerated pretensions, such as the right of search; you would suggest that our external policy should be one of non-interference in Europe, but that we should continue to be the pioneers of commercial civilization and Christianity throughout the rest of the world. Though these are great principles, M. Malvoisin, I think I speak the common opinion of my friends at this table, and we do not doubt your concurrence in them."

"In all that comprehensive scheme of public policy I see no dangers over which the genius of this great nation will not triumph. In pursuing this path, your ardour will occasionally lead you into the embarrassment consequent on a glut of the then existing markets. But the tendency of invention will be greatly to cheapen the manufactures which you will export; and that of enterprise, combined with cheapness, wonderfully to enlarge the circle of your commercial relations, and so to absorb the transiently surplus production. You will also have embarrassments from European wars or convulsions, from great revolutions in your own vast colonial empire, and even from the rivalry of foreign competitors to whom you sell your machinery. But over these I am confident of the triumph of your race. There are, however, two or three sources of disaster, to which I never look without alarm."

" Are they political or social dangers ? " inquired Mr. Roger Sutcliffe.

" They are of a mixed character," answered Malvoisin. " First, I watch the enormous strides which your manufactures have made since the invention of the steam-engine, and I ask myself whence the raw material for further progress at the same rate is to be derived. It is not, at present, clear to me whence you are to obtain your wool. But to depend for your cotton mainly on the slave produce of the United States, is to place the destiny of a vast population in this country at the mercy of an institution inconsistent with the theory of the republican constitution, and which must either perish or cause a dissolution of the Union."

" We must confess, said Mr. Roger Sutcliffe, " that while our religious communions preach the abrogation of slavery, our manufacturing system supports it."

"The next great danger which I apprehend, is from the influence of puritanism, in leading a large part of your population to oppose the martial training of your people, and especially the maintenance of the police of the seas, by an armament equal to a contest with the combined navies of the world. No economy, also, would be so false as that which should induce the merchants of England to grudge the payment of the charge required to protect their commerce in every quarter of the globe. As for yourselves, gentlemen, your manufactories are not worth six months' purchase if England lose the command of the ocean."

"We should be," said Mr. Habergham, "in the midst of an unemployed population, ourselves ruined, and exposed to the worst acts of their despair."

"Then, gentlemen," continued Malvoisin, "if you ask me what other dangers there are, you must permit me to explain that I have, for many years, made the state of your workmen a subject of careful study."

"M. Malvoisin," Sir Guy remarked, "has visited this district from time to time, especially in great crises of trade; and he is, perhaps, more familiar than any one at this table is, with all the elements which compose our complex machine, as regarded from a scientific point of view."

" My apprehensions of the social condition of your population are always much relieved when I live among you, and observe the wonderful compensating instinct of your race; else, I should truly tremble for the coarse, semi-barbarous state of your people. They are illiterate, sensual, and ignorant; their manners are rude, and their training is confined to that of the workshop; yet they are collected in masses. They represent, therefore, a great brute force. Wesley and Whitfield have been your greatest modern benefactors, for they have made manifest the power of religion on this rude power. Raikes and the Sunday school have opened to view the alliance of religion with the culture of the intelligence. But a large part of Europe has, since the peace, carried on a work of civilization, in which, in England, you have taken only the first steps."

" We have been accustomed in England," said Mr. Cliderhow, " to entrap our soldiers, and to press our sailors, and to drill them by a somewhat harsh discipline; and in our manufactories we import our raw material from the moors, or from Ireland, and exact order, not, certainly, in the same way as in the King's service, but by a peremptory rule."

" And there can be no doubt," said Malvoisin,

" that the habits of punctuality, implicit obedience, subordination, and respect for property, in which your rude workmen are trained in your factories, have been one chief source of order in this country."

" You think, however," said Mr. Cliderhow, " that would not be a sufficient security in a period of combined political and social discontent ? "

" Imagine a combination of disasters," said Malvoisin. " Conceive an insurrection of slaves in the southern States of America to coincide with the influence of some democratic demagogue of great ability either in the political or in the trades' unions. Wouldn't that be a favourable opportunity for preaching a holy war for a distribution of the accumulated labour of the people?"

" But," said Mr. Walmersley, " would any amount of discontent or suffering cause the success of such a doctrine ? "

" When you see the trades' unions successfully enforce submission to an equality of earnings, irrespective of strength, skill, or character—when you find they can compel a tariff of wages adapted to this equality—when they are found to preach, not simply an equal interest in the wage fund, but also in the profits of capital—there can be no doubt that the logic of ignorance would as easily lead them to a community of goods to be attained by a new distribution."

"Then, your view is that the greatest danger to this country is the want of an intelligent Christian civilization for the labouring classes?" said Sir Guy.

"Certainly," said Malvoisin. "The future history of capital and labour may be described to consist in the successive steps of the solution of their mutual relations. At present, this relationship is a partnership in which the respective shares of the partners are ill defined. The tendency, through a series of struggles more or less violent, will be to make these relations more and more definite. The first step will probably elevate the skilled and intelligent workmen into positions giving them a more immediate interest in the profits of the whole enterprise. Subsequent steps will probably lead slowly to the admission of other classes of workmen to a more direct participation in the results. They will be assured wages so long as the factory is carried on; and when there are profits, they will have an additional remuneration proportionate to the profits. But it is clear that only a very intelligent class of workmen could be admitted into such a participation of the profits, for it would involve an audit of accounts on fixed principles. The rate of progress towards such a form of co-operation between master and servant must, therefore, be proportionate to everything which tends to raise the moral and mental condition of the workmen. But the principle of co-operation, as contrasted with that of the discipline of which Mr. Cliderhow has spoken, will be the distinguishing feature of two eras of civilization."

"Our warehouses in Manchester are certainly conducted on this principle," said Mr. Cliderhow; "and I hear that some services of the most highly skilled branches of trade, such as among the machine-makers their overlookers, and first class of mechanics, are remunerated after this principle. The fact that the salesmen in the several departments of the warehouses, and the overlookers and mechanics, are of much higher intelligence than the common operative, illustrates your conception."

"You have doubtless given your attention to the *Conseils des Prud'hommes* at Lyons and in other cities of France, which settle questions of wages and regulations of labour between masters and workmen? Give us, if you please," said the duke, "your opinion on these *Conseils*."

"The *Conseils des Prud'hommes*, in France, duke, are principally occupied with disputes as to wages, for which the English common, and statute law provides an easy and inexpensive remedy before the justices of the peace. So far, the justices are a

Conseil des Prud'hommes. As respects the much more embarrassing question, raising a social war between the trades' unions of the workmen and the associations of the masters, as to the hours and conditions of labour and the rates of wages, the justices are also charged with the preservation of the peace. It is their duty to afford protection to every individual to dispose of his labour without the arbitrary interference of any associated body. As to actual open breaches of the peace, the law, with the aid of an efficient police, is sufficiently stringent. But as to moral intimidation, the law is almost powerless, and I don't see what any *Conseil des Prud'hommes* could do to prevent it. I am also very doubtful indeed, whether either masters or workmen would consent to any arbitration of their differences. There could be no harm, however, in affording legal facilities for such arbitrations."

" You are aware," said Sir Guy Scarsdale, " that the establishments of my guests are, probably, among the best regulated in Lancashire, as respects ventilation, the hours of labour, precautions against mutilation by the machinery, and the regulations as to the employment of women and children. Do you see any reason why the selfish and short-sighted class of manufacturers, many of whom have risen from the ranks, should not be compelled, by law, to assimilate their factories, in all these respects, to the best-conducted mills in the trade?"

"On the contrary, that is a policy," said Malvoisin, "required equally for the protection of the capitalist, who refuses to wring his profits out of the physical and moral sufferings of his workmen, and for that growth in civilization, which is indispensable to the future liberty of your country."

"I agree with you, M. Malvoisin," said Lord Pendleborough, "in relying to a great extent on the spirit of independent action and voluntary association. But the security of property, public peace, a sound social organization, national order and progress, ultimately depend on the steady growth of a high Christian civilization among the working classes of this nation. Are you then disposed to confide that result to our purely provincial and local efforts, unaided by the law? Or would you apply the resources of the executive government, and expect that the interference of the legislative authority would be required to stimulate and guide the independent exertions of individuals and associations, to remove obstacles from their path, and to give expression to the will of the most enlightened classes, as to this crisis in the fortunes of the State?"

"I cannot conceive that these great improvements. which suppose the creation of so extensive and novel an organization throughout the country, can be accomplished without legislative interference."

The conversation then becoming more special, as to the expedients to be adopted at the public meeting on the morrow at Bacup, the duke, Lord Pendleborough, and M. Malvoisin, rose, and leaving Sir Guy in conference with his guests, withdrew to rejoin the ladies, whither, about an hour afterwards, they were followed by the rest of the party.

CHAPTER III.

THE NEW BAILEY PRISON AT MANCHESTER.—AN ADVENTURE IN SCARSDALE CLOUGH, AND ITS CONSEQUENCES.

THE light of noon streams, by a single slanting ray, through a small unglazed window barred with thick iron stanchions, on to the muscular frame of Floi-bi-Neet, lying on a heap of straw, at the bottom of a narrow but deep cell in the New Bailey at Manchester. As a man of desperate life, charged with belonging to the gang of assassins of the machine-breakers' union, and caught in an act of burglary, he is manacled round each ankle by a ring, riveted to a chain hanging from handcuffs at his wrists. He lies sullenly on some boards raised four inches from the flagged floor, and gazes through the gloom, sometimes on the bare brick walls, and sometimes, through the high aperture in the wall, on the light clouds floating in the sunlight.

There are steps in the adjacent passage: they approach the door; a key is inserted into the lock—

Floi-bi-Neet raises himself upon his elbow in an attitude of expectation—the key is turned, the door opens, and the vicar of Assheton gravely enters the cell.

The door has been again closed, and the vicar has seated himself on a small wooden stool, near the prostrate form of Floi-bi-Neet.

"The chief constable sent me a message which reached me at an early hour this morning, that you desired to see me, James Haworth. Whether it be for your soul's health, or the ease of your conscience, or the good of others, I am here, having lost no time in obeying your summons."

"Parson, oi'm i' yore debt, yo see; yo seed fair play i' yon ugly job o' Giles' woife, an' yo geet me cawt o' th' gate (out of the way) o'erneet (over-night) when t' Ratchda' folk were'n fur teying me wick or dead (alive or dead), to work their will on me."

"I told you, Jem, plainly, that though I thought you, wittingly or not, the cause of that woman's death, you had a right to the safeguard of the law, and should have it."

"Yo were'n o above booard, parson—reglar John Bull—an' oi'll tell nowt to nobody bur to yo; as for this savage big Sladen an' his runners, oi'll noan trust thooas chaps."

" Jem, you know I can hear nothing from you by which the ends of justice can be gained, which I am not bound to tell again. It were, perhaps, a different matter, if you were truly sorry for your misdeeds, and sought by confession one means of making your peace with God."

" Moi thowts (thoughts) is rough thowts, parson; bur, yo see, oi were bred on Squoire Scarsdale's lond, an' when owd Holte and t' Ratchda' 'torney 'ud a harried me off yon bit o' waste wheer moi heause wur, t' squoire looked into th' job for hissel. An', says he, Jem's a poacher, fur sure, an' a rough chap, says he, an' he'll maybe get into wur mischief, says he, bur then here's bin some sooart of a pleck (place) on this greaund (ground) o moi toime, an' o moi feyther's (father's) an' gronfeyther's toime, an' whether it were robbed fro' Scarsdale lond a hunderd year bygone nother yo nor ony mone on say; bur a poacher shall have fair play fro' me, an' oi winnot harry a poor mon wi' law."

" That's strictly true," said the vicar; " but who told you that, Jem?"

" Woi, it wur a reet thing to do, bur who should do it but Meaustur Holte hissel, for tho' it made again him, he thowt oi should poach less, yo see, i' th' squoire's londs."

" Mr. Holte is a just man, and, though with rather narrow views, always faithful to Sir Guy."

" Well, nother t' squoire nor Meaustur Holte were'n wur worse off fur that, yo may be sure."

" You let them alone ? " said the vicar.

" Oi nother robbed Holte henroost, nor drove his sheep, nor poached i' Scarsdale for years. Well, then, oi'n summut verra feaw (something very wrong) to tell yo, vicar."

" Remember, Jem, that whatever you tell me which can help the law I shall tell again."

" Yore loike (you must do so). Bur then, yo see, o eawr gang bur one chap is ketched (caught). Teyn o been ketched weel armed i' th' verra act, an teyn shot at t' runners, an' tey'rn o sure to be transported or gien to Jack Ketch."

" That's true : you can do those who are taken up no harm, for there is proof enough against every one o' them."

" Then this chap, as wur to hae bin at High Collor Fowd, wur a keeper at Scarsdale, an' he wur bagged (sent away) for thieving game, drinkin', and makin' a pie (a collusion) wi' poachers."

" You mean Ascroft, the ruffian whom I sent to gaol for theft a year ago?"

" The verra same chap. He had woaned (dwelt) i' Scarsdale o his days, had eaten t' squoire's bread o his loife, bur he's a bloody divil. An' eawr gang 'ud noan listen to owt as oi said, bur a fortneet sin orthers were gien to kill t' squoire fur yon job at t' Eagle Mill, an' t' lot fell on this bloody divil."

"You don't think it possible, Jem, that he'll try to take Sir Guy's life!"

"Oss (try) to tak' it! he'll tak' it as sure as yore'n wick (alive), parson, if yo connot ketch him. For, yo see, he kneaws o th' ins an' eawts o' Scarsdale; he wur allays preawling abeawt th' ho (prowling about the hall), an' yon owd bit o' th' castle, an' oi kneaw not what he's fun', bur yo kneawn, parson, there's o macks o' moudiwarp hoiles (all kinds of mole galleries) abeawt them owd warld hos (old world halls). Oi'd hae yo get some o' Sladen folk up yon; tey'rn cute chaps (clever fellows); teyn smell eawt Ascroft, or set a gin for him. Put t' squoire on his guard, neet an' day, nur yo'n teyn (taken) this bloody divil, Ascroft."

"Then, Jem, I understand that your conscience compels you to prevent this crime if possible."

"Oi'll noan hae Sir Guy's blood to anser for, parson."

"You also can trust me, Jem?"

"Tho yore'n a parson an' a justice, an' oi'm a poacher, an' wur (worse), oi'll tak' yore word for owt, whether yone (you will) tey moin or not."

"You will help me to the utmost to stop Ascroft's bloody errand, if I keep from the police what you tell me about your chums and hiding-places on the moors."

"That's a bargain, parson."

"Then, Jem, I promise you to give no such information to the police, but I can receive no confession of any crime or conspiracy on such a condition."

"That's o reet, parson."

"Well, then, Jem, I have learned from Mr. Sladen, as I entered the New Bailey, that on the morning on which you left High Collor, Swart Ned returned with his string of 'gals' from Deerden. On the way, he had met Ascroft at a lonely homestead at the edge of the Marsden moors. Ascroft had lost his way in the dark over Boulsworth, from the moors above Heptonstall, and had not reached Briercliffe till just before dawn. He was then afraid to go forward to High Collor, but, before retreating to some hiding-place beyond Extwistle, he gave Swart Ned a paper, on which he had scrawled some figures which are a puzzle to the police. This was to be delivered to you, but before Swart Ned found out what had occurred at High Collor, it got into the hands of Silly Neddy."

"Eh, that were'n a fawse (cunning) felley fur sure," interrupted Floi-bi-Neet, rubbing his hands, and laughing at the trick which had been played upon him.

" Well, Silly Neddy has a guess at the meaning of this document, and if you see no reason to withhold it from him, or from me, this may lead to the capture of Ascroft."

" Han yo getten it wi' yo ? "

" Yes, Jem, here it is," said the vicar, producing a dirty bit of paper, on which were rudely traced, with a bad pen, or a skewer dipped in ink, the following hieroglyphs in one line. First, there was a rude representation of a tree, then one of a large hooped barrel with a bung at the top, resting on its side, then a mark like the capital letter **Y**, then three strokes thus **| | |**, and then a half-moon cut off thus **D**. The whole missive was on a large coarse scale like the following drawing :—

Floi-bi-Neet laughed again when he saw the scrawl, and his eyes still twinkled with delight when he turned to the vicar.

" Woi, this is as plain as a pikestaff, and yon Silly Neddy hasn't o th' gumption as oi'n gien him credit for, an he connot mey that eawt, nae he's getten it into his honds."

" Well, I know how Silly Neddy reads it, and I will tell you, Jem, whether his reading is right, if you can give me yours."

" Yo see, parson, as Ascroft couldna coom forrud to High Collor, he sattles a pleck (place) an' toime weer oi or cawr chaps con leet on (find) him. Nae connot yo read it."

" I think Silly Neddy's reading will prove right, Jem."

" Eh, he's a cute un (clever one) fur sure. Well, parson: yon tree means *ash*, then theer's a *tun*; then a three lone-eend—that means Assheton three lone-eends; the three strokes is three days, and yo see the moon hasn't risen."

" Then the scrawl may mean Assheton three lane-ends, three days hence, just before the moon has risen?"

" As true as gospel, parson."

" Well, Jem, that exactly agrees with Silly Neddy's reading; may I tell him that he is right?"

" Wi' o my heart yo may; an' if yo lay a gin fur Ascroft, at t' three lone-eends on Assheton Moore to-morrow neet, yo mun think on, ut a landcrake cry mun be answered by un cawl skrike (shriek of an owl), an' then yore chaps mun mey moore-feawl chirps, nur Ascroft's fun cawt weer teyr'n liggin."

(till Ascroft has found out where they are lying down).

"Now, Jem, I always saw some good in you, though your lawless pursuits, reckless habits, and now and then signs of a savage nature that did not shrink from blood, have made me fear you would meet a felon's death. This is a manly act, without any mixture of baseness in it, Jem, to try to save Sir Guy's life, and I hope, for your conscience sake, it will succeed. The first act of penitence, James Haworth, may be the first step of the prodigal back from the husks on which the swine feed, to his father's house. I pray Almighty God that it may be so in your case. May God, who has given you grace to do this manly, honest deed, shed on the better thoughts that are in your heart the influence of His Holy Spirit, and like His rain, which descends on the just and the unjust, may the divine power quicken these thoughts of gratitude and mercy, this conscious shrinking from the guilt of returning murder for kindness, into a complete change of heart and conscience."

"Yo connot mey (make) a silk purse eawt on a sow's ear, parson. Oi'm booked oather for Jack Ketch or Botany Bay, bur no mon ever did me a koindness i' this world beawt moi stroivin' at leäst to be cawt on his debt."

"That is something, Jem—nay it is much; but the Gospel goes even further—it teaches us to forgive our enemies, to pray for them that despitefully use us and persecute us;—I will ask the chaplain, Jem, to explain these things to you."

"Oi kneaw it ud pleasure yo, parson, an' tho' oi reckon it'll do me nae good, oi'll year what yon prison parson has to say, for yore sake."

Mr. Hollingsworth kneeled down by the side of Floi-bi-Neet, and prayed briefly, but fervently, that he might be led to a true penitence and renewal of life. He then took his leave. When the door of the cell was shut, Floi-bi-Neet drew his sleeve across his eyes, saying,—

"Dang yon parson, he's made me blubber."

The vicar had a conference with Mr. Sladen. Philp had brought the intelligence from High Collor, having left there Robert Dewhurst, with Swart Ned, and one experienced constable. It was agreed, that as soon as it was dark, Philp and two constables should follow the vicar to Scarsdale. Mr. Hollingsworth then mounted his horse, and rode slowly homewards, pondering much on the measures to be adopted. He found Sir Guy returned from the morning meeting of manufacturers at Bacup. His daughter, and the duchess, and Lord Pendleborough had visited the Mere Clough with Miss Hollingsworth, the duke having proposed a drive to Lord Salmesbury, and Miss Wilmslow. M. Malvoisin and Deloisir were gone to Rochdale, to pursue some inquiries as to a growing combination among the flannel weavers, ostensibly for an advance of wages, but also for a group of impracticable objects, which were to be accomplished by a general " shuttle gathering," that is, by a stoppage of the whole flannel weaving of the valley of the Roche, by the collection of all the shuttles by a mob.

Mr. Hollingsworth briefly related the information which he had obtained to Sir Guy Scarsdale without reserve.

" Without my experience of guerilla war, or this police agent Philp's cunning, this ruffian, if one exercises common skill, will run his head into the hangman's noose," said Sir Guy.

" To one so experienced in hazardous enterprises as you are, Sir Guy, I need say nothing about the precautions to be adopted against assassins. But Mr. Sladen wished me to request you not to be abroad at night, not to walk or ride alone, to avoid paths near thickets, and to allow Philp to have his own way in guarding the house, and ensnaring this villain."

" To no part of which have I any objection, provided we can conceal that we are upon our guard.

Lord Pendleborough's experience of adventure among savage tribes has given him a quickness of sense, and a fertility and promptitude of resource, which, combined with his singular natural daring and coolness, make his aid invaluable in such an affair," said Sir Guy. "Let us go, therefore, and see whether he has returned from his ride with the ladies."

They found Lord Pendleborough in a small room adjoining his bedroom. He appeared somewhat fatigued and absorbed, but rose with his usual calm and slightly reserved manner on their entrance. Sir Guy and Mr. Hollingsworth step by step related to him what had occurred at High Collor, the vicar's interview with Floi-bi-Neet in the gaol at Manchester, the character of Ascroft, and the suggestions made by Floi-bi-Neet, and emphatically pressed on their consideration by the police, that this ruffian might have knowledge of some secret passage to the ancient keep, and by some lateral gallery to the house. If this were not the fact, then, one so conversant as he with the whole building, might be aware of some other method by which the Hall could be entered.

Lord Pendleborough seemed in no degree surprised by these communications. He interrupted the narrative by occasional inquiries, and asked if any plan of the house existed, which he could study. Sir Guy promised to give him all the plans in his possession, and remarked that though they contained no evidence of any hidden passages, they would enable him to concert with Lord Pendleborough and the police the best mode of guarding the mansion.

The conversation then took this form :—

" I have seen a man with a wiry form," said Lord Pendleborough, "with a singular hooked nose, very dark and fierce eyes, and with a wound dividing one eyebrow, and marking the brow with a red line slanting outwards."

" That is Ascroft," said Mr. Hollingsworth.

" Then I think there is an end of him," said Lord Pendleborough ; " for I chased him to earth this afternoon, and he leaped from the top of a cliff, in what I understand is called the Kestrel Cove. No doubt his body will be found at the foot of the cliff, and he must have lost either life or limb."

This was said so calmly, and with such a complete absence of emphasis, as to provoke a quiet smile on Sir Guy's face, but to fix Mr. Hollingsworth's eyes on Lord Pendleborough with a deepening intensity of expression.

" What has happened, Pendleborough ? " said Sir Guy.

" I accompanied the duchess and Miss Scarsdale in their ride this afternoon to Assheton Vicarage. On our way we rode through the upland farms, by the fields which skirt the edge of the wood. Miss Scarsdale wore a scarlet scarf tied round her neck, and then brought, like an officer's sash, over one shoulder across the chest, and tied in a knot at the waist."

" According to the pretty caprice which prevailed during our visit to Madrid," remarked Sir Guy.

" This caprice, however, seemed to infuriate a savage bull in a field between our road and the wood ; it bellowed furiously, galloped towards us with its head stooping, and was stopped only by one of your rough stone walls. Protected by this wall, we rode leisurely enough along, for my two companions have no lack of nerve, but our prolonged presence maddened our ferocious enemy. I was, therefore, glad when he was separated from us by an inner cross field wall."

" He is a dreadful brute, Sir Guy," remarked Mr. Hollingsworth, " and ought to have been killed a couple of years ago, for he is now quite maddened with answering the echoes of his own fierce bellowing from the clough."

" I suppose he belongs to the Northwood Farm,"

said Sir Guy. "He shall certainly be killed without delay."

"As we rode from this scene, I saw a man," continued Lord Pendleborough, "half hidden by a holly bush, at the skirt of the wood, close to a gate opening into the clough. I should have taken him for one of your keepers, but that he drew back, as though he sought concealment. Not, however, before my hunting sight had caught a glimpse of a scar over his eyebrow."

"Did he appear to be armed?" asked the vicar.

"We rode rapidly on to the vicarage, and except this hurried glance, which exited no suspicion in my mind, I saw nothing. Miss Hollingsworth joined us at the vicarage, in a walk down the valley, and we proposed to return thither on foot from the Mere Clough, and then to ride home by some other road."

"Relieve us," said the vicar, "by saying whether any accident has occurred to any of your party."

"Thank God, to none," said Lord Pendleborough. "The ladies are much fatigued, and are, I hope, all retired to rest, for we brought Miss Hollingsworth hither, vicar."

Sir Guy was silent, fixing his quick eyes, with a smile of satisfaction, on the impassive face of Lord Pendleborough, who continued,—

" We had got about half way to the Mere Clough,
and were in a deep wooded ravine with a stream
tumbling over the rocks and bolders below, when
I caught sight of the bull about three hundred yards
in front, and, when I first saw him, I had a glimpse
of the same man in the wood, near the road, irritating
the bull, to chase him up the valley towards us.
The furious brute was bellowing, and, at sight of
our party, seemed to be to the last degree infuriated.
His tail was extended stiffly behind, slightly curled;
he was trotting forwards; the next thing I knew
would be a rush.   I cut Miss Scarsdale's scarf from
her shoulder, and, sending the ladies back up the
road, I walked down to meet the mad creature, recalling all my matador experience at Madrid.   You
know, Sir Guy, I have the habit of carrying with
me one of those Indian bamboos, which are almost
as heavy, and are as strong as a bar of iron, and
that my cane is also loaded with lead.   I provoked
the beast to the utmost fury by waving the scarf,
taking care to stand three paces in front of a
great oak which grew on the edge of the road.   As
I expected, the monster made a mad rush with
his head down, and just before he reached me
I stepped aside, so that he came with his whole
weight and force against the trunk of the oak.
I think he must have broken his skull or his neck;

but to make sure of it, I cut his throat with my hunting-knife."

"Well done!" said Sir Guy.

"I had scarcely done this, when it occurred to me to look out for the man I had twice seen in the wood. Perhaps it required a hunter's eyes to detect a head which was suddenly withdrawn behind the trunk of a great tree. It flashed across my mind, at once, that this fellow had, from some sinister motive, let the bull into the clough, and led him up the road down which we were descending. By an incontrollable impulse, I sprang into the wood, and rapidly approached the tree, which was within one hundred yards. I walked quickly, but deliberately, for I did not want to lose my breath; and twice the head dodged, and was withdrawn, until, as my purpose was clear, the man whom I have described, and whom you call Ascroft, stood from behind the trunk, calling out, ' What do you want with me ?' I was within fifty yards, so I answered this appeal by a rush. This seemed to leave the ruffian no alternative but to draw a pistol from his breast, and to fire at me, when he turned and ran. He evidently depended on his wiry frame, practised agility, and knowledge of the wood, to escape. He certainly put to proof my training, for he dashed through bogs and threaded brakes; and as I was climbing a steep rugged path to a ridge of rocks, he turned, and, taking deliberate aim, fired at me again, and even paused a moment as though certain of his game. The ball grazed my shoulder, and has left two holes in my coat.   But this pause was, I think, fatal to the villain.   We had run about two miles, at the top of our speed, through very difficult ground, leaving the Mere Clough far behind on the right, and we were so near Scarsdale, that the wretch was clearly in a desperate position.   At any moment he might encounter a keeper or foresters, and I was close on his heels.   He made a sudden dodge to the right, rushing, with a last effort, to what I knew to be the Kestrel Cove, for I have passed it two or three times in our rides.   He was for a moment hid from me by the close thicket of holly, bramble, and hazel, which covers the slope towards the cliff, and the edge of the precipice.   One or two glimpses I got of him as he dodged through this labyrinth, and I am by no means certain that I chose the same path.   My last sight was attracted by a shout, which accompanied a leap into the air.   In a minute or two I was on the same ground.   I found there a steep face of the cliff, overgrown with ivy hanging in immense tods, but otherwise a sheer descent of two hundred feet into the wood and copse below.   I searched the edge of the precipice, and found marks of boots armed with iron, which corresponded with the traces in the thicket, but no divergence to the right or left. I looked down the face of the cliff, and saw the ivy tods torn below, as though by some heavy body, which had either fallen among them, or swung through them. I remained some time searching for a means of descent, but finding none, and fearing that the ladies might need my protection, I returned, breathless, through the wood, to find them all safe, but much fatigued, at the vicarage."

The vicar's grave and thoughtful gaze had been fixed intently on Lord Pendleborough during this narrative. He drew in a deep breath at its close.

"I thank God," said he, fervently, "that you were spared a struggle with this desperate man, which would have left the forfeit of his life, however doomed, upon your hands; for as he knew the Kestrel Cove well, I cannot but think he has swung himself down the face of the cliffs into some hiding-place among the ivy tods. May God, who took David from the sheepfolds, consecrate your intrepidity, Lord Pendleborough, like that of our own Alfred, to the service of the Church and nation."

"Pendleborough's pluck, promptitude, and vigour would make him a terrible commander of a rifle brigade, or of light horse, and will stand him in good stead in taming his Irish Peep-o'-day Boys.

Can anything be done, vicar, to catch this ruffian in his earth?" said Sir Guy.

" As it is already dusk, I fear he will have slunk out of it before the Cove can be reached; but your keepers are such expert Kestrel hunters, that I would have his trail followed at once."

" All that shall be arranged instantly," said Sir Guy; " for your Cock of Rossendale, vicar, Markland, and Broxup, are in the servants' hall, at this moment, waiting a summons from me."

" The fellow must have more than the nerve and vigour of an Orkney bird-catcher," said Lord Pendleborough, " if he have succeeded in swinging himself down that cliff, by the ivy branches clinging to the face of the rocks."

" I have a dim recollection of some talk of a mine adit in that cliff," said the vicar.

" We must have Seth Diggle in council," said Sir Guy. " He has some stories about a subterranean passage from the keep to the cliff. He and our Kestrel hunters must know of this."

They all rose to adjourn the conference to Sir Guy Scarsdale's private room of business, whither the keepers and Seth Diggle were summoned. Before we relate what occurred there, we have other scenes to which to introduce our readers, and which are necessary to the completion of our narrative to this point.

On the return of the duke from his drive, which had been prolonged by the beauty of the weather, to the foot of Blackstone Edge, the duchess's maid informed him that the ladies had been exposed to some great danger and fatigue during their ride, and that the duchess, though she had retired for an hour or two's repose, would be glad to see him, and to assure him personally of her well-being. The duke, therefore, entered the duchess's private apartment, and found her resting on the sofa. His natural gallantry, and the polish of his manners had received an expression of tenderness from his gratitude for the duchess's gentle solicitude during his illness, and the grace with which she acknowledged the accomplishments and the good qualities, which her noble instincts discovered in her lord. The beauty, self-devotion, and delicate tact of the duchess, were exactly the traits of character most fascinating to his fastidious nature. As, therefore, he had told Lord Pendleborough, with his usual sarcasm even when the sting was directed against himself, he was in no little danger of falling in love with his own wife—a catastrophe involving an entire revolution in his life and being; for such a love was, like a reconciliation with Heaven, only consistent with purity, gentleness, and the abandonment of his sceptical epicureanism. Malvoisin's profound penetration foresaw the possibility of such a conclusion, when he sought to place the duke in relations favourable to its development.

The duke approached the duchess, therefore, not only with his usual courtly bearing, but with a natural expression of solicitude, in which the tenderness of a father seemed to melt somewhat into that of the lover.   In answer to his anxious inquiries, the duchess rapidly related to him the incidents of their ride, until the death of the bull and the disappearance of Lord Pendleborough, expressing a warm admiration of the singular presence of mind, daring, and vigour of Lord Pendleborough.

" I think, duke, I have made a little discovery," the duchess continued, with a radiant smile.

" Oh, of some heart secret?" replied the duke, with evident curiosity.

" Certainly.   I could not but remark, though but an instant elapsed, when Lord Pendleborough cut the scarf from Miss Scarsdale's shoulder, the intense expression which his face wore: he said, as plainly as expression could say, though no words were uttered, ' Farewell! I gladly give my life for yours!'"

"Are you sure, dear Marie?   That explains much!" said the duke.

" The expression was one of devoted love, taking its last inspiration to a feat of great daring, from the

eyes of his mistress, and saying, with a smile,—
'Farewell!'"

"How did Miss Scarsdale answer that look?" inquired the duke.

"She turned deadly pale. As Lord Pendleborough advanced, waving the scarf, she remained fixed to the spot, with her hands clenched and teeth set, and her eyes glaring so that her beauty looked like the terrible beauty of Judith."

"Well," said the duke, intensely interested; "and were not you disturbed for the fate of your brother, ma douce sœur angélique?"

"Strangely, duke, I had a perfect self-possession, and a sort of prophetic anticipation of the result. My attention, too, was fixed on ma belle rose de Lancastre, who was now as pale as a lily, and who, when the bull rushed on Lord Pendleborough, even uttered a slight sob, followed by a deep, deep inspiration, and a flood of tears, when the monster lay bleeding, with his throat cut, upon the road."

"What happened when Pendleborough sprang into the wood after the ruffian?" inquired the duke.

"Mabel quivered from head to foot at the pistol-shot, and watched the pursuit, pale and trembling, as long as they were in sight. Then she, for the first time, seemed to revive to a consciousness of our presence. She turned her gaze on me as though she had awakened from a dream. She kissed me, and then Miss Hollingsworth. 'Thank God, you are safe, my dear friends!' she said, and at once made a great effort at self-command, and resumed her usual stately bearing, and, even to us, the *fierté* which she shows to those who are not within the circle of her intimate friendship."

"Ah! can it be, then, that Lord Pendleborough has not proposed to her?" said the duke. "I had no suspicion whatever that she had any affection for him, though I had pretty well penetrated his secret."

"I have another explanation, duke. I fancy I see a great struggle in Mabel's mind. I have had no doubt that he has long been attached to her, and that last look proves to me that he has declared his attachment, not merely by the steady attention of years of friendship with her father and herself, but, perhaps, recently in words. But Mabel has not only a great natural *fierté*, which would cause her long to question her own heart before she yielded to one whose position, immense possessions, original character, and personal attractions, have made him, as I hear, the glass of fashion in foreign courts; but she has also a horror of the idea of a life devoted to even innocent pleasures, in the absence of an overmastering sense of higher duties. Probably she has put her knight to this proof; for, from his conversations with me, I gathered, in France, that he has, for more than a year past, been a diligent disciple of Malvoisin."

" Oh, mystery of mysteries! " said the duke; " that subtle intelligence of woman, which, by intuition, solves every riddle! Ma douce et belle Marie, a thousand thanks for this charming solution of a puzzle, on which my crass intellect has pondered witlessly and vainly."

" During our walk to the vicarage," continued the duchess, " Mabel was very silent, but she recovered her self-possession to a great extent before we arrived there; and when Lord Pendleborough returned—probably more fatigued with his exertions than his almost stern bearing betrayed, she received him with the most graceful courtesy, and a warm expression of thanks, in which we all joined, but without any sign of emotion on her part which was not at least equally exhibited by both Miss Hollingsworth and myself."

" How did Pendleborough comport himself under this reception ?" asked the duke.

" Almost sternly: he was paler than I have ever seen him, reserved almost to silence; he seemed chiefly satisfied that we did not appear much fatigued, and then he took charge of us, as though we were under his command, ordered out Miss Hollingsworth's pony, declared that Miss Scarsdale could not dispense with her society that evening, and, directing us to ride before him in a group, hurried us home."

" Did he say what had become of the ruffian ? "

" Not a word."

" Perhaps he had killed him," said the duke.

" Merciful Heaven ! I hope and pray not."

" That, at least, would account for his sternness, silence, and anxiety that Miss Hollingsworth should accompany Miss Scarsdale."

" Oh ! I pray you, duke, resolve this doubt; I cannot bear to think what Mabel would suffer."

" That I will at once," answered the duke.

As, however, the duke rose to leave the room, the duchess's maid entered with a card, on which Lord Pendleborough had written, " Dear duchess,—You and our two friends will be glad to learn, that it is probable the ruffian whom I chased in the wood will be captured to-night."

When the maid had left, the duchess put the card into the duke's hand, who, on reading it, remarked,—

" This clearly explains that Pendleborough on his return thought he had killed this ruffian, and now finds that he has escaped. Pray let Miss Scarsdale see the card at once; it is obviously his intention to relieve her mind from an oppressive apprehension."

"I will go to her without a moment's delay," said the duchess, and, rising, she left the room.

On the arrival of the riding-party at the hall, Mabel had carried Miss Hollingsworth with her to her own private sitting-room. She had maintained during the ride homewards the same almost queen-like bearing which the duchess had described, and had renewed to Lord Pendleborough warmly her acknowledgments for his presence of mind and gallantry, without which some shocking catastrophe would doubtless, she said, have befallen them.

"My father, the duke, and the vicar will know better how to thank you, Lord Pendleborough, than I can; but there is nothing in life worth having, without that personal satisfaction which you have, of true and generous deeds."

Lord Pendlebrough took her hand and lifted it to his lips, while he stooped to kiss it, this time un-covered with a riding gauntlet, nor did Mabel rebuke the warmth of feeling which he revealed. He was, however, quite silent, and, bowing to the duchess and Miss Hollingsworth, retired at once to his own room. When Mabel and Helen were alone, it was soon apparent that Miss Scarsdale was suffering from a violent headache. Her friend, having persuaded her to undress and lie down, gave her some ammonia, and sat by the bedside bathing her temples with eau-de-Cologne and water.   After awhile, Mabel said,—

" Helen, I have a terrible thought."

" What is it, dearest Rose ? perhaps I can relieve your apprehension."

." Have you noticed how stern and silent Lord Pendleborough has been since he returned to us ? "

" But, Queen Mab, you don't know how majestic you have been in the smiles and favour with which you have acknowledged his prowess."

" Oh, no, my dear Helen, Lord Pendleborough knows the terms on which we are, and that it is not the lion heart which is not quite proved in him, nor, to whisper you a secret, dearest Heather-Bell, his tried love for his friend's daughter. I read something else in his impassible, stern .presence : he had killed that man ! "

" That is a terrible thought indeed, dear Mabel."

" Oh, I know: there is an awful instinct which enables us to read the thoughts of those—those—who —who would seek to put their natures in harmony with ours, which makes one sure of the meaning of every discord.   He had the consciousness of a terrible act on his mind, when he came back so stern and pale."

" But, dearest, he had been away from us an hour,

and his pallor and silence were perhaps simply fatigue from intense mental and physical exertion."

" Did you observe the hole in his coat over the shoulder, and the corresponding hole a little way down the back ?"

" What of that ? "

" They were clearly the results of a pistol-shot, for I have often examined my father's peninsular uniforms, which are torn with balls in the same way."

" Well, then, the man must have fired on him a second time."

" So I think, and probably provoked a crushing blow from Lord Pendleborough, to which his life is a forfeit."

" Though I am but a simple maiden, and though deeds of blood are shocking to me, yet if my father had so defended his own life, I might grieve and suffer, dear Mabel, as you do, but with patience and prayer the pang might pass."

" Perhaps ; yet the doubt, the suspense, the vagueness of everything torment me sadly, Helen ; the image of that pale, stern man, speaking brief, peremptory words, afflicts me. Surely there is some shocking tale to unfold ; I doubt not, a history of righteous wrath, with ruthless guilt, but perhaps a savage man sent to his account suddenly by one swift blow of vengeance."

" Oh, Mabel, Mabel, fear not to find Lord Pendleborough all that your inner consciousness has proved him to be. He is self-possessed in the extremest peril. In such men danger is an inspiration which places them under the guidance of genius. Even if the man have perished, be confident Lord Pendleborough has been true to his own noble generous nature."

" I will not rebuke you, dear Heather-Bell, though your words imply that I have unconsciously such an interest in Lord Pendleborough as I have never confessed even in my prayers and secret communings. He has done much this year or more past under my father's example and guidance to rise higher and higher towards the supreme objects of life, and he has made me conscious that he seeks my love."

" Thank God, dearest Rose, for if my inexperience dare to speak, it is only to second the opinion of my father, who always calls him either David or Alfred when we are alone."

" My sweet Helen, I know not whether I have yielded my heart or not, but this day's terrible agitation makes me fear that I have struggled vainly to repress this sentiment until I had complete proof that Lord Pendleborough had acquired a full sense of the vast responsibilities of his station and possessions, and had determined to train and devote himself to meet them."

"Dear queen, your *fierté* has undergone a terrible trial, but I cannot but congratulate your majesty on having at least preserved from all but your little privy councillor the interest you take in the champion who, having been victor in all the lists, is by his virtue to rescue some thralls from a wicked enchanter ere he can win the acknowledgment of your love."

"Nay, my pretty privy councillor, you are privileged to see the mortal weakness of a moment of agony, but doubt not that I will be true to my highest allegiance until this brave and generous man prove that he will devote his life to God and his brethren as a soldier and servant of Christ."

"Well said, my dear sister in heart and friend in trouble; we are of one mind. God give you grace to be true to Him!"

A pause ensued. Helen still sat by the bedside holding Mabel's hand, who shut her eyes, the long dark lashes of the lids being moistened with tears. The room was quite still for half an hour. Then there came a gentle tap at the door. Helen rose to open it softly, and the duchess entered holding Lord Pendleborough's card in her hand. Helen read it, smiled, and pointing to Mabel, who seemed asleep, gently and silently exiled the duchess from the room.   When the door closed, Mabel opened her eyes, and, seeing the card, anxiously asked,—

" Any relief, Helen, to my terrible anguish ? "

" Complete, my dear Mabel ; Lord Pendleborough writes for our relief that he hopes the ruffian will be caught to-night."

" Thank God, then, he is not killed !"

" Assuredly not."

" But it is clear that in some way Lord Pendleborough conceived that he was dead, when he returned to us—else, why so stern, so pale, so peremptory ? "

" Probably your instinct divined accurately, and this anxiety to reassure you that a life has not been sacrificed is a sign that the discord which caused such a jar in your heart, vibrated also in Lord Pendleborough's.   He has answered your stately courtesies by the genuine anxieties of love."

" Oh, Helen, how has he bribed you to tempt me to be impatient with my vow to Heaven ?"

" Or rather, dear friend, to assure you that your vows will be reconciled with your love."

There was again silence.   Mabel closed her eyes and with a muslin handkerchief moistened with eau-de-Cologne and water on her broad brow, seemed to doze.   Helen sat by the fire musing, looking from time to time at her friend, and sometimes sighing. She, too, had her vow. Sustained by her father, by prayer, faith, and active charity, as well as by cheerful studies, in which the vicar was her guide and teacher, she had borne her long trial with more than resignation, with a trustful confidence in the mercy of God's righteous providence. She possessed her spirit with the patience of the saints, waiting for the manifestation of His will. But something of the agitation of her friend's mind penetrated her own. She had been gradually made aware of the exact nature of the accident which had happened to Colonel Vavasour. Her father had revealed to her the imminent peril in which his life had been. He had even familiarized her mind with the details of Oliver Holte's timely interposition. Since Colonel Vavasour's return to Assheton Manor, he had been in too critical a state to see any one but Oliver Holte, who remained entirely with him, as friend and confessor quite as much as physician. The devotion of Oliver Holte to his friend knew no limit. He read to him; sustained his spirits by cheerful conversation; communicated with Mr. Hollingsworth and the principal tenantry; and especially as a physician to the wounded conscience of the sufferer poured in the balm of holy thoughts, aspirations, and prayers. All this was known in detail to Helen, for the vicar considered his daughter entitled to the fullest knowledge of all that transpired. She had, therefore, pursued her studies, home duties, and charities, if with a suffering yet with a grateful mind. The chief trouble—the fear of an impenitent death—that was undergoing a gradual relief. Mr. Holte's faithful discharge of his complex functions was a source of deep gratitude. So her mind had retained much of its usual condition of tranquil confidence in the mercy of Heaven. This sudden vision of the half-blown flower of the love of her friend awaiting the light and warmth of the assurance of duty to burst into full bloom agitated her. She sighed deeply from time to time. Had she really reconciled herself to the one final wish that Colonel Vavasour should be reconciled to Heaven by a true penitence? Had she really given up her early love, asking only that God in His righteous providence would so order events as to bring the prodigal son home to his Father? Had she quite, quite given him up to God? Was there no lingering selfish wish? Might not the reconciled penitent live to fulfil the vow of his youth?

CHAPTER IV.

A LEAP FROM THE CLIFF OF THE KESTREL COVE.
—A NIGHT IN THE LAIR.—BLOODHOUNDS ON
THE SCENT.

THE native population of East Lancashire, though
only partially civilized thirty years ago, and, consequently, rude and untamed, was not vindictive.   The
secret societies of the trades' unions had generally in
them some extraneous element.   Not unfrequently,
Ribbonism, or Whiteboyism, had, by the Irish immi-
grants, contributed some Milesian blood.   Silas
Whitaker, by his mother's side, was of Hibernian
extraction, and had been much mixed with the tur-
bulence of the Irish colonists at Manchester.   Ascroft
had another origin.   He belonged to a family, some
members of which had been hanged at Lancaster for
a brutal murder of two servant-girls, in the open day,
at Pendleton, within a few yards of one of the most
thronged approaches to Manchester.   He was then a
youth, and the public horror which overwhelmed a
family, in which a ruthless ferocity seemed to work

like a fierce animal instinct, drove him into the country. In the recesses of Rossendale, pursuing his vocation as a journeyman handloom-weaver, he joined gangs of poachers on the moors, gratifying the impulses of his nature in the savage contests with keepers in the pursuit of game.

The young poacher is not unfrequently promoted to be a watcher, or under-keeper; and, as Ascroft was sober, active, and daring, he was soon selected by Sir Guy Scarsdale's head-keeper to aid in watching the moors above Scarsdale and Assheton. In this capacity, his pluck and hardihood were equal to any trial; but the ruthless savagery of his blood broke out in a fierce conflict on the moors, in which he was, with the utmost difficulty, separated from an antagonist, on whose throat he had fastened, with a gripe which would have been speedily fatal. After this occurrence, he was distrusted. Removed to the preserves near Hurstwood, and regarded with apprehension, he was tampered with by dealers, and having been detected in the disposal of the game entrusted to his care, he had been dismissed, about two years before the machine-breaking riots. Resuming his occupation of handloom-weaver, and now familiar with the Scarsdale and Assheton manors, he had become a formidable poacher. Naturally, he was an object of peculiar suspicion and vigilance to the keepers of these manors. The irritation caused by such vigilance, by occasional detection and punishment, and by night conflicts, fermented in the desperate nature of Ascroft. In one of these encounters, he had received a stunning blow from a bludgeon, which had not only left him an insensible captive, but had divided the eyebrow and scalp by a deep contused wound, which had only slowly healed in the hospital of the prison, leaving an indelible red scar. Probably, the injury from this blow, though it left his physical vigour unimpaired, had aggravated the natural ferocity of his character by a new source of internal irritation. Certainly, from this time forth no enterprise seemed too ruthless for this fierce man. Silas Whitaker, therefore, in whom cunning was combined with his reckless qualities, relied mainly on Ascroft, in the execution of the bloody designs of the secret gang. He was the man who fired with a deliberate aim on Oliver Holte, when he rode down Scarsdale through the mob, sending a ball through his hat. Ascroft had been knocked over by Oliver's horse, and severely contused by his fall. His vindictive fury, inflamed by this event, and worked upon by Silas, disposed him to obey the orders of the secret gang. This had led him to waylay Oliver in the wood, and to fire upon him a second time, a few nights after the outbreak. The belief that he had then been recognized caused his flight to the moors above Heptonstall, where he had since lain, concealed by some of the associates of Floi-bi-Neet. We have seen how he escaped the capture which awaited the rest of the gang at High Collor. This was the man to whom the order to assassinate Sir Guy Scarsdale had been issued by the remnant, in their secret conferences in the Yorkshire moors.

On the afternoon on which Lord Pendleborough had chased Ascroft through the wood, Oliver Holte had left Assheton Manor-house, to visit the suffering cottagers of Mere Clough. The great prostration of their strength seemed to yield neither to the more generous food provided by Sir Guy Scarsdale, nor to the prophylactic remedies intended to avert marsh fever. Something in the air of the cottages and of the Mere, combined with this continued debility, induced Oliver to conceive that an outbreak of some unmanageable form of typhus could not be avoided unless the cottagers could be removed from the clough to higher ground. He therefore determined to prolong his walk to the hall, and to suggest to Sir Guy Scarsdale that a range of handloom cottages, now in disuse, on one of the upland farms, should be at once appropriated to the reception of the inhabitants of the Mere Clough. With this view he had walked down Scarsdale by the forest road towards the hall. The main road followed the course of the stream, at a slight elevation above it, so as to preserve a straighter course and a more regular descent. The wood was dense, and filled with undergrowth on every side, and a mile below the Mere Clough the steep slopes of the ravine, on the east, were from time to time broken by rocky projections, which at length showed themselves to be the outlying bluffs of a rampart of precipitous crags. About two miles from the Mere, this cliff swept backwards in a deep semicircle, with a span of a quarter of a mile, and a perpendicular face of rocks 250 feet high. The forest timber sprang from the very talus of this precipice, and the rocks were singularly overgrown with ivy, whose knotted stems climbed the lower strata in rugged forms, the growth of centuries. Sixty or eighty feet from the talus, huge tods of ivy overhung, probably from projecting rocks, and hid the higher part of the cliff from any one standing at its foot. At a distance, however, glimpses of the whole face of the precipice might be obtained through the forest, and everywhere it was thickly clad with ivy. This was the Kestrel Cove—so called because it was the haunt of the sparrow-hawk, and the scene of daring feats of keepers, in pursuit of this ravager of their preserves. Oliver Holte was a diligent naturalist, and he had diverged from the road to examine the line of stratification, as he descended the ravine. His observations led him, step by step, into the recess of the Kestrel Cove. He was busied in the examination of as much of it as was not covered by the strong stems and knotted branches of the ivy, or concealed by the huge tods, which hung in masses from the face of the cliff. While thus occupied, he heard a loud cry at the top of the scarp. Looking up through the oaks, ash, and sycamores, which grew close to the foot of the rocks, he saw, a moment later, the closely-clustered ivy disturbed by some heavy body descending through it, and struggling desperately. Instantly afterwards, it was clear that some man was in the agony of an effort to prevent a frightful fall, by clutching the ivy branches. One knotted stem, torn by his weight from its hold on the rocks, was yielding rapidly, and, though breaking his descent, threatened, as it grew thicker, to become less lithe, and to snap off where it was dry and brittle with age. The falling man, therefore, grasped resolutely the thickest branches of the ivy tods, to lessen the strain on the stem which he still clutched. A few seconds only elapsed in these desperate efforts, ere, mass after mass yielding, and at length the stem itself breaking abruptly, the man fell forty feet, on to the talus at the foot of the cliff.

The ground was softened with the moisture exuding
from the strata, otherwise, though two hundred feet
of descent had been accomplished with only a few
scars, this last fall of forty feet must have been fatal.
So nimble and self-collected, even to the last moment,
was the victim, that he had balanced his descent so
as to alight on his feet, but so heavily, that he was
at once thrown, with a rude shock, backwards—his
shoulders and head striking the earth violently.
When Oliver came up, he was quite insensible.

Oliver Holte instantly recognized, by the scar on
the brow and the marked features, the man who had
deliberately fired upon him, with such precision as to
pierce his hat with a ball, and whom he had ridden
down. He was the man, too, suspected of having
shot at him at the edge of night in the wood between
Scarsdale Hall and the Eagle Mill. He was help-
less, and Oliver was both brave and compassionate.
His only impulse, therefore, was to employ the resources of his art to save a life. He dragged the
body from the wet and steep talus to a dry bank at
the foot of an oak, and then carefully laid bare the
neck and chest. The heart laboured heavily, and
there was a slow partial respiration. He cut the
sleeve of the coat, bound the arm, and opened a vein.
As the blood flowed, the breathing became deeper and
more free, and the pulsation of the heart less op-

pressed. He interrupted the flow of blood, now and then, to afford time for the observation of the effects produced. In half an hour an almost natural respiration was established; the arm was bound up, and the body slightly raised from its prostrate position. Another hour passed, with little change, except an occasional moan—a quiver of the lips and eyelids—and at length deep sighs. But soon afterwards, Ascroft—for it was he—opened his eyes, as though awakening from a deep sleep, and gazed with a dimly-awakened consciousness on Oliver. The gaze was prolonged and silent. He saw, he knew not what. By slow degrees consciousness dawned. He turned his eyes, which had been fixed on Oliver, to the forest, and thence to the foot of the cliff, and then back to his attendant. On him he gazed again, long and silently, while Oliver, drawing from his pocket a case of medicines, administered a cordial to him. When he had taken this, Oliver examined the limbs with care. None seemed to be dislocated or broken. As his patient now seemed conscious, he asked him whether he felt pain anywhere. There was no answer, but another prolonged gaze from the dark eyes, and a slight shudder. Oliver therefore continued his examination with a gentle solicitude. He could discover no severe contusion, no fracture of the ribs. By and by the sufferer stretched out his limbs, as though to relieve a sense of weariness. It was clear that he was recovering from the stunning effects of his fall.

But more than two hours of the autumnal afternoon had rapidly sped away. Twilight gloomed over the wood. Ascroft could not be left there through the night. The hall was not half a mile distant, but the path round the southern extremity of the Kestrel Cove was a steep zigzag; and Oliver doubted whether he had the strength to carry a burly man through the boggy ground of the Cove-wood and up this abrupt path. At least he could strive to carry him to the foot of it, and he could then rapidly ascend and secure assistance from the hall to bear his patient to a shelter for the night. He therefore addressed himself to Ascroft, who had not spoken a word.

"Your kestrel hunting has nearly been fatal to you. You owe your life to your skill in dropping on to your feet from the last forty feet of your fall. But you were stunned. I have taken some blood from you, and if you are now strong enough to hold on I will carry you on my back to some shelter, where I can take care of you for the night."

Ascroft made no answer.

"I cannot leave you here. The cold would be fatal to you. Can you stand?"

There was no reply.

" Strive to hold on by my shoulders while I carry you on my back to some place of shelter."

He had reared Ascroft in a sitting position against an oak. He now raised him so as to stand with his back leaning against the tree. Stooping, he lifted the knees of his patient so as to throw his trunk upon his own back. Ascroft seemed to second his effort by placing his arms on Oliver's shoulders. Having thus adjusted his burthen, he staggered forward through the boggy ground of the wood at the foot of the Cove.

When Ascroft first opened his eyes to fix his gaze on Oliver Holte, consciousness only slowly dawned. He did not at first recognize him. As his sense of his position gradually awakened, he gazed on the wood and the cliff, and began to have some faint recollection of the occurrences which had immediately preceded. Then he recognized Oliver with a shudder. He was in the power of a man whose life he had twice attempted. By and by his consciousness was almost complete, and with it his natural astuteness and ferocity returned. He pondered sullenly on the course to be taken. He was too weak for a struggle with his attendant; yet to remain in his power was to expose himself to a certain capture; in a short time he would be in the hands of the police, and given up to justice, for two attempts to kill the man who had now strangely saved his life. He could not escape this fate by force—he might by subtlety, or by some means which his unsuspecting deliverer, but certain betrayer, might place in his power. He therefore feigned a greater degree of unconsciousness and debility than he suffered. He observed Oliver's movements. They were all those of a thoughtful physician, who sought only his recovery; he therefore would have no suspicion of his design to escape by whatever means. When Oliver placed him on his back he still feigned an almost helpless condition. But, in truth, though he was weakened, his consciousness was now completely restored. He remembered his vindictive attempt to expose Sir Guy Scarsdale's family to the fury of the bull—his efforts to escape from Lord Pendleborough —his intention to reach the ledge in the Kestrel Cove —his struggles when the ivy stem was separated from the face of the cliff by the too sudden impulse of his abrupt descent. All this passed rapidly through his mind. If taken, his life was therefore thrice forfeited to the law. He must escape at whatever hazard, by whatever means. He remembered, too, that, bound by the terrible oaths of the secret gang, he had been ordered to take Oliver's life, and had fired upon him in the Scarsdale Wood. The ferocious instinct had become in him an insanity.

He felt, too, the terrible and immediate peril of his position. What, then, was the measure of his strength. When reared against the tree he found his limbs lithe and free. He could clutch either hand firmly. His arms seemed to have recovered their force. He feigned, however, still to be help-less, that he might choose his own opportunity.

Oliver stepped warily down the dry bank to tra-verse the boggy ground with his heavy burthen. Ascroft perceived, in a short time, that the direction in which he moved was in a straight line with the steep zigzag which ascended to Scarsdale Hall. The shelter of which Oliver had spoken was not in some woodman's cottage. Had he the design of furtively delivering him into the power of Sir Guy Scarsdale? Had he tended him only to reserve him for ven-geance, and for the punishment of his crimes? These thoughts gathered into a tumult in his mind, just as Oliver reached the zigzag. They roused the murderous impulse in his heart to so fierce a fury, that he suddenly clutched his hunting-knife in its sheath in the breast pocket of his coat, and lifted his arm in the air. At the same time he leaned back-wards, holding Oliver's shoulder with his left hand, and would have buried the knife deep in the spine of the neck, if the suddenness of the motion had not wrenched his legs from his bearer's grasp, enfeebled by his struggle through the deep, wet ground. Before, therefore, Ascroft could strike the neck, he fell heavily to the earth, grazing the back with his knife.

Ere Oliver had turned round he had buried the weapon by a sudden blow deep in the leafy soil. The twilight had gloomed. They were at the foot of the zigzag. Oliver, conceiving that some convulsion had occurred, at once left his patient on the ground, saying, " I will bring back help to carry you to a shelter in a quarter of an hour." He then rapidly climbed the zigzag to the hall.

Oliver appeared at Scarsdale at the moment when the head keeper had been summoned by Sir Guy Scarsdale, to receive orders as to an immediate search for Ascroft. Sir Guy and Lord Pendleborough heard the intelligence, and communicated in a few brief words to Oliver the chief occurrences of the afternoon. While, therefore, Oliver returned with the least possible delay with the keepers, expecting to find Ascroft at the bottom of the zigzag, Lord Pendleborough sent to the duchess the card which it will be remembered she received from him.

Oliver was no sooner out of sight than Ascroft rose, and looking round warily in the gloom, he removed his highlows, and stole along the hard ground where his feet would leave little or no trace. Thus, among bushes of hazel and thickets of thorns and briar, he crossed the spur on which the zigzag led to the hall. Descending on the southern side, he came to the foot of another precipice, called the Scarsdale Crag, on the top of which stood the ruins of the keep. This crag was a cliff of the same strata of rocks as those which formed the Kestrel Cove. But here, the face of the precipice was not a semicircle, but an irregular line broken by bold pillars of rock. Stepping from stone to stone so as, if possible, to leave no footmarks, Ascroft approached a dense thicket of holly, briar, bramble and mountain ash, growing close to the foot of the cliff. Behind this he crept, until he got to the centre. There he tilted backwards a large bolder which lay against the rock. Beneath this was a hole like the mouth of a drain, into which he crept, thrusting his feet under the rock, and gradually wriggling backwards, until his shoulders were under the edge of the cliff. Then stretching out his arms he drew the bolder over the mouth.

A few yards farther back the passage, into which he had thus painfully entered, was less encumbered with *débris*. It soon became apparent that the mouth of a subterranean gallery had been nearly choked by the splinters which, perhaps, centuries had accumulated at the foot of the cliff, since the arch had been cut in the rock. Six yards within, the cavern was high enough to enable a man to walk in a slightly stooping posture. It entered the rock in a straight line for about twenty yards. At the end of this gallery at a right angle on the left hand was another, containing a flight of steps cut in solid stone, which ascended to a small chamber. Here he groped in the blackness of the gloom for a strong oaken door covered with the clenched heads of iron bolts, but without handle, keyhole, or hinge on the exterior. Having found this door, with which he seemed to be familiar, he stretched himself on the floor of this chamber, weary and weak, and was soon fast asleep. He slumbered with the profound stupor of fatigue and of the consequences of his fall.

After his interview with the duchess, the duke of Chatellerault retired to his own apartment in a mood deeply reflective. The courtesy which belonged to him as one of the ancient noblesse of France, his gallantry to a beautiful and charming woman, who had watched his illness with the pious devotion of a sister of charity and the tenderness of a daughter, gave an air of grace to his intercourse with the duchess, which masked the terrible struggle by which his inner nature was torn. In the presence of such purity he felt self-condemned. The simplicity and truth of the guileless character of his wife rebuked the subtle spirit of her lord. There was within him a sense of honour, which made life itself a small price to pay for his plighted word. He saw the divine instinct of the duchess which gave her an implicit trust in this proud faith of the noble of Old France. But all else within him wanted harmony with the sanctity of that virgin nature, whose aspirations sought to spiritualize all the relations of life, so as to sublimate them by faith and hope and charity to an anticipation of a better world. Charmed by the beauty and grace, subdued by the piety and gentleness of the duchess, won by her saintly tenderness, he felt oppressed by the impossibility of offering more than a paternal affection, and of reconciling even that with his inner self corrupted by long use. When his thoughts recurred to the associations with which his epicurean life had surrounded him in Paris, he felt that the frivolity, and the debasing sensuality of his career could not be exposed to the gaze of that being, whom Vavasour had described as an angel, whom he had brought within his house to look with heavenly eyes on all his ways. Thus, though the distractions of his voyage, of change of scene, and of an association with Sir Guy Scarsdale's family had afforded a respite, the duke gloomily reflected that the catastrophe of his errors was not the less sure. He asked himself the terrible question :—Shall I add to all the regrets of my wasted life, the remorse of the ruin of the happiness of a saint, whose beauty, grace, and purity appeal to *me* in whom the honour of a French noble survives?

Every means which had suggested itself to the subtle intelligence of the duke, as a way of escape from this catastrophe, seemed to have proved abortive. He reflected, one by one, on each. His reflections raised his estimate of the motives of Lord Pendleborough, of Malvoisin, of the duchess, and plunged him into a profounder gloom, when he analysed the selfishness and sensuality of his own. He felt, that whatever the inbred politeness of his rank might suggest, however the restless curiosity of his active mind might place him temporarily in relations with English society, his whole experience and habits were in discord with this domestic practical life, composed of familiar and social duties, interwoven with traditional pursuits. By and by his inquisitive interest would be exhausted; he would soon become weary of this provincial routine. The sarcastic *dénigrant* spirit would disturb the calm of his courtesies. The critical analytic severity of his nature would pierce with its poisonous fang, even the charities of this serene existence. His irritable nerves, disturbed by gout and tortured by remorse, would, against his will, cheat him into some outbreak of fury. Could he even protect the duchess herself from his sarcasms, his tendency to see and expose faults, or to imagine them where they did not exist? Even, if his affection should grow, could he protect her from the severities of an insane jealousy? Could he always look some illusion of his imagination as to her fidelity in the face, until the monstrous phantom disappeared under his steady gaze? Or, must he be maddened by the growth of a love, contrary to his plighted word, but the strength of which might be to him an unquench-able fire, the torment of an undying worm? Under the torture of these reflections, the duke writhed, as he had often before spent hours of agony in La Vendée, before he was soothed and aided by Malvoisin. The duke rung for his valet, and directed him to inquire whether M. Malvoisin could permit him to wait upon him before dinner. The servant brought a courteous reply from M. Malvoisin, that, as soon as he had changed his riding dress, he would prefer to do himself the honour of visiting the duke. After a short interval, M. Malvoisin entered the duke's room. The duke briefly related the events of the afternoon. He dwelt emphatically on the confirmation which they gave to the assurances of Malvoisin, as to the feelings of Lord Pendleborough towards the duchess. He only glanced by a passing allusion at a possible solution of Lord Pendleborough's *farouche* indifference to the homage of fashion in the capitals and courts of

Europe. He then spoke in despair of the reflections into which he was plunged by an analysis of his position.

"You found me dying in La Vendée. It was an act of cruel kindness to prove a too skilful physician to a mind poisoned past cure by the corruptions of my life, and a strength exhausted by an unbridled career, and unequal to struggle with this vulture of remorse. Why, oh why did I not expire in La Vendée? To have so died would have been some sort of expiation! It would have been a sort of suicide by the pangs of conscience! I have regained a strength which feeds the thoughts that prey upon me."

"Such a revulsion of feeling was to be expected, duke. The tide of our being seems to suffer a partial ebb, even when it is flowing. You are suffering, either from physical or from moral causes, a transient recoil of doubt and distress. You have not yet learned confidence in the new course of life, of which you are making trial."

"On the contrary, I am convinced that my whole nature is poisoned by a fatal virus, which will work its own hideous results in a moral deformity—a depravity of temper and manners—which will consume my being, and make me loathsome to the angelic purity of this saint, whom I have invited to shed the light of heaven even on my inner self

—eaten by the ulcers of a life which, in retrospect, is a long disease."

"Let me speak as frankly to you, duke, as if I were your confessor."

"I invite you to do so."

"You have spent a magnificent fortune—your constitution at forty-five is so exhausted that, without repose, your career will soon end—while in art, literature, and science, your subtle and acute mind has rare accomplishments, you have permitted your moral nature to be averted from the highest aims of life, to an epicurean existence, in all respects beneath your natural gifts and station. The taint of this life rankles like a poison in your conscience. You cannot expel this virus at once. Time is required for its elimination. I encourage you to believe, that the irascibility, suspicion, and critical malignity of which you complain will, in a calmer life among wholesome associations, gradually subside. You will gain strength of body, and mental power to control these terrible results of a reckless addiction to so-called pleasure. Let me be your physician, and believe that, with time, all will improve."

"But already I am impatient of the *niaiseries* of this provincial life. To touch the secret springs of European civilization—to float among the statesmen, diplomatists, and men of genius in the capitals of

Europe—has become to me a necessity of existence. I cannot away with this *fade* succession of duties in the seclusion of a wild region of forest and moor."

" By and by, Sir Guy Scarsdale will visit London. There, as elsewhere, he has the *entrée* of the highest and most intellectual society. Accompany him, duke. You will—separated from associations which drag your life downwards—find, in the highest regions of English life, all that you justly say has become necessary to your existence."

"Malvoisin! you would have made a great general— or a greater Superior of the Order of Jesus; for your presence is so calm—your intelligence so lofty—your range of vision so wide, that you have the transient power to make me obedient to your will. I submit, because I know that my mind is diseased—my thoughts are unnatural, they border on phrenzy—you have the power to control me, as the lunatic is controlled by the eye of his keeper, or as a beast of the forest is awed by the gaze of man."

So saying the duke sank back upon his sofa exhausted. Malvoisin, knowing his moods, remained silently by his side. After the lapse of an hour, the bell rang, and the duke's valet entered to dress him for dinner. Then, without uttering another word, Malvoisin noiselessly retired.

The party which Sir Guy Scarsdale assembled at

a late dinner included, besides the vicar and Mr.
Oliver Holte, Mr. Cliderhow and Mr. Balderstone,
with some of the oldest manufacturers of the valleys
of the Irwell and Roche, and of the forests of Rossendale and Pendle. These were men who had risen
from the ranks. Whose progenitors had either been
small yeomen, or tenant farmers, with a few looms at
work in their homesteads; or even industrious, thrifty,
handloom weavers, who had gradually increased the
number of journeymen in their *loom-shops*. The
memory of some of his guests, therefore, extended to
period of the invention of the " spinning-jenny," and
" water-frame." They remembered the early riots
by which these machines were driven from Blackburn
and the valley of the Calder, into Nottingham and
Derbyshire. They could speak of the gradual con-
version of corn-mills, moved by water power, into
spinning mills, and of the absorption for manufactures of this motive force through the hill valleys—
of the introduction of Watt's steam-engine — the
building of mills in villages, and the rapid growth of
new and flourishing towns.

The conversation during dinner was led backwards
by Sir Guy Scarsdale and the vicar, for the information of Malvoisin to the traditions of an earlier period.
His guests, speaking a broad Lancashire dialect—
being themselves men of the simplest habits, and of

manners which, though frank and courteous, were otherwise unpolished—related how their fathers had conducted the first steps of the staple manufacture, about the period of the invention of the fly-shuttle by Kay, of Bury. A century only had elapsed, since the roads through the valleys of the Irwell and the Roche were so rude, that they were little traversed by carriages. The products of the quarries and mines, and of the loom were carried on the " pack-saddles" of horses. Thus also the cloth woven in the forest and moorland homesteads and cottages, not required for home consumption, was carried to Manchester or to Leeds. By the fly-shuttle, about a century ago, a great impulse had been given to the power of the production of the loom as compared with that of the spinning-wheel. The wages of the women and girls employed in spinning rose. Every effort was used by yeomen, farmers, and small manufacturers having *loomshops* to stimulate the production of the "yarn," for the warp, and of the "weft" for the tissue of the cloth. Their agents went from house to house distributing cotton or wool to be cleaned, carded, and spun, and collecting the woollen or cotton "weft" or "yarn." Hence the whole country was traversed by such paths from one homestead, or cottage, to another, along which these collectors travelled, either with wicker baskets, called "skips," on their backs, or with donkeys or ponies, and large wicker panniers. The roads are to this day known as "Jersey roads"—that is, paths used by the collectors of the woollen thread spun for the flannel, baize, or blanket loom, and called "Jersey."

The difficulties of thus providing warp and weft for the looms, whose productive power was so greatly increased by the invention of the "fly-shuttle," were, however, insurmountable. Without the successive inventions of the "spinning-jenny," the "water frame," or "throstle," the cylindrical carding machine, the steam-engine, and the "mule," the vast commercial and social development of Lancashire would have been arrested at successive periods of progress.

In conversation during dinner, the vicar aided Sir Guy Scarsdale in drawing out from his aged guests, in their quaint vernacular, a series of interesting anecdotes, illustrating these traditions. Sir Guy translated them to the duke, to whom the dialect was unintelligible, and succeeded gradually, with the aid of Malvoisin, in awakening the duke's interest in the narratives.

The conversation was garnished with accounts of strangely rude customs and habits. The guests related how the inhabitants of the forest valleys— especially boys—had been clad in clothes formed of sheepskins, the wool of which was worn inwards, and the half-tanned skin outwards. They related the primitive condition of the dwellings—the rudeness of rural pastimes—the savageness of personal combats, and of the frays caused by village feuds—the grossness of certain provincial superstitions and usages. Even in their own experience they had narratives of adventures or rides from the forest valleys to the Manchester market, along deeply rutted roads crossed by perilous quagmires; and, in winter, choked by drifts of snow. Such a journey required that the manufacturer should be in the saddle at four or five o'clock in the morning, according to the distance he had to ride; and as the roads were not always safe, they often came from Manchester in the evening in parties riding ten or a dozen miles in company, for protection against footpads, and then dispersing on their separate moorland routes.

The vicar also elicited curious stories as to the habits of small squires, who had, a century before, inhabited the humbler class of mansions, built in the style of James the First, so many of which still remain as monuments of a state of society now past. The coarse, convivial habits of this class of gentry were related, as well as their addiction to cock-fighting, bull and bear baiting, dog-fighting, and the better sports of hunting the otter and the fox.

It was late ere Sir Guy rose and conducted his

guests into the drawing-room, where, after a welcome
from the ladies, they were again soon left alone; the
fair hostess, fatigued with the events of the day,
having been urged by the duchess to retire.

There had been a marvellous growth of wealth
within a century. Indeed, a century and a half
before this time, these moorlands had been only sheep
pastures and deer forests. The annual value had
increased a hundred, or five hundred fold, or even
more throughout entire districts. Malvoisin had,
throughout the entire conversation, pressed a series
of inquiries as to the amelioration of habits—the
decrease of superstition—the increase of self-control
in all classes,—which had accompanied the growth
of physical well-being.

The duke suggested cynical doubts ; gradually
roused himself to propose the problem that the deer-
keeper of the ancient forest, the shepherd, or hind,
of the trackless moorland, the herdsman of some
solitary upland glen, were, two centuries ago, simpler
better, stronger, and happier, than the race now
crowding the valleys and plains. He spoke in French
as follows:—

" To increase in numbers, in activity, in wealth,
or even in knowledge, is not certainly to make progress in happiness, nor necessarily to rise to a higher—
it may be only a different, form of civilization. These

handloom weavers are surely not happier than the
forest hinds, shepherds, and huntsmen. Are these
manufacturers superior to the small gentry and
yeomanry who inhabited, in the seventeenth century,
the scattered rural halls ? Are the people more
loyal, pious, obedient to the laws, or more intelligent
promoters of the national welfare ?"

" Such improvements," answered Malvoisin, also
speaking in French, " are slow. Material prosperity
may be the growth of scientific discoveries, combined
with local advantages, concurring with public policy.
It is possible to conceive a vast increase of wealth,
commercial activity, and power, without an elevation
of the standard of public or private morality—without the growth of a national literature—without the
improvement of political or social institutions. But
I think the century of scientific discovery and invention has also been an era of legislative, political,
social, and domestic improvement. I differ from the
common estimate, for I regret to think that moral
progress has not kept pace with that which is purely
intellectual, nor Christian civilization developed society, in all its forms, with the rapidity with which it
has advanced in physical comfort, and power over
the natural forces. Wealth is not heroism ; nor is
national power to be measured either by men or
money, without the indomitable valour—the love of

truth—the faith and moderation—of the progenitors of this great nation."

" I wish," replied the duke, " that I could imbibe so cheering a philosophy. History rather teaches me that society revolves in cycles, than makes any true progress through a series of developments. I can look back to periods of history in which I would rather have lived than at present."

" But I," said the vicar, " must discard Christianity—must disbelieve the gradual substitution of the law of Christian brotherhood, or love, for the antagonistic spirit of all preceding forms of society— if I do not cling firmly to the conviction, sanctioned, as I think, equally by historical and by philosophic induction, that the principle of Christian brotherhood is, in the slow growth of secular changes, glowing like a dawn through these eighteen hundred years—the dawn of a better state of society."

" If the eras of social change are as vast and as majestically gradual as the geological ages of transition, I may be won," said the duke, " to a dim faith in development."

" Take care, duke," said the vicar, with a gravity which had in it something of a rebuke, " that you do not place yourself in the light of the prophetic denunciation of St. Peter, and be reckoned among those ' scoffers ' who shall ' come in the last days, saying, Where is the promise of His coming? for since the fathers fell asleep, all things continue as they were from the beginning of the creation.'"

"I am but too much inclined," replied the duke, "to fulfil both that part of the apostle's words which describes the 'scoffers walking after their own lusts,' and which you are scarcely faithful in not repeating, and in questioning whether the Saxon thanes and Norman lords, with their serfs and villeins, cared not as much for the well-being of the common people as these manufacturers for their starving weavers."

"The law has displaced the rule of force, and the caprice of individual will among the strong," said Malvoisin. "There is no rapine, no law of feud— the common people are not chattels—they fare better, are better clad and housed, and have more liberty and intelligence. The instincts of the governing class are more humane—those of the comparatively subject less brutish. There is more security for life and for property, even for the feeble and solitary."

"There is, therefore, a dawn," said the vicar, "and St. Peter warned the Church, saying, 'Beloved, be not ignorant of this one thing, that one day is with the Lord as a thousand years, and a thousand years as one day.'"

After an interview with Sir Guy Scarsdale, Oliver

Holte had returned, with two keepers, down the steep zigzag, between the Kestrel Cove and Scarsdale Crag, to the place where he had left Ascroft. The twilight had meanwhile rapidly thickened in gloom, and night was at hand. There was, however, just light enough to identify Oliver's footsteps, deepened by his heavy burden in the soft earth, and the impression of Ascroft's body where he had fallen. To their surprise, he was no longer there. The head-keeper restrained them from moving from the spot, in order that no fresh mark might be left on the soil, and, if possible, the direction of Ascroft's retreat might be traced. The night had become so dark, that it was even difficult to climb the zigzag back to the hall. Up this the baffled party returned, to await the arrival of the police, who, as Sir Guy had informed them, were on their way from Manchester.

A couple of hours later, Philp and Martin arrived at Scarsdale Hall. Oliver had remained in Sir Guy's library, at his request, to concert measures with them for the night. Philp had a long conference with Oliver, made numerous inquiries from the keepers, and examined plans of the hall, and of the wood, Cove and crag. At length, he suggested that Oliver should spend the night in Sir Guy Scarsdale's dressing-room; that one watcher, without shoes, should move noiselessly about in the hall and passages on the ground floor; and that others should be stationed, one in the long gallery and corridors of the floor occupied by the family, and the other in those occupied by their guests. He suspected that Ascroft had some place of concealment close at hand. He therefore determined that he and Martin, each accompanied by a keeper, should watch through the night in the wood—one in a thicket, at the foot of the southern horn of the Kestrel Cove; the other, at the southern end of the Scarsdale Crag. Deloisir offered his services, and he, with the Cock of Rossendale, was stationed in a thicket, half way up the zigzag, at a point which both prevented any escape in that direction and overlooked the precipitous declivity which, on either side, descended to the Kestrel Cove and the foot of the Scarsdale Crag. Every watcher was well armed with pistols and a dirk, and provided with a dark lantern, with a bull's-eye glass and reflector.

This arranged, Philp quietly stationed the watchers in the house, and gave to each detailed instructions and cautions. He then took some refreshment with Martin, and walked forth, with Deloisir and the rest of his party, with the stealthy step of a tiger-cat, apparently certain of his prey.

Meanwhile, Ascroft slumbered soundly in the chamber of the subterranean gallery. Exhausted by

his rapid run of two miles through the rough and
boggy ground of the wood, by the agony of his
frightful struggle on the face of the precipice, and by
the consequences of his fall, a profound sleep came
to the relief of his vigorous and healthy frame. He
slumbered on, hour after hour, through the night.
At length, he was awakened by hunger, for he had
not eaten anything from the preceding noon. He
awoke in the black darkness of his cavernous lair,
and groping about found the studded door, and soon
remembered where he was. Crawling down the flight
of steps cut in the rock, and then along the gallery
towards the entrance, he slowly removed the bolder
to refresh himself with the air, and to watch what
was stirring without. The sun had some time risen,
the birds were singing their matins in the wood, the
light glanced from the trunks of the forest trees, and
glittered on the leaves. As seen from the cavern, it
had a green sheen, like that of a pale emerald, or like
the sea-water in the inlet of a rocky shore. Even
the ruthless instincts of Ascroft had not blunted his
mental perceptions, so as to make him indifferent to
natural beauty. This sense, and the power of observation, together with the craft, daring, and romance
of adventure, often lie at the root of the poacher's
impulses, and nourish them with an aliment stronger
than the profits of their moonlit and stealthy enter-

prises. With the astuteness of a watcher for deer, and with somewhat of the pleasure of a naturalist, Ascroft lay on his breast, with his head barely protruding from the narrow mouth of the secret gallery, hidden in front by the thicket which grew close to the foot of Scarsdale Crag. Stealthily, his eyes searched the wood, through the interstices of this close undergrowth. For a long time, nothing stirred, except the rabbits, which bobbed about from hole to hole, showing the white fur under their tails—the hares, which passed with slower and longer bounds, nibbling as they went—the pheasants, which fed under the Spanish chesnuts, and among the bushes of Mahonia—the wood-pigeons and magpies, each with their peculiar flight and note—and the colony of rooks, which careered overhead from the vast sycamores and limes which surrounded Scarsdale Hall. Ascroft found much of peculiar interest to him in all that he saw, but these were not the objects of his watch.

What was that in the thicket, near the foot of the zigzag? A man, whom he could not recognize, was busy, like a hunter, in the examination of the ground. He advanced slowly, with a microscopic scrutiny. Step by step, every blade, pebble, and leaf, seemed to be observed. Had he found some trace of Ascroft's footsteps of the preceding night, even though he had

taken the precaution to remove his highlows? No
other person was in sight.   But this stranger, stooping to the earth, and advancing slowly, with singular
care and skill, followed traces of the path along which
Ascroft had threaded the thickets to the stony talus
of the cliff.   The progress of the searcher was very
tardy, but it seemed to be sure.   By trifling marks,
the pressure of his feet on the leafy soil under the
forest trees seemed to be detected.   His path, however, had been purposely devious, and he had struck
the talus of stones fallen from the cliff above two
hundred yards beyond the entrance of the gallery.
Even if the searcher should be successful in tracing
his footsteps to this point, he must have singular
acuteness, and marvellous power of observation, if he
could retrace his strides from one large angular stone
to another, as far as the thicket and the mouth of the
cave.

To prepare himself, however, for every alternative,
Ascroft pulled from his pocket a large hunch of bread
and some bacon, the common resource of poachers.
When he had eaten a part of this, and swallowed two
or three mouthfuls of whisky from his flask, he withdrew farther into the gallery, and, by the light of the
entrance, carefully reloaded a double-barrelled pistol.
Assuring himself that his knife was safe, and that he
had in his possession a piece of iron, like the key of the

nut at the head of a screw, he returned noiselessly
and cautiously to his post of observation.

In the interval, the first stranger had been joined
by a second, and their proceedings were observed by
a group of the Scarsdale keepers whom he knew,
and who stood at the foot of the zigzag. The two
strangers were clearly upon his traces. They had
followed, with strange skill and accuracy, the very
devious path by which he had threaded the undergrowth. At their rate of progress, however, it
would take them an hour, at least, to reach the rocky
border of the talus of the Scarsdale Crag. Having
satisfied himself of this, Ascroft cautiously replaced
the bolder on the mouth of his place of concealment, crawled back into the gallery, and, creeping
along it, ascended the flight of steps to the chamber,
in which was the oaken door, thickly studded with
bolts. Here, with a flint and steel, he struck a spark
on to some tinder, lighted a match, and then a candle
—all which simple apparatus was contained in a
small tin box, carried in his pocket, for his midnight
poaching rambles. Having thus lit up the chamber,
he pulled from his coat the iron key, and, examining
the square studs which projected from the face of the
door, fixed upon three. He first applied the key in
succession to two of these—one, near the edge of the
door, was turned round about twenty times; the

second, which was about half way towards the centre, only six times, and in an opposite direction to the first. The key was then applied to a stud much higher up, the rows which intervened having first been carefully counted. This higher stud was turned round also about twenty times. When Ascroft had finished this last manœuvre, he pulled the heavy oaken door slowly open with the help of the key, so that he could insert his fingers at the edge, and then cautiously exerting his strength he dragged it towards him, till he could pass through the interval.

On the other side appeared the bottom of a deep well, cut through the rock of the crag, but with no lateral opening below, except this door. This well and postern had, apparently, formed a safe and secret means of communicating with the country, when the keep and its castellated precincts were beleaguered above. The door was doubly secured. In the interior were massive bars, bolts, and props, which, combined with the great strength of the door itself, would prevent an entrance to the well by this means. To enter the bottom of the well, without possessing the means of ascent for upwards of 250 feet, was, however, to be in no better position that at the foot of Scarsdale Crag. The means of ascent and descent were commanded by a chain hanging from a thick oaken trunk above, on which it was wound by a winch handle, within a lateral chamber, at the summit of the well. Communication could thus be maintained with the exterior without danger to the keep, and intelligence and supplies were thus within reach. The means by which Ascroft had effected his entrance consisted of an arrangement for the return of a confidential messenger to the keep. By the turning of the first two studs Ascroft had worked an internal rack, liberating the massive bar of a latch from two perpendicular bolts which held it down. Having thus freed the latch, it was lifted by turning another rack, by means of the third stud to which the key was applied.

When Ascroft entered the bottom of the well, he carefully examined the rust-eaten chain which hung in the centre. He knew it to be still strong enough to bear his weight. On the chain loops of cord had been fastened to the links, at intervals within a moderate stride upwards. By means of these loops, the chain could be ascended, and the chamber at the top of the well could be reached.

Having completed his observations, Ascroft re-entered the chamber at the top of the flight of steps, leaving the oaken door partially open; then he descended the steps, blowing out his candle at the foot, and replacing it in his tin box. Thence, stealthily and cautiously, he crept to the entrance.

There he lay a quarter of an hour without disturbing the bolder, listening in silence.   Hearing nothing to deter him, he again carefully removed the stone, and raised his head to the edge of the soil in the thicket. After searching for some time he at length discovered that the two strangers had threaded their way through the copse nearly to the place where his path had first struck the large stones at the foot of the talus. By and by, Philp and Martin—for they were the two strangers watched by Ascroft—reached this point. After carefully examining the soft ground on every side along the foot of the talus, they returned in about half an hour to the point of the stony border to which their quest had led them. There, sitting down on a mass of rock, they whistled. The group of keepers then approached from the foot of the zigzag, about a quarter of a mile away. Some refreshment was distributed to the whole party, for it was afternoon. During their meal they talked in whispers. After a respite of twenty minutes thus occupied, the keepers dispersed, arranging themselves at intervals which enabled each man to see his neighbour, and in a line stretching from the foot of the zigzag to a point about two hundred yards below the place where they had eaten their meal.

The cunning of a red Indian in pursuit of the trail

of an enemy or of game could not surpass the skill of Philp, in similar combinations, on the track of offenders against the law. From his conferences on the preceding evening, and from his scrutiny of the plans of the hall, he had felt certain that Ascroft was acquainted with some hiding-places, or even possessed secret means of access to the hall. From the condition in which he had been left at the foot of the zigzag, Philp had no doubt that he had crept to one of these crypts. From this covert he expected him to be compelled by hunger to come forth, after some hours' rest. Through the night, therefore, the Kestrel Cove, the zigzag, and the Scarsdale Crag wood had been watched. When the morning broke without any sign of the assassin's position, Philp, having sent only one man for their breakfast, maintained the watch from a part of the zigzag which overlooked both the Cove and the crag. He then commenced a careful examination of the ground, and, after some time, found faint traces of the steps of a man walking in coarse ribbed stockings over the leafy forest earth. The course taken was devious. It threaded the thickets, so as to confirm his suspicion that Ascroft had chosen an intricate route to baffle pursuit. Filled with this conception of his cunning, when he had assured himself that he was on the right track, he had summoned Martin to assist him, and to

be ready for any emergency. If flight from the
wood had been Ascroft's intention, he certainly would
not have chosen so tortuous a path. He must, therefore, be hidden somewhere near. The morning, as
we have seen, was consumed in this scrutiny.

Ascroft still lay watching at the mouth of the
passage when Philp and Martin resumed their
search. At this point, probably, the quest must
have been without further indication, if a slight trace
of blood had not been discovered. Here and there
along the footmarks a drop of blood upon a leaf had
assured Philp that the marks were those of Ascroft's
devious track. A few yards nearer to the mouth of
the thicket, another drop of blood had fallen on the
stone from the sleeve of Ascroft's coat. From this
point, the progress of the searchers was so rapid, that
Ascroft withdrew from the opening, replaced the
bolder with extreme caution, and remained just
within to listen. He again refreshed himself from
his flask of whisky and his lunch of bread. Within
twenty minutes, he heard a voice outside about
thirty yards from the thicket say, " Here is another
drop. The scent lies strong. He cannot be far off."
These ominous words were the signal for retreat to
Ascroft.   He slid noiselessly backwards into the
gallery along which he crept. Then, climbing the
steps, he passed through the chamber and the oaken

door which he had left ajar to the foot of the well.
Here he closed the door, with the help of a massive
iron handle which hung from the inner side. Then
lighting his candle, he worked the rack on the
inside which closed the latch, and afterwards he
fastened it down by the two perpendicular bars.
Having, however, strange proofs of Philp's cunning,
he further slid a massive oaken bar into a hole in the
rock on one side of the door, and then into iron rests
fastened to the back of the oak, and into a ledge
in the rock on the opposite side. This barred all
progress without the destruction of the door, which
was double planked, and bolted with iron studs.
Here, therefore, Ascroft waited to ascertain whether
his pursuers had found his place of refuge.

He had not to wait long. Philp and Martin,
warmed with the excitement of their rapid discovery
of the traces of blood on the stone, were soon in the
thicket. They found a smear of blood, from the
sleeve of Ascroft's coat, along the face of the rock at
the foot of the cliff. On the moist talus in the
thicket were faint indications of footmarks. The
bolder had been too often moved to escape the
signs on its surface of having been turned over on to
the soil. They lifted it at once from its place, and
discovered the entrance to the secret passage. Both
silently raised their hands at this discovery, and

Martin was at once despatched for the head-keeper.
A brief conference occurred. The keeper knew
nothing of this gallery in the rock. He was sent
to draw the rest of the watchers into a narrow circle
round the mouth. As soon as this had been done,
each was questioned as to what he knew of the
cavern. But all were equally surprised at the discovery. Little time elapsed in these inquiries.
Meanwhile Philp and Martin had examined their
weapons carefully. Each lighted his police lantern,
and, followed by Deloisir, they entered the secret
gallery.

In the mud at the foot of the entrance, the marks
of Ascroft's bootsoles were at once recognized. He
had, therefore, put on his boots in the gallery, and
had probably not left it, for no traces of highlows
were to be found outside. Along the gallery the
wonder-struck party tracked the footmarks up the
steps to the chamber. Here the floor was again
smeared with blood from Ascroft's sleeve. The floor
of the chamber also betrayed that the oaken door
had been recently opened. There were, however,
no apparent means for this purpose, no keyhole, no
handle. The secret of the mode of opening the
postern might perhaps be read, but this would require
time. Philp examined the whole surface with his
lantern patiently and with care. Some signs on one

50—2

of the bolts which had been turned, did not escape his scrutiny. But there was a necessity for immediate action, and some hours at least would be required to unravel the mystery—even if meanwhile the door, as was most probable, had not been fastened within by means only accessible on the inner side. Philp, therefore, decided that the door must be broken, and no means but gunpowder were likely to be prompt and effectual enough. He withdrew from the chamber with Martin and Deloisir, and despatched the keepers for all the canisters of powder in their possession, rough canvas bags, and a slow match.

Not a word had been exchanged by the three who had entered the chamber, lest Ascroft should be listening on the other side of the postern. In the thicket on the outside they concerted their plans. More than an hour elapsed, the afternoon had passed, and twilight again come, ere the keepers had been able to collect powder enough to fill two strong bags made of sailcloth. A slow match was put in the mouth of each. They were carefully tied up, and Philp and Martin then entered, and, groping their way in the dark, placed the bags of powder at the foot of the oaken door. The slow match was then laid to the head of the flight of steps; both returned to the mouth of the passage, and Philp, taking his lantern, re-entered, cautiously lighted the match, and

escaped from the gallery. All withdrew from the
side of the cliff to await the explosion. The match
burned in five minutes, a loud heavy sound ensued:
earth, stones, and smoke were blown from the mouth
of the gallery, and the ground quivered as from a
heavy shock, but nothing was displaced from the
cliff. After the first puff of smoke, the air seemed
to enter the gallery as though it circulated through
some inner shaft. This current inwards was so
strong as to blow a flame to an acute angle. After
a short interval, the gallery was nearly free from
smoke.   Philp, Martin, and Deloisir re-entered,
leaving the keepers at the mouth. They found the
oaken door broken into such fragments that, with the
help of a hatchet, its removal was the work of half an
hour. Within, they discovered the bottom of the
well, without any other portal, and no apparent means
of ascent. Casting the light of their lanterns up the
shaft, they could dimly discern the rusted chain,
eighty yards above, wound round a huge beam.
Was it possible that Ascroft could have climbed this
chain, and then wound it on to the rude windlass
at the top of the well? If so, where was he now?
The smoke of the explosion was driven by the
current of air up this shaft. Where was it escaping?
If this could be observed, some clue might be got to
the mystery of the secret passages about the keep

and in the walls of the ancient castellated structure which had been built in to the western side of the hall. Philp pondered. A watch must be left in the chamber at the foot of the well, but he must immediately return to the hall, to warn Sir Guy Scarsdale and his guests, and to take precautions against a new form of danger, and, if possible, to entrap Ascroft in his burrow. Martin and a keeper were, therefore, left in the chamber, and a watcher at the entrance of the cavern, while Philp, Deloisir, and the rest returned to Scarsdale Hall. As they ascended the zigzag, the gloom had thickened into night.

CHAPTER V.

"PEEP-O'-DAY BOYS." — VISITS TO ASSHETON
MANOR-HOUSE.—A LOVER'S ADIEU.—AWAKEN-
ING INTEREST.

THE day, the lapse of which to evening in the
Scarsdale Wood was described in the latter part of
the last chapter, was marked by events in the hall
which must be interwoven into the tissue of our narrative before we proceed.

At the breakfast-table, the adventure of Oliver
Holte with Ascroft, and his subsequent escape,
formed a chief topic of conversation. Oliver had
left with dawn for Assheton Manor-house. Mabel
was radiant; it was a conscious though unavowed
subject of satisfaction to her that Ascroft had not
been killed by his fall from the cliff, to which he had
been chased by Lord Pendleborough. The duchess
and Miss Hollingsworth reflected their friend's brilliant mood, which overflowed in conversation full of
wit and grace. Sir Guy with his usual cheerfulness,
the duke with his sparkling sarcasm, and the vicar

with his grave and quaint sagacity and humour,
entered the lists. Lord Pendleborough, though
serene, was silent, and replied in little more than
monosyllables, even when Malvoisin endeavoured to
draw him into the gay *mêlée*.

When the party rose, the gentlemen retired into a
deep bay, and there, ere long, the causes of Lord
Pendleborough's preoccupation of mind transpired.
He had received letters from Ireland, rendering
an early visit to his estates in the west imperative.
The letters described some of the worst consequences
of the cottier system, which had been fostered by
agents during his minority. The cultivated land
was thickly peopled by a class of small tenants, who
had built their own cabins on diminutive holdings.
This system had displaced in some generations the
previous forms of tenancy. As it involved no fresh
outlay by the landlord, and was attended by an
immediate increase of rental either from money or
service, the agents of proprietors, who were to a
great extent absentees, blindly fostered the settlement
of a population without capital, almost without
wages, and chiefly supported by the cultivation of the
potato, the feeding of pigs of an inferior breed, and
the raising of young stock on the bogs, heaths, and
mountain pastures, or other land not broken up for
the potato culture. The tendency to the exhaus-

tion of the land by this form of cultivation was
rapid. The half-idle population, deteriorating in
condition, became more and more lawless, and, with
the Celtic tendencies to secret association, formed
" Ribbon," " Whiteboy," or " Peep-o'-day " lodges,
which soon conspired to convert the occupation of
land into possession with service, or even to refuse
the payment of either rent or service. Agents of
neighbouring properties, who had rigorously enforced
the payment of rent, and exacted the customary
labour, had been threatened, waylaid, and had suffered from malicious injuries. This rigour, however, was resented less than any interference with the
occupation of land. This morning brought to Lord
Pendleborough the disastrous intelligence of the murder of a Scotch farmer who had settled on a group
of conacre and small holdings, consolidated into a
moderate farm, on which a well-constructed homestead had been built. The displaced cottier tenantry
had been liberally supplied with the means of emigrating to Lord Pendleborough's own property in
Canada, and had there been each established in the
management of an allotment of land, with a pro-
vision of implements, and paid labour for the first
year. The Scotchman had been warned to interfere
as little as possible with local customs and habits.
But the necessities of regular husbandry, and some-

thing in the habits of the lowland farmer, had made him more exacting as to the regularity of his labourers, and as to the quality of their work, than was consistent with popularity. When to this source of vexation was added the fact, that every plot of conacre, and every holding which fell vacant by death, or from which the occupants could be induced to remove, was added to the farm, it became apparent, that this was only the first step in a process of absorption. The idea of converting occupation into possession, which was the bond of the secret societies, was thus brought gradually face to face with that of a partnership, in which the landlord provided the permanent capital in buildings, roads, drainage, fences, and plantations, and the tenant the moveable stock of implements, cattle, and the transient capital of seed and manure. A barbarous idea of usurpation was brought into conflict with the law and force of society tending to a gradual amelioration. The secret societies issued their order, and the Scotch farmer had been shot, in his own fields, in the open day, in the midst of labourers, none of whom discontinued their work, even to carry the corpse to the house, much less to pursue the assassins. The body was removed in a cart by the farmer's own brother.

This was the news brought to Lord Pendleborough by the morning's post, and which had kept him silent

and self-absorbed during the breakfast. All the
party were aware that Lord Pendleborough contemplated an early visit to Ireland, personally to direct
the improvements on his estates, on the nature and
extent of which he had, after a year's inquiry and
observation, resolved. The condition of this property
and the means of preventing an imminent catastrophe, ruinous alike to the tenantry and to the
proprietor, had formed the subject of constant correspondence with Lord Pendleborough's agents and of
discussion with Malvoisin. This had been also the
motive of visits to those parts of Germany which
had been transformed by the policy of Hardenberg,
to the small farms of Belgium, to the properties of
the Béarnais in the Pyrenees: and to the Lothians,
Lincolnshire, and Norfolk, to examine the results
of capital and skill. Since his arrival in Lancashire, Lord Pendleborough had taken every opportunity of testing his own conclusions, by comparing
them with the experience of the vicar, ripened by
many years of successful management of Assheton
Manor, and with that of Sir Guy, whose clear, active
mind at once combined the facts, and whose early
and later experience made him no mean judge of the
mode of avoiding a useless or wasteful outlay, and
especially of governing men. The group in the
bay window, therefore, excepting only the duke,

was a group of Lord Pendleborough's private coun-
sellors.

"What are your accounts, Pendleborough, of
your Irish settlers in Canada?" asked Sir Guy.

"They are excellent. Briscoe seems a splendid
fellow. He has employed the settlers to fell the
timber on the farms, which they are to occupy, and
paid them wages in kind, sufficient to sustain them
until they have built their own log houses, and
shanties for cattle, fenced in their arable land, and
sowed their first crops. Such of the timber as was
of proper size and near the lake, he has got into
rafts, and sold for a sum which has defrayed a fair
proportion of the cost of the clearing and buildings.
He has advanced to the tenants stock and implements, for which he is to be repaid by instalments.
As there is to be no rent for three years, and then
only a moderate rent to those who have actually
repaid this loan, I have no doubt of the result. The
cost has not amounted to half the sum which I
placed at his disposal. The rent at the end of three
years will be five per cent. on my whole outlay and
the price of the land."

"Are the tenants satisfied? and have they
written in that spirit to Ireland?"

"Of that I have as yet received no assurance.
The disruption of habits and associations may be

too recent for such a result. Yet I fancy my poor Scotchman would not have succeeded in persuading some conacre tenants and small farmers to follow the rest to Canada, if accounts of their well-being had not been received."

" Doubtless that is so," said Malvoisin, "though no confession of such satisfaction will at present transpire in Ireland. The Peep-o'-day boys will throw discredit on any prosperity which hinders the success of their intention to usurp, by a system of terror, the possession of the land."

" The dawn of the millennium of St. Peter, vicar," said the duke in French, " would appear to require ages as vast and numerous in Ireland as in English forests and moors, inhabited by starving weavers, represented by secret clubs of assassins."

" Yet to the eye of faith," said the vicar, gravely, " there is a dawn, even in the fact that this population migrates to England—emigrates to America— exhibits a strength and tenderness of domestic sympathy equal to any sacrifice, a valour, a religious faith, and a patriotic spirit, which, whatever we may think of their objects, are never appealed to in vain. Be assured this is the dawn, in which Providence will employ the growing humanity, charity, and intelligence of English civilization to create, perhaps in some great crisis, a new era for Ireland."

"But I, who am a scoffer, have not observed that what are called revolutions are any other things than the crumbling into ruin of structures gnawed by the tooth of time. I believe in law, in order, and, if you allow me ages like the vast geological periods of transition, I believe in social progress. But crises are prepared through long antecedent time."

"That is doubtless the truth," said Malvoisin, "and we perhaps might form some estimate of the rate of social progress by comparing the condition of those races which have apparently exhausted, while unmixed, the force of development, with the dominant races in which it is still active. How long a time was required to build up the civilization of the Chinese, the Hindoos, the Affghans, the Persians, or the Arabians? Why is their progress arrested? What events do they await?"

"At least nothing can be more certain than that the Christian faith, operating through the Circassian and European races, tends to disseminate itself throughout the world," said the vicar. "Its triumph is in Europe contemporaneous with the revival of letters and art, and the discoveries of inductive science. Its impulse has explored and colonized the world. The stagnant races are everywhere dominated by Christians. Is not this the dawn of a new era?"

"The era of the slave trade," said the duke, "of the

supply of the staple of this district, and of some of the modern necessaries of life, such as sugar and coffee, by slave labour;—the era of the opium trade to China, and of a revenue raised in this Christian country by an excise on the brutal habits of a semi-barbarous people;—the era of the extinction of the aborigines of America and Africa by the small-pox, brandy, and the rifle;—the era of the pillage of empires, by a ruthless Christian soldiery, who do not even restore the tanks and canals of their Maho-metan predecessors. A true dawn of the gospel of peace and good-will."

" The era, let me also say," replied the vicar, " of the suppression of piracy on the high seas; of the spread of commerce to the remotest regions, where every trader is safe under the protection of the Christian flag; of the sway of law and order, with whatever defects, over Eastern nations, which had fallen into a sensual anarchy. Let our nation conceive rightly, in the spirit of its Christian faith, what is its mission, and these conquests will be the dawn of which I speak. Doubt it not, duke. We have each of us in our own spheres at home to make this central light and heat of England the collected force of pure Christian homes and communities, and the world will be the better for the valour, endurance, and enterprise of our race."

"The vicar expresses my own faith," said Sir Guy; "and Pendleborough, by taming these Irish Kernes, and then civilizing them, will do something to make this kingdom the sun of Christian civilization."

"I am resolved to be in Kerry with the least possible delay," said Lord Pendleborough. "But I should not like to leave without seeing Colonel Vavasour. Are you disposed for a ride to Assheton, vicar?"

"My duties carry me thither without delay," replied the vicar.

"I pray you to leave Miss Hollingsworth at Scarsdale, as my daughter's guest, and to return yourself to-night," said Sir Guy.

The vicar consented; horses were ordered; and Lord Pendleborough and Mr. Hollingsworth were soon on their way across the upland farms to Scarsdale Head. Before noon they entered the fold of Assheton Manor-house.

On the night before, when Oliver Holte found that it was proposed by Philp that he should remain all night in Sir Guy Scarsdale's dressing-room, he sent Seth Diggle to the Tim Bobbin at Scarsdale Head, where he knew that Barnabas Collier was a guest, with a note, requesting Barnabas to spend the night at Assheton Manor-house.

He promised that if Colonel Vavasour continued, on the following day, as well as he had recently been, Barnabas should have an interview with his old patron and companion in moorland rambles. He entrusted him also with an explanatory note to Colonel Vavasour, who was thus left for the night to the care of his valet, aided by Dame Parkinson, with Barnabas at hand, as counsellor in case of emergency. The night, however, had passed, and a couple of hours after dawn Oliver entered the manor-house, while Colonel Vavasour yet slept. After breakfast with Oliver, Colonel Vavasour resumed his favourite seat on the broad cushioned ledge in the oriel, overlooking the western fork of Scarsdale to the Mere Clough. The eastern sun had risen high enough to make a mirror of the Mere, the sheen of which penetrated the foliage in the extreme distance of this branch of the ravine. The brook sparkled here and there through the trees. His own rooks careered in a throng, as busy as a Parliament about to disperse for the moors, and similarly intent on their own game in the stubbles and pastures. His own thoughts reverted to the early times of his innocent youth; to the gradual corruption of his manners at school and college; to the tenacity with which, through all, he had clung to his reverence for his guardian; his early love for his foster-sister Helen; his romantic memory of the wild sports of the cloughs and moors, with the *gamin* of the glen for his creel-bearer, and to carry his game; and of the long tramps with Barnabas to scenes of traditional interest.

Meanwhile, Barnabas, unseen, had crept within the door of the room, limping, and afraid to disturb his patron. He seemed staggered to find the slight youth developed into a man, whose strongly knitted frame told of endurance; whose thick dark eyebrows, and compressed, delicate lips, revealed a character of unusual vigour and firmness. Still more did he wonder at the signs of refinement in the fastidious, feminine expression of the great, calm eyes; of luxury, in the delicate hands, on which was one massive ring set with large diamonds; and of fashion, in the velvet dress with bright silver buttons, in which his former friend was attired. The irregular profile had developed from the soft outlines of youth into a craggy series of prominences, which gave a singular individuality to the handsome face. Barnabas had approached no such man. What, thought he, will he have to say to the scraggy, withered, limping pedagogue, shrivelled with penury, worn by tramps through these forest dales, wasted by holding forth in cottage conventicles, and teaching in the foul air of ranters' Sunday schools?

Is there anything left in common, between this glass of fashion and mould of form, and myself, the cobbler, sign-painter, ranter, and pedagogue?

By-and-by, while Barnabas still stood, unwilling to advance, Colonel Vavasour turned his head from the day-dream inspired by the view from the oriel, and was himself staggered to see within the door a meanly-dressed man, with a lean face furrowed by deep lines, and the muscles of which were gathered in cords about the mouth and jaw. The small grey eyes twinkled, a smile gathered on the haggard features, and the withered hobbling figure limped towards him.

"Barnabas," said Vavasour, stretching out both his arms, and grasping the horny fingers with his own delicate hands—"Barnabas, the casket in which the jewel of thy noble spirit is locked for a time, my old friend, is strangely battered. What ill chance has robbed thee of the little flesh that clothed thy wiry limbs when we were lads?"

"No ill chance, Colonel Vavasour. Partly, I have but a meagre frame at best, a poor stomach, and a fidgety spirit. I am always on the tramp among the little flocks of the Great Shepherd and Bishop of our souls, in the hand-loom weaving hamlets, teaching, praying, ranting, tenting the unwary, helping the sorrowful and needy, painting village shop signs, cobbling shoes, and boarded and lodged here and there."

"Ah, I remember well, Barnabas, our excursion over Assheton Moor to Bacup, and through the Dule's Gate to Studley Pike. I must, graceless though I was, needs meet Deacon Crabtree at a prayer-meeting in Todmorden, and then, forsooth, sleep in the clean chamber of a widow, who assuredly was a lineal descendant of Dorcas; and then, alack the day! witness a baptism by thy unconsecrated hands in a pool in the Dule's Gate, after a holding forth in a cottage in that wild glen."

"True, colonel; but do you remember Deacon Crabtree's admonitions on the way from Todmorden through the Dule's Gate?"

"I have never forgotten them. He told me, like a prophet or evangelist, that I should find no peace till I became a soldier and a servant of Christ."

"He is dead. He sent for me to his deathbed. An hour before he died, he turned, and said: 'Has the vicar news of the lord of Assheton Manor?' 'Yes,' I said, 'his regiment has been through our fortresses in the Mediterranean, and he is now colonel, and at Corfu, whence he is visiting Greece and the Holy Land.' 'May the grace of God reach him there! Tell him, that it was the last prayer of old John Crabtree, the deacon of the Baptist church of Assheton Moorhoyles. His father suffered us to build our little Zion; his guardian the vicar, is a large-hearted man, and has left us to work among the poor in peace. May the blessing of those ready to perish, for their sakes, descend on our brave but wild young lord.' "

" Amen!" said Vavasour, gravely. There was a slight pause. Then the colonel, turning to Barnabas, said cheerfully: " Art thou still a catgut scraper, a rhymster, a leader of choral festivals at charity sermons, as in times past, Barnabas? "

" Truly, in my poor fashion, colonel, I still distract my own fidgets by shrill and harsh catgut scraping, which would scare any professor, but passes for a work of genius in these wilds; I write epitaphs and hymns, and I train our Sunday scholars for their annual choral charity meetings."

" And hast thou found no resting-place for the sole of thy foot, thou bird with the olive-branch? "

" Colonel and friend, thou touchest the most sacred secret of my heart."

" Nay, I would not pry, Barnabas, into thy inner thoughts; but with such a treasure of poetry and self-sacrifice in thy nature, there is the heroism which attracts a true and faithful woman to native nobility of heart."

" My good lord of Assheton, and old friend and

patron, your words of sympathy unlock the hidden chamber where lies my secret. For six years past, I have watched and trained a fair scholar in my Sunday class in Scarsdale. She has grown under my eye in knowledge and goodness. Her father was a graceless man, who kept the Tim Bobbin, and farmed the intack at Scarsdale Head. But the mother was always a decent body, and these six years past, being a widow, she has, helped by me and old Tummus of Scarsdale Head, kept a reputable house. Of late years, I have been more and more her guest. She has become a communicant at Assheton Church. So is her daughter. We are plighted each to the other, and we are to be wed ere long, for Susan is now twenty years of age."

"Thank God, Barnabas! And thou art, if I mistake not, thirty-two; for ten years have passed since I was last at Assheton Manor."

"Ten years! Is it so long?"

"I came back to Lancashire, not intending to visit Assheton. Man proposes and God disposes. Here I am, smitten by the hand of God; a wreck, barely escaped from the immediate danger of the storm; but, thank Heaven, at least ashore, though it be but to rot away, in my own ancestral home, among old friends, of whom, Barnabas, I reckon you not the least."

Oliver here entered the room, and approached Colonel Vavasour. He sat for a time by his side, while the conversation drifted onwards, and then Barnabas, at a concerted sign, bid his old friend good morning, and retired with strong injunctions to repeat his visit. When he was gone, Oliver counselled complete repose; and while he wrote at the table in the middle of the room, Colonel Vavasour lay wrapped in a maud on the cushioned seat, and ere long fell into a doze. A couple of hours after, some refreshment was brought, and Colonel Vavasour seemed to have quite overcome any fatigue caused by his interview with Barnabas. About half-past one, Oliver was called from the room, and found Lord Pendleborough and the vicar below stairs. The immediate departure of Lord Pendleborough for his estates in Kerry, appeared to Oliver to justify an interview. The vicar understood that the period of his own access to his ward must depend on the effects of preliminary interviews such as these. Oliver, therefore, returned to Colonel Vavasour, gradually broke to him the emergency which precipitated Lord Pendleborough's visit to Ireland, and his anxiety to be admitted before he left. Colonel Vavasour was eager to see his friend. While, therefore, Oliver remained below in conversation with the vicar, the servant led Lord Pendleborough to the

room. Colonel Vavasour sat up to welcome his
visitor, but excused himself from advancing, by
saying,—

"I am a cripple, Pendleborough, in the hands of
our good friend Holte, who forbids me to walk or
even to stand, until I have made some further progress in the reparation of the hurt which I got in our
midnight interview at Deerden. Do not measure
my courtesies by my infirmities, which alone prevent
my doing more than offer my hand as a welcome to
my old manor-house."

"Vavasour! you are a soldier, and I am a hunter.
When men have perfect faith in each other's sincerity
and truth, they know that old friendship is like old
wine—it needs no bush."

"Though an uninvited guest, Pendleborough, none
is more welcome."

"I leave by to-night's tide from the Mersey for
Ireland, and I was unwilling to do so without seeing
you. Are you aware that the Duke and Duchess of
Chatellerault are at Scarsdale?"

"Only within two days has my cautious physician
permitted me to know."

"The duchess and Malvoisin have acquired a
wonderful influence over that impious old wretch.
I have been able to keep my hands from the faithless
roué, who is torn with remorse. Not a word of re-

proach has escaped me, though he tried my self-command strangely by the most infamous insinuations, and flagrant proposals."

" What is the character of Malvoisin's influence ? "

" To do the duke justice, there is in him the true *trempe* of the old noble of France. His reckless career and conventional morality have precipitated him into the catastrophe of a great crime. He detests priests ; he likes philosophers : he is an epicurean *encyclopedist.* Malvoisin has the art to keep out of sight his own profound religious convictions. The duke therefore constitutes him his confessor. Malvoisin subdues him by calmly speaking the truth, which his profound analytic spirit enables him to discern. He points out to the duke, step by step, the means of reparation. He has kept him from suicide. But anything like reformation in a being into whom corruption has crept, like gout into the blood, would seem like a ' new birth.' "

" My guardian would say that, to God all things are possible. Have you had any conversation with the duchess ? "

"Not a word about the duke. She seems to regard her marriage vow as the one supreme motive of her life, and to bend all her grace and beauty, her angelic sanctity and insight, to subdue the duke to a preference for English society. She has, doubtless, been guided in this by Malvoisin's sagacity and knowledge of the world. The duke seems to hide his torments from her since they have arrived at Scarsdale. She is, therefore, comparatively tranquil and satisfied in the society of Miss Scarsdale."

" Where will this tragedy end, Pendleborough ? "

" I dare not speculate, Vavasour. I cannot conceive that the duke should reform his life completely. I can foresee that the duchess is capable of sacrificing herself to the duties imposed upon her by her vow, and living a long martyrdom as a heavenly ministrant at the side of this reckless miscreant. Malvoisin says that time alone can determine whether the moral abyss will swallow all their fortunes in a common ruin."

" I do not wonder, Pendleborough, that you, who witnessed the first scenes of this tragedy, and vehemently struggled to prevent its progress, should look with blank horror on all its issues. I am inclined to say with Malvoisin, Let us wait and watch ! No man knows the path through which, by the mystery of providential guidance, he will be led."

" Have you been able to form any plans for yourself, Vavasour ? "

" To know whether this swift rebuke was to issue in life or death, has first required patience and self-control. That, Pendleborough, has been a useful discipline, and Holte has been to me in a double sense a physician. Now that Oliver gives me some prospect of life, I wait to ascertain whether I am to be a cripple. Until I know that, I strive, Pendleborough, to revive the early training of my guardian, and to keep myself in humility and submission. This I may say, that if it please God to restore me, I shall live chiefly at Assheton."

"I am glad to hear that, Vavasour; for I, too, have a growing conviction that the true pleasure of life is attained only by the highest conception and most faithful discharge of its duties. Farewell."

So saying, Lord Pendleborough shook Colonel Vavasour warmly by the hand, and descended to the room below stairs, where the vicar and Oliver Holte awaited him. He found them in earnest conversation; hastily but warmly bid them both adieu, and, mounting his horse, rode rapidly back to Scarsdale.

Sir Guy Scarsdale sat writing outside the porch, which opened from the centre of the south front of the Hall upon a stone terrace fenced by a pierced parapet of geometric design. The afternoon was calm and sunny. From his position he overlooked the garden court, and saw through the gate of twisted iron far down the grand avenue of lines. On the terrace near him paced a keeper, with a carbine under his arm, and pistols in his belt. A brace of pistols also lay upon Sir Guy's papers on the table before him. Among the walls of trim verdure formed by the clipped yew hedges, might occasionally be seen his daughter, with the duchess and Miss Hollingsworth, issuing from some green archway into the court of a fountain surrounded by flower-beds, or resting in an arbour on a seat, to which cushions had been brought from the Hall. The lofty screen of majestic limes which surrounded the court was so still that scarcely a leaf fluttered in the air.

The door opened in the recess of the porch at Sir Guy Scarsdale's side, and Lord Pendleborough approached.

"I found Vavasour calm, and quite equal to an interview with me, though still forbidden to walk, if indeed he be yet able to do so. I have bid him farewell. Now also the time presses, and I must bid you too a soldier's adieu."

"So soon! Must you leave to-day?"

"I intend to be out of the Mersey with the tide to-night, and I have, with unavoidable delays, a journey of five hours to Liverpool."

"I will not say a word to hinder the execution of a generous resolution. There are the ladies. Will you not bid them too farewell?"

Sir Guy pointed, as he spoke, to the three ladies

then walking in one of the courts. Instantly Lord Pendleborough descended from the terrace. He was glad to have no time to think before he bid Mabel good-bye, It was better to leave everything to the inspiration of the moment. The fair group turned as they heard steps behind them. The duchess was the first to speak.

"Can it be that you are compelled, as Sir Guy says, by urgent affairs to leave soon for Ireland?"

" My estates in Kerry require my immediate presence to inspire confidence in my agents, to overawe some conspirators, and to teach my tenantry what are their true interests. I am come to bid you farewell, ladies."

"Miss Scarsdale," said the duchess, "we desire you, in our name, to impose on Lord Pendleborough, for this abrupt departure, some impossible feat of heroism, under the *peine forte et dure* of our supreme displeasure."

She then turned and drew Miss Hollingsworth away, leaving Miss Scarsdale alone with Lord Pendleborough.   Mabel had turned very pale.

"I did not expect that you were leaving to-night," she said.

" Though I leave suddenly, under the compulsion of a stern necessity, I have, for a year past, matured my plans with care, and my prompt action is the result of a resolution arrived at by slow and painful steps."

My father tells me, what I was quite unconscious of, that for two years past you have been examining similar questions, and that much of the past year, in which we have seen less of you, has been spent in inquiries which have satisfied you as to the measures required on your Irish property."

"Sir Guy's own example led me into this path. Let me not leave without some hope that you will welcome me, if I prove worthy of that friendship with which your father has honoured me."

Mabel was very pale while she replied,—

"Lord Pendleborough, I have suffered very much since the scene in the Scarsdale Clough the other day. I know not what my sentiments are, for they are entirely new to me. But I reproach myself bitterly, if I have ever said or done anything which should lead you to expose wantonly a precious life, or to arrest a career which I feel will be full of honour, for a weak woman like me. Give me your promise, my lord, that you will do nothing from mere chivalry. Say that all shall be done from a sense of duty to God and your country. I cannot consent that my poor favour should be made a gage of battle. Be worthy of yourself."

"I would not that you should suffer one pang of

anxiety or regret for any such cause. I promise solemnly that you shall be in my thoughts only to prompt me to acts of tenderness and mercy. Farewell."

"Farewell; and God be with you. I know not what I feel; but I am disturbed that a man so brave, so simple, so generous, should make my poor favour in any respect the motive of his life."

"To win your favour, Miss Scarsdale, will be a proof to me that I have risen nearer to the favour of Heaven. Farewell!"

He did not turn to greet the other ladies, but hurriedly bidding Sir Guy Scarsdale adieu, hastened to his carriage, which awaited his arrival in the quadrangle.

To hide her agitation from the duchess, whose reception of Lord Pendleborough, and sudden withdrawal, betrayed that she had, with feminine acuteness, penetrated the nature of their present relations, Mabel turned in an opposite direction to that taken by the duchess and Miss Hollingsworth. She threaded the avenues and courts under the high walls of clipped yews, slowly and in deep reverie, concealed from all but her father, who anxiously observed her movements from the terrace. After half an hour spent in a solitary promenade in the garden court, Mabel approached the terrace and ascended the flight of steps to the porch, before which her father was writing. Sir Guy rose, and putting her arm within his own, while he caressed her hand, accompanied her without a word to her own room. There Mabel seating herself, fatigued and agitated, drew from her dress the locket-portraits of her grandfather and grandmother, given to her, with so solemn a message, by her father's nurse, Judith, on the day before her death.

"Dear father," at length, after a long pause, she said, "I fear I have committed a great error."

"How so, my daughter?"

"I have no confessor but you, dear father! Listen with patience to my trouble."

"Speak without reserve, dearest Mabel."

"It is not that I have formed a premature estimate of the character of Lord Pendleborough, or that, being unconscious of what you tell me of his long preference, I have met even my father's friend with an independence of bearing which was, I hope, not unbecoming in your daughter. But I fear I may unwittingly have given an impulse to his chivalrous daring which may precipitate him into a hazardous career."

"How has this fear been inspired dear Mabel?"

"Oh! to none but yourself, dear father, could I possibly disclose the agony which I suffered from the look which Lord Pendleborough gave me, before he, with such awful courage, met the rush of that maddened bull, and baffled it by his coolness."

" No doubt you felt, dearest, that he exposed his life for you, and that he bade you a possible farewell, with a supreme devotion."

" Oh, what words, dear father! I can accept no such homage. That is an idolatry! I only ask God to give me, if I am to ally myself in marriage, a soldier of Christ for my husband. I am too weak and frail to be the star of the faith of a strong, brave, stern man, who should rather devote himself to Heaven than to me."

" Yet, Mabel, let me say, that the high estimate which my daughter has formed of the objects of life, and the very *fierté* with which she has repelled all mere personal homage, and especially from those, who, with every endowment of person and ability, and every gift of fortune, had yet failed to raise themselves to the same level, has had a marked influence on the career of Lord Pendleborough."

" Oh, do not tell me so, dear father."

" My daughter, the time has come to speak the truth without reserve. I have for years observed your influence on Lord Pendleborough. He has constantly returned from his perilous travels to our circle, like a moth to the light, unable to resist the unavowed attraction. You have met his advances with an unconscious indifference, which, while consistent with courtesy to your father's friend, has kept him on the outer boundary of the circle of privileged acquaintance."

"Father, I hope I have not been unfeminine or unkind to your friend."

"Never, my child; but you have seen Lord Pendleborough surrounded by courtly homage to his rank and possessions, and you have disdained to imitate the servile or sordid throng of fashion."

"Then, I wonder that I have not repelled Lord Pendleborough."

"You have mistaken, among other things, the *trempe* of his character. He is not a man to shrink before difficulties. You have rather thrown him back on self-examination. He has sought to discover in what he had failed to make himself acceptable to you."

"There, oh, there, dear father, is the source of my alarm."

"Listen, my daughter. I have watched Pendleborough carefully. His is a simple, frank, noble nature; he has had a filial attachment for me. My experience of life has been of some service in preserving him from the dangers and errors of his perilous position. Escaping these—living a life of singular purity and simplicity, he has gradually become conscious of the higher responsibilities of his station and possessions. With this consciousness, the gulf which separated him from you has been revealed, as though by the absorption of a mist. The last two years have been devoted to a careful preparation for the discharge of the duties of which he has now, I think, a true conception."

"Certainly, dear father, we have seen almost nothing of him for a year."

"But he has been in constant correspondence with me, he has been a diligent disciple of Malvoisin, and his mind has now grasped a scheme of life which his heart and conscience approve."

"And which I trust he will pursue from a sense of allegiance to the Power from on high, to the teachings of conscience, and the relations of his spiritual life, and not for the favour of your daughter."

"That I believe to be the settled purpose of his life; but not the less to win your love, my child, as his help-meet in its execution."

Mabel clasped her hands upon her brow to hide a flood of tears, which betrayed the deep emotion which she suffered. As she did so, the locket with the portraits fell into her lap. Some secret spring of the jewelled case seemed to be touched, for an

inner part opened, and from it fell a closely compressed packet of tissue paper, oiled to preserve them
from moisture. Sir Guy Scarsdale picked up the
paper which had dropped to the floor, and, attracted
by some marks which he perceived on it, spread it
out on the table, and discovered, to his surprise, that
it contained a plan of the keep and of the hall, distinguishing the ancient walls which had belonged to
the castellated structure that had preceded the mansion, and part of which had been incorporated with
it. This was evident at a glance. A more careful
scrutiny disclosed many curious details.

After some time, Mabel rose and joined her father
silently in his survey. Step by step, they traced
narrow secret passages in the thick ancient walls
of the house, which had formed part of the old
castle on the edge of Scarsdale Crag. There appeared to be three secret chambers, one of which
was marked—

"Secret closet of Peregrine Erskine of Dun. His court dress
hangs here."

Another was marked—

"Secret chamber of the Lady Mabel."

On a third was written—

"Herein was sheltered Oliver Heywood in the time of the
Nonconformist trials."

Both the father and daughter were so deeply absorbed in these researches, that twilight overtook them in the examination of the plans. It became too dark to decipher the inscriptions. They were about to ring for candles, when the house quivered to its foundations, as with the sudden shock of an earthquake, and a heavy sound, followed by a long, dull reverberation, diverted their attention.

Sir Guy was unwilling to leave his daughter alone, when the duchess and Miss Hollingsworth entered the apartment from the garden court. At that moment there were two sharp shots in the house. Unable to explain these sounds, Sir Guy hurried into the corridor, called the armed watcher who waited there, and placing him at the door of his daughter's room, hastened, for a reason which will become apparent, to the private cabinet of the Duke of Chatellerault.

CHAPTER VI.

THE DUKE GRAPPLES WITH HIS FATE.

On the same day as that on which the events related in the preceding chapters occurred, the duke, after luncheon, had withdrawn M. Malvoisin for a *tête-à-tête* during a promenade in the Long Gallery. Philp had requested Sir Guy to restrain his guests from rides and walks beyond the hall and its courts, until he had cleared up the mystery of Ascroft's whereabout. The watchers were left in the corridors, and the gentlemen were requested to carry arms. These precautions were founded on Philp's conviction, that Ascroft was in possession of some secret mode of entrance into the hall. He even suggested to Sir Guy that the ladies should be induced to take exercise in the garden court, so positive was his belief that Ascroft had feigned extreme prostration, and was lurking in some hiding-hole of the ancient structure. Both Malvoisin and the duke, therefore, were armed with pistols, and the duke wore his rapier at his side. He revived the conversation respecting the duchess which he had held with Malvoisin on the preceding evening.

The duke, by outbursts of venomous analysis of his own life, seemed to illustrate the fable of the scorpion surrounded by a circle of fire, stinging itself to death. To soothe this self-inflicted torment, Malvoisin led him to contemplate the restoration of the duchess to cheerfulness in the society of Miss Scarsdale. He gradually diverted the conversation to inform the duke that Colonel Vavasour had, with the consent of his physician, requested an interview with Malvoisin. The duke inquired, with marked interest, as to the colonel's condition. Malvoisin then led the conversation to an account of the care which Mr. Hollingsworth had taken of the manor of Assheton; so that, during ten years, the mines had been successfully explored and worked, producing a revenue which had removed all incumbrances, and had enabled the vicar, as the colonel's trustee, to restore the farm buildings and house, and to improve the farms by drainage and lime.

"Ah, then!" said the duke, "the speculation of the Marquise de Buron was not ill founded. She might, if she had succeeded in her intrigue, have found a wealthy English husband for her daughter."

"Had she ever such a design?" said Malvoisin.

" Undoubtedly; and she set about it in the most original manner. It is sufficiently notorious," said the duke, " that when the marquise was distinguished by youth, wit, the fascinations of beauty, and the most seductive manners, I was not without preference in the circle of her admirers."

" Twenty years ago, I remember you, duke, riding with the marquise in the Bois de Boulogne, and waltzing with her in the balls of the court circle."

" She was always most lavish in her expenditure. She ruined the poor marquis, and made a great breach in my fortunes. Then, as such resources diminished with the gradual fading of the exquisite freshness of her personal charms, her income ceased to satisfy her lavish expenditure. The subtlety and audacity which had made her triumphant in intrigue then led her to adopt other expedients to replenish her means."

" I have heard," said Malvoisin, " that she had received of late some private warnings from the minister of police."

" Nothing more true. But our *liaison* had been notorious, and my receptions were so comprehensive, that, though I had been made aware of these practices, I always included her in my circle."

" What, then, was her plot against Colonel Vavasour ? "

" She had, I fancy, ascertained—for she had good means of information—that his dilapidated fortunes were restored. She sought to make him her prey. But she had a double design. If she could burthen him with debts of honour, by losses at play, she intended to make these the *dotation* of her daughter, whom she was bent on marrying to Vavasour."

" Are you sure, duke, that she was capable of such a plot?"

" Capable both of the design and the execution; and that she had conceived it, I know, for I was partially sounded by her confederate the Comte de Marne, whom I stopped by treating his approaches as a *plaisanterie*, in which he should not indulge, lest any *niais* should conceive the marquise to be gliding into the arts of *escroquerie*."

" Did you put Vavasour upon his guard?"

" Vavasour was not a child, he was a quick-witted man of the world, well acquainted with the *ruses* of the unscrupulous part of the *haut-monde*; and I neither thought it necessary to warn him, nor quite an act of friendship to my friend the marquise, to give any currency to the evil reports which made a scandal of her name."

" Permit me to say it, duke, as you have allowed me always to speak the truth, that you ran some risk of creating for yourself a subject for re-gret."

"Most penetrating moralist! you have touched one of the ulcerous spots of self-reproach which rankle in my conscience."

" What happened, duke ?"

" One night, in a most brilliant assemblage in my *salons*, by the merest accident, I observed that the marquise had entrapped Vavasour to a game of cards, in which the Comte de Marne and M. de Busset, two of her confederates, had joined. Through a friend, whom I saw watching the game, and whom I sent for to a remote part of the *salon*, I found that the play was high, and that Vavasour had already lost about fifteen thousand francs."

" A most unpleasant crisis !" said Malvoisin.

" To the last degree; for I had not been a good guide to Vavasour, yet I was under infinite obliga-tions to him for courteous and delicate services in some affairs of honour."

" What could you do, duke ?"

" I could not hesitate. Fortunately, the minister of police was present. After a few words from me, he despatched a gentleman, who was known to the marquise as the medium of previous communica-tions, with a note to Colonel Vavasour, requesting an immediate interview, for a moment, on matters of urgency; and also saying that, in the interval, the gentleman who carried the message would, with the consent of the party, take his cards. Vavasour came, and was at once informed of the plot into which he had fallen."

" Had he lost much ? "

" Before the play was interrupted, about twenty thousand francs; but the *mouchard* who had taken Colonel Vavasour's cards showed to him the trick by which he had been robbed. The minister forbade him to pay that night's losses."

" Do you think he obeyed ?"

" I doubt it very much. But I discovered that this was not the first loss. On some previous night, the marquise had won from him, in my own *salons*, a large sum, unobserved by me."

" There is a Nemesis, duke, in all evil," said Malvoisin, gravely.

" Am I not a living victim, impaled by the spirit of evil, to perish, in the agony of remorse for error, brought about by the catastrophe of my marriage ? "

" These losses will account, to a great extent, for Colonel Vavasour's embarrassments in Paris," said Malvoisin.

" How did you know," said the duke, " that he had suffered any embarrassment ? "

"Colonel Vavasour has himself told me that, since Mr. Hollingsworth has, through his physician, made known to him the state of his affairs, he is agreeably surprised to find that he has it in his power at once to repay the loans which some of his friends made to him, to save him from usurers."

"I did not know that he had contracted any loans; but I know that Colonel Vavasour has friends in France who would share their last franc with so manly and generous an ally."

"Duke, he reckons you among those friends; and as he accepted your aid at a moment when he conceived himself erroneously to be without resources, he feels assured that you will perceive that his honour requires him to repay to you what you lent him."

"I lent him nothing; nor is he under any obligation to me. I am bankrupt in everything, except in the sense of the honour of my order; and of that, as the sole treasure left to me, I am so sensitive a guardian, that I cannot permit Colonel Vavasour to deprive me of the satisfaction of reflecting that, in wiping away a stain from my own reputation, I was of some service to him."

"Bear with me, duke, if I say that your mind seems to me so overwrought, that you forget that Colonel Vavasour may also feel it to be impossible to accept an assistance which he finds he did not need."

"Malvoisin! I am almost mad with the retrospect of a wasted life; but I never committed a *poltronnerie*, much less have I winked at an *escroquerie*. I have, however, the consciousness of faults, not to say crimes, which make me unfit to be a judge even of cowards and *escrocs*; for a judge should be pure, not merely from the errors which he punishes, but should be conscience free. I could not punish or expose the marquise; but I will refund to Vavasour the loss which occurred in my house."

"Some reflection, duke, will, I trust, make you feel what is due to Colonel Vavasour."

"He is under no obligation to me," said the duke, with a passionate energy; "but he has no right to deprive me of this poor salve to an ulcerated conscience."

"Nevertheless, I enter so fully into Colonel Vavasour's feelings, that I have readily consented to place in your hands, duke, this cheque on his banker for the amount of your aid to him, and to say that, as early as he is permitted, he hopes to express to you personally his strong sense of your generous friendship."

Malvoisin, as he spoke, had drawn from his pocket a cheque for two thousand pounds, which he placed in the duke's hands. The attitude of the duke, in receiving it, was one of passionate defiance. He gazed at Malvoisin as though he had received a deliberate insult; the veins swelled up in his forehead; his cheeks were coloured each with a purple spot; his lips became livid. There was a pause, in which he seemed to control himself to repress some outburst of fury, when, striking his cane perpendicularly on the floor with violence, he walked steadily to the fire, and, turning to Malvoisin, thrust the cheque into the flames, saying, in a strange whisper between his teeth,—

"So perish any man who may, from whatever motive, renew to me a proposal to part with the memory of an act of expiation."

The expression of the duke's eyes reddened with wrath, the pale, quivering lips, the thin white left hand clenched on the top of his cane, and the right hand extended and quivering, with his outstretched arm—thrilléd through Malvoisin as signs of an unbridled fury, bordering on insanity. In the same metallic whisper, the duke continued,—

"Tell Vavasour that I remember him ten years ago, when I had warm red blood in my heart, and not this thin fermenting virus of gout. He was my guest, my companion, my disciple; and if I have failed to make him, like myself, a spendthrift of

health, life, fortune, and conscience, he owes it to
his early training, and not to me. But I will not
suffer him to rob me of one spot of light in the
blackness of my past career."

The duke still stood gazing, with fixed and glaring
eyes, on Malvoisin.

" Listen to me. I feel, in this act, the strength
to tell you what is my resolution as to this marriage.
It maddens me. I cannot endure the terrible
presence of a purity and sanctity which penetrates
my inmost being with a heavenly light. I see all
the foul cavernous secrets of my heart. The loathsome thoughts crawl about like reptiles, surprised
in their stygian darkness. I will not suffer it. The
marriage shall be cancelled. The *dotation* shall be
returned, if I beg my bread, with a wallet, from
door to door, and die in a ditch. Anything were
preferable to this spectre-haunted fever of the brain.
A self-inflicted penance of penury, or a cell in a
convent, with the maceration of vigils, fasts, and
flagellations—this, I can endure. But to be linked,
the pure to the impure—a dead body rotting on
the same stem with a living one; to poison by
corruption the life of a saintly nature, or to affright
it with impieties, or to waste it in the dreary penance
of a hopeless vow ;—am I a fiend, think you, that I
can endure this? I am a man !—a noble of old

France! My honour is unsullied. My crimes have been self-inflicted. I will not be the demon to destroy a saint. Perish the thought!"

He struck his brow passionately, staggered, and would have fallen to the ground fainting, if Malvoisin had not caught him in his arms, and carried him to an ottoman. The duke was, for a few minutes, insensible, but revived without convulsion, beyond a slight quiver in the lips. Malvoisin, who had been a diligent student of medicine, loosened his dress, drew a case from his pocket, and applied ammonia to the nostrils. When the duke partially revived, he gave him a cordial. Slowly, the leaden pallor left the face, which was again warmed with a faint livid hue of life. In about half an hour the duke sat up on the ottoman, supported by cushions, and, in a low tone, resumed his conversation, without the frenzy which had caused the fainting fit.

" You all seem like angels in a dream, on a great beam of light, ascending and descending. But I cannot obey the heavenly summons. My path is there—downwards," said he, pointing to the floor. " Our Catholic faith, indeed, affords a somewhat more sympathetic refuge, in these crises of life, than the cold dogmas of Calvinism which pervade our French Protestant Church. But I detest equally cunning priests, and unctuous or severe *pasteurs.*

Since I have no blood to spill—and since, if I had, there is no worthy cause for which to give a worthless life in the *mêlée* of battle—and since, if there were, I have no faith left in man or principle—I will betake me to some garret in Paris, where thou, Malvoisin, who art the only Christian whose philosophy I could endure, shalt, in my poverty and solitude, be my confessor until my last crust is eaten, and I fall back on my solitary pallet a wasted corpse."

Malvoisin made no reply, but held the duke's hand in his own, sympathetically, during this whispered soliloquy. After a considerable pause, the duke continued,— .

" As for this marriage, my *notaires* shall have immediate instructions. I will restore the duchess to entire freedom. Her fortune shall be repaid to the last shilling. I shall be a beggar, and I will betake myself to my garret and my crust."

Malvoisin still sat silent by the duke's side, unwilling to ruffle this impetuous current of thought by interposing any statement of difficulties, or any form of remonstrance. The afternoon had waned, and the sun was descending rapidly in the west. He encouraged the duke to take a few turns in the gallery, rang for his valet, and directed him to bring a cup of tea and a small glass of brandy.

After this refreshment, the duke seemed to shake off the frenzy, which had visited him like a sudden squall, with whirlwind and gloom. Standing in a bay overlooking the garden court, they witnessed Lord Pendleborough's adieus to the ladies; but the duke withdrew from the window, when he saw that Lord Pendleborough was left alone with Miss Scarsdale, saying, sarcastically, that in his own *affaires du cœur*, he preferred the absence of even the most interested friends, and had never chosen a garden, with a vigilant father on the terrace, as a place of farewell.

Perceiving that the duke was now thoroughly calm, Malvoisin led him to his own private apartment, surprised at the elasticity with which his vigorous nerves, released from spasm, regained their force. The duke walked with more than usual firmness— he was gay—he directed his valet to wait in his ante-chamber, and, telling Malvoisin he would take some repose, unsheathed his rapier, laid his double-barrelled pistol at his side, and lay down upon his couch.

The duke revolved resolutely the rapid expressions of his frenzied will. Vehement as they had been, even to defiance and wrath, they were the expression of the calmer convictions of his self-tortured mind. He, therefore, pondered only on the steps to be taken to carry them into execution. Not a day should be lost. On the morrow, he would instruct his *notaires* to take the first steps for a declaration of the nullity of the marriage. He would pursue these with an unflinching hardihood. The duchess's fortune should be restored. For this purpose, his estates, houses, gallery of paintings, collections of art and *virtu*, should be sold without reserve. There would be residue enough, probably, to provide him with the income of a cadet. If not, he would shroud himself in some obscurity, till a not distant death released him. Meanwhile, he disciplined his mind to conceive what was due to the duchess, as expressive of a paternal solicitude for her—what to his own sense of gratitude, for her pious care during his illness—what became the awakening love, from which he shrank with the terrors of conscience. The twilight deepened. From the flickering fire, the portrait of Peregrine Erskine of Dun, in his velvet court-dress, was lit by a reflection—bright though fitful—from the hangings of the bed, where they were open at its foot. The pale, delicate features, the high forehead, and the large eye full of romance, attracted his attention. He dwelt on the history of the concealment, by his sister the Lady Mabel, of the lover of his queen, as it had been sketched to him by Miss Scarsdale. This somewhat diverted the current of his thoughts.

"I am not in the condition to be cheated by my imagination with a visit either from 'la vieille dame de Chatellerault' or from 'the Lady Mabel.' But I have never yet tried the effect of a *coup de pistolet*," suggested his cynical spirit, "either on 'la vieille dame' or on 'the Lady Mabel.'" The duke smiled, with a grimace which seemed to be eager for the experiment.

These thoughts were humorously coursing each other through his mind, when the dull subterranean boom of the explosion, followed by a quiver like the tremor of an earthquake, made even the glass on the dressing-table jingle. The duke was aroused; he grasped his pistol instinctively, and raised himself in an attitude of attention and expectation. There was a short, breathless pause, in which he hesitated whether to rise, so completely was he disturbed in his reverie.

But what was that sound? A rusted hinge grated. The duke assumed an eager attitude, glancing rapidly from side to side. A door was shut. There was a heavy step on the floor on the side where the tapestried hangings of the bed were drawn. Would the Lady Mabel visit him again? Let her beware! An instant after, a figure, in the velvet dress of Peregrine Erskine of Dun, stood at the foot of the bed! Rapidly as a flash of lightning, the duke perceived a red scar on the forehead of the visitant, whose features had no resemblance to those of the delicate portrait. His pistol was in his hand, ready for an expected emergency. Scarcely ten seconds elapsed before, with the promptitude of a practised duellist, he had discharged both barrels at the head of the phantom, not doubting that it was Ascroft. The assassin, believing that he had before him Sir Guy Scarsdale, had mounted on to the couch at the foot of the bed to precipitate himself, knife in hand, on his victim. The duke, rising, met him with a vigorous rapier-thrust, which pierced the right side of the breast; and, as the heavy frame of Ascroft fell forwards, brought the hilt with force against his chest, having pressed the rapier through the body. But, in falling, the ruffian aimed a desperate blow at the duke, which must have been instantly fatal, if the weight of the assailant had not carried the duke backwards. The knife, instead of penetrating immediately behind the collar-bone into the great arteries shielded by it, which it would inevitably have done, had the duke been in a more upright position, was buried deeply in the muscles between the shoulder and the neck, where it pierced till it struck against the blade-bone.

The duke's pistol-shots and rapier-thrust had,

however, taken such effect, that Ascroft fell heavily upon him, covering him with blood, which flowed profusely from his face, where both balls had entered the mouth.

A moment later, the duke's valet entered, and lifted the heavy body of Ascroft to the floor. Ere this was done, Sir Guy Scarsdale, followed by Malvoisin, came, and both were busied in the examination of the duke, who was conscious, but bleeding. Malvoisin counselled him not to move till he returned, and, leaving the knife in the wound, speedily brought a case of surgical instruments from his own room. He then skilfully withdrew the knife—tied up such arteries as were within reach, and, though blood still oozed, assured Sir Guy that the main sources of the bleeding were secured. The duke had, meanwhile, fainted, and he required restoratives. Applied with patience and caution, these, ere long, restored animation. The wound, though wide and deep, had not injured any of the larger arteries, and was made by a sharp weapon which had cleanly divided the muscles.

The body of Ascroft had been carried out; and when Malvoisin could leave the duke, he found that the balls had passed through the palate, cutting some large bloodvessels, which bled profusely, and that the rapier had, probably, pierced towards the root of the lung, through large pulmonary arteries. He had died, apparently, in a quarter of an hour, from internal bleeding.

While the disorder of the duke's apartment, and the signs of conflict and blood, were in course of removal, Sir Guy Scarsdale carefully prepared his dress, and, after a little interval, left Malvoisin to watch the duke, while he executed the difficult task of revealing this tragedy to Miss Scarsdale and her guests.

Sir Guy Scarsdale passed slowly and thoughtfully down the corridor to his daughter's room, which was on the south front of the hall. He released the watcher at the door, and entered calm and self-possessed.

"I cannot clear up the mystery of that noise, Mabel, unless some explosion has happened in those vaults of which you have the plan before you. That is a probable solution, for the west wing is full of the smell of gunpowder."

"But what were those shots, Sir Guy?" said the duchess.

"I have to compliment you, duchess, on the perfect presence of mind and prompt action of the duke; for though this assassin, for whose appearance we have been watching, entered his room from a secret passage, like the phantom of Peregrine Erskine,

whose dress he had assumed, the duke fired on him
so instantly as to deprive him of the power to com-
mit his intended crime."

"That the duke should have baffled this ruffian,
after his thrice repeated attempts at murder yesterday, and his previous efforts to assassinate Mr.
Oliver Holte, makes us all his debtor," said Mabel,
who had observed the anxious look with which Sir
Guy regarded the duchess.

"I trust," said the duchess, gravely, but calmly,
"that no life has been sacrificed."

"This assassin was so desperate in his assault,
that the duke could only save his own life by in-
flicting mortal wounds."

"Is the man, then, dead?" inquired the duchess.

"His death, or that of the duke, was the only
choice," replied Sir Guy; "and I rejoice to say the
duke has escaped with a wound, which, though
severe, is not desperate."

"Ah! Is the duke, then, wounded? I may, I
hope, at once attend on him!?"

"M. Malvoisin is with him. The duke needs
some repose. When he can see you, duchess, without agitation, you will, of course, assume your place
at his side. But, for his sake, a few hours of complete repose, in M. Malvoisin's care, are indispensable."

The duchess sank into a chair, pale, and in a deep reverie; while Sir Guy, observing her attitude, drew his daughter away with Miss Hollingsworth to the polygonal bay which overlooked the garden court, where he continued the conversation with them in a low voice.

The first impulse of the duchess had been a horror that the duke should have the responsibility for a life upon his hands to deepen the troubles of his stricken conscience, whose workings had not been hidden from her in La Vendée. Then the stern necessities of the case, briefly but conclusively stated by Sir Guy, and the fact that the duke had received a severe wound, agitated her. She was too saint-like even to think that, if the event had been reversed, she would have been released from the life-long purgatory of her marriage. The idea of her vow was ever present, to shut out any thought inconsistent with its obligations. She had no love for the duke. Though she knew nothing of his vices, she shuddered at his cynicism, his sceptical raillery, his utter want of faith, his cold-blooded estimate of human motives on the level of instinct, passion, or sordid interest. On the other hand, as we have seen, she had a clear insight into his sense of honour, his valour, and a certain chivalry of spirit which shrank from completing the sacrifice of her happiness. She had come to regard him, as a daughter might watch a father sick to death with a malady consequent on a debauched life. She was not, therefore, agitated with a passionate feeling for the risk and suffering of the duke, so much as with a profound self-examination whether she rightly apprehended what was now required of her by her vow, and was ready, with a pure, simple, and entire self-devotion, to discharge the duties which awaited her. She felt the necessity of being alone. After, therefore, remaining some time in this self-absorbed attitude, she rose, and, approaching the group in the window, said, in a low voice, that if Sir Guy saw no obstacle, she would prefer to spend the interval before dinner in her own apartment. Sir Guy at once offered his arm to conduct her thither, and gently led her away from her two friends.

Meanwhile, Malvoisin watched the duke with anxiety. His own study of medicine, though profound, had been necessarily rather theoretic than practical. Bearing in mind, therefore, the agitation which the duke had suffered during the day, the fainting fit which had supervened, and the considerable loss of blood, as well as the great expenditure of energy in his conflict with the assassin, he regarded the duke's condition with deep apprehension.

He seized an instant to write and despatch an urgent
note to Oliver Holte, explaining the absolute necessity of his prompt return to Scarsdale, to give the
aid of his careful and prolonged hospital training
to rescue the duke from his imminent peril. The
note was scarcely despatched ere Malvoisin observed
a slight tremor in the muscles of the duke's face,
and a shaking of the head, which were the obvious
precursors of an attack of convulsions. This he for
the moment arrested by the prompt administration of
restoratives. When the duke recovered complete
consciousness, he beckoned to Malvoisin, after an
interval in which he had kept his eyes fixed with
a calm gaze upon him. Malvoisin bent down his
ear to the duke's mouth, and in a faint whisper listened, not without emotion, to his words.

"I wished for some worthy cause on which to
spend a worthless life. Mine was a wish inspired
by destiny, or if you will, by Providence. I am
content to have given my life to protect this family,
which was my refuge in the storm of retribution."

There was a pause, during which Malvoisin perceived that blood still oozed from the wound, which
he had closed with sutures. He could not staunch
the blood, which exuded from vessels too small to
be tied; nor could he command the main artery,

without making the wound gape, and embarrassing
the feeble respiration. He tried some pressure upon
it in vain.

"Give me the cordial again," said the duke; "I
have that to say which must be said soon."

Malvoisin administered a strong dose of the re-
storative, and again bent his ear to the livid lips
of the sufferer.

"I am forty-five years of age. Twenty years
have passed since the only vision of true love has
shed its light on my life. I have two daughters
who do not bear my name. Thrust your hand into
my breast, and you will find there a locket with
the portrait of their mother, and of her two children.
There is also within my last testament——"

The duke paused, exhausted, and Malvoisin,
putting his hand into the duke's dress, found in a
breast-pocket, a golden locket of the most exquisite
workmanship. Within was the portrait of a charming woman of radiant beauty, and of two infant
children. All were profusely set in diamonds of
extraordinary size and brilliancy, and of great value.
Beneath the portraits of the children, Malvoisin found
the duke's will, written on tissue paper, and beneath
that of the lady, a lock of hair twisted into a ring
with a superb diamond. The duke, following him
attentively with calm eyes, asked again for the cor-

dial. Malvoisin complied. As soon as he had drank the dose, the duke said,—

" The secret of the marquise is safe in your hands, my confessor. My testament provides for the re-payment of the *dotation* of the duchess, by the sale of all my estates and possessions of whatever kind, except these diamonds. The residue of the sale of my property, as far as it will not be claimed by my heirs-at-law, I bequeath to my daughters. But these diamonds are not mine. They are the *dotation* of my daughters, entrusted to me by their mother, and preserved with a pious care. I entrust them to you, Malvoisin, as my confessor and friend. The marquis wasted his estates to the last sou, and perished in the retreat from Moscow. The two charming daughters of his wife are in the convent of the Religieuses dans la Vendée, which I have endowed during my lifetime, so as to provide them an asylum as long as they and you may desire. You, have I made the guardian of their fortunes, and with you I have united the Duchess of Chatelle-rault. This will was made in La Vendée, when I thought myself dying."

The duke had spoken with a calm and deliberate emphasis, but in a faint whisper, which became almost inaudible ere he ceased. Malvoisin withdrew the pillow, sponged the duke's face with ice-cold water, applied warmth to the feet. The tremor of the head returned; for a moment the eyes were inverted to the inner angle of the orbit, and the mouth was distored with spasm. But this partial convulsion passed away; by-and-by the duke again fixed his calm and steady gaze on Malvoisin. The livid lips moved, and Malvoisin bent down his ear again.

" My will encloses a separate document in which I express my desire that the Duchess of Chatellerault will take charge of the Mesdemoiselles de Clairvœux, as a proof that she knows that, this tie to life transferred to her better keeping, I have no business here to stand between her and happiness. I welcome death. I have this faith, Malvoisin, that my expiation of my life of egotism is in part accomplished by my desire to withdraw the blot of my pollution from the purity of this saint."

These words were scarcely uttered, when the possible agitation of his thoughts caused a violent and prolonged convulsion, which threatened to be fatal. Malvoisin sent the duke's valet, whom he summoned from the adjoining room, for Sir Guy Scarsdale, and then requested him to break as early as possible to the duchess the fact of the extreme peril in which the duke was. Sir Guy went to find his daughter, and to entrust this delicate duty to her.

Meanwhile, the strange vigour of the sufferer's

constitution for a time struggled with the grim enemy. He slowly revived from the insensibility and convulsions which he had suffered. He again fixed on Malvoisin the same calm and steady gaze. At length, after a long pause, he said,—

" My hour approaches. I wish to bid the duchess farewell, if she will not be too much shocked with my condition."

Malvoisin made a sign for perfect silence and repose. Then, by degrees, he gave the duke a cup of green tea with brandy, and, waiting to observe its effects, he at length despatched the valet again to Sir Guy Scarsdale, and, on his arrival, communicated the duke's wish to him.

Miss Scarsdale had cautiously caused herself to be announced to the duchess. When she entered her apartment, she found her pale, grave, but calm, sitting before her table with a book of prayers spread open upon it. She rose, as though she had by some saintly power a divination of the tragic scene passing in the adjacent room. Miss Scarsdale saw her dilated eye and exalted mien. She felt how transformed the duchess was by the brief space for self-communion, prayer, and the recall of all the inner resources of her piety. At once she recognized that the cheerfulness with which she had joined in the pure satisfactions of their recent domestic intercourse had only hidden from external observation a consciousness of the tragic fate which seemed to await her. Now, in the presence of this swift messenger of Providence, such reserve was no more possible, than in the supernatural light of an angel's form. Miss Scarsdale saw at once into the depths of her friend's sense of her life sacrifice, and recognized all her pious self-devotion. She therefore said little. By a few brief hints, she confirmed the duchess's intuitive anticipations of the duke's state. It was even no surprise to her to learn that his life was in imminent peril. When she knew that he wished to see her, in order to confide some sacred trust to her, she eagerly obeyed. She appeared equal to any emergency; to be appalled by no scene of suffering or death to which she was summoned by duty. Perceiving all this, Miss Scarsdale requested her father to announce to M. Malvoisin the duchess's approach.

The duke received her with a smile of tenderness. She placed her hand in his, and he locked it in a feeble grasp. After an interval, in which he gazed upon her placidly, he said,—

" Marie, my gentle, pious Marie, you have gained a strange power over my wayward spirit. So discontented am I with the past, that I welcome the future, which is first death, and then, as I think, the completion of my expiation! Help my conscience, Marie, in this supreme hour. Your estates are restored. Whatever else I can, I bequeath to my two daughters, the Mesdemoiselles Clairvœux. Their mother's portrait, in a case of precious diamonds, will augment their slender fortunes. You, Marie and Malvoisin, are my executors. He has my will. But, hear my last request! Make my daughters like yourself in purity, in piety, in self-devotion. They are your wards. I confide them to you alone."

The duke's voice sank as he spoke. The energy of a vigorous will alone enabled him clearly to utter, after a pause between each sentence, this final injunction. He continued to gaze on the duchess, as though he bade her farewell, with a last expression of admiration and confidence.

"I have heard and understood all, duke," she said. "I call God to witness that I accept, and, with his help, will discharge, the trust which you have confided to me."

He smiled, and endeavoured to utter the words, " Adieu, Marie," but no sound escaped; she thought she read them on his lips. A quiver passed over his face; she lifted her eyes in prayer. When she turned to him again, he was no more.

The duchess kneeled, bowed upon the bed so long, that at length M. Malvoisin entered, and discovered her still holding the duke's lifeless hand pressed to her forehead, which was bent upon it. Gently and patiently he withdrew her to her own room, and then confided her to the tenderness of her two sympathizing friends.

We pass from the days of sad preparations, the detail of unavoidable arrangements, the history of a crisis in the life of this beautiful and saintly woman. The body was confided to the charge of the duke's confidential servant, to be conveyed to La Vendée.

After a fortnight's seclusion with her friends, the duchess, attended by a lady of the convent in which she had been educated, and who had arrived from France for the purpose, left Scarsdale for France, to take charge of her young wards.

Before this narrative closes, we will again follow her steps for a brief space; but the lesson which her purity and angelic sanctity had to teach, is mainly told. We only, by and by, desire to inform our readers as to the drift of her future life.

We have not ventured to interrupt the tragic story of this chapter by any explanation of the sudden appearance of Ascroft at the foot of the duke's bed, in the disguise which he had assumed. During

Sir Guy Scarsdale's absence he had been, as under-keeper, much employed by Mr. Holte as a watch-man at the hall. The range of buildings round the quadrangle was so large, that one keeper or watcher, in succession, occupied a room on the ground floor, and visited every apartment of the house at nightfall, at midnight, and in the morning. In the discharge of these duties, Ascroft had found in the drawer of an " escritoire," a plan of the secret passages and chambers in that part of the old castellated structure which was incorporated with the hall. Having obtained the clue, he explored them with care, ex-amined their entrances, learned the trick of their fastenings, descended the shaft of the keep by making loops on its rusted chain, discovered, on the inner side, the means of opening the postern at the bottom, and found the mouth of the gallery in the thicket. He had thus in his power a secret means of lurking about the hall for plunder, or for any other sinister object. The apartments, now occu-pied by the duke, had originally been those of the Lady Mabel, and in respect for her memory, were regarded as the lord's rooms, or the apartments des-tined for the head of the house. Sir Guy had occu-pied them at every previous visit ; but he had now, knowing his daughter's tastes, chosen for her some rooms overlooking the garden court, with deep polygonal bays to the south, and had his own cabinet next to hers. Whereas, the rooms occupied by the duke and duchess were on the west, overlooking the ravine from Scarsdale Crag, and were in part formed by the west wall of the old fortalice. In this wall, and in some cross walls at right angles to it, were the secret passages and chambers.

When Philp, and Martin, and Deloisir penetrated to the studded door in the secret gallery at the foot of Scarsdale Crag, Ascroft listened attentively for some signs of their intentions. As they did not speak, before he heard their retreating footsteps, he determined to leave nothing to risk, lest they should adopt some means of forcing the door. He, therefore, ascended the shaft by the loops on the chain, wound it up by the windlass at the top, and at once proceeded on his bloody errand ere his retreat should be discovered. In one of the chambers he disguised himself in the velvet court-suit of Peregrine Erskine of Dun, hoping thus to appal his victim as a phantom, and to be aided by the traditional superstitious legends in effecting his escape. He expected to find Sir Guy Scarsdale, at the edge of night, in the cabinet adjoining the bedroom into which the secret passage entered. He crept to the thick door of oak, covered, on the side opposite the passage, by the "napkin paneling" of the room.

He cautiously lifted the latch, and thrust open the door, the hinge of which grated with rust, and which, notwithstanding his precautions, shut with some noise. He advanced, therefore, more rapidly, intending to pass to the door of the cabinet; when, on arriving at the foot of the bed, he was startled and disconcerted by seeing, as he thought, his victim on the couch. His knife was in his right hand, and before he had time to draw his pistol from his breast, he received two rapid and decisive shots just as he was in the act of springing from the sofa to plunge his weapon into his prey. He had never seen Sir Guy Scarsdale, and the duke, therefore, received the stab intended for another.

CHAPTER VII.

COLONEL VAVASOUR'S FIRST INTERVIEW WITH
HELEN. — FEVER IN THE MERE CLOUGH. — A
NEW LIFE IN MABEL PERPLEXED AND INTER-
RUPTED.

OCTOBER had rapidly embrowned and thinned the
foliage of Scarsdale Clough. The November frosts
had withered, and its winds had whirled the leaves.
Colonel Vavasour had been permitted by his vigilant
physician to descend to the garden terrace of Assheton Manor-house, whence he could overlook the
western fork of the ravine. There, leaning on
Oliver Holte's arm, or from time to time on the
sturdy support of the Cock of Rossendale, or occasionally on the unequal and halting aid of Barnabas,
he delighted to inspire at noon the still, tranquil,
autumnal air; to gaze on the scenes of his boyish
freaks and youthful adventures; to talk over with
his humble friends the sports, mountain rambles, and
daring feats of early days. He gathered strength
so steadily, that at length, on a sober cob pony

belonging to Mr. Parkinson, he ventured forth to make some visits to neighbouring homesteads, the pony being led either by Nathaniel, or by the Cock of Rossendale. Then his physician sanctioned an interview with Sir Guy Scarsdale, and finding no ill consequences from this, one morning he gradually led the conversation with Colonel Vavasour towards the long postponed interview with his guardian.

Colonel Vavasour was resting after breakfast in his favourite cushioned seat in the eastern oriel, whence he could gaze down the once leafy labyrinth of the western fork of the Clough, now partially ravaged by frost and storm, but still, on sunny days, wearing its brown garniture, almost glorious in the yellow rays of the midday and western sun.

" From what I see of the homesteads, and the state of the pastures, fences, and plantations, my worthy guardian, besides paying all my debts, and providing for me a large unappropriated balance in my banker's hands, has left me little to do in the material improvement of this manor."

"The vicar has, in ten years, almost made a revolution in the property, and your mines are now so productive that the rental is doubled; but these material improvements are but the rude foundation of a much slower and more difficult moral amelioration."

"Assuredly, if, as you tell me, the struggle with semi-barbarous superstitions, coarse and sensual habits, and half-brutish ignorance is painfully toilsome in the hands of my guardian, I can have little hope to increase the rate of progress either by effort or example."

"If you realize what you tell me has been the dream of your life, and make Miss Hollingsworth your wife, you will unite the experience of the vicar's faithful ministry with your own larger survey of life, and may, with God's grace to help you, worthily continue his pious labours."

"God grant it! But you forget that I have not, as you, Malvoisin, and Pendleborough have, either inquired or thought on these subjects. Schools, poor colonies, penitentiaries, the reclamation of wastes, the civilization of serfs, cottiers, and villeins—these have been no part of my interests in life."

"You will begin. You will toil up the hill, with such help as you can get. There is this faithful Barnabas at hand, with his earnest, sagacious aid. You will convert such a man as Jonah Ingham into an instrument of much good. By slow and painful steps you will break the ground, clear it of weeds, prepare it for the seed, and then, by your prayers, and by your life, in conformity with your communion with God, you will invoke the sun and rain of his spiritual blessings on what you have sown."

"Your teaching, Holte, revives the deep impressions of my early youth in my guardian's vicarage. The seeds of his example and instruction must have lain half dead in my heart, since they stir now with a new life under the discipline of Providence and the influence of my physician."

"The vicar knows what your purposes are. He heartily approves your intention of making Assheton Manor your home. He believes that your dependants will derive only advantage from your presence."

"That is a message which prepares me to receive my guardian without any of that alarming emotion which has been one of the symptoms of my malady."

"I am satisfied that you might now see Mr. Hollingsworth with perfect safety, if you will be careful to avoid any recurrence to the past."

"That I will do; and, if he makes his usual morning call, it would be most natural for both of us that he should come upstairs, without further preface."

Within an hour, the vicar rode into the fold of Scarsdale Manor, and found Oliver Holte, who had heard the sound of his horse's hoofs, at the door of the manor-house, waiting to take him upstairs to his former ward. When the vicar entered, Colonel Vavasour advanced eagerly across the room to embrace him, and Mr. Hollingsworth warmly folded him in his arms as though he had been a son. They sat down without speaking, the colonel still holding the vicar's hand, and gazing earnestly on his face.

"Time has dealt leniently with you, vicar, in these ten years. Your black hair and eyebrows are grizzled, and the stormy climate of our moorlands has made you more swarthy. But your eye is as bright, your figure is as erect, and your step as elastic, as when we last met."

"To you, my godson and ward, these ten years have been a growth in strength, grace, and manly bearing. I read in your features and manners the cultivation of the camp and the court."

"Read nothing else, vicar, unless you can also give me hope that the rebuke of Heaven has chastened my spirit, ere it broke the spring of life."

"I have been present with you in spirit, colonel, all through this sharp trial, and have known from your physician all that has passed. God, of his great mercy, has smitten you, as a father his child."

"You were ever ready to receive and kill the fatted calf for your prodigal son. Holte has told you what are the plans of my future life, and he assures me of your approval, so that I shall not trespass on the promise which I gave you."

"You will not, Colonel Vavasour."

" Nor will you now forbid me access to your family."

" Miss Hollingsworth will welcome you as her foster-brother. Let us be quite frank with each other. My daughter is quite prepared for any change of sentiment on your part. Mr. Holte has made me aware of your own views. But ten years is a long interval of separation; it is necessary that you should meet as friends, not as former lovers. You are free in all respects; so have I striven that my daughter should be free. Her feelings are chastened into a desire, before all things, to do that which shall be in harmony with her spiritual life, and her reverence and affection for her father."

" That is exactly what I hoped you would say, my dear vicar. Miss Hollingsworth may find me changed from the ideal of her youth. She is entirely free ; but I gather from you, that if I recover, I too am free to win her, if I can."

The vicar made no reply, but perceiving some emotion in his former ward, at once rose, obeying the injunction of Oliver Holte, and bidding him adieu, assured him of an early return.

Ten days later, as the Cock of Rossendale was walking at the side of Nathaniel Parkinson's pony, on which Colonel Vavasour was mounted, he found

that, for the first time, the pony's head was directed
by the rider down the steep road which wound from
the abrupt cliff, on which the manor-house was built,
into the western fork of Scarsdale Clough. Colonel
Vavasour seemed bent on visiting the scenes of his
early sports and rambles, when "the Cock" as the
gamin of Scarsdale, carried his creel and landing-
net, or held his setters in leash. As they threaded
the leaf-strewn road through the wood, they recalled
the feats which each pool had witnessed. They
gazed at the scars which they had climbed, they
lingered at the rock whence they had watched a
brood of otters, kennelled under the roots of a huge
alder, issue to sport and fish; they stopped at a sand-
bank burrowed with rabbit-holes, to chat of their
success in depopulating this warren with the help of
ferrets and terriers. Then, passing the Mere Clough
and its row of weavers' cottages, they wandered up
the narrow and embowered glen which led to Scarsdale Head. Midway, was a huge bolder, as big as
a house, beneath which it had been their custom to
make a fire, and, on the glowing wood-ashes, to fry
the trout they had caught for a midday meal. Here
Colonel Vavasour dismounted, in a mood for thought,
and sent his attendant into the wood with the pony,
to let it graze.

Though scarcely a breath of air stirred, the frost-

withered leaves were pattering through the branches
to the dry and leafy ground, flecked everywhere
with bright gleams of the last sunlight of November,
through the thin and faded foliage.

The torrent sang to him, as in days when he had,
as a child, wandered hither with his foster-sister,
or, when a youth from college, he waylaid her as
a lover. There was not a rock, a tree, a turn
in the tortuous road, unconsecrated by some emotion of this pure passion of early life. How often
had these scenes recurred in the splendour of courts,
in the gayest haunts of fashion, in moments of
supreme temptation or error, always to restrain,
always to revive the better nature—even to dash
from his lips, with remorse and horror, the polluted draught with which he was about to poison
his being! Would to God he had never left his
native valley! Would to God he had lived a
simple life in these wilds! Oh that, guided only by
his early training, he had altogether preserved his
life from the stains of a career of passion! How
could he, even though penitent, approach the sweet
and gentle piety of Helen, from whose trustful love
he had wandered, to bring back only a life withered
by the rebuke of Heaven, and a heart, if constant,
still one that had wearied her affection by his wayward career, if he had not alienated it by his pro-

digality. She was before him, in his mind's eye,—
a beautiful girl, barely seventeen, with large beaming eyes, fair hair, an exquisite mouth, an air of
simplicity, tenderness, and grace, without the slightest consciousness of the power of her beauty and
truth. The hue of health was in her lips, and on
her cheek, and in the step with which, like a roe,
she ran to greet her foster-brother. He had bent
his head upon his hand, the better to drink in this
mental vision, and to contrast it with the proud
rivals of fashion, which had sought to displace it
from his heart. No! Marquise de Buron, your
daughter, though radiant as Aurora, and seductive
as Venus, fresh from the foam of ocean, did not so
open heaven in all its purity to me, as Helen my
foster-sister had the power to do.

He sat on a moss-grown stone beneath the huge
bolder, hidden from the upper winding of the road,
buried in this profound reverie. There was a sound
of footsteps in the thick carpet of leaves, and of
voices close at hand. His attention was aroused;
he rose, and disturbed by familiar tones, stepped
hurriedly into the road, and stood suddenly in front
of Miss Scarsdale and Miss Hollingsworth, who
were walking from the vicarage to the Mere Clough.
A moment before, he had been gazing in reverie on
the vision of his early love; now, he stood face to

face with the gentle lady, whose affection he had put to so rude a probation.

There stood before him no longer the girl of seventeen, who had yielded herself involuntarily to the love of the companion of her childhood, but a beautiful woman, with calm and beaming eyes, a clear though not expanded brow; the same exquisite grace, simplicity, and purity, but a self-possession now, not merely the result of a perfectly guileless nature, but, alas! of severe discipline in suffering, and of a self-conquest over unavailing sorrows. The gentleness and simplicity were developed into a serene wisdom; the grace and beauty were dignified by mental culture; the purity was now not so much a sensitive shrinking from evil, as a sense of the ever-present help of God to the prayer of faith. Colonel Vavasour felt at a glance how Helen had more than fulfilled every promise of her youth.

Even the contrast of Miss Scarsdale's rare beauty, in all the pride and power of an earlier bloom, made brilliant by every grace of fashion, and provoking by the *fierté* which repelled all homage of lip or manner, rather, to his mind, enhanced the charms of Helen's womanhood. He was, for an instant, staggered by the suddenness of their meeting, and then recovering, with his wonted *aplomb* and courtesy, he approached Helen, and taking her hand, raised it to his lips, and then greeted Miss Scarsdale.

Helen had, as we have seen, been carefully disciplined by her father. He had, by a perfectly truthful narrative of the main circumstances of Colonel Vavasour's condition, preserved her from any needless agitation. Securing this serenity, he had buoyed out her path faithfully. He had counselled her, that she could not know whether Colonel Vavasour could now inspire the affection she had once felt for him. He must, by whatever effort of self-command, be received as an old friend, entitled to every courtesy, and to the most friendly interest. But it must not be presumed that he would seek more, nor could it be taken for granted that more could be conceded. Miss Scarsdale had seconded these counsels of the vicar most earnestly, and had contributed greatly, by her high spirit, to maintain the cheerfulness with which Miss Hollingsworth awaited the issue of her trying position. The vicar had, however, said nothing whatever of the change which he himself recognized in Colonel Vavasour.

When, therefore, from behind a rock, a tall and handsome man, with irregular features, dressed in a suit of velvet, approached them, and taking Miss Hollingsworth's hand, raised it to his lips, she had not, until the last instant, recognized him. This was not the slender active youth whom she had met in the glen, and whose image had so long filled her imagination. The graceful figure of the gentleman before her was that of the highest *ton*. The strong, well-knit frame of the man had seen service in war. These polished manners had been trained in court. This luxury of dress, and fastidious expression had been caught in the haunts of fashion. Had time then put this interval between her boy lover and herself? If this, perhaps more? Was this the change against which her father had warned her to hold her thoughts in equipoise?

Miss Scarsdale with feminine tact had come to her relief.

"My father brought so good an account of you, Colonel Vavasour, that we all hoped you would get abroad before the winter weather wraps us in storm and mist. But this visit to the clough is beyond our most sanguine hopes."

"Thank you much, Miss Scarsdale. I have ventured hither on Nathaniel Parkinson's cob attended by a young man, who was my creel-bearer in these cloughs a dozen years ago. I have been musing among familiar scenes, and sat here to rest."

"We are on our way to the Mere Clough cottages. Are you strong enough to come with us?"

"I think so, but I am still under orders not to

walk except on level ground, and then only for a short time. Give me leave, ladies, to call my Cock of Rossendale and the cob, and to mount and accompany you."

Mabel had foreseen that such a meeting afforded great advantages to Helen, to slide gracefully into terms of intercourse with Colonel Vavasour, consistent with the friendship which her father counselled, and enabling her to hold entirely in reserve her decision as to the further progress of their intimacy. Miss Scarsdale, therefore, as they walked down the clough, gradually drew Helen into the conversation, and ere they reached the Mere she had begun to recognize some of the once familiar tones of his voice—some traits of expression in his features; and to devise in her own mind, how the comparatively smooth profile of his youth had changed into the craggy outline which gave an original character to the face of the man.

When they reached the cottages, Miss Scarsdale would not let him dismount—but telling him that they were about to tend to some sick people, seemed, with a radiant smile and the utmost courtesy of manner, about to counsel him to avoid the chilling evening air of the clough, when Oliver Holte and Barnabas issued from the cottage which they were about to enter.

Mr. Holte approached Miss Scarsdale and Miss Hollingsworth, saying,—

"My apprehensions are all confirmed. It is greatly to be regretted that the roof of the cottages at the Northwood uplands proved so unsound, and had to be renewed. There is a case of malignant typhus in this cottage, and I fear almost every household will be a prey to this terrible malady this week. I must most earnestly dissuade your entrance, ladies; any contact with this form of the disease is dangerous. Barnabas will discharge your self-imposed duties, and I will attend the sick."

This was spoken in a gentle tone of voice, but with the quiet decision of a man accustomed to be obeyed in the exercise of his profession, and who, as Miss Scarsdale knew, had been the resident physician of large hospitals.

She paused, and turning to Miss Hollingsworth, took her hands.

"This, I suppose, is not a matter in which we can have any discretion, Helen. Your father and mine must be consulted. We must refer Mr. Holte's advice to them."

"Mr. Holte's advice has an emphatic form, Miss Scarsdale," said Colonel Vavasour, "which I hope the vicar and Sir Guy will interpret as an interdict."

"Let me also, ladies, dissuade you at present from

visiting the Mere Clough. The fall of the foliage
of the woods, its rapid decay, the chilling mists of
the evening, and the natural insalubrity of the
marsh round the Mere, combine to create a source
of danger.' Colonel Vavasour, I must induce you
also to make your excursions on the uplands; and
now to return to Assheton Manor."

There was a polite decision in Oliver's manner
which secured an immediate compliance with his
suggestions. They bade each other adieu, the ladies
returning to the vicarage, and Colonel Vavasour
pursuing his road homewards by the western fork
with his attendant, while Oliver and Barnabas continued their visitation of the cottages. They found
the traces of an outbreak of malignant typhus in
almost every house. The whole afternoon was occupied in making arrangements for the nursing of
the sick, for the supply of wine, and other necessaries, and for the removal of some who were capable
of bearing the change to that part of the row of
cottages at the Northwood uplands, which had been
repaired and furnished.

Colonel Vavasour was too just and manly to be
dissatisfied with his reception by Miss Hollingsworth.
It would be a consolation to be restored to her
friendship. To his wounded conscience it would be

a satisfaction to know that the happiness of his early
mistress had not been sacrificed by his wayward
career and long neglect. Even if the budding hope
of renewed love should not bloom, might he not
find peace? He must hold his passionate nature by
a firm rein; he must discipline his spirit to patience;
he must still this throbbing tumult of thought. What
right had he to offer the wreck of his constitution,
the dregs of his youth, the wasted gifts of a bountiful
nature to her who had loved him only in his un-
corrupted prime? Her father had been faithful to
his guardianship. His daughter had received him
calmly and gently as an early friend. He would
accept this position: let the future bring what it
might, it should, with the help of God, bring no fresh
pang to his conscience. These were the thoughts
which, not without visible emotion, thrilled through
him on his way homewards, and during the evening,
while he awaited his physician's return from the
typhus-haunted cottages of the Mere Clough.

He had dined ere Oliver arrived. Then he
listened to the narrative of suffering and impending
calamity among the families of weavers. Barnabas
had found a lodging in the naturalist's cottage a little
higher up the glen, in order that he might personally
superintend the execution of the medical directions.
Deloisir would join him there, so that each might

watch during every alternate eight hours. They would thus be able to devote twenty-four hours out of every forty-eight to sleep and exercise in the open air. These arrangements, with nourishing diet and constitutions prepared to encounter contagion by previous exposure, seemed a probable source of safety. Colonel Vavasour highly commended their devotion, and placed all the resources of his own household at his friend's command.

From day to day, the malady thenceforth made rapid progress through the families of the Mere Clough, worn as they had been by labour and want, and with blood poisoned by the miasmata of the marsh. The previous abundant help from Scarsdale, combined with the vigilance and skill of Oliver and his assistants, doubtless mitigated the ravages of the disease, and saved many victims; but no day passed without a death. In the course of three weeks twenty-four of the fever-stricken weavers had been buried in Assheton churchyard. The vicar was assiduous and faithful in his ministrations. Putting on a suit in the cottage of the naturalist which, when he exchanged it, was hung some hours in the open air, he paid daily visits to the sick and dying. Colonel Vavasour, knowing his habits, appeared at the vicarage almost daily to welcome him on his return from his morning visits, by awaiting him in the garden. He then entered with him, and took luncheon with Mr. Hollingsworth and his daughter. Thus he was soon on his old footing of intimacy. He made no apparent effort to be received as a lover. By degrees, therefore, Helen acquired confidence that she would not be perplexed with premature proposals. She was astonished at the change which ten years of intercourse with the courts and camps of Europe had made in her boy lover. The fascination of Colonel Vavasour's polished manners—the indications of a wide experience, accomplishments,—an acute insight into the springs of action, among classes of which she had no knowledge; and, at the same time, of a brave, truthful, manly spirit, deeply interested her. She observed with what reverence and gratitude he treated her father. When the vicar spoke on subjects of faith and duty, he listened like a son or a disciple, but was silent. He volunteered no indication of the workings of his own mind either on his past life, or on their previous associations. To herself, his demeanour was full of a delicate courtesy, with almost a tinge of melancholy in his tone, when he addressed her, if they chanced for a brief period to be alone.

Her father treated him with entire respect and confidence. He placed no bar on Colonel Vavasour's intercourse with her, but his own fastidious sense of honour. But he obviously never sought to be alone with her, and the only sign of the object of his visits to the vicarage was their frequency, which appeared to indicate that he wished her to have the fullest opportunity of observing what change had occurred in him. Yet she was not disturbed. The discipline of sorrow, aided by the training of her father, had enabled her to form a juster estimate of the aims of life. Oh what cause for joy, that this prodigal brother had been restored to his home! If she could not welcome him with the caresses of a sister, she could every night pour out a thanksgiving for answered prayers.

When a youth, Colonel Vavasour had, as the vicar's ward, taught every Sunday in the school which was held in an old chauntry in the church-yard of Assheton. Thither it had been her constant habit to repair. One Sunday morning, on entering, she observed the tall figure of Colonel Vavasour by the side of Barnabas Collier, who was teaching the class of young men which the colonel had formerly instructed. He remained a calm and silent observer of Barnabas's teaching, and went out with the class to church, without appearing to observe her presence. This was the first day on which he had attended the parish church since his return.

The news of his early ride to the school had spread, and the churchyard was filled with groups of tenantry and labourers anxious to welcome him, and to assure themselves of the recovery of the lord of the manor. Leaning upon the arm of Nathaniel Parkinson, and quietly conversing with him and Barnabas, he approached each group to return the hearty congratulations of his neighbours and dependants. Helen observed all this, as she slid like a sunbeam through the churchyard to her quiet corner in the vicar's pew.

Miss Scarsdale had not visited the vicarage for a week. This was so unusual an interval, that Helen persuaded her father to accompany her in a visit to Scarsdale Hall. They found Sir Guy Scarsdale at home, but anxious and disturbed. Miss Scarsdale had during the preceding week been very weak, sleepless, and far from well. One evening a violent shivering fit had occurred, followed by severe headache, delirium, and other alarming symptoms. M. Malvoisin had left for Glasgow, whither he had been summoned, by one of his agents, in consequence of some shocking outrages of a secret society. Sir Guy had sent to Assheton for Mr. Holte on the evening when the shivering occurred. On his arrival Sir Guy was deeply disturbed by a confirmation of his fears. His daughter had caught the contagion in the Mere Clough, and was certainly attacked with fever. Mr. Holte had urgently pressed Sir Guy to summon a physician from Manchester, and he was now anxiously awaiting his arrival. Helen was greatly disturbed, and the vicar grave and silent.

The vicar and Miss Hollingsworth remained to luncheon, at which they were joined by Mr. Holte. To the vicar he explained that the symptoms of Miss Scarsdale's attack were alarming, that he had met the emergency with promptitude, but that he felt the responsibility deeply. He anxiously expected the arrival of the physician from Manchester. Mr. Hollingsworth observed that he looked worn and distressed, which he attributed to the harassing duties, that he had recently discharged in the Mere Clough. He was unusually silent. He had heard the sound of the physician's carriage before they were aware, he rose abruptly, and left the table, and soon afterwards the noise of the horse's hoofs and of the wheels in the quadrangle, explained his sudden departure.

"What if Mr. Holte should a third time save Miss Scarsdale's life!" said the vicar.

"I pray God that it may be so. Oh, how terrible a calamity to Sir Guy!"

"And if I mistake not," said the vicar, "to Lord Pendleborough?"

His daughter made no reply, but with a feminine intuition suggested, " Did it ever occur to you, father, to imagine why Mr. Holte avoids living at Scarsdale,—why he has refused Sir Guy's offers to place him in Parliament—and why he intends, notwithstanding his very varied experience and sympathies, to devote himself solely to medicine in a provincial town?"

" I have, at Sir Guy's suggestion, endeavoured to shake his resolution, my child. His plea is, that his father, when he was a boy, under the influence of his Puritan faith, destined him to become a Christian minister among the Nonconformists. His own convictions and experience interfered with the accomplishment of this intention, which had almost the form of a vow. Though, therefore, his father has left him free to follow his own sense of duty, he conceives himself bound to adopt a profession closely in harmony with his vow."

" I have no doubt also," said Helen, " that in becoming a physician to the body, he will live the life of a confessor. But, dear father, are there not some other motives mixed with his resolution ? "

" None that I can discern, my daughter."

" I have a vague suspicion that the romantic hardihood with which he has twice rescued Miss Scarsdale from most imminent peril, is a sign of an admiration for her, which he deems it his duty to suppress. He will, therefore, resolutely exile himself from her society."

" That would certainly add cogency to his motives for separating himself from all associations with Sir Guy's family."

" If I am right in my suspicions, no trial could be more severe to him, than that he should have charge of Miss Scarsdale in this terrible illness. I pray you therefore, dear father, to use every proper influence to secure a daily visit from the physician."

" If needful, I will not fail to impress that on Sir Guy Scarsdale, on any obvious general grounds."

When the physician had visited Miss Scarsdale he requested an interview with Sir Guy, who received him with a calm but grave manner, as one who would meet an evil fate with becoming dignity.

" I regret to say that I find Miss Scarsdale is suffering from continued fever, with a sudden and remarkable prostration of vital power, requiring the most constant attention."

" My domestic physician is a gentleman of such experience, that I have the utmost confidence the results of your daily consultations will be most diligently and skilfully executed."

" No doubt, if he felt himself equal to the task; but he informs me that he is much exhausted by attendance at all hours in a hamlet on your estate, which has been ravaged by typhus; and he fears Miss Scarsdale might suffer from his weakness and loss of nerve."

" I will not venture to risk a life precious to me, as having twice been put to grave hazard for my daughter. Can you point out any mode of meeting the emergency? "

" Mr. Holte has suggested that I should submit to you the expediency of recalling M. Malvoisin from Scotland, and until he arrives, that I should spend every night at Scarsdale. I am quite disposed to do so, if that be in accordance with your own wishes."

" I am most grateful, and at once accept your generous offer. I have, however, no hope that M. Malvoisin can return, and I hesitate to make such a claim on his friendship."

It was then about three o'clock. The physician left, promising to be back soon after ten o'clock, so as to visit his patient before midnight. Alice, as a trained nurse, was to spend the night in her mistress's room; the doctor was to be summoned from an adjoining room twice in the night; he was to see his patient again in the morning with Mr. Holte, and then to leave her in his charge for the day.

Helen eagerly pressed her father and Sir Guy
to permit her to attend Miss Scarsdale during the
day. But Sir Guy resolutely forbade her; and,
at Mr. Holte's suggestion, himself, aided by his
housekeeper, undertook this latter duty. Mr. Holte
proposed to confine his visits to every fourth hour,
in the absence of the physician.

The vicar and his daughter, from these arrangements, perceived at once how critical was the condition of Miss Scarsdale. Mr. Holte explained that
the hope of saving her life depended mainly on the
vigour of her constitution, and on the minute accuracy with which the remedial measures were executed. They left Scarsdale with heavy hearts.

In all matters of feeling, women are infinitely more
quick-witted than men. They seize and combine
with the swiftest intuition indications which escape
masculine faculties. Thus, in the unrestrained freedom of their charming friendship, Miss Hollingsworth had come unawares, from time to time, on the
traces of an anxiety for Mr. Oliver Holte, which
lurked deeply seated in Miss Scarsdale; and, like
a remembrance or a presentiment of evil, troubled
her consciousness with a sudden pang. Helen
loved her friend too tenderly not to ponder what
this could mean. She knew that for four years Oliver
had, as Sir Guy's physician, been their constant

companion in travel. Two years ago, at the source
of the Garonne, while Sir Guy was himself engaged
with a brigand, Mr. Holte, by a prompt and dex-
terous act of gallantry, had rescued Miss Scarsdale.
Sir Guy had written a full account of this to the
father, expressing strongly his sense of the manly
bearing of his son. Helen observed that the colour
faded in Miss Scarsdale's cheek on the slightest
allusion to this incident. Then Mr. Holte's eager-
ness to run any risk to save Miss Scarsdale from
the mob of machine-breakers on the day of the
attack on the Eagle Mill, though most gracefully
acknowledged by her friend, was never alluded to
without the recurrence of the same ominous pallor.
She was aware that Oliver, declining to avail himself of Sir Guy's friendship, even sought as early
as possible to separate from his family. She saw
how steadily Sir Guy sought to bring the influence
of the vicar, and of Oliver's father to second his
own wish to give to his young friend's ability and
high cultivation, a sphere of action more promising
than that of a provincial physician. Miss Scarsdale
evidently felt a grave anxiety for the success of this
intervention, though she took no part in it. This,
too, was one of the subjects which, if even casually
introduced, banished the radiant smile of youth and
beauty from her face, and clouded it with the gloom

of care. What did this mean? Helen asked. .Why did this sudden pang seize her friend's heart like a mortal spasm? Why, in this elastic nature, so fancy free, so gay, so instinct with a vigorous will, did the torpedo shock of a secret dread seem, now and then, to benumb her otherwise hopeful life?

She was too much troubled on account of her friend, not to observe Mr. Holte. His absence at Deerden, and subsequently at Assheton Manor, seemed welcome to him. These duties—attendance on the sick weavers—not unfrequent consultations with her father, and with Barnabas, and Deloisir, on the condition of the weaving population, and brief visits to his own family absorbed his time. He was seldom or never at Scarsdale Hall. Did he avoid it? His manner was habitually calm, cheerful, without the slightest tinge of melancholy. Her father spoke of him as a man of settled purpose. One in whom a resolution once deliberately taken, was not reviewed, but acted upon with an unswerving decision. These were the elements on which Miss Hollingsworth, thinking much and anxiously, came to the conclusion suggested by her to her father. She believed that Miss Scarsdale had become aware that she was the object of a hopeless attachment from her father's friend. She then divined the intense will which must have repressed the exhibition of this affection, so that even Sir Guy seemed to be quite unconscious of it, and that it had been chiefly revealed to Miss Scarsdale by Mr. Holte's chivalrous hardihood, combined with his resolution to separate himself from her father, to whom he had shown such devotion.

The father and mother of Oliver have occupied the background of our picture of Lancashire life. They represented the link between the old yeomanry of the county with their not infrequent puritan faith, and the classes growing into wealth and power by manufacturing enterprise. To them the deep interest taken by Sir Guy Scarsdale in the education and career of their son was a subject of unmingled gratitude, for they had confidence in the generosity of Sir Guy's motives, as well as in his wisdom. Their inclination, therefore, was to adopt his friendly suggestions, and to avail themselves of his aid to place their son in a position for which he was well fitted by education and habits of thought, and in which the fortune, accumulated by their patient enterprise and thrift, would enable him to persevere. They had, however, watched the growth of his intelligence and character, and they felt that the decision ought to be his own. They could not do more than make him aware that they were disposed to regard Sir Guy Scarsdale's suggestions with favour.

On the day after the adventure in Scarsdale Clough with the bull, Mistress Holte, with the motherly solicitude of a Lancashire matron, sought a personal interview with Miss Scarsdale. There hung about the hall the peril of this disaster, the mysterious appearance and precautions of the police, the constant watch in the corridors, the courts, and in the wood. The worthy dame sought admission to the young lady of the squire.

"Mistress Holte," said Mabel, rising eagerly, as Oliver's mother was announced to her in her boudoir, "you are very welcome; I long to have a chat with you."

"Well-a-day, my dear young lady, neither Mr. Holte nor I could close our eyes, till the night was far spent, for dread. We were glad Oliver should be with Sir Guy."

"Your son is always prompt, brave, and generous; and if he would give my father the satisfaction of promoting his fortunes in proportion to his merits and to our gratitude, he would afford us all a heartfelt gratification."

"His father and I think Sir Guy's plans as wise as they are kind; but Oliver is more capable to judge than we are, for he has seen more of life."

"Has he not the impression that you devoted him to the ministry of the Gospel, and that he must fulfil that vow—if not as a healer of the spirit, then as a physician to the body?"

"Doubtless; but his father says, Christ has ministers and teachers in every walk in life. Now Oliver cannot gainsay that; but as nathless he wills to take this humbler path, he may fear some temptation of Satan if he were carried to an exceeding high mountain, or to a pinnacle of the temple."

"What," said Miss Scarsdale, in a low voice—"what temptation, Mistress Holte, can he fear?"

The tone of this question caused Mistress Holte to raise her eyes to Miss Scarsdale's face as she replied,—

"He says he fears a worldly ambition, or an unrighteous and selfish presumption."

But the pallor of Miss Scarsdale's face shocked the worthy matron so much, that she rose instantly from her seat, and approaching her hastily but tenderly, said,—

"Ah, well-a-day! that terrible bull! You are not yet well, my dear young lady!"

In fact, Mabel resorted to her *vinaigrette*, while Mistress Holte dipped a muslin handkerchief in eau-de-Cologne, and applied it to her temples.

"Truly, dear Mrs. Holte," said Mabel, by and by recovering, "the events of yesterday have somewhat unnerved me. But let me say," she added, with her hand strongly tightening its grasp on Mrs. Holte's caressing palm, "I too have some right to assert an interest in your son. He has twice saved my life; he will make me happier, if he will let my father and Lord Pendleborough place him in the position for which he is fitted by natural gifts and accomplishments."

"Lord Pendleborough has seen my husband, and has urged his strong belief that Oliver is well fitted for success in public life, and has promised that nothing shall be wanting on his part to put him forward."

"That, I fear, has not shaken your son's resolution."

"On the contrary, Miss Scarsdale, Oliver sought out Lord Pendleborough and thanked him heartily, but told him that it was his fixed resolution to devote some years to the work of a physician among the poor of a great trading town, until he had satisfied his conscience that any other path was safely open to him."

The worthy matron was surprised when the beautiful young lady, of whose courtly manners she stood somewhat in awe, drew her towards her on the sofa, and kissing her with an emotion which betrayed itself in her moistened eyes, said,—

"You have a noble and generous man for your son; let us not doubt that in satisfying his conscience he will find an enduring happiness. But events march quickly past our will; and let us hope, that as God's will is manifested, your son may gratify us all, by accepting my father's and Lord Pendleborough's advice and aid."

Mrs. Holte was not prepared for such emotion or tenderness in the spirited and courtly young lady, whose beauty and charms radiated from her to awe as well as to attract. The devotion of Lord Pendleborough, though cloaked in his almost austere manners, and in the reserve which he had imposed upon himself, was so marked by slight acts of a constant homage, that all the dependants of the family accounted him the suitor of Miss Scarsdale. None conceived that a man of his remarkable presence and vast possessions would fail in such a suit, when he possessed the friendship of the father, and had long enjoyed the intimacy of the daughter. To Mrs. Holte, therefore, nothing could be more natural than that Lord Pendleborough should seek to fulfil the grateful wishes of perhaps his affianced mistress. Why, then, this trouble? Would Miss Scarsdale's marriage to Lord Pendleborough remove any obstacle to her son's entrance on a parliamentary career? How so? These thoughts flashed through Mrs. Holte's mind as she received the tender embrace and the kiss from Miss Scarsdale, as from a daughter to a mother.

The summer of Mabel's life was climbing above her horizon every day in wider circles of fire, like the path of the sun converting the polar winter darkness into light. Under the new power, emotions hitherto controlled by a maidenly reserve, by a fine instinct sustained by a quick and vigorous will, asserted their power, breaking the bonds by which they were held. The deep fountain of a woman's sympathies welled forth—to the poor, to the gentle friendship for her sweet friend Helen, to new emotions such as she had never known. What meant this painful anxiety for Oliver Holte's happiness? What was this agonizing thought that Lord Pendleborough would rashly spend his life to win her love?

The matron and her beautiful young lady sat some time in silence, till Miss Hollingsworth came in to invite Mabel to a walk in the garden court with the duchess. What happened there has been related in a previous chapter.

CHAPTER VIII.

THE TAMING OF THE KERNES IN THE GLENS OF DUNKERRON.

THE agent whom Lord Pendleborough had selected for the management of his Irish estates was an Engineer officer, the cadet of an English family of distinction, whom he had met in Paris. There this gentleman occupied the leisure afforded by peace and half-pay in the study of strategy and fortification. He had visited the chief battle-fields and fortresses of Europe. He had also profoundly interested himself in the great social revolutions accomplished by Hardenberg, and in the different systems of the tenure and descent of property, and of its cultivation. These latter pursuits had naturally brought him into the society of Malvoisin, and there he had met Lord Pendleborough and Sir Guy Scarsdale, about a year and a half before the opening of our narrative. After some months' acquaintance, Lord Pendleborough, having first consulted Sir Guy Scarsdale, proposed to Major Piers Harcourt that he should undertake the direction of the measures of improvement by which Lord Pendleborough intended to transform his Irish property.

Major Harcourt had now been one year resident in Kerry. During this time he had been chiefly engaged in collecting information, ascertaining upon whom he could depend for aid in the promotion of the changes which were to be introduced, making himself familiar with the character and habits of the people, with their prejudices, superstitions, and the social or national feelings likely in any way to embarrass his operations. He found formidable obstacles to the plans which were contemplated, and these he had regularly communicated to Lord Pendleborough in systematic reports during the year. These exact and comprehensive documents had been submitted to Malvoisin, and had been the subject of anxious discussion. Harcourt strongly urged that the first steps of these improvements should be introduced by Lord Pendleborough in person. He relied on the influence of the traditional homage to his name, and on the effect of personal manifestations of sympathy on the impressionable Celtic race. He thought that the proofs of such interest in their welfare would affect the imagination and hearts of the cottiers, who would be inaccessible to the most demonstrative facts and reasoning. When, therefore the catastrophe of the assassination of his Scotch farmer occurred, Lord Pendleborough was prepared by a long train of preceding inquiry and deliberation for immediate action, and he left Scarsdale without delay for Kerry.

His yacht, which had been lying in the Mersey, floated with the tide to sea, on the night on which he bade adieu to his friends; and in a few days he entered the harbour of Valentia, and proceeded at once to his castle, between the Inveragh and Dunkerron mountains. A fortnight elapsed before even brief tidings of his successful voyage reached Scarsdale. About a week later, a letter from Harcourt to Malvoisin gave the following account of the first steps:—

" I calculated pretty accurately the period of Lord Pendleborough's voyage, and I had only to wait one night in Cahirciveen. As soon as he put foot on shore, he sprang into his saddle, and we rode across the Inveragh and the valley of the Inny to the slopes of the Dunkerron, and reached the castle about an hour after sunset. He seems to have a frame of iron; for even before taking any refreshment he would visit every principal room. He seemed both surprised at the lavish outlay on this immense pile, and full of regret that the revenues of the property had not been used for objects more allied to the well-

being of the tenantry. It was half-past eight before
we sat down to dinner. As soon as we were alone,
he planned the work of the following day. At five
o'clock the following morning he had breakfasted.
He was dressed in a plain velvet shooting suit. He
would have no attendant but a 'spalpeen,' whom I
selected to show him the way. With a loaded
bamboo as his only apparent weapon, but also well
provided with a brace of double-barrelled pistols, he
left the castle on foot soon after five o'clock, to ascend
a wild glen in which live many of the near relatives
of his new tenants in Canada. His intention was to
enter their cabins alone, to read to them accounts of
the condition of the absent members of their families,
to make himself personally familiar with the state of
each household, and by such intercourse to lead them
to rely on his wisdom and generosity. I have since
learned that he took them all by surprise. His
handsome figure, fearless bearing, frank, yet dignified
demeanour, and the confidence with which he came
among them unattended, appealed irresistibly to some
of their higher sentiments.

"But this vigorous and brave lord of these
wretched serfs sat down in a miserable cabin, in the
smoke and dirt, surrounded by the wild, unkemmed
kernes, who crowded around him, and at the door, with
an insatiable curiosity. He drew out letters from his

Canadian agent, describing exactly what had been done for the emigrants, and their position and prospects. He gave them familiar anecdotes of the adventures and successes of individuals, interspersed with traits of personal character, some humorous and some pathetic. By degrees, the cunning of the half-outlawed savage yielded to this sympathetic intercourse. It appeared that letters had been received, dictated by their absent relations, which had been read for them by a hedge schoolmaster. Lord Pendleborough's statements came only in confirmation of what they knew of the condition of their friends. He, however, explained to them in simple language his whole scheme, and described what he hoped would be the position of his Irish emigrants in three or four years. From a plan and picture of the log-houses and farm buildings already built, he showed them the use of every room, and of every separate structure. A day's work for a backwoodsman was described—in his first year,—in his second year,—and in subsequent periods. He gave them accounts of the sledge journeys in winter, of the trapping of wild animals, the poisoning of the wolves, the hunting of the deer and buffalo, the 'bees' for mutual assistance.

"The crowd had become so great, early in his narrative, that he had found it necessary to sit at the door of the cabin, and the half-savage cottiers from the whole of the glen hurried thither. He formed them into a circle, round which they sat on the ground, on their haunches—eager, from genuine concern for their absent relations, to hear all that their lord had to tell them.

"Towards noon, Lord Pendleborough asked the mistress of the cabin if he might join their meal; and half an hour after, a smoking bowl of potatoes, with pieces of bacon in honour of his visit, was set before him, with many hearty, if homely apologies. He made a meal before them all, and, giving a handsome largess to the dame, proceeded to visit every cabin in the glen, followed in his whole route by the respectful, if ragged and noisy crowd. As there are two hundred of these wretched cabins in this glen alone, it was twilight before this work was done. Then, refusing any escort, and accompanied only by the 'spalpeen,' he walked six miles back to the castle, arriving just in time to dress for an eight o'clock dinner.

"In four succeeding days Lord Pendleborough visited four other glens, from each of which some emigrants had gone to his Canadian estates, though fewer than from that which he first visited. The day was in each case spent in a very similar manner to that already described, varied, of course, by incidents characteristic of each glen, too numerous for this sketch. The effect of these visits has been to produce a conviction that their lord has taken great personal pains to secure the well-being of those who entrusted their fortunes to him in Canada. Lord Pendleborough has been very careful to avoid any hint that he is disposed to promote further emigration. Even to such applications as were made to him, he has replied that he will make due inquiries as to the motives, capacity, and character of those who are desirous to join their friends. The suspicion that he has come hither to clear the land, or simply to detect and punish the assassins of Mac Vie, will be lulled. At present, it is still rampant. But the complete occupation of Lord Pendleborough's time in these visits to the cottier tenantry of the glens—his fearless bearing—the total absence of all apparent precautions for his personal safety—his reliance on their loyalty to his family—their gratitude for his help to their relatives—and the proofs of personal sympathy as to their condition—have produced a singular ferment in their excitable temperaments.

"On two other days Lord Pendleborough has been on horseback with me. We have taken a general survey of the whole property, and he has called upon each of the Catholic priests, has sat an hour with them, and left an ample sum to be expended in blankets, clothing, and necessaries for the sick during the ensuing winter. We have spent every evening in the review, in detail, of the plans which are to be carried into execution. Until next week Lord Pendleborough has postponed some acts of a very different character, for which he is obviously preparing himself, by the information which I can give him, and by his private communications with the police—the head of which force is here every night for a couple of hours. But yesterday was Sunday, and he waited to ascertain what the priests would say to their flocks from the altar. I have had a report from each chapel. The visit to each of their reverences, and the personal explanations made to them, had conciliated their good-will, and every address recommended confidence in Lord Pendleborough, and congratulated the peasantry on his visit to his great ancestral estates."

There was also a brief letter from Lord Pendleborough to Sir Guy Scarsdale, in which he said that he found the condition of the cottiers in the glens of the Dunkerron and Inveragh as low as anything which he had seen in Poland or Russia, but that he saw no difficulties in the execution of his plans which were not to be surmounted by patient perseverance, sagacity, and vigour.

Ten days elapsed before any other communications were received. Then a letter to Malvoisin from Harcourt arrived, of which the following is an extract :—

"One of the most difficult things to be done here is to grapple with the conspiracy to convert occupation, with rent and service, into possession with or without those accessories. The work of the secret societies has been shown in the death of Mac Vie, and in the refusal of either rent or service by some desperate outlaws. The information of the police coincides with my own, that this conspiracy against rent had its origin, or was mainly fostered, by a man who inhabits a solitary house in one of the wildest recesses of the Dunkerron mountains. He is known to combine the respectable vocations of cattle-stealer, whisky-stiller, and poacher. Upon circumstantial evidence, he is suspected of encouraging the resistance to any change of occupation, and to the payment of rent and service. The suspicions of the police point to him as either an active member of the secret society by whose orders Mac Vie perished, or at least as a main source of information by which it is guided. This man is the son of a hedge schoolmaster, who discovered and worked a mine in the wildest glen of the Dunkerron. Since his father's death, ten years ago, this ruffian has paid no rent either for his mountain 'holding' or for the mine. The agents of the property have been intimidated by anonymous letters, by malicious injuries to their stock, and by the fierce, resolute bearing of this daring outlaw, who never appears at market without the stock of a horse-pistol ostentatiously protruding from his frieze coat. The den of this rascal is at ten miles' distance from the castle, and he lives there with two miners, who work his lode, and two shepherds, all equally fierce outlaws with himself. Lord Pendleborough had obtained from the head of the police very accurate and minute information of the habits of this wild household, and I had shown him the lower part of the glen during one of our rides. It was the custom of Patrick Macguire to attend a fair at Kenmare, with a faction party of hill farmers and shepherds, and by routes purposely varied to return across the Dunkerron in the night. As this fair came off four days ago, Lord Pendleborough laid his plans accordingly.

"He started alone from the castle in the night, rode five miles by a route with which he had become familiar, to a police station in the valley, near the mouth of the glen. Here he left his horse, and thence, still alone, he followed the wild road by the side of the torrent, through the hamlets of cabins, which extended two miles up the ravine; and then, leaving them behind him, penetrated three other miles, concealed by a singularly dark night, into the desolate and bare region from which the stream fell among the wild recesses of the Dunkerron. With the first gleams of dawn he was able to recognize the hut of the outlaw, and to steal, with the practised skill of a deer-stalker, to a rock, where he lay concealed in the heather, and whence he could watch the proceedings of the household.

"A more savage scene of rock, torrent, and desolate, heathery mountain steeps, it is scarcely possible to imagine. Here Lord Pendleborough lay an hour, without a sign of any living thing. Then, from the cleft of a narrow dell, through which the stream chafed, he saw a man, on a strong and active hill pony, emerge, approach the house, dismount, place his nag in a shieling, and then enter the hut. After the interval of half-an-hour, two men issued with ' picks ' on their shoulders, and wandered up the glen. They were scarcely out of sight ere two others, each eating a hunch of bread, and taking a pull at a whisky flask, separated at the door, and climbed the steep slopes on opposite sides. These were the shepherds. In half an hour they also were out of sight. Lord Pendleborough waited yet awhile, but perceiving no other sign, he cautiously made a circuit, and stole to the house. He listened at the door. There were no footsteps. There was no other noise within, except a sound like a low moan. Through a narrow window, in the wall of rough bolders, he could see the light of a turf fire in the gloom of the interior. He went round to the back of the hut, and to the outbuildings. There was no other entrance. He could make out nothing of the interior by peering into another narrow window. There was but one opening in the roof, and from that the smoke of the turf fire issued. Forming his own deductions from these observations, he again cautiously approached, and listened at the door. All was yet still—no motion within—no sound but the dull moan, which, by comparing it with his own breathing, he made out to be the snoring of a man asleep, near the fire. He hesitated no longer, but slowly and cautiously opened the door, wide enough to creep into the hut.

"It was lighted only by the rude and scanty opening of the window, and the glimmer of a turf fire. But this gleam, with that from the half-opened door, showed him the large frame of the outlaw, in a frieze coat, stretched in a deep slumber on a sack, thrown on some heather in a corner of the room. From habit, the ruffian's hand had been on his horse-pistol, the stock of which protruded from the pocket of his coat, but, oppressed with fatigue, the hand had fallen from this position.   Lord Pendleborough's quick glance at once perceived this, and advancing stealthily, he withdrew the weapon without awakening his antagonist, who snored loudly.   He thrust the pistol into his own pocket, opened the entrance widely, and seating himself on a three-legged stool, so that the light might fall full upon his person, he gave the outlaw two or three pokes with his bamboo, and roused him from his sleep.   The ruffian sat up in his bed, staring with astonishment on his visitor, whom, from popular report, he at once recognized as his lord.   Involuntarily, his right hand sought his pistol in the pocket of his frieze coat, and he **was** daunted when he found it gone.   Ere he could recover from his surprise, Lord Pendleborough said,

" ' Macguire, I am come in person to settle a long account with you.   Pay me at once the rents which you owe, or get up and go with me to gaol.'

" The answer to this was a fierce rush at Lord Pendleborough, who, thoroughly on his guard, had risen as he spoke, and now met the onslaught by so rude a thrust with his bamboo into the stomach of his assailant that he was instantly doubled up, and, before he could recover, was slightly stunned by a blow on the side of the head.   Before he was sensible, Lord Pendleborough tied him hand and foot, and enveloping him in the sack which lay on the heather, secured it about his neck, brought out his own pony, threw him across it, and tied the sack securely to the girth. Just as Macguire revived to a sense of his position, he found himself a prisoner, carried on his own pony down the glen.

" The action of Lord Pendleborough had, however, been so prompt, skilful, and vigorous, that no alarm had been given, and he threaded the first three miles of this wild glen, with his prisoner secured to the saddle of his own pony, unmolested from the scattered huts on the hills. Below this, hamlets of cabins succeeded each other, and then the straggling street of a village of cottiers. Lord Pendleborough had insisted that the police should take no precautions against a rescue, lest the moral effect of his personal and unaided capture of this outlaw should be impaired. A great excitement soon prevailed. The fierce features of Macguire were recognized, protruding from the sack. A few days before, Lord Pendleborough had purposely ridden through these groups of cabins, and visited some of them. He was, therefore, well known. The wild kernes rushed from their huts, summoned by familiar outcries, but though Macguire uttered loud and fierce appeals, and the crowd gathered in tumultuous throngs, yet, when Lord Pendleborough stopped occasionally, and warned them that no one could be permitted to approach, they hesitated to answer the appeal for a rescue which would bring them into personal collision with their lord.   He had no weapon but his bamboo, but there was something in the calm, stern vigour of the man, together with the antecedents of the preceding fortnight, the fame of which was in every mouth, that overawed and subdued them.

" The position was, however, most perilous.   I had impressed, from time to time, on Lord Pendleborough, the danger which he ran, in his solitary visits, from the excitable character of the population.   Of his plan for the conduct of this midnight expedition, I knew no details.   All he had said was, that he would quell the ruffian in his den.   In our ride in the glen, I had, however, pointed out one hamlet, near the mouth, which was reputed to be the abode of men who were in the Peep-o'-day plot, and might have been accomplices in the murder of Mac Vie.   The most dreaded of these desperadoes was a fellow with one eye.   The chief of the police confirmed my warnings of the influence which this wretch had on the tenantry of the glen, and of his reckless character.

" Turning, from time to time, to keep the yelling crowd at bay, Lord Pendleborough had passed through four miles of the glen.   There was still more than a mile to the police-station, when he saw two wild, half-naked slips of lads running at the top of their speed down the road towards the hamlet, of the character of which I had warned him. As he approached it the excitement of the crowd became fearful. They answered the screams of Macguire by frantic gesticulations, brandishing their shillelahs in the air, and dancing, as though to lash themselves into frenzy. But a wild, fierce yell of wrath and vengeance broke from the whole mass, as a one-eyed man came from a hut, with a horse-pistol in his hand, and advanced coolly and steadily to meet Lord Pendleborough, who was driving the pony before him with his bamboo. His prisoner and the beast formed a screen, over which it was difficult to fire, with the crowd only a few yards behind, without more risk of killing one of the peasantry than himself. With this advantage, Lord Pendleborough walked steadily on till he was within six paces of his opponent, when, rushing past the pony, he struck the pistol from his grasp with so severe a blow from his loaded bamboo, that he broke the bones of the hand; whilst the wretch was writhing with the agony, he hit him heavily on the back of the neck, and tumbled him into the brook.

"The excitement of the mob was so wild, that it was necessary for a moment to turn upon them. Lord Pendleborough walked calmly towards them, and, as he advanced, they paused, and even retired some paces. The frantic gestures and yells became less menacing, and they seemed to recover, in some degree, their self-possession, in the presence of this grand courage.

" I cannot, however, conceive that this frenzy could have been thus kept in control many minutes longer. Probably it would ere this have broken out into an ungovernable fury, if some of the more respectable cottiers, whose cabins Lord Pendleborough had visited with me some days before, had not exerted themselves to calm and restrain the tumult. Eight or ten of these wild, but honest men, seemed to have been made friends by the familiar talk in their huts. They had gathered into a group, and with courage and decision stopped every attempt to make a rush to rescue the captive. Contrary, however, to Lord Pendleborough's express commands, the chief of the police had ordered some of his men to creep in the night into the cabin of a man, who had been placed in the hamlet as a watch on the suspected members of the Peep-o'-day-Boys' plot. At this juncture, Lord Pendleborough was surprised to see the crowd falter and retire some paces with a loud shout, and to find himself, a moment later, surrounded by ten policemen, armed with carbines, cutlasses, and pistols. Between this group and the discomfited rout of the mob, remained a dozen stalwart fellows, who had exerted themselves for his protection.

"Having first directed the attention of the police to Mahoney, who lay stunned on some bolders at the edge of the torrent, Lord Pendleborough advanced, with a smile of thanks and an extended hand, to the men who had voluntarily become his body-guard. He thanked them heartily, and sitting on a rock, by the side of the road, at once inquired their names, and entered them in his pocket-book.

"He discovered that they corresponded with a list of the most peaceable, industrious, and thriving of the tenantry with which he had been furnished. He, however, observed about an equal number of this list had remained at home in their cabins. To the group before him, he at once explained that it was his intention, at the same time that he enforced the observance of all legal obligations, to make great improvements in the glen. He briefly stated, that he had decided to provide labour and wages during the ensuing winter for the entire population, by making a good road through the ravine—by enclosing fields with stone walls for pasture, meadow-land, and tillage; and by building better dwellings. He therefore directed them, together with the other men in his list who had not left their cabins, to be at the castle in the morning, when he would explain to them his plans in detail. Then giving them each a small present of money for their help, he sent them back to the mob, who crowded round them, with eager curiosity as to the results of their interview.

" While this conference was in progress the police remained stationary, but another party of constables had made a swoop into the hamlet of cabins in which the suspected members of the Peep-o'day-Boys' Association lived, and had taken five men, who had long obstinately refused to pay rent, and against whom warrants of ejectment and outlawry had been issued. Their huts were at once unroofed, the cabin walls thrown down, and the furniture seized; but the families were carried away in carts to a sort of hospital, which had been made in an old barrack, close to the police station. Lord Pendleborough stood by, and personally directed these measures of rigour. Then, while the police was placing the families and their poor effects in the carts, amidst the wild wailing of the women and the screams of the children, he entered some of the cabins of the better-disposed tenantry pointed out to him by the police, and there again briefly explained, that, while by these acts he was determined to rebuke disorder and vindicate the law, he intended to protect and encourage the industrious and well-disposed. He invited two men from this hamlet also, to come to the castle on the morrow, to hear an explanation of his intentions.

" The whole events of the morning, combined with those of the preceding fortnight, were well adapted to move the excitable imaginations of these half-savage tenants of the glen. The ferment everywhere bordered on frenzy, and time alone could subdue it to reason. They were in the hands of a resolute man, whose generosity was not akin to fear, and was, therefore, no bribe to procure peace and submission. The ignominious way in which the champion of the anti-rent party had been, with a strange hardihood, paraded as a captive down four miles of the glen— surprised and bound like a wild beast in his own house, and without the aid of the police tied like a calf on his own nag, and driven past the cabins of his confederates, had first stunned, then maddened, and now subdued them. With such a lord who could strive? If he were cruel, they must suffer, and watch for their opportunity. If he were rash and inconsiderate, what could they do against such determination and power? They wailed loudly at the thought. But he might be merciful—even gracious and wise. So thought the group with whom Lord Pendleborough had conversed, and as they wandered up the glen talking with tumultuous throngs of half frenzied men, some part of their confidence was inspired into individuals among the mass. Agitated, distressed, and full of strange suspicions, the rest spent the day in vociferous wrangles, which left them when night fell tormented with mingled apprehension, anger, and sullen projects of revenge. Some had, doubtless, also crept away to secret rendezvous.

"Meanwhile, Lord Pendleborough spent a great part of the day in personally superintending the arrangements made by the police in the barrack for the families whose huts had been dismantled. Here I joined him, and in the evening we rode back to the castle, perceiving everywhere, in the five miles of our route, that the whole country was in a state of excitement with the events of the day. Whether to intimidate by a palpable sign of an extensive combination, or to assemble some sudden meeting of the conspirators, I know not; but at eight o'clock, beacons blazed out simultaneously on half-a-dozen peaks of the Dunkerron and Inveragh: and on two great heathery slopes, on opposite sides of the valley of the Inny by some unknown combination were fired large circles of heath, which must have been cut for the purpose in the twilight.

" Our plans had been taken deliberately, and Lord Pendleborough had executed them with wonderful daring and skill; but it was clear that the leaders of the conspiracy, though taken by surprise, were not daunted. Twenty of the twenty-five men invited from the glen, appeared at the castle on the ensuing day. But it appeared that attempts had been made to fire the thatch of every man who had interfered to defend Lord Pendleborough by thrusting a burning turf into the windward side. In only two instances was the thatch dry enough to ignite, and in both these the roofs of the huts were destroyed. The police had at once removed the families, and their effects to the barrack.

"Lord Pendleborough had provided a substantial meal for his visitors in the servants' hall. When they had warmed themselves with this hospitality, and a glass of hot whisky toddy, he explained in simple language his plans.

"He intended to make a well planned and firm road up the glen. To create twenty-five hill farms, each with a decent new house, cattle sheds and barn, and a cottage for a labourer's family. Thus fifty families, out of the hundred and fifty inhabiting the ravine, would be better provided for. He intended to develope the working of the mine, and to proceed to enclose large sheep pastures on the mountains. There would likewise be labour in works of drainage, and in the clearing of land from stone, scrub, and heather. For all these works, he intended that regular wages should be paid at fair rates for piece work; but from these wages, which would be settled every week, he would deduct instalments until, with the exception of cases of misfortune, all arrears of rent were repaid. He would not dispossess any con-acre tenants, who faithfully fulfilled their engage-ments, unless men of enterprise and vigour desired to push their fortunes in Canada. Then, if they had not been convicted of crime, and had given proofs of steady industry in carrying out these improvements, he would, as a reward for such qualities and services, give them the same chance of bettering their condition as those already settled in Canada. For the twenty-five new hill farms, he would select those men whose previous character, conduct and fidelity, in the dis-charge of their engagements, had given him the greatest degree of confidence. He only refrained, he said, from naming them at once, lest, till the excite-ment of the people had somewhat calmed, they should become objects of suspicion or malicious injury.

" After a long conversation on all these topics, Lord Pendleborough took his guests over the castle, and showed them everything in it which was a subject of interest. He kept them to an early dinner, and then walked with them through the grounds. Then, amply compensating the men whose cabins had been destroyed, and sending a winter cloak to each of their wives, he dismissed them, full of wonder, to spread their story through the glen.

"On succeeding days, Lord Pendleborough assembled a similar party from each of the other glens of the Dunkerron, and made corresponding explanations to each; giving them a reception like that which I have described; and sending them home agitated, but with a dawn of confidence in the wisdom and kindness of his intentions. This work has consumed a week, and has kept us within the circuit of the castle and its precincts. I am glad of this, for I have alarming intelligence of the activity of the secret societies. The fires have been repeated nightly on the surrounding peaks, and the circles of light glow suddenly where they are least expected on the mountain slopes. No vigilance of the police penetrates the secret of these manœuvres. We shall, however, at once commence the formation of one of the roads, and the building of two homesteads in one glen near a police station, whence our first operations can be protected. For this first step, I have, during the week, organized two strong gangs of labourers on whom I can depend, who will work, one in quarrying and carrying stone for the farm buildings and a bridge, and the other in cutting the road, blasting rocks, breaking stone, and preparing the foundations of the bridge and the farmstead. In a few days more I expect to have a third gang at work, walling in the enclosures. Each gang consists of twenty-five men and a foreman, and as rapidly as I can, I shall organize others. I shall, therefore, be too busy to write soon, or to say much. We shall know ere long whether Lord Pendleborough has broken the neck of this desperate conspiracy or not."

The letter from Lord Pendleborough to Sir Guy Scarsdale was very brief. He had, he said, got into the heart of his work. He had grappled with the glens first, because their population was most lawless and miserable. As soon as his plans were in successful operation in every glen, he would commence the improvement of the cultivation of the valley. He, however, doubted whether Harcourt would not have as much in his hands in the glens during the ensuing winter as he could properly superintend. He conceived, therefore, that the works in the valley would have to be postponed to another year.

October had passed away since Lord Pendleborough left Scarsdale, but December had arrived before other tidings were received. Harcourt's letter sketched in briefer terms their proceedings since his last account. He had first organized three gangs of workmen in the glen which was the scene of Lord Pendleborough's capture of the outlaw. These gangs had gradually been developed into four, including one hundred men. In the glen which Lord Pendleborough had visited the day after his arrival, little difficulty was experienced in forming five gangs in the course of a fortnight. Four other glens had each four gangs of twenty-five men. Harcourt visited one of the glens daily without notice, and often by circuitous routes, always well armed, and sometimes attended by one or two men on horseback. He was always back at the castle before four o'clock in the afternoon.

Lord Pendleborough had given a supper at the Castle to the workmen from each glen in separate parties, and had familiarly explained his plans to them. To men who worked with zeal, or who were promoted to situations of trust, he had remitted part of their arrears, and had directed Harcourt to proceed with such remissions as a reward for good service. As the works advanced, the assertion of the rights of property became more and more apparent, by an exercise of them, beneficial to all. This tended to their practical vindication. The sullen and subtle spirit of conspiracy, goaded into malignant excesses by misery, partially gave way to a growing satisfaction with the substantial benefits offered. Where this feeling existed, greater confidence was manifested in the narratives of the success and well-being of their relatives in Canada. Applications were renewed for facilities to emigrate. Lord Pendleborough had, therefore, selected about twenty families, recommended by their loyal feeling and good conduct, and as a boon to them he revived in their favour the arrangements which he had made for the first settlers on his American property.

He had ordered his yacht round to Cork, to be ready for sailing within an hour of his arrival, and had drawn out minute instructions to Harcourt, for his guidance during the rest of the winter. Efforts were to be made to organize successive parties of emigrants, by offering such aid, as the prize to be attained by persevering labour, and perfect fidelity in the new works. The improvements in the glens were to be extended as far as Harcourt found it practicable, consistently with perfect subordination, and the thorough execution of the works. From every man engaged, punctuality, regularity, and steady application were to be required. Loiterers, idlers, and uncertain men were to be dismissed, and not to be put to work again, until after the interval of a month. This discipline, combined with encouragement by a gradual remission of arrears, with presents of meal, of clothing, or of blankets for the winter, would gradually prove a stimulus, the force of which would, it was hoped, be more and more acknowledged.

Notwithstanding the improved feeling consequent on the gradual introduction of these measures, all the efforts of the police to discover a trace of the

murderers of Mac Vie, known as they must be to
many of the tenantry, received no apparent aid from
the population.

Some remarkable circumstantial evidence had
transpired. The impression of the boot-soles of the
men who had shot Mac Vie had been traced, and
carefully copied, with exact measurements. The
pattern of these boots was found to correspond with
those worn by Macguire, but not the size. He was
not, therefore, one of the assassins, but might be in
league with them. The maker of Macguire's boots
was found to be a man driven from the town by his
constant collision with the police ; who had a cabin
at the edge of a bog, and was a notorious still-
keeper—combining this vocation with his original
handicraft of shoemaker. The chief of the police,
ascertaining that Lord Pendleborough had possessed
himself of Macguire's horse-pistol, carefully unloaded
it. The ball was weighed, and found to be heavier than
those with which poor Mac Vie had been dispatched.

This fact confirmed the previous impression that
Macguire was not one of the murderers. But the
paper with which this pistol was loaded was part of
an incendiary tract, which had been circulated in
the county; and another portion of the same publication, forming the wadding of the pistols with which
the Scotch farmer had been dispatched, had been

found entangled in the hole made in his dress. Every
effort was made to apprehend the shoemaker, but he
had absconded. His house was searched. Some of
the incendiary tracts were found in it, but none from
which any pages had been torn. In a deserted turf-
built still-house, on the hills between Macguire's hut
and Mac Vie's farm, however, a half-consumed tract
was found among the soot of the chimney, built
of bolders from a neighbouring brook. Though
charred, and blackened with soot, with careful hand-
ling it was made clear that this was the tract from
adjoining pages of which the wadding both of
Macguire's pistol and of that of the assassins had
been torn. Beyond this the police could get no
trace. They induced Lord Pendleborough to take
precautions for the security of his agent and foreman, by placing in every gang one labourer on
whom the police conceived they could rely. But
signs of the under-current of the secret association were not wanting. Many sullenly held aloof
from the wages, rewards, and promotion offered. The
improvements were watched, sometimes in silence,
by men who looked on, in their frieze coats, and
lounged about half the day doing nothing; or at
other times, by clamorous groups, who chattered in
their native tongue like monkeys.

Lord Pendleborough's courage, promptitude, and

skill in the use of his weapons had inspired awe. But the police were in constant apprehension of some attempt on his life. Unknown to him, therefore, precautions were taken. It was his habit to ride to the mouth of a glen, leave his horse at a police-station, or at a farmstead, with his groom, and walk to the several gangs of labourers at work on the improvements. The police contrived that the rough copses and groups of rocks should be scoured at the usual period of his visit. The chief of the police examined his arms, and selected for him a brace of long double-barrelled pistols, with hair triggers, locked by a bolt, and sighted, with which Lord Pendleborough had been accustomed to practise. Nothing, however, seemed to daunt his daring. The vigilance which had with him become habitual in travel in wild regions; the quick habits of observation, which such adventures had cultivated to a skill equal to that of a Red Indian; the prompt action with which he had learned to repel sudden danger;—rather seemed to give him confidence, that if opportunity offered, he should do his agent a final and critical service, by personally baffling any attempt of the secret societies.

The last week of his residence approached. All the foremen of the gangs were assembled at a dinner at the castle, at which Lord Pendleborough promised to reward faithful services by promotion. He explained his plans in general terms. He intended to make such improvements on the property, in buildings, enclosures, drainage, and plantations, as would provide labour for years for all disposed to work. As he provided wages, he would enforce the regular fulfilment of all engagements of labour, rent, and service, as well as respect to every right of property. He would grant the means of emigrating to his Canadian estates to such as deserved such aid, but to none who were idle, factious, or turbulent. He would continue the remission of arrears as rewards for extraordinary zeal, skill, or fidelity.

He had received anonymous letters of every description. One series, professedly written by a friend, and which had given intimation of circumstances which had subsequently transpired, he had privately shown to the chief of the police. This series constantly warned him to beware of Molly Macguire; told him when and where he had been waited for by assassins. The police discovered many confirmatory facts, and endeavoured fruitlessly to prevent Lord Pendleborough's further visits to the glens.

"Am I," he replied, "to leave Harcourt exposed to a danger from which I shrink myself? Rather let me find the opportunity to crush it."

He had determined to give a final largess to each of the six hundred labourers now employed on the improvements, and money had been sent to the foreman of each gang, which Lord Pendleborough was to distribute personally to every man in the open field. For this purpose he had visited three of the glens, and as the time pressed, he had ridden to each field, leaving his horse with his groom at the roadside.

He had thus, one afternoon, ridden to the top of one of the glens, and distributed his largess to three gangs of men; there remained two other gangs lower down the ravine. He entered a rough stony field, where the men were digging up bolders, and blasting superficial rocks, with which to build a dry wall of enclosure, and to prepare materials for a homestead. According to a habit, which had become an instinct, he took a rapid survey of the field. The men were busy in four or five groups towards one corner. There was a piece of rough copse, with outcropping rocks, within two hundred yards. His quick eye detected something unusual in the attitude of the labourers, and the mode in which, after a sudden glance, they applied themselves to their task without again looking up. By a deviation from his path, he placed two of the groups immediately behind himself, so that, as he advanced, he kept the rocky copse clearly in view. He unbuttoned his coat, and, as he ascended the field, pierced with a searching eye every opening of the copse which presented itself. Turning suddenly to the two groups of labourers, in front of which he stood, he detected two or three men looking up from their work, with an expression varied in each, but which was to him a sign of some unusual event. On turning again, he caught sight of something stirring in the copse, which instantly disappeared. He at once approached the labourers, and so mingled with them, as to make it impossible for a shot, even from a rifle, to be otherwise than full of risk to the men by whom he was thus masked.

While inspecting their work, and with the aid of the foreman, giving to each his largess, he kept his eye on the copse. In crossing to the next group, which was nearer the rough ground, he carried with him the foreman, and another man. All the other groups were at a greater distance from the broken wooded land. Lord Pendleborough again caught a glimpse of a creeping lurker in the copse. He, therefore, turned round, and stooping down to examine a rock about to be blasted, he started again to his feet suddenly, with a pistol in his hand, in time to confront and fire, at a distance of fifty feet, upon two figures, in women's clothes, but whose size, motions, and boots showed that they were men, who were rapidly advancing on the group of workmen.

They were, however, apparently unprepared for the sagacity and vigilance which had detected their motions. They were obviously staggered by the sudden apparition of their victim, armed and determined. Lord Pendleborough was an unerring shot, and had the advantage both of surprising his antagonists and firing from the group by which he was masked. The ball of his first barrel took effect in the shoulder of the foremost of the two men, who stumbled forwards. The second man received the shot in his arm, and, being thus disabled, dropped his weapon, and turned to run away. Drawing a second pistol, and calling on his foreman to help him, Lord Pendleborough rushed on the first assassin, whom he struck to the ground, as he attempted to rise. While Lord Pendleborough disarmed him, the foreman chased the other into the copse.

The conduct of the workmen did not escape him. After a moment's pause, some advanced from the two nearest groups, and helped him to secure the ruffian. The rest, after looking on a minute, sullenly resumed their work. A similar demeanour characterized the men in some of the other working parties. As soon as the assassin was secured, Lord Pendleborough personally separated the men who had shown a sullen spirit from the rest, and proceeding from man to man, took down every name and the place of his abode. In like manner he took down the names of all who came to his aid.

In a short time his foreman returned from an unsuccessful chase of the second assassin. The two pistols, however, were secured. Notice was sent to the police, who took charge of the prisoner, and hotly pursued the chase of his comrade. Lord Pendleborough rode down the glen, visited the other gang of workmen, distributed his largess, and returned to the castle.

In the evening he directed Harcourt to dismiss every man who had, by a sullen spirit, shown a sympathy with the assassin, and to remove them from the estate.

CHAPTER IX.

THE TEMPEST-TOSSED STAGGERING INTO PORT.

THE sun was rising in the rime of a winter's gale
as Lord Pendleborough's yacht caught the fuller
force of the blustering south-wester, when rounding
the Roche Tower Light, in mid-Channel, from the
Cove of Cork. The good vessel, buoyant as a bird,
but able to carry little sail in the fierce breath of
the storm, bounded forwards over the long swells of
water, the necks of which were crowned with waves
of foam. As the morning advanced, and the more
open sea of St. George's Channel was gained, the
green hollows were deeper, and the roll of liquid
emerald between each curled into a sharper ridge,
and would have toppled over, if its white crest had
not been blown away by the blast. By and by, the sea
became a plain of angry white waves, tossing rudely,
and broken against each other, in constant clash and
agitation, till the whole was lashed into foam. A
blinding spray was whirled across the deck ; the

bitter storm-wind made a loud harp of the rigging, through which it roared like a wild animal eager for its prey.

By turns, Lord Pendleborough and the master kept the poop, and the sailors relieved each other from time to time in their duty on deck, so piercing and cold was the wind. Few words were exchanged. Scarcely any sail could be carried, but the gale swept them wildly onwards towards the north. Now and then, glimpses were obtained through the rack of vessels labouring in the storm. Confident in their seamanship, and in the tried qualities of their craft, the day wore away and night came. The crew had been kept in good condition, their strength was in no degree exhausted; though, therefore, the force of the gale increased, the precautions needed for the night were taken, and Lord Pendleborough, listening only to his impatience to be at Scarsdale, disregarded the remonstrances of the master, and, trusting to the sailing powers of his vessel, and to his own skill and vigilance, ran before the wind, watching the white crests of the waves which chased the yacht, as though they strove to bury it under the mass of their waters.

He remained on deck all the night, during which the poop was twice swept by a following sea, under the heavy blow of which the little vessel reeled and groaned. As there was still no sign of the abatement of the gale, the master urged that it would be impossible to make the port of Liverpool, and strongly dissuaded Lord Pendleborough from attempting to round the Isle of Anglesea for shelter under the Orme's Head. Lord Pendleborough admitted the risk to be great, if the force of the storm continued. They, therefore, shaped their course for Holyhead, and, at the close of the afternoon of the second day, staggered out of the hurly-burly of the strife of wind and water into the calm land-locked harbour. As they approached the coast, Lord Pendleborough had changed his dress, and, as soon as they were in smooth water, he descended the ship's side, secured a carriage, and, as fast as horses could carry him, hurried to Scarsdale.

This impetuous determination had been caused by the receipt of intelligence from Oliver Holte of Miss Scarsdale's critical illness. As soon as Oliver had ascertained that she was attacked by the Mere Clough fever, he had not hesitated to despatch Lord Pendleborough's courier with a letter urging his immediate return. This, he well knew, would have Sir Guy Scarsdale's approval, for he had long penetrated the relations of Lord Pendleborough to Sir Guy's family.

Lord Pendleborough had remained on his estate

a week after his defeat of the attempt at assassination. He had daily visited the working gangs, alone, or riding only with Harcourt. He had personally directed such measures of rigour as he thought expedient against the men who had remained in sullen indifference to his defence or the capture of the murderers. Having produced the impression which he intended of a fearless determination to carry into execution his plans of improvement with generous promptitude and unflinching vigour, he rode down the valley of the Inny on his way to Cork. In the Gap of Dunloe he encountered his own courier riding post, with the despatch from Oliver Holte; and at once bidding Harcourt adieu, he hastened, with all the force of an iron frame and an indomitable will, to reach Scarsdale. What was happening there?

The calm and cheerful mien of Sir Guy Scarsdale had seldom been ruffled or clouded in the worst straits of war. In harassing duty, in the rear-guard of Sir John Moore's army in its retreat through an exhausted country, no voice was more gay, no smile more radiant than his. And if, in the sterner command of battle, his expression was more thoughtful, it was always serene. Even in scenes of carnage and horror, a dire necessity had compelled the suppression of emotion: the breach must be won; the flag of England must be defended; the enemy must

be repelled by grape, *mitraille,* or the bayonet.   But
in the first pause, the same charming equanimity
evinced itself in the most casual remark that fell
from his lips.   How was it, then, that he soon
found himself martyrized by the self-imposed duty
of watching at his daughter's side?

Her mother had died when she was an infant.
Except during his campaigns, this only child had
been his constant companion.   Educated under his
eye, everywhere with him in his visits to the capitals of Europe, he lavished on her bringing up
every resource.   She grew up a marvel of beauty,
grace, and accomplishments; devoted to her father,
reflecting his opinions, feelings, and objects in life;
gathering from his frank, manly bearing a native
independence and vigour; full of animation, high
spirit, and health, which made her a hardy companion in travel, even in rude countries.   She was
conscious of no hope or wish separate from her
father; she compared all who approached her with
him.   If they wanted his simplicity, manliness, or
unostentatious depth of purpose, they had no hold
upon her sympathies.   She had no vanity; she had
not only no desire for admiration, but repelled all
homage by the unconscious *fierté* with which she
sought only to be worthy of him.   Lord Pendleborough she had regarded as a noble child of nature,

in whom the highest instincts of his being were not
developed. Her father's obvious interest in him
failed to make her conscious of the fact that she
had repelled his approaches to herself. She was not
aware that the determination to win her hand in
marriage had powerfully stimulated the growth of
his own mind, and determined the objects to which
he would devote his life. This very unconsciousness of her power had vastly increased her influence
over Lord Pendleborough, who met the interested
or obsequious courtesies of fashion with the reserve
of a profound distrust. Hitherto her life had been
an unsought and unconscious triumph. To her
father she had been a constant source of life and
joy. She had seldom suffered even transient illness.
When, therefore, days of *malaise* and weakness, and
sleepless nights, were followed by a violent shivering
fit, and a rapid prostration of strength, a spasm of
fear cramped her father, and sat like a hideous night-
mare on his thoughts. The country general practi-
tioner had been summoned to attend her in the first
days of her distress. When Oliver Holte was sent
for, on the occurrence of more marked symptoms,
he at once recognized the influence of the contagious
fever of the Mere Clough. Sir Guy still, by a severe
self-control, hoped to be equal to the duty of watching his daughter in the day. But this was one of

those rare cases of fever in which the collapse is
sudden and great. He was not prepared to witness
the terrible change from vigour to helpless weakness;
from the animation of beauty and health to an ex-
pressionless vacancy. He could not stand by and
see his child pick the bed-clothes to remove imagi-
nary motes, or look upon him without a smile of
recognition. The parched lips, the arid tongue, the
altered traits, the terrible stillness of the sick room,
broken only by the unnatural mutterings of delirium
—all, all were insupportable to him. He scarcely
dared to approach the door; he sat in an ante-room,
and, feeling that his agony was eating into his mind,
he forced upon himself tasks of mental occupation,
alternated with rapid walks in the garden court, yet
unable to refrain from a constant reference to his
watch, that he might return to secure Oliver Holte's
next report as to the state of the sufferer.

Twice in the day Oliver Holte rode to the Mere
Clough, to visit the perishing weavers' families, and
give instructions to Deloisir and Barnabas. There
the vicar met him in the morning, eager, besides his
daily ministration to the sick, to obtain the last news
from Scarsdale. These duties, a walk in the park,
and brief conversations with his father or mother,
filled up the intervals of Oliver's visits to the sick
chamber. As he passed through the ante-room, Sir

Guy invariably sat there writing. On his return, he went on tiptoe with Oliver into the corridor, silently, and, without question, to receive his report. Miss Hollingsworth rode over, anxious and troubled, every afternoon. The suspense wrung all hearts. At a late hour, every evening, appeared the physician, and, after his visit and consultation with Mr. Holte, Sir Guy awaited him at dinner. The flame of life flickered. Any day it might be blown out. Nothing but an unrelaxed vigilance, a minute care to feed it from hour to hour, without error or excess, could enable the youth and vigour of Miss Scarsdale's constitution finally to eliminate the poison. The physician praised the attendants, assured Sir Guy that no fault had occurred; but for days the scale hung quivering in the balance, without perceptible change.

A week had now elapsed since the courie nad been despatched to Lord Pendleborough. The weather had been wild, but Oliver Holte reckoned certainly on his arrival. He therefore told Sir Guy what he had done, and received his hearty thanks. This was one of the critical days of the fever, and on it the two physicians prognosticated a change. When, therefore, they entered the sufferer's room at dawn, Alice told them that Miss Scarsdale had awakened from a profound sleep, and had asked, after days of unconsciousness, to see her father. They found the pulse somewhat fuller, a calm intelligence in the eye, and all the symptoms slightly improved. She repeated to them her desire to see Sir Guy. They at once sanctioned a compliance with her wish, and awaited the result in the anteroom. When Sir Guy entered, and stooped to kiss his daughter, she said,—

"How long have I been ill, dear father?"

"A fortnight, my child."

"Have you sent for Lord Pendleborough?"

"He will be here, ere long."

"Tell him that I wished him to come."

She was too weak to say more, and Sir Guy put his finger to his lips in token of silence. He felt a deep relief in this returning sense of the interests of life, as evinced in her anxiety to spare pain to Lord Pendleborough. He found that he could, without emotion, read to her a few verses from the Scriptures, and a short prayer for the sick. This done, after an interval, he returned to the physicians, to express to them his deep gratitude for the dawning hopes of life.

Meanwhile, Lord Pendleborough encountered, during the night, such obstacles in obtaining relays, that, with the utmost exertions of his courier, the morning was half spent before Sir Guy, who watched anxiously on the terrace above the garden court, saw a carriage with four horses advancing at their utmost speed up the long avenue of limes. He descended from the terrace, and passed through a postern in the wall of the court, in time to meet and stop them in the avenue before they drove round the mansion. He feared lest his daughter's awakened consciousness should be disturbed by the sound of wheels near her window in the eastern wing. Lord Pendleborough, bronzed by his exposure in the Kerry mountains, descended, grave but collected, from the carriage, and took Sir Guy's hand with a look of anxious inquiry.

" You are welcome, Pendleborough. I trust the crisis is passing. My daughter, this morning, awakening from many sad days of unconsciousness, inquired if you had been sent for, and told me to say that she wished you to come."

Lord Pendleborough felt deeply the manly promptitude with which Sir Guy had at once poured the best balm into his wound. He said nothing, but walked with Sir Guy silently through the garden court to the hall. A late breakfast was served, at which Oliver Holte joined them on his return from his morning ride to the Mere Clough. To Lord Pendleborough's anxious inquiries, he replied, by assurances that, as the fever was not complicated by any local congestion, forty-eight hours of steady progress in the present train of symptoms would enable them to form a favourable prognosis. Then, the crisis might be regarded as past. The further arduous steps towards the restoration of strength would still be full of risk, and would require the most delicate care. He strongly counselled his two friends to be much abroad, on horseback, so as to prevent the suspense still inevitable from straining their spirits. Lord Pendleborough at once proposed to Sir Guy to ride to the vicarage and to Assheton Manor; and the suggestion, seconded by Oliver as an opportunity of conveying the news of the hopeful change, was acceded to by Sir Guy Scarsdale.

In half an hour, therefore, they were on horseback, and about one o' clock they entered the vicarage. They found that Colonel Vavasour, according to his almost daily custom, had arrived a few minutes before them, and was seated with Miss Hollingsworth. The vicar was expected to return from his round of parochial visits to luncheon.

Malvoisin had forwarded all Harcourt's letters to Colonel Vavasour, after they had been read at Scarsdale, and they had been perused also by the vicar and Miss Hollingsworth. After, therefore, Sir Guy had made known to his friends the hopeful change which had occurred in Miss Scarsdale, the conversation drifted from this absorbing subject of anxiety into inquiries addressed to Lord Pendleborough as to all the incidents of his visit to Kerry, the state and character of the population, his plans, and their progress. After the intense preoccupation of their minds with one painful thought, it was a relief both to Sir Guy and to Lord Pendleborough to discuss this new subject, and the vicar on his return an hour later, found them thus engaged.

After luncheon, Colonel Vavasour announced that he intended to call at the Tim Bobbin at the Scar Head, to make acquaintance with Barnabas's intended bride. The vicar proposed a walking party to accompany the colonel. All readily acquiesced, and in a few minutes they were on the moorland road, behind the vicarage. Sir Guy Scarsdale and the vicar, walking on either side of Nathaniel's cob, in conversation with Colonel Vavasour, left Miss Hollingsworth and Lord Pendleborough some little distance behind.

"I fear," said Lord Pendleborough, "that the agitation caused by the shocking catastrophe of the duke's death may have rendered Miss Scarsdale more susceptible to contagion."

" She has been much disturbed, Lord Pendleborough ; but, frightful as that event was, her mind was too much preoccupied by other fears to dwell even upon that tragedy."

"Tell me, Miss Hollingsworth, if you may, what was her apprehension."

"I think I may, for she avowed it to you in the garden court. She had a fixed dread which haunted her night and day, and made her tremble when the post arrived, that you would chivalrously expose yourself to danger, and meet with some tragical disaster."

"Did she tell you the promise which I made to her.?"

"She did, and she believed it; but she could not shake off a strange prognostication of evil. The accounts, too, contained in Mr. Harcourt's letters were not reassuring. Your daring seemed to her reckless, and she feared that she had impelled you on this career."

"Certainly, next to the approval of my own conscience, there is no hazard which I would not run to win Miss Scarsdale's favour, but I fulfilled my promise. I thought of her only in deeds of mercy. She would not have had my love for her unman me when sterner work was to be done."

"So have I endeavoured to suggest to her, and so her reason told her; but the deep impression once made, her equanimity was at an end."

"Perhaps I am rash in making the suggestion, but latterly, may not the disturbance of the terrible contagion of this fever have prevented a complete conquest over this impression?"

"I have no doubt of that."

"May I congratulate you, Miss Hollingsworth, on the steady progress of my friend Vavasour's recovery?"

"Doubtless. He was my foster brother, and earliest companion in life."

"Let me not intrude on any heart secret, but, since I speak freely to you of my own hopes, let me say that Vavasour's illness at Deerden revealed to me the constancy and force of the affection which in youth he avowed, and which he has always cherished for his foster sister."

"He has resumed his place in my father's house, Lord Pendleborough, after ten years of absence, in which we have all passed through a bitter trial—chastening the spirit, and changing the objects of its aspiration."

"Am I too rude, then, if I say, that I know Vavasour will suffer intensely if you have ceased to love him?"

"The discipline of anguish and fear, and the education through which my father has trained me, first to bear, and then to conquer them, have

perhaps made me satisfied with a calmer happiness."

"I tremble for Vavasour. Do not interpret him
by the gentleness of his manners, and the almost
effeminate fastidiousness of his bearing. If he has
forfeited your love, or if he cannot revive it, his
despair will reckon it as retribution."

"I meant to say, Lord Pendleborough, that I have
so complete a satisfaction in seeing my foster brother
the object of my father's confidence and affection,
and in his society from day to day, that I do not
permit the thought of a love which he has not avowed
to me to enter my mind."

"Colonel Vavasour acts with great delicacy, Miss
Hollingsworth: if he has not avowed an affection
which, in his fiery nature, has triumphed over every
other impulse, doubtless, he waits till his recovery
is complete; doubtless, also, he wishes you and your
father to ascertain how the life of courts and camps,
and the discipline of illness have moulded his
character. He is the very soul of honour. His
lightest breath is truth. If, as I see, he is a constant
guest at the vicarage, these are his motives. He
would not offer you a life withered in its prime, or a
love the freshness of which had faded. He waits till
you can believe that, true as the magnetic force in every
devious path, has been his love for his foster sister."

Lord Pendleborough, impelled by his simple, strong nature, had spoken with earnestness, but without calculation. When he paused, Miss Hollingsworth made no reply. After an interval he glanced at her, and found her face expressive of deep emotion, and flooded with tears.

"A thousand, thousand pardons," said he, hurriedly. "I forgot you, my dear Miss Hollingsworth, in thinking only of Vavasour. I had no right to plead his cause to the point at which the answer can be only made to him. But some day I will, with his leave, justify myself. I cannot without his leave give you conclusive proof that I have rightly interpreted the strongest human motive which governs his life."

Helen was still silent. She walked on with downcast eyes, meekly striving to become the mistress of her emotion. So they lingered somewhat behind the foremost party, and ere they reached the Scar Head she was again calm and self-possessed.

The conversation between the party which accompanied Colonel Vavasour, was suggested by the object of his visit.

"The ungainly, halting, withered frame of our friend Barnabas, is the casket of an apostle's spirit," said the vicar. "I thank him for having made me more tolerant.   Years ago, I thought these dissidents from our church a swarm of mosquitos; and I was impious enough, because of their stings and nasal trumpeting, to regard them as simple nuisances, having no office in God's providence, and to be simply smoked out."

" But he has, from time to time, taken his place in the Church Sunday-school, and even received the sacrament from your hands, vicar," said Sir Guy.

" I believe, partly as a lesson to me in Christian charity ; and, I own with shame, that my first impulse was to banish him from the school, as an unauthorized intruder on the function of Christ's ordained ministers, and to refuse him the sacrament as a preacher of heresies at the Pool of Siloam."

" Is he aware of that ? "

" I sent for him to the vicarage ; I told him my doubts as to my duty.   He was humble, patient, and deferential, but asked me this formidable question, ' Whether the Church forbade her lay members to teach, to watch at sick beds, to try to gather in the wayfarers from the hedges and lanes to the wedding supper of the Lord ? '   I sent him away, and pondered on this question, and the result was, I let him have his own way."

" He has done a good work," said Colonel Vavasour, " at this rough, moorland tavern."

"Four years ago, in the life of the father, the Tim Bobbin was the resort of all the roughest 'tramps,' poachers, and drunkards in the forest of Rossendale. Barnabas watched at the sick bed of the father, having been brought thither by Susan, who was in his class at the Sunday-school. Roger Moorhouse had been a rude, riotous tapster, had lost his nose in an 'up and down' fight, and had jumped from his bedroom window in a fit of delirium tremens, and crushed his feet and ankles in his fall."

"It was a strange mission, to convert this family into the home of the self-constituted village mission-ary," said Sir Guy.

"Once there, Barnabas never faltered," answered the vicar. "Roger lingered through all the stages of a wasting liver disease. Barnabas was unob-trusive, kind, consoling, full of pity and help, and step by step, led the wretched man to regret, to listen, to think, even to pray. Then he reconciled him to me; he brought me in as the authorized pastor, to lead home the lost sheep to the fold. My belief is, that the penitent man died in the faith of Christ."

"Barnabas has given me some brief hints about his courtship, but I should like to have a fuller history from you, vicar," said Colonel Vavasour.

"Susan was always a pretty, modest, gentle girl. She shrank from the coarse uproar of the riotous tavern, and found refuge in the Sunday-school. I think she must have been six years in Barnabas's class, his favourite scholar; the most diligent, docile, and intelligent. In her little cold bedroom at the Tim Bobbin, she worked at her Bible tasks, her catechism, her writing and arithmetic, and brought to Barnabas weekly proofs of steady improvement."

"That was a sure way to creep like a dove into a warm corner of the limping apostle's heart, and to nestle there."

"They neither of them thought of love, but they came to love each other insensibly. The dying man in my presence enjoined his widow to put her house in order, under Barnabas's guidance, as my helper; to prefer poverty to ill-gotten gain, to think more of the farm than the tavern."

"She has certainly followed his advice," said Sir Guy; "for Mr. Holte informs me, that she has done more to fulfil the usual conditions of the draining and improvement of the farm, than any other moorland tenant."

"I do not think she could have done it if Barnabas had not lent the widow money to buy stock and horses," said the vicar.

"I have had great satisfaction in improving the

farm buildings, and in preparing a house for Barnabas and his wife," said Sir Guy. "The tavern has shrunk to small dimensions, and is now literally a licensed victualler's house for refreshment, and the farm will gradually flourish more and more. No one has had more than a pint of beer in the house for years."

"I have robbed you of the Cock of Rossendale, Sir Guy," said Colonel Vavasour. "He clings to his old companion of the cloughs and moors, and I have made him head keeper of Assheton Manor, and established him, and his devoted Nancy, in the fold at Assheton."

"So I hear," said Sir Guy; "but I am content to have Robert Dewherst in his place, in my preserves at Scarsdale Head, and glad to know that as soon as Jonah Ingham can return from his hidingplace at the Pool of the Wyre, he will be installed as Barnabas's farming man at the Tim Bobbin."

"Robert Dewherst was married two months ago," said the vicar, "and he is now in training for his work as keeper."

Sir Guy's and Lord Pendleborough's horses had been led by their grooms in the rear of the walking parties, and as they approached the tavern, both looked anxiously at the declining winter's sun, and after the exchange of an expressive glance, bid adieu to their friends, and suddenly mounted before they reached Scarsdale Head, riding at a rapid pace up a woodland road on their return to the hall.

Oliver Holte was evidently taking exercise on the Park road where he would be sure to meet them on their return from the vicarage, with the earliest intelligence respecting Miss Scarsdale. There had been a steady progress during the day. Miss Scarsdale had slept, had taken food, had gained strength, had been quite conscious. She had asked again to see her father.

They dismounted outside the quadrangle, and Sir Guy hastened to comply with his daughter's wish. He entered her room noiselessly, but found her awake, with calm eyes, whose beaming intelligence was made ampler in their orbits by the waste of sickness, and a transient, febrile excitement. He took his daughter's hand, kissed it, and returned her gentle, loving pressure with a smile.

"Father, you remember your dying nurse's message when she gave me the portrait locket bequeathed to me from your mother."

"Yes, my child."

"The message has sunk into my heart, and the image of my grandame is pictured on my brain."

"She was a lady full of dignity, thought and grace."

"I suppose it was a dream, for my nurse had seen nothing, yet I thought she had been here, and stood beside my bed, graciously, and lovingly."

"What seemed her purpose, my child?"

"She came, she said, to tell me that I should return to life; to bless me, for that I had taken her message to heart; to tell me that Lord Pendle-borough was a true man, a servant of Christ, who would make a reverent son to my father."

"Has this message left you tranquil, my child?"

"Further, she said, that the step which I heard in the corridor was his; that he had come back from Ireland, like a St. George after his combat with the dragon: she bade me sleep and awake in peace. At the waving of her hands, I fell asleep, and awakened a little while ago quite tranquil, dear father, but she was gone. Was it a dream?"

"Whether it were a vision or a visitation, let us confide in it, my child. The certainty that the proved love of a man whom your father regards as a son, waits to welcome **you** back **to** life, will soothe, nourish, and strengthen you."

He kissed her as he spoke.

She held his hand tenderly, gazing at him long in silence.

"Nothing must separate the child from her father," at length she said.

"Nothing, my daughter; I will live with you and for you, till my latest hour, my charming Mabel."

"Will not Lord Pendleborough be jealous of my devotion to my father?"

"He will only see in that a proof of your constancy and unselfishness, which are among a wife's chiefest virtues."

There was again a long pause, during which, the twilight deepened, until the room was lighted only by the flickering of the fire. Sir Guy still sat by his daughter's bed. The soft pressure of her hand slowly relaxed. The gloom, the silence, and her weakness had prevailed—she had fallen into a gentle slumber. The nurse crept in on tiptoe with some refreshment, but put it on the trivet at the fire. She slept an hour calmly, and awoke with a feeling of hunger, felt for the first time. The nurse was ready with her beef tea and wine, and even a few crumbs of bread. All were relished, and, as soon as taken, the lovely sufferer lapsed again into a tranquil repose, during which, Sir Guy Scarsdale stole away.

·CHAPTER X.

ALL SAFE IN PORT.

THE midwinter of the Lancashire and Yorkshire border is wild and stormy. Tempests rage from the Irish Sea, and deluge the moorlands with storms of rain. Floods sweep through the river valleys, often destroying the weirs—uproot the forest trees, and bearing the massive trunks and great crowns of branches of a century's growth on an impetuous rush of waters. The level Ings are flooded into lakes, and in the narrow gorges, as under Whalley Nab beneath Morton Hall, or at the Orr under Hoghton Tower, the roar of the furious river is hoarse as a threat of ruin. In the night, the wind seems to wrestle with the towers of the country mansions like a ghostly contest between the spiritual world in anarchy, and the material in its repose of ages. The day dawns late, and often in an almost black gloom brooding on the moors. Night swoops down like a bird of prey, with dark wings outspread over the sky, and seems suddenly to shut the world up in a cavernous blackness.

It was through these months of tempest and gloom that Mabel's convalescence slowly recruited her strength. Her father was her constant visitor and frequent attendant as soon as she could bear to be read to for a short time. By and by the physicians declared that all danger of contagion was at an end, and then Miss Hollingsworth was daily admitted. But all was still done under some restriction. The wilder whirl of the wintry war had subsided into the piercing winds of February and March, ere the beautiful sufferer sat up in the boudoir adjoining her sleeping apartment. Here she daily took some exercise, leaning on Sir Guy's arm—she listened to his reading, or that of Helen. She was calm, gentle, grateful and tender. Much had happened to tame the *fierté* of her nature, as the fair startled creature of the forest or the waste is brought within domestic rule. She had been brought face to face with the dread realities of life. To suffer, to 'reach the confines of the other world; to be conscious of an overmastering love in others; of an incontrollable sympathy; to struggle fruitlessly against this sentiment; to find it become more potent than the will—a new ghostly influence rising within the soul and asserting an irresistible dominion; to be thus,

as it were, possessed, all this at first had excited
the most determined resistance in Mabel. She
could not—she would not yield herself to this
possession. Hers was a virgin nature. Her own
sweet empire ; her father's demesne. None should
encroach on these sacred precincts. What violent
man was this who dared to assert a claim on her
affections? She had permitted none to think that
within this bound any one could reign but only her
father, and herself as the châtelaine of a keep
placed too high to be scaled. Who was this man
who had silently for years beleaguered the fortress,
had gained her father, studied her own estimate of
life, trained himself patiently to win her love; was
formidable, not more by his silent homage, than his
chivalrous daring? She had been unconscious, then
astonished, then disturbed ; now, what should she
do? Is this then the fate of woman? Is it not
enough that I am a daughter, loving, devoted?
Have I also another destiny? can I not avoid it ?
must I love? can I not shake off this fascination ?
Why will he grow always something better, higher,
stronger, nobler in my imagination, and claim my
love by a devotion which counts life as nothing to
my preference? What, oh! what shall I do? Father,
dear father, cannot your experience of life teach me
that there is some other form of existence for

woman, than to be a ministering angel, with an overpowering sympathy which folds her nature into another's being?

Something of this kind, perhaps, is felt in many natures, ere the mystery of life, the marriage of two souls into one, has triumphed over every other force. But, in Mabel's life, everything combined to render the struggle formidable, and it may even be doubted whether it would soon have ceased, if the terrible messenger of Heaven had not come to chasten the sweet pride of this virgin spirit.

As her convalescence restored her to the sympathies of life, she knew that she had ceased to be her own mistress. She had become subject; that strong chivalrous nature had won her by its purity, nobility, and devotion. She had known herself only as her father's daughter, full of reverent affection. How was it, that in so short a time—a few weeks or months, with a growth of tenderness towards her father, had also grown in her heart a more agitating and a more engrossing love, with a sense even of subjection, to a will stronger than her own, and obedience to a more commanding being? The struggle was over. She had ceased to be her own! She was another's.

To this, during her convalescence, succeeded a new phase of feeling. To bring her new life into harmony with her old; to make the love of the affianced wife a part of the love of the devoted daughter; that Lord Pendleborough should be as reverent a son as he had been a grateful friend and disciple of her father; to add to her father's treasures of affection another warm heart and noble nature; to tend and guard his future with a strength and wisdom greater than her own; to surround his home with new honours and homage; to carry the wealth of her affections, and with them their most cherished idol, into even a higher sphere; to gild all the decline of his life by the vision of his daughter's happiness. These were the motes that floated like golden dust in the sunbeams of her reveries. Hope had dawned upon the night of doubt and struggle. She had yielded; but she had won! Won! yes, won a noble son for her father;—a friend,—oh, dearer title than friend—a husband for herself!

Oh, marvellous mystery of the tender virgin nature—who shall ever truly paint its sacred repose, its serene heavenly constancy, pure as the azure, or its saintly emotions, which throb like the magnetic pulses of nature, all pervading and dominant? Oh, Ondine of crystalline purity and transparent truth, whose repose reflects heaven and all natural beauty, and whose agitation sparkles with light, ripples into music, murmurs harmony, whispers peace! Why, oh why, Ondine, art thou ever fickle, frail, or treacherous! a deep pool in which swell the bloated corpse like victims of despair! or a shallow shoal on which the heart lies torn and bleeding?

Daily from Lord Pendleborough her room was replenished with the choicest exotic flowers, from his own conservatories. Her father rewarded him with her thanks. He did not approach her himself, but he selected passages in favourite authors which Sir Guy or Miss Hollingsworth read to her. As her strength was restored, and she had become familiarized, by the interchange of these courtesies and of messages, with his not remote presence; he wrote to her daily. At first brief notes only; then fuller accounts of his own feelings during her illness. By and by, a history of the first implanting and the deep growth of the sentiment which had become a part of his being. Of the influence of her unconsciousness and indifference upon him; his self-examination, his comparison of himself with Sir Guy, his counsels with her father, his studies, pursuits, researches, and the gradual development of his principles and plans in life, in all which she had formed a part.

Her ideal of a noble man had been his model. He had striven long and arduously to rein in the untamed physical vigour and hardihood of his nature, to develop the contemplative, the philosophical, and to weld together the wild active strength and growing intellectual force. Then he spoke with gratitude and reverence of Sir Guy Scarsdale; of the value of his wisdom, fidelity, and counsels in guiding his inexperience; of the influence which his soldier-like frankness, tolerance and manly bearing had in winning his [entire confidence, and of his example and maxims of life on his character.

Later, he ventured to pour forth a confession of the fascination which her beauty, grace, and indifference to all the homage which they attracted had on one *blazé* with interested adulation, and in search of truth and sincerity.

Mabel permitted herself to reply to his letters about her father. She told him that his reverence for Sir Guy and her father's esteem for him were the first things to awaken any interest in Lord Pendleborough, which his own chivalrous nature had afterwards deepened into a profounder feeling. To his letters respecting herself she replied, that she knew not how, but she believed and accepted this homage now, which a few months ago, would have seemed to her an illusion or an interested and insincere adulation, but now was a pledge to her of undeserved future happiness.

One morning, Miss Hollingsworth entered. with a rich casket of the rarest medieval workmanship;

a *chef-d'œuvre* of Benvenuto Cellini. The golden straps with which it was bound were all exquisitely decorated in relief. The padlock was a gem of art. The key itself was a miracle of intricate beauty. In a plate of gold was set in diamonds this inscription:—

"MABEL, COUNTESS OF PENDLEBOROUGH."

Within was a treasure of the rarest jewels. A mine of diamonds, emeralds, sapphires, rubies, turquoises, garnets, agates, pearls in necklaces, bracelets, earrings, stomachers, clasps, brooches, rings, and coronets. There was a note from Lord Pendleborough to say that he had not prepared the inscription on the casket, without her father's permission, after the receipt of her last notes, and that it contained only the hereditary bridal ornaments of his family; while those which were to be his personal gift, he reserved till he could present them himself.

He had written to the Duchess of Chatellerault an account of all that had occurred, and he enclosed the duchess's heartfelt congratulations that the love which, on the banks of the Allier, he had told her he felt for an English lady, had met with the reward which his pure and chivalrous nature deserved.

A day or two later came a letter to Miss Scarsdale, from the duchess herself, with warm expressions of heartfelt sympathy and joy. She spoke of her own

unlimited trust in Lord Pendleborough; of his scru-
pulous honour and delicate tact. Of the reserve
with which he had withdrawn, even from his fraternal
relations to her, as soon as he found she could avail
herself of M. Malvoisin's hints. Of memoranda
left by the duke, proving how deeply she was indebted to Lord Pendleborough for the duke's right
conception of her own character and motives. She
thanked Mabel for endowing "her brother" with
the rich treasure of her love and life. No earthly
fate could, she thought, be fuller of fair promise than
the marriage of two such lofty and harmonious natures.

She had found the duke's late wards in the
Convent of Religieuses, near Napoleon (Bourbon)
Vendée. They were under the care of ladies of
gentle blood and great accomplishments, who devoted themselves, like the former community of
Port Royal, to the education of the highest classes
of society. She had herself apartments in the convent, and aided in the training of her wards. She
rode with them daily, when the weather permitted;
herself conducted part of their instruction; spent
all her leisure in their society. They were very
beautiful; with the duke's arch spirituality of feature
and a Greek grace superadded. Volatile, restless,
like fireflies in a tropical night, full of wit, sarcasm,
and a searching, analytic spirit, which made the

whole convent the victims of their humour. Carica-
turists of the most fertile and acute power, writers
of pasquinades and epigrams, nothing, not even the
duchess, escaped their criticism. Sometimes they
caricatured her as giving alms to an *escroc*, or endowing a charity the almoner of which was em-
bezzling the funds, or pouring water into a vase
without a bottom, or praying for them behind a
screen, while they caricatured her on the other side.
Perplexing, fascinating, loveable, they caressed the
duchess as a sister, but treated her as an equal;
exposed to her all their little escapades, deceptions of
the " sisterhood," wild fancies, romances and dreams,
and seemed thunderstruck at the depth of her tenderness for the memory of the duke—at the elevated
sanctity and exquisite gentleness of her nature—at
the love which led her to devote herself to them,
and which no caprice or folly could disturb. She
thought she had acquired influence by the greater
solidity and extent of her own acquirements, by the
equipoise of her judgment, and the loving tolerance
of their eccentricities. They had in some degree
ordered their own lives after her example. Their
reading was guided by hers; their devotions, which
had been acts of obedience to custom, had acquired
a new character, in which the imagination and feelings had been aroused, and now needed to be guided

by careful instruction. Her task was difficult. It absorbed her time and thoughts. But, as they were young, she hoped, in the two years which must elapse before she introduced them to life, to lay the foundation of future virtue and usefulness. When her task began in Paris, she said she trusted that Sir Guy Scarsdale would bring the Earl and Countess of Pendleborough to launch her lovely and charming wards the Mesdemoiselles de Clairvœux on that maelström of life.

When Mabel had shown this letter to her father, she sent it by Helen to Lord Pendleborough, who wrote with deep interest his comments on the whole narrative. These Mabel forwarded to the duchess.

So the winter drifted into the arid and searching winds of the spring; and May had come before more than the buds swelled, and some few leaflets peeped from their sheaths, as though distrusting the inhospitable rebuke of the nipping air. The physicians had been informed of Miss Scarsdale's implied engagement, but had forbidden the lovers to meet until she had for a time visited the coast. Lord Pendleborough had hired a country seat near Fleetwood, and filled it with every luxury. He had brought his yacht round to the Wyre, and about the middle of May, Mabel, stretched in her father's travelling britschka, and accompanied by Miss Hollingsworth, with Sir Guy Scarsdale and Colonel Vavasour on the box, travelled on a sunny day to " The Warren," near Rossall.

To some this scene has an aspect of bleak and pitiless desolation. To our mind, it is never inhospitable. Morecambe Bay always welcomes us with a radiant smile. The screen of the lake mountain range on the north reminds us, by its picturesque outline, of a not distant fairyland, where every rock, tree, cottage, and stone is a picture, and the whole a magical combination of beauty. The rim of the sea, along which labour the steamers, and flit the white-sailed ships from Barrow, Whitehaven, Workington, and Maryport, to Liverpool and Wales; the fishing and pilot boats tossing on the horizon; the vessels cautiously threading their way through the buoys to round the Pigeon-house Light, nestled on piles far out in the waters of the bay; even the level, sandy waste of the shore and beach, and the barren warren within, have to us a character which we would not exchange for other more popular scenes. If the hotel had been built at Rossall point of Morecambe Bay, with ample windows to the south, one façade to the north, another to the west, and a long drive upon the sea-wall towards Blackpool, with easy means of descent on the firm sands beyond the breakwaters, this would have been the most popular bathing-place in the north of England. It would have combined the sanitary advantages of Blackpool and Scarborough with those of Southport. In Morecambe Bay—the screen of the lake mountains—excursions to Furness—boating on the pool of the Wyre and in Morecambe, and driving or riding on the hard sands of the west coast—sources of enjoyment and health would have been found which no other watering-place possesses. Unfortunately, the capacious hotel has been built close to the mud at the entrance of the harbour, far away from the hard sands and good bathing ground—and with the air of the muddy river's mouth, instead of that of the open sea.

Lord Pendleborough had long appreciated both the beauty and salubrity of the Rossall Point, and, supported by the opinion of the physicians, had selected " The Warren " as the place for Mabel's complete restoration to health. He lived on board his own yacht, and cruised in the bay, and along the coast to Barrow, Whitehaven, the Solway, and the Isle of Man ; while his future countess regained, on the hard sands of the western coast, between Blackpool and Morecambe, the vigour which the almost fatal poison of the Mere Clough had undermined. Here, on horseback, from day to day, accompanied by her father, Miss Hollingsworth, and Colonel Vavasour, she gradually extended her rides. When June came, they frequently took luncheon at Blackpool, and returned to dinner at "The Warren." Then, when Miss Scarsdale's health was quite restored, they rode down to Lytham, spent the night there, and returned to "The Warren." They crossed the bay in Lord Pendleborough's yacht to Barrow, visited Furness, and returned to Fleetwood. All this while, Lord Pendleborough kept out of the way; though daily, when ashore, letters reached Mabel from him, full of devotion.

Colonel Vavasour had been inseparable from the party. His strength was so far restored that he joined, without fatigue, all their rides and excursions. His manner to Miss Hollingsworth had been that of a brother—always thoughtful, attentive, and kind, but never trespassing on any expression of the tenderness of a lover. The fact that he was always in her society, with an unobtrusive solicitude which revealed no deeper feeling by any look or act, and only by its consistent though measured homage gave proof of the depth of its source, marked both the delicacy with which he awaited the time when he could offer a life restored from great peril, and purified by trials. It seemed as though at least a friendship which should link the past of his early

youth with the present, was necessary to his conscience.

There was nothing to indicate that, whatever
might be the dominant wish of his heart, he had
not the power to control it, so as to seek happiness
in this friendship with his foster-sister, if no more
tender relation were possible. In fact, he had imposed on his fiery nature this penance, that he should
do nothing whatever to endanger the growth of such
a friendship to the utmost limits of personal confidence and regard, though Helen might never be to
him nearer than a foster-sister—tender, gentle, and
true.

Nor had the vicar uttered to his daughter one
word revealing to her that Colonel Vavasour had
a warmer wish. Helen's conversation with Lord
Pendleborough, at the end of the autumn, was the
only positive expression of Colonel Vavasour's love
which had occurred. The intercourse which he had
constantly had during Miss Scarsdale's convalescence with herself and her friend—their reading,
conversation, discussions, descriptions of life and
manners—had laid bare the range of his opinions
and feelings the more certainly, because his was a
frank, manly nature which scorned a veil, and
which, with whatever polish of manner, never hesitated to reveal his convictions and emotions. The

two friends, therefore, had a certainty that they knew Colonel Vavasour well. With this, grew in Miss Scarsdale's mind a confidence in his truth and honour—in the perfect sincerity of his love for Miss Hollingsworth, and his desire to make her happy— as well as of the power of self-control, which he had gained under the discipline of a terrible rebuke, and the influence of early training, and a deeply-seated affection. Mabel, therefore, treated him with a continually growing confidence and respect; but she was careful not to utter one word to influence Helen's decision, whether she could accept the life-long friendship which Colonel Vavasour offered, or whether that awoke in her heart the throbs of an emotion which had once possessed her entire being, but which her father's careful counsels, and the training of years of prayerful anguish and silent endurance, had enabled her to bring within the control of conscience and reason.

To Helen Hollingsworth, the constant presence, the unobtrusive attention, the implied homage and regard of her foster-brother, brought a balm for deep-seated wounds. She was thus assured that she had not cheated herself with an illusion. In that fervid time of his earnest youth, he had felt a passionate regard for his foster-sister. His was really a true, sincere spirit, incapable of guile; and the memory of their love, in that early prime, dwelt in natures still in harmony with each other. There was not only a deep repose in this friendship, but much more. The agonizing fear, that a reckless career had perverted the heart and corrupted the principles of her former lover, was assuaged in that daily intercourse in which every thought and feeling, not too sacred for expression, found utterance. This mutual confidence—the complete restoration of Colonel Vavasour's filial relations with the vicar—the friendship which grew up between him and Miss Scarsdale—all satisfied her of a harmony of thought and hope which made them a group of congenial friends. With this mixed no agitating fear or wish. She did not dread that Colonel Vavasour should change. His was not a capricious nature. She did not permit herself to wish for more than the friendship which restored to her the foster-brother of her youth, polished by his intercourse with the world—ripe in experience—a man of refined accomplishments, great grace, manly sincerity, and true to his early associations—rewarding her father by the growth of the principles which he had so carefully sown—more than rewarding the daughter by returning with the deep-seated influence of an early love, now, perhaps, chastened into a sincere and enduring friendship.

The two friends, Miss Scarsdale and Miss Hollingsworth, were seated alone in a sheltered cove in the sand-hills of the coast, on a warm, still morning.

"We shall return to Scarsdale to-morrow; but I shall always carry with me the remembrance of our visit to the Warren. It has been to me a source of unmingled satisfaction, dearest Helen, to see that the heartache, which you so long suffered about your foster-brother, is at an end by his restoration to you in every sense."

"I am again his sister. I have unwavering confidence in his sincerity, truth, and manly uprightness. His filial reverence for my father, and his brotherly solicitude for myself, link the past with the present," said Helen.

"But, dearest, is it to end there? Will you not permit Colonel Vavasour to make you his wife?"

"Are you sure that he does not prefer this calm confidence of friendship, after all the agitating incidents of his past life?"

"Of this I am sure, dearest Helen, that unless some thrilling accident reveal it, he will be slow to avow to you the deep love which he feels, lest he should endanger a friendship necessary, as I think, to his conscience and his life."

"He has never, either by look or word, expressed

any such sentiment, though I am bound to say that Lord Pendleborough also assured me that Colonel Vavasour had not wavered in the attachment which we confessed to each other in our early youth."

"Nothing has given me greater confidence in him than his willingness to rein in his fiery nature, and to accept just as much affection as you can give him; though his entire being is, I am sure, possessed by the memory and presence of his only love. Lord Pendleborough in his letters confirms to me this impression; and says, that he has the most positive and irrefragable grounds for this certainty."

"I never dare to question my own heart. No woman ought to yield it where it is not sought. I am happy in our friendship, and I do not fear its interruption."

"But there are always great risks in such friendships which do not ripen into marriage. Theirs must be rare natures in which such friendship can endure for years without the agitation of jealousy—the necessity for a more confidential intercourse—the growth of an irrepressible impatience for a more perfect communion of spirit. Where there is no insurmountable obstacle, such friendship should have a growth of tenderness, in which the marriage of two lives becomes an imperious want."

" When, however, there is such an obstacle, and, especially, when there has been the discipline of prolonged trials chastening the spirit, and humbling the aspirations for earthly happiness," said Helen, with a beaming smile full of piety, " surely, with God's grace to help, this may be ! "

" There may come, however, such trials as illness —prolonged and perilous illness—in which separation will be a long agony! Or, which God forbid! you may lose the protecting care of your father. It would be well to be safe in port before these storms blow."

A few days later the whole party were reassembled at Scarsdale. The vicar and Pendleborough also were in the circle. They had ridden from Poulton up Wyresdale, and through the Trough of Bowland to Whitewell, where Lord Pendleborough had, for the first time, joined them. They remained for the night at Whitewell. Here they had wandered along the Hodder; and while Lord Pendleborough separated Mabel from the party to pour into her ear the story of his own devotion, Colonel Vavasour climbed, with Sir Guy and Helen, the wooded hill on the west, which overlooks the embowered river, where it murmurs through an umbrageous solitude. They suddenly missed Sir

Guy, who had discreetly slipped away through the thickets. Colonel Vavasour had placed his arm within Helen's, and clasped her hand.

"All must be risked, my dearest Helen," he said, "rather than the best prize not be won."

She was silent.

"My nature is as passionate as ever, Helen. It has been true to you through life. I can no longer withhold this confession. Your friendship is necessary to my conscience; but your love, dearest, is necessary to my happiness—nay, to my life."

"Say not so, Percy!"

"It is the truth, Helen. I risk all. I must win you—my life, my happiness, my all!"

"Oh, you are not changed, Percy, since the happy days long passed away!"

"I fear I have still the same impetuous, headlong nature; for, to win you, Helen, as my wife, has become an imperious necessity, for which I risk all —all—even these conscience-calming days of friendship and peace; even they must cease, if you cannot be my wife."

"Oh, Percy, there is no need that they should cease!"

"Yes, there is! I cannot any longer control my fiery nature—I love you, Helen; you are to me more than a friend—I cannot bear any longer the more measured relation. Either we are one in heart, in spirit, and in life—wedded in soul, and joined in being; or, I feel the terrible, heart-crushing alternative—we must part; for, I am no longer able to control the expression of my love."

" Oh! we cannot part, dearest Percy."

He folded her in his arms, and kissed her.

They sat down on a knoll. The first outburst of passionate daring past, the confession made in her gentle reply to his agonizing utterance, he became calmer. He put a strong control on the tempest of his feelings. He called up every solemn sentiment in his soul to hallow this supreme hour. It was a relief to give expression to these thoughts, as he held Helen's hand clasped in his own.

"Oh, gentlest and best! Type of all tenderness and love! Thou canst, then, dearest Helen, be sinned against for long years, by the absence of thy wayward lover, yet believe that, in every aberration, the light of thy own faith and purity drew me with an unseen but omnipotent attraction! Then there is pardon! Then there is mercy! For even thou, dearest, canst not be more forgiving than the All-merciful! Oh, messenger from the blest!—from the highest!—I take thy love, my own Helen, as the first gift of Heaven to its penitent! Teach me; lead me, like a messenger of light, out of the frailties and faults of this clouded lower world into that serener life in which we have lived of late, and in which I would ever live with thee as my wedded wife!"

So on—much more of the same fervid thoughts poured like a Geyser in tumult and heat from the long-pent-up fervour of his fiery spirit. Helen recognized her boy-lover again. The natures were the same, but the man had been taught by suffering, even by error, to rein in and master the passionate impulses which, unbridled, had wrought so much wrong. Nay, of late, the tropical heat of his soul had ripened, in one brief spring, the latent seeds of example and principle long ago sown by his guardian. His early love itself was become a part of the deep religion of his heart. He looked at Helen as an angel sent to help him to spiritualize and elevate his being.

They were all reassembled at Scarsdale. The day on which three weddings were to occur was fixed. Barnabas and Susan were to be married by the vicar at the same altar with Lord Pendleborough and Miss Scarsdale, and with Colonel Vavasour and Miss Hollingsworth.

The Mere Clough fever had burned itself out. A better trade had come. The weavers were fully

employed at fair wages. The bounty of Sir Guy
and the colonel, of both of which the vicar was
the almoner, had greatly mitigated the crisis. Oliver
Holte, released from all his anxious duties, had
settled in Manchester as a physician. He wrote
almost daily to Sir Guy Scarsdale, with a filial
veneration and gratitude, describing his new duties
among the poor of one of the then unsewered and
unpaved districts haunted by typhus. To his father
and mother, his letters expressed the deeper workings of his conscience, and satisfied them that he
was wisely seeking "the peace which passeth knowledge" in this new path.

He often visited Floi-bi-Neet in the cell, where he
awaited the orders of the Secretary of State for his
transportation beyond the seas. Sir Guy had provided the means to enable Floi-bi-Neet's wife to
follow him to Botany Bay, and to live as near to
him as the authorities would permit. A full history
of Floi-bi-Neet's disclosures, duly attested by the
vicar, and an account of the service thus rendered
to the police, signed by Sladen, were sent by Sir
Guy Scarsdale to the Secretary of State, and dupli-
cates of them to the Governor of the colony. It
was thus hoped that, after some probation, Floi-bi-
Neet would be sent into the bush as a convict-shep-
herd, and allowed the company of his wife.

The Yeoman of High Collor, cherished by his daughter's aunt and by the child, seemed to take a new lease of life. He received the visits of Mr. Hollingsworth from time to time, not only without repugnance, but with a growing sense of satisfaction. Swart Ned was now getting too old and too bewildered to guide his *" Gals,"* which were sold; and, as the Yeoman was persuaded by the vicar to part with his cocks, and to regulate his diet by Mr. Braithwaite's counsels, Ned found less to terrify him in the Yeoman's frenzied moods, and whispered to the vicar, " T' Yeoman's as meek as a lamb ! "

Of course Sally Parkinson had chief charge of the grand wedding-breakfast to the tenantry, colliers, quarry-men, farm-servants, and labourers of the two manors, and to the children of all the Sunday schools.

The Cock of Rossendale and Nancy, Jonah Ingham and his wife, and Robert Dewhurst and Judith, had each charge of tables ; and Nathaniel presided at the feast of the Assheton tenants, while Mr. Holte (the father) would not accept any other office than that of head of the Scarsdale tenants. The bray of the bands in Scarsdale Clough was deafening. The processions of tenantry, workmen, and Sunday scholars seemed interminable. All assembled in Assheton churchyard, where Barnabas and Susan humbly awaited the arrival of several carriages, three of which were drawn by four horses, attended by gentlemen on horseback as outriders. Barnabas had repectfully but firmly declined to occupy the third carriage with Susan, which therefore came empty, but with peremptory orders from Sir Guy and Colonel Vavasour, that Barnabas and his wife, and Betty o' th' Scar Yead, were to be brought back in it. The young farmers who had been his Sunday scholars surrounded this carriage on their moorland ponies.

Sir Guy Scarsdale gave away Susan as well as his own daughter. The vicar was assisted in the ceremony by a clergyman from Bolton-le-Moors, whose mild and reverent mien impressed all. The vicar left the church with Barnabas—gently enforced his entrance into the carriage amidst the shouts of the people—handed in Susan and Betty himself, and then occupied the remaining seat. Lord Pendleborough, as soon as the ceremony was over, despatched a servant to Oliver Holte with a letter, and a most costly keepsake, inscribed,—

Sir Guy Scarsdale and the Earl and Countess of Pendleborough, to their tried friend Oliver Holte, July, 1827.

Another casket, containing a less lavish but beautiful present, bore this inscription,—

Percy and Helen Vavasour, to the Physician and Confessor of 1826.

Are there any of our readers who would wish to follow the fortunes of Oliver Holte, Malvoisin, and Deloisir?   For the present the Oracle is dumb.

THE END.

London : Printed by Smith, Elder and Co., Little Green Arbour Court, E.C.

65, *Cornhill, London,*
April, 1860.

CLASSIFIED CATALOGUE

OF

NEW AND STANDARD WORKS

PUBLISHED BY

SMITH, ELDER AND CO.

CONTENTS.

THE CORNHILL MAGAZINE.
Edited by W. M. Thackeray.

Price One Shilling Monthly, with Illustrations.

CONTENTS :

No. 1.—JANUARY, 1860.

Framley Parsonage. Chaps. 1, 2 and 3.
The Chinese and the " Outer Barbarians."
Lovel the Widower. Chap. 1.
Studies in Animal Life. Chap. 1.
Father Prout's Inaugurative Ode to the Author
   of " Vanity Fair."
Our Volunteers.
A Man of Letters of the last Generation.
The Search for Sir John Franklin.
The First Morning of 1860.
Roundabout Papers.—No. 1.

No. 2.—FEBRUARY, 1860.

Nil Nisi Bonum.
Invasion Panics.
To Goldenhair (from Horace).
Framley Parsonage. Chaps. 4, 5 and 6.
Tithonus.
William Hogarth : Painter, Engraver, and Philo-
   sopher. I. Little Boy Hogarth.
Unspoken Dialogue.
Studies in Animal Life. Chap. 2.
Curious if True.
Life among the Lighthouses.
Lovel the Widower. Chap. 2.
An Essay without End.

No. 3.—MARCH, 1860.

A Few Words on Junius and Macaulay.
William Hogarth. II. Mr. Gamble's Apprentice.
Mabel.
Studies in Animal Life. Chap. 3.
Framley Parsonage. Chaps. 7, 8 and 9.
Sir Joshua and Holbein.
A Changeling.
Lovel the Widower. Chap. 3.
The National Gallery Difficulty solved.
A Winter Wedding-party in the Wilds.
Student Life in Scotland.
Roundabout Papers.—No. 2.

No. 4.—APRIL, 1860.

Lovel the Widower. Chap. 4.
Colour Blindness.
Spring.
Inside Canton.
William Hogarth. III. A Long Ladder, and hard
   to climb.
Studies in Animal Life. Chap. 4.
Strangers Yet.
Framley Parsonage. Chaps. 10, 11 and 12.
Ideal Houses.
Dante.
The Last Sketch—Emma.
Under Chloroform.
The How and Why of Long Shots and Straight
   Shots.

Voyages and Travels.

A Visit to the Philippine Isles

in 1858-59.

By Sir John Bowring,

Governor of Hong Kong, and H.M.'s Plenipotentiary in China.

Demy 8vo, with numerous Illustrations, price 18s. cloth.

"The work of Sir John Bowring on the Philippine Islands is exhaustive in scope, if not in substance. It does not pretend to set forth all that is known of the islands; but, in a series of condensed chapters, connected together by the author's reminiscences, presents a brilliant view of that rich region of sun and colour."—*Athenæum.*

"Anything coming from the pen of the ex-Governor of Hong Kong is entitled to a welcome and a hearing. He has brought back a fund of information of the utmost value, ranging over the four heads of history, politics, literature, and commerce. The information it contains is of the highest value. It is profusely illustrated."—*Morning Post.*

"This book upon the Philippine Islands is very welcome, because it describes a part of the world, about which very little is really known."—*Critic.*

Life in Spain.

By Walter Thornbury.

Two vols. post 8vo, with Eight Tinted Illustrations, price 21s.

"Two volumes of more entertaining and instructive matter are not discoverable in the literature of the day. They unite the charms of travel and romance."—*Leader.*

"Mr. Thornbury's book will be acceptable to a very large class of readers."—*Morning Post.*

"The book is to be recommended as a wholesome body of light reading, from which plenty of substantial knowledge may be gleaned."—*Examiner.*

"The sketches of character with which this volume abounds are amusing and effective."—*Morning Herald.*

Heathen and Holy Lands;

Or, Sunny Days on the Salween, Nile, and Jordan.

By Captain J. P. Briggs, Bengal Army.

Post 8vo, price 12s. cloth.

"Freshly and naturally written; the landscapes are graphic, and the personal anecdotes are adventurous."—*Daily News.*

"This volume has the peculiarity that it introduces us into the Holy Land from the other side of the world. . . . . The Captain's descriptions are those of an eye-witness, and of a keenly observant one. They are admirably graphic, full of genuine enthusiasm, and of fine feeling."—*Illustrated News of the World.*

"It is seldom we meet with a book of travels so original as this."—*Leader.*

"This book is extremely well written, and its descriptions have a vigorous freshness about them which would reflect no discredit upon a much more 'practised' hand.—*Morning Herald.*

Through Norway with a Knapsack.

By W. M. Williams.

With Six Coloured Views.

Second Edition, post 8vo, price 12s., cloth.

"Mr. Williams will be an excellent guide to all who wish to travel as he did, on foot, and with the least possible expense. They may also place thorough reliance on all he says, his good sense never allowing his enthusiasm to dazzle him and delude his followers. It is a useful and trustworthy book."—*Athenæum.*

"The book is amusing; the author saw much that was new. There is frank graphic writing, and much pleasant thinking, in his volume, which is elegantly produced, and liberally illustrated with tinted views and woodcuts."—*Examiner.*

"'Through Norway with a Knapsack' is a work of intrinsic interest, very instructive and amusing. Mr. Williams is a model pedestrian traveller, and his book is the best guide we know of for those who intend to explore Norway on foot."—*Spectator.*

"A very instructive book on Norway, and the manners and customs of its inhabitants."—*Literary Gazette.*

"Every chapter of it will be read with interest."—*Morning Post.*

Voyages and Travels—*continued*.

Voyage to Japan,

Kamtschatka, Siberia, Tartary, and the Coast of China, in H.M.S. *Barracouta*.

By J. M. Tronson, R.N.

8vo, with Charts and Views.   18*s.* cloth.

"The able and intelligent officer, whose work is before us, supplies the first authentic information on the present state of Japan and the neighbouring settlements. . . . An extremely interesting book."—*Athenæum.*

"The book possesses all the qualities of a book of travels, with the prominent advantage of breaking comparatively, and in some instances altogether, new ground."—*Illustrated London News.*

"Mr. Tronson writes well, and imparts a great deal of new and useful information. The clear and beautiful charts and sketches, accompanying the volume, are of great value."—*Globe.*

"It contains a great deal that all the world ought now to know."—*Morning Herald.*

"We cordially recommend it."—*British Quarterly Review.*

To Cuba and Back.

By R. H. Dana,

Author of "Two Years before the Mast," &c.

Post 8vo.   Price 7*s.* cloth.

"Mr. Dana's book is so bright and luscious, so pictorial and cheerful, so essentially pleasant and refreshing, that even the rule of a Spanish capitan-general appears tolerable where the subjects are so courteous, and the strangers so gracefully petted. Mr. Dana has a pen to paint such pictures well. His voyage and residence occupied scarcely a month, yet he has written a volume not only fascinating from its warmth and glitter as a narrative, but also intelligent, instructive, and of obvious integrity."—*Athenæum.*

"Mr. Dana does not spare his faculty of description. The pictures he gives of the Cuban metropolis itself, with its tropical luxuries and laziness, its dirty and dainty ways of existence, the Spanish grandiosity of its national manner, and the pettiness of its national character, are pleasantly and forcibly drawn. A coasting voyage to Matanzas, and a railroad journey, brought him into closer contact with the essential characteristics of the country and its history."—*Saturday Review.*

Life and Liberty in America.

By Dr. C. Mackay.

Second Edition, 2 vols. post 8vo, with Ten Tinted Illustrations, price 21*s.*

"A bright, fresh, and hopeful book, worthy of the author, whose songs are oftenest heard on the Atlantic. Dr. Mackay writes as healthily as he sings; describing 'Life' as he saw it, and 'Liberty' as he studied it, in the North and in the South."—*Athenæum.*

"We recommend these volumes to perusal, as the result of careful and diligent observation, assisted by personal association, well calculated to facilitate the attainment of truth."—*Leader.*

"Dr. Mackay's volumes are eminently readable and amusing."—*Press.*

Life in Tuscany.

By Mabel Sharman Crawford.

With Two Views, post 8vo.   Price 10*s.* 6*d.* cloth.

"There are many traces of quiet, genial humour, brilliant and harmless as summer lightning, which agreeably relieve the more serious portions of the work. Miss Crawford's reflections are as sound and practical as her perceptions are lively

and acute, and she has succeeded in contributing a really valuable addition to that otherwise redundant department of literature."—*Press.*

"The peasant life in Tuscany has, perhaps, not been so well photographed before."—*Athenæum.*

Voyages and Travels—*continued*.

Narrative of the Mission

From the Governor-General of India to the Court of Ava in 1855.
With Notices of the Country, Government, and People.

By Captain Henry Yule, Bengal Engineers.

Imperial 8vo, with Twenty-four Plates (Twelve coloured), Fifty Woodcuts, and Four Maps. Elegantly bound in cloth, with gilt edges. Price 2*l*. 12*s*. 6*d*.

"Captain Yule, in the preparation of the splendid volume before us, has availed himself of the labours of those who preceded him. To all who are desirous of possessing the best and fullest account that has ever been given to the public, of a great, and hitherto little known region of the globe, the interesting, conscientious, and well-written work of Captain Yule will have a deep interest, while to the political economist, geographer, and merchant, it will be indispensable."—*Examiner*.

"A stately volume in gorgeous golden covers. Such a book is in our times a rarity. Large, massive, and beautiful in itself, it is illustrated by a sprinkling of elegant woodcuts, and by a series of admirable tinted lithographs. . . . . We have read it with curiosity and gratification, as a fresh, full, and luminous report upon the condition of one of the most interesting divisions of Asia beyond the Ganges."—*Athenæum*.

Hong Kong to Manilla.
By Henry T. Ellis, R.N.

Post 8vo, with Fourteen Illustrations. Price 12*s*. cloth.

"The narrative fulfils the object of the author, which is to present a lively account of what he saw, heard, and did during a holiday run to a rarely visited place."—*Spectator*.

"Mr. Ellis has given to the public a most valuable and interesting work upon a race and country little known to English readers."—*Illustrated News of the World*.

Antiquities of Kertch,

And Researches in the Cimmerian Bosphorus.

By Duncan McPherson, M.D.,
Of the Madras Army, F.R.G.S., M.A.I.

Imperial 4to, with Fourteen Plates and numerous Illustrations, including Eight Coloured Fac-Similes of Reliques of Antique Art. Price Two Guineas.

"It is a volume which deserves the careful attention of every student of classical antiquity. No one can fail to be pleased with a work which has so much to attract the eye and to gratify the love of beauty and elegance in design. . . . ."

The book is got up with great care and taste, and forms one of the handsomest works that have recently issued from the English press."—*Saturday Review*.

Captivity of Russian Princesses in the Caucasus.

Translated from the Russian by H. S. Edwards.

With an authentic Portrait of Shamil, a Plan of his House, and a Map
Post 8vo. Price 10*s*. 6*d*. cloth.

"A book than which there are few novels more interesting. It is a romance of the Caucasus. The account of life in the house of Shamil is full and very entertaining; and of Shamil himself we see much."—*Examiner*.

"The story is certainly one of the most curious we have read; it contains the best popular notice of the social polity of Shamil and the manners of his people."—*Leader*.

"The narrative is well worth reading."—*Athenæum*.

Biography—*continued.*

The Life of Charlotte Brontë

(CURRER BELL),

Author of "Jane Eyre," "Shirley," "Villette," &c.

By Mrs. Gaskell,

Author of "North and South," &c.

Fourth Edition, revised, one vol., with a Portrait of Miss Brontë and a View of Haworth Parsonage. Price 7s. 6d. ; morocco elegant, 14s.

"All the secrets of the literary workmanship of the authoress of 'Jane Eyre' are unfolded in the course of this extraordinary narrative."—*Times.*

"Mrs. Gaskell's account of Charlotte Brontë and her family is one of the profoundest tragedies of modern life."—*Spectator.*

"Mrs. Gaskell has produced one of the best biographies of a woman by a woman which we can recall to mind."—*Athenæum.*

"If any one wishes to see how a woman possessed of the highest intellectual power can disregard every temptation which intellect throws in the way of women—how generously and nobly a human being can live under the pressure of accumulated misfortune—the record is at hand in 'The Life of Charlotte Brontë.'"—*Saturday Review.*

"Mrs. Gaskell has done her work well. Her narrative is simple, direct, intelligible, unaffected. No one else could have paid so tender and discerning a tribute to the memory of Charlotte Brontë."—*Fraser's Magazine.*

Life of Lord Metcalfe.

By John William Kaye.

New Edition, in Two vols., post 8vo, with Portrait. Price 12s. cloth.

"A work which occupies the highest rank among biographies of the great men of modern times."—*Observer.*

"The new edition contains new matter of the utmost value and interest."—*Critic.*

"One of the most valuable biographies of the present day. This revised edition has several fresh passages of high interest, now first inserted from among Lord Metcalfe's papers, in which his clear prescience of the dangers that threatened our Indian empire is remarkably shown."—*Economist.*

"This edition is revised with care and judgment. Mr. Kaye has judiciously set forth Lord Metcalfe's views of the insecurity of our Indian empire."—*Globe.*

"A much improved edition of one of the most interesting political biographies in English literature."—*National Review.*

Life of Sir John Malcolm, G.C.B.

By John William Kaye.

Two vols. 8vo, with Portrait. Price 36s. cloth.

"The biography is replete with interest and information, deserving to be perused by the student of Indian history, and sure to recommend itself to the general reader."—*Athenæum.*

"One of the most interesting of the recent biographies of our great Indian statesmen."—*National Review.*

"This book deserves to participate in the popularity which it was the good fortune of Sir John Malcolm to enjoy."—*Edinburgh Review.*

"Mr. Kaye's biography is at once a contribution to the history of our policy and dominion in the East, and a worthy memorial of one of those wise and large-hearted men whose energy and principle have made England great."—*British Quarterly Review.*

The Autobiography of Lutfullah,

A Mohamedan Gentleman; with an Account of his Visit to England.

Edited by E. B. Eastwick, Esq.

Third Edition, small post 8vo. Price 5s. cloth.

"This is the freshest and most original work that it has been our good fortune to meet with for long. It bears every trace of being a most genuine account of the feelings and doings of the author. Lutfullah is by no means an ordinary specimen of his race."—*Economist.*

"Read fifty volumes of travel, and a thousand imitations of the Oriental novel, and you will not get the flavour of Eastern life and thought, or the zest of its romance, so perfectly as in Lutfullah's book."—*Leader.*

Art.

WORKS OF MR. RUSKIN.

The Elements of Perspective.

With 80 Diagrams, crown 8vo. Price 3s. 6d. cloth.

"Mr. Ruskin, seeing the want of a clear and accurate code on the subject, has set himself to the task of arranging and explaining the necessary rules in a form as nearly approaching the ideal of a popular treatise as can be managed consistently with the object of practical completeness. No better way of blending the two purposes could, we believe, have been found than the way Mr. Ruskin ingeniously discovered and has ably worked out. A careful perusal of the work will enable the intelligent student not only to solve perspective problems of a complexity greater than the ordinary rules will reach, but to obtain a clue to many important laws of pictorial effect less than of outline."—*Daily News.*

"This book, provided by Mr. Ruskin for the use of schools, bears its recommendation on the title-page. The rules are arranged in a short mathematical form, which will be intelligible to students reasonably advanced in general knowledge."—*Leader.*

"The student will find in this little book all that is necessary to lay the foundation of a thorough scientific knowledge of perspective."—*Illustrated News of the World.*

"To the practical student it is likely to prove a most valuable manual."—*Literary Gazette.*

The Elements of Drawing.

Sixth Thousand, crown 8vo, with Illustrations drawn by the Author. Price 7s. 6d. cloth.

"The rules are clearly and fully laid down; and the earlier exercises always conducive to the end by simple and unembarrassing means. The whole volume is full of liveliness."—*Spectator.*

"We close this book with a feeling that, though nothing supersedes a master, yet that no student of art should launch forth without this work as a compass."—*Athenæum.*

"It will be found not only an invaluable acquisition to the student, but agreeable and instructive reading for any one who wishes to refine his perceptions of natural scenery, and of its worthiest artistic representations."—*Economist.*

"Original as this treatise is, it cannot fail to be at once instructive and suggestive."—*Literary Gazette.*

"The most useful and practical book on the subject which has ever come under our notice."—*Press.*

Modern Painters.

Vol. I., 6th Edition. Price 18s. cloth. Imperial 8vo.

Vol. II., 4th Edition. Price 10s. 6d. cloth.

Vol. III. OF MANY THINGS, with Eighteen Illustrations drawn by the Author, and engraved on Steel. Price 38s. cloth.

Vol. IV. ON MOUNTAIN BEAUTY. Imperial 8vo, with Thirty-five Illustrations engraved on Steel, and 116 Woodcuts, drawn by the Author. Price 2l. 10s. cloth.

"A generous and impassioned review of the works of living painters. A hearty and earnest work, full of deep thought, and developing great and striking truths in art."—*British Quarterly Review.*

"Mr. Ruskin's work will send the painter more than ever to the study of nature; will train men who have always been delighted spectators of nature, to be also attentive observers. Our critics will learn to admire, and mere admirers will learn how to criticise : thus a public will be educated."—*Blackwood's Magazine.*

"Every one who cares about nature, or poetry, or the story of human development—every one who has a tinge of literature or philosophy, will find something that is for him in these volumes."—*Westminster Review.*

"Mr. Ruskin is in possession of a clear and penetrating mind; he is undeniably practical in his fundamental ideas; full of the deepest reverence for all that appears to him beautiful and holy. His style is, as usual, clear, bold, racy. Mr. Ruskin is one of the first writers of the day."—*Economist.*

"All, it is to be hoped, will read the book for themselves. They will find it well worth a careful perusal."—*Saturday Review.*

"Mr. Ruskin is the most eloquent and thought-awakening writer on nature in its relation with art, and the most potent influence by the pen, of young artists, whom this country can boast."—*National Review.*

"This work is eminently suggestive, full of new thoughts, of brilliant descriptions of scenery, and eloquent moral application of them."—*New Quarterly Review.*

"Mr. Ruskin has deservedly won for himself a place in the first rank of modern writers upon the theory of the fine arts."—*Eclectic Review.*

"The fourth volume of Mr. Ruskin's elaborate work treats chiefly of mountain scenery, and discusses at length the principles involved in the pleasure we derive from mountains and their pictorial representation. The singular beauty of his style, the hearty sympathy with all forms of natural loveliness, the profusion of his illustrations form irresistible attractions."—*Daily News.*

"Considered as an illustrated volume, the fourth is the most remarkable which Mr. Ruskin has yet issued. The plates and woodcuts are profuse, and include numerous drawings of mountain form by the author, which prove Mr. Ruskin to be essentially an artist. He is an unique man, both among artists and writers."—*Spectator.*

"Such a writer is a national possession. He adds to our store of knowledge and enjoyment."—*Leader.*

Art—*continued.*

WORKS OF MR. RUSKIN—*continued.*

The Two Paths:

Being Lectures on Art, and its relation to Manufactures and Decoration.

One vol., crown 8vo, with Two Steel Engravings. Price 7s. 6d. cloth.

"The meaning of the title of this book is, that there are two courses open to the artist, one of which will lead him to all that is noble in art, and will incidentally exalt his moral nature; while the other will deteriorate his work and help to throw obstacles in the way of his individual morality. . . . They all contain many useful distinctions, acute remarks, and valuable suggestions, and are everywhere lit up with that glow of fervid eloquence which has so materially contributed to the author's reputation."—*Press.*

"The 'Two Paths' contains much eloquent description, places in a clear light some forgotten or neglected truths, and, like all Mr. Ruskin's books, is eminently suggestive."—*Literary Gazette.*

"This book is well calculated to encourage the humblest worker, and stimulate him to artistic effort."—*Leader.*

The Stones of Venice.

Complete in Three Volumes, Imperial 8vo, with Fifty-three Plates and numerous Woodcuts, drawn by the Author. Price 5l. 15s. 6d. cloth.

EACH VOLUME MAY BE HAD SEPARATELY.

Vol. I. THE FOUNDATIONS, with 21 Plates. Price 2l. 2s. **2nd Edition.**
Vol. II. THE SEA STORIES, with 20 Plates. Price 2l. 2s.
Vol. III. THE FALL, with 12 Plates. Price 1l. 11s. 6d.

"The 'Stones of Venice' is the production of an earnest, religious, progressive, and informed mind. The author of this essay on architecture has condensed it into a poetic apprehension, the fruit of awe of God, and delight in nature; a knowledge, love, and just estimate of art; a holding fast to fact and repudiation of hearsay; an historic breadth, and a fearless challenge of existing social problems, whose union we know not where to find paralleled."—*Spectator.*

"This book is one which, perhaps, no other man could have written, and one for which the world ought to be and will be thankful. It is in the highest degree eloquent, acute, stimulating to thought, and fertile in suggestion. It will, we are convinced, elevate taste and intellect, raise the tone of moral feeling, kindle benevolence towards men, and increase the love and fear of God."—*Times.*

The Seven Lamps of Architecture.

Second Edition, with Fourteen Plates drawn by the Author. Imp. 8vo. Price 1l. 1s. cloth.

"By 'The Seven Lamps of Architecture,' we understand Mr. Ruskin to mean the Seven fundamental and cardinal laws, the observance of and obedience to which are indispensable to the architect, who would deserve the name. The politician, the moralist, the divine, will find in it ample store of instructive matter, as well as the artist. The author of this work belongs to a class of thinkers of whom we have too few amongst us."—*Examiner.*

Lectures on Architecture and Painting.

With Fourteen Cuts, drawn by the Author. Second Edition, crown 8vo. Price 8s. 6d. cloth.

"Mr. Ruskin's lectures—eloquent, graphic, and impassioned—exposing and ridiculing some of the vices of our present system of building, and exciting his hearers by strong motives of duty and pleasure to attend to architecture—are very successful."—*Economist.*

"We conceive it to be impossible that any intelligent persons could listen to the lectures, however they might differ from the judgments asserted and from the general propositions laid down, without an elevating influence and an aroused enthusiasm."—*Spectator.*

The Political Economy of Art.

Price 2s. 6d. cloth.

"A most able, eloquent, and well-timed work. We hail it with satisfaction, thinking it calculated to do much practical good, and we cordially recommend it to our readers."—*Witness.*

"We never quit Mr. Ruskin without being the better for what he has told us, and therefore we recommend this little volume, like all his other works, to the perusal of our readers."—*Economist.*

"This book, daring, as it is, glances keenly at principles, of which some are among the articles of ancient codes, while others are evolving slowly to the light."—*Leader.*

𝕽𝖊𝖑𝖎𝖌𝖎𝖔𝖚𝖘.

Expositions of St. Paul's Epistles to the Corinthians.

By the late Rev. Fred. W. Robertson.

One thick Volume, post 8vo.   Price 10*s.* 6*d.* cloth.

"These lectures were the last discourses that Mr. Robertson ever delivered from his pulpit. High as is the standard of thoughtfulness and originality which we expect in everything that comes from the pen of this preacher, these pages are not unworthy of that high standard. This single volume in itself would establish a reputation for its writer."

Sermons :

By the late Rev. Fred. W. Robertson, A.M.,

Incumbent of Trinity Chapel, Brighton.

FIRST SERIES.—Seventh Edition, post 8vo.   Price 9*s.* cloth.
SECOND SERIES.—Seventh Edition.   Price 9*s.* cloth.
THIRD SERIES.—Fifth Edition, post 8vo, with Portrait.   Price 9*s.* cloth.

"There are many persons, and their number increases every year, to whom Robertson's writings are the most stable, exhaustless, and satisfactory form of religious teaching which the nineteenth century has given—the most wise, suggestive, and practical."—*Saturday Review.*
"We recommend the whole of the volumes to the perusal of our readers. They will find in them thought of a rare and beautiful description, an earnestness of mind steadfast in the search of truth, and a **charity pure** and all-embracing."—*Economist.*
"They are very remarkable compositions. The thoughts are often very striking, and entirely out of the track of ordinary sermonising."—*Guardian.*
"We feel that a brother man is speaking to us as brother men; that we are listening, not to the measured words of a calm, cool thinker, but to the passionate deep-toned voice of an earnest human soul."—*Edinburgh Christian Magazine.*

Sermons :

Preached at Lincoln's Inn Chapel.

By the Rev. F. D. Maurice, M.A.

First Series, 2 vols., post 8vo, price 21s., cloth.
Second Series, 2 vols., post 8vo, price 21s., cloth.
Third Series, 2 vols., post 8vo, price 21s., cloth.

" Is it not Written ? "

Being the Testimony of Scripture against the Errors of Romanism.

By the Rev. Edward S. Pryce.

Post 8vo.   Price 6s., cloth.

The Province of Reason ;

A Reply to Mr. Mansell's Bampton Lecture.

By John Young, LL.D., Edin.,

Author of " The Mystery; or, Evil and God."   Post 8vo.   Price 6s., cloth.   [*Now ready.*

𝔐iscellaneous.

On the Strength of Nations.
By Andrew Bisset, M.A.
Post 8vo.　Price 9s. cloth.

" We can safely recommend the perusal of this work to all who have not maturely considered the subject. It will set them thinking in the right direction."—*Daily News.*

" Frequent concurrence with him, and general sympathy with his views, even where we do not accept his principles, dispose us to recommend Mr. Bisset's book for perusal."—*Spectator.*

"Mr. Bisset has dealt with this important subject in a way that will be equally acceptable to the scholar and the true economist."—*Morning Star.*

" We commend most heartily Mr. Bisset's able volume."—*Examiner.*

"A work exhibiting considerable research; many of the author's views will be found correct, and valuable at the present moment."—*Literary Gazette.*

Social Innovators and their Schemes.
By William Lucas Sargant.
Post 8vo.　Price 10s. 6d. cloth.

"Mr. Sargant has written a very useful sketch. His book is impartial, pleasantly written, and excellently arranged."—*Saturday Review.*

" It has the merit of going deep into the subject-matter at one of its most vital points; and it is this merit that constitutes the special value of Mr. Sargant's book. His views are sensible and sound, they are brought forward clearly and dispassionately, with quiet vigour and telling illustration."—*Press.*

Lectures and Addresses.
By the late Rev. Fred. W. Robertson.
Post 8vo.　Price 7s. 6d. cloth.

" These lectures and addresses are marked by the same qualities that made the author's sermons so justly and so widely popular. They manifest the same earnest, liberal spirit, the ardent love of truth, the lucid eloquence, the wide sympathy, and singleness of purpose."—*Lit. Gaz.*

" They throw some new light on the constitution of Robertson's mind, and on the direction in which it was unfolding itself."—*Saturday Review.*

" In these addresses we are gladdened by rare liberality of view and range of sympathy boldly expressed."—*Daily Telegraph.*

Quakerism, Past and Present :
Being an Inquiry into the Causes of its Decline.
By John S. Rowntree.
Post 8vo. Price 5s. cloth.

*** This Essay gained the First Prize of One Hundred Guineas offered for the best Essay on the subject.

The Peculium :
An Essay on the Causes of the Decline of the Society of Friends.
By Thomas Hancock.
Post 8vo.　Price 5s. cloth.

*** This Essay gained the Second Prize of Fifty Guineas, which was afterwards increased to One Hundred.

India and the East—*continued*.

Papers of the late Lord Metcalfe.
By John William Kaye.
Demy 8vo. Price 16*s.* cloth.

"We commend this volume to all persons who like to study State papers, in which the practical sense of a man of the world is joined to the speculative sagacity of a philosophical statesman. No Indian library should be without it."—*Press.*

Personal Adventures
During the Indian Rebellion in Rohilcund, Futtehghur, and Oude.
By W. Edwards, Esq., B. C. S.
Fourth Edition, post 8vo. Price 6*s.* cloth.

"For touching incidents, hair-breadth 'scapes, and the pathos of suffering almost incredible, there has appeared nothing like this little book of personal adventures. For the first time we seem to realize the magnitude of the afflictions which have befallen our unhappy countrymen in the East. The terrible drama comes before us, and we are by turns bewildered with horror, stung to fierce indignation, and melted to tears. . . . . We have here a tale of suffering such as may have been equalled, but never surpassed. These real adventures, which no effort of the imagination can surpass, will find a sympathising public."—*Athenæum.*

"Mr. Edwards's narrative is one of the most deeply interesting episodes of a story of which the least striking portions cannot be read without emotion. He tells his story with simplicity and manliness, and it bears the impress of that earnest and unaffected reverence to the will and hand of God, which was the stay and comfort of many other brave hearts."—*Guardian.*

"The narrative of Mr. Edwards's suffering and escapes is full of interest; it tells many a painful tale, but it also exhibits a man patient under adversity, and looking to the God and Father of us all for guidance and support."—*Eclectic Review.*

A Lady's Escape from Gwalior
During the Mutinies of 1857.
By Mrs. Coopland.
Post 8vo. Price 10*s.* 6*d.*

"A plain, unvarnished tale, told in the simplest manner."—*Press.*

"This book is valuable as a contribution to the history of the great Indian rebellion."—*Athenæum.*

"The merit of this book is its truth. . . . . It contains some passages that never will be read by Englishmen without emotion."—*Examiner.*

The Crisis in the Punjab.
By Frederick H. Cooper, Esq., C.S., Umritsir.
Post 8vo, with Map. Price 7*s.* 6*d.* cloth.

"The book is full of terrible interest. The narrative is written with vigour and earnestness, and is full of the most tragic interest."—*Economist.*

"One of the most interesting and spirited books which have sprung out of the sepoy mutiny."—*Globe.*

Views and Opinions of Gen. Jacob, C.B.
Edited by Captain Lewis Pelly.
Demy 8vo. Price 12*s.* cloth.

"The facts in this book are worth looking at. If the reader desires to take a peep into the interior of the mind of a great man, let him make acquaintance with the 'Views and Opinions of General Jacob.'"—*Globe.*

"This is truly a gallant and soldierly book; very Napierish in its self-confidence, in its capital sense, and in its devotedness to professional honour and the public good. The book should be studied by all who are interested in the choice of a new government for India."—*Daily News.*

India and the East—*continued*.

British Rule in India.
By Harriet Martineau.

Sixth Thousand. Price 2*s.* 6*d.* cloth.

.•. A reliable class-book for examination in the history of British India.

"A good compendium of a great subject."—*National Review.*

"A succinct and comprehensive volume."—*Leader.*

The English in Western India:
Being the Early History of the Factory at Surat, of Bombay.
By Philip Anderson, A.M.

Second Edition, 8vo. Price 14*s.* cloth.

" Quaint, curious, and amusing, this volume describes, from old manuscripts and obscure books, the life of English merchants in an Indian Factory. It contains fresh and amusing gossip,

all bearing on events and characters of historical importance."—*Athenæum.*

"A book of permanent value."—*Guardian.*

Life in Ancient India.
By Mrs. Spier.

With Sixty Illustrations by G. SCHARF.

8vo. Price 15*s.*, elegantly bound in cloth, gilt edges.

"Whoever desires to have the best, the completest, and the most popular view of what Oriental scholars have made known to us respecting Ancient India must peruse the work of Mrs.

Speir; in which he will find the story told in clear, correct, and unaffected English. The book is admirably got up."—*Examiner.*

The Parsees :
Their History, Religion, Manners, and Customs.
By Dosabhoy Framjee.

Post 8vo. Price 10*s.* cloth.

"Our author's account of the inner life of the Parsees will be read with interest."—*Daily News.*

" A very curious and well-written book, by a young Parsee, on the manners and customs of his own race."—*National Review.*

"An acceptable addition to our literature. It gives information which many will be glad to have carefully gathered together, and formed into a shapely whole."—*Economist.*

Tiger Shooting in India.
By Lieutenant William Rice, 25th Bombay N. I.

Super-royal 8vo. With Twelve Plates in Chromo-lithography.
10*s.* 6*d.* cloth.

" These adventures, told in handsome large print, with spirited chromo-lithographs to illustrate them, make the volume before us as pleasant

reading as any record of sporting achievements we have ever taken in hand."—*Athenæum.*

Indian Scenes and Characters,
By Prince Alexis Soltykoff.

Sixteen Plates in Tinted Lithography, with Descriptions.
Edited by E. B. EASTWICK, Esq., F.R.S.

Colombier folio. Prints, 10*s.*; proofs (only Fifty Copies printed), 15*s.*

Naval and Military.

England and her Soldiers.
By Harriet Martineau.

With Three Plates of Illustrative Diagrams.   1 vol, crown 8vo,
price 9s. cloth.

"The purpose with which Miss Martineau has written about England and her soldiers is purely practical, and equally so is the manner in which she has treated the subject. There is not in her whole volume one line of invective against individuals or classes. No candid reader can deny that this effort has been made opportunely, ably, and discreetly."—*Spectator.*

"The book is remarkable for the clear, comprehensive way in which the subject is treated. Great credit is due to Miss Martineau for having so compactly, so spiritedly, with so much truth of detail, and at the same time so much force, placed the matter before the public in this interesting and well-timed volume."—*Shipping and Mercantile Gazette.*

"Miss Martineau has worked out her subject with courage, power, and conscientiousness. Faithful in fact and rich in suggestion, she has given us in this volume a very valuable addition to our present store of knowledge as the conduct and condition of the Crimean troops."—*Literary Gazette.*

Narrative of the Siege of Delhi.
By the Rev. J. E. W. Rotton,
Chaplain to the Delhi Field Force.

Post 8vo, with a Plan of the City and Siege Works.
Price 10s. 6d. cloth.

"A simple and touching statement, which bears the impress of truth in every word. It supplies some of those personal anecdotes and minute details which bring the events home to the understanding."—*Athenæum.*

"'The Chaplain's Narrative' is remarkable for its pictures of men in a moral and religious aspect, during the progress of a harassing siege and when suddenly stricken down by the enemy or disease."—*Spectator.*

The Defence of Lucknow:
By Captain Thomas F. Wilson, 13th Bengal N.I.
Assistant Adjutant-General.

Sixth Thousand.   With Plan.   Small post 8vo.   Price 2s. 6d.

"The Staff-Officer's Diary is simple and brief, and has a special interest, inasmuch as it gives a fuller account than we have elsewhere seen of those operations which were the chief human means of salvation to our friends in Lucknow.

The Staff-Officer brings home to us, by his details, the nature of that underground contest, upon the result of which the fate of the beleaguered garrison especially depended."—*Examiner.*

Eight Months' Campaign against the Bengal Sepoys during the Mutiny,
1857.
By Colonel George Bourchier, C.B.
Bengal Horse Artillery.

With Plans.   Post 8vo.   Price 7s. 6d. cloth.

"Col. Bourchier describes the various operations with a modest forgetfulness of self, as pleasing and as rare as the clear manly style in which they are narrated."—*Literary Gazette.*

"Col. Bourchier has given a right manly, fair, and forcible statement of events, and the reader will derive much pleasure and instruction from his pages."—*Athenæum.*

Fiction.

Transformation;
or, the Romance of Monte Beni.
By Nathaniel Hawthorne,
Author of the " Scarlet Letter," &c.   Third Edition.   In 3 vols.

" One of the most remarkable novels that 1860 is likely to give us either from English, French, or American sources. Such an Italian tale we have not had since Herr Andersen wrote his 'Improvisatore.'"—*Athenæum.*

" No one but a man of genius could have written this novel. The style is singularly beautiful. The Americans may be proud that they have produced a writer who in his own special walk of English has few rivals or equals in the mother country."—*Saturday Review.*

" Never before, unless our memory be greatly at fault, has Italy inspired a romance writer with a work like ' Transformation,' so composite in its elements, so perfect in their organic harmony."—*Spectator.*

" ' Transformation' is a book of marvellous fascination, full of wisdom and goodness, of pure love of the beautiful, of deep and intense thoughtfulness, of sound practical piety."—*Art Journal.*

" The impression produced by Mr. Hawthorne's wonderfully vivid description of the associations and reflections evoked by a residence in Rome is keenly pleasurable; he makes you see the place and breathe the air."—*Morning Post.*

" There is no work of this class on Rome and its treasures which brings their details so closely and vividly before us. It is worth all the guide-books we ever met with, as regards the gems of Italian art, the characteristic features of Roman edifices, and the atmosphere of Roman life. In fact, we conceive it calculated in many instances to impart new views of objects with which travellers may have imagined themselves already too familiar."—*Times.*

Netley Hall;
or, The Wife's Sister.   Foolscap 8vo.   6s., cloth.

" The author is heart and soul in his work, writes vigorously, and with earnestness."—*Morning Chronicle.*

" ' Netley Hall' is an excellent story.'—*Illustrated News of the World.*

Against Wind and Tide.
By Holme Lee,
Author of " Sylvan Holt's Daughter."   3 vols.

" The reputation which ' Kathie Brande' and ' Sylvan Holt's Daughter' won for their author will be crowned by ' Against Wind and Tide.' A more charming novel has not proceeded of late years from the press."—*Morning Herald.*

" This novel is by many degrees the best specimen of fiction that has been placed in our hands."—*Literary Gazette.*

" This is one of the few good novels that deserve permanent life."—*Examiner.*

" Full of animated scenes and rich in clever description."—*Press.*

" To all who appreciate a powerfully concentrated work, this one may be fairly recommended."—*Sun.*

Greymore:
A Story of Country Life.   Three volumes.

" The author of ' Greymore' is fairly entitled to our congratulation on her first appearance as a writer of fiction. Her volumes contain much that is positively good in performance, and better still in promise."—*Spectator.*

" ' Greymore' is a very pretty story, and one that may be given to the younger members of a family, or be read aloud, with the certainty that it will give a wholesome tendency to the interest it excites."—*Athenæum.*

Esmond.
By W. M. Thackeray.
A New Edition, being the third, in 1 vol. crown 8vo.   Price 6s. cloth.

" The book has the great charm of reality. Queen Anne's colonel writes his life—and a very interesting life it is—just as a Queen Anne's colonel might be supposed to have written it. Mr. Thackeray has selected for his hero a very noble type of the cavalier softening into the man of the eighteenth century, and for his heroine, one of the sweetest women that ever breathed from canvas or from book since Raffaelle painted and Shakspeare wrote."—*Spectator.*

" Once more we feel that we have before us a masculine and thoroughly English writer, uniting the power of subtle analysis, with a strong volition and a moving eloquence—an eloquence which has gained in richness and harmony. ' Esmond' must be read, not for its characters, but for its romantic plot, its spirited grouping, and its many thrilling utterances of the anguish of the human heart."—*Athenæum.*

Recent Publications.

VOYAGES AND TRAVELS.

Visit to Salt Lake.

Being a Journey across the Plains to the Mormon Settlements at Utah.
By William Chandless.
Post 8vo, with a Map. 2*s.* 6*d.* cloth.

"Mr. Chandless is an impartial observer of the Mormons. He gives a full account of the nature of the country, the religion of the Mormons, their government, institutions, morality, and the singular relationship of the sexes, with its consequences."—*Critic.*

"Those who would understand what Mormonism is can do no better than read this authentic, though light and lively volume."—*Leader.*

"It impresses the reader as faithful."—*National Review.*

Memorandums in Ireland.

By Sir John Forbes.
Two vols. post 8vo. Price 1*l.* 1*s.* cloth.

The Argentine Provinces.

By William McCann, Esq.
Two vols. post 8vo, with Illustrations.
Price 24*s.* cloth.

Germany and the Tyrol.

By Sir John Forbes.
Post 8vo, with Map and View.
Price 10*s.* 6*d.* cloth.

"Sir John Forbes' volume fully justifies its title. Wherever he went he visited sights, and has rendered a faithful and extremely interesting account of them."—*Literary Gazette.*

The Red River Settlement.

By Alexander Ross.
One vol. post 8vo. Price 5*s.* cloth.

"The subject is novel, curious, and not without interest, while a strong sense of the real obtains throughout."—*Spectator.*

"The history of the Red River Settlement is remarkable, if not unique, among colonial records."—*Literary Gazette.*

"One of the most interesting of the romances of civilization."—*Observer.*

Fur Hunters of the West.

By Alexander Ross.
Two vols. post 8vo, with Map and Plate. Price 10*s.* 6*d.* cloth.

"A well-written narrative of most exciting adventures."—*Guardian.*

"A narrative full of incident and dangerous adventure."—*Literary Gazette.*

Campaign in Asia.

By Charles Duncan, Esq.
Post 8vo. Price 2*s.* 6*d.* cloth.

The Columbia River.

By Alexander Ross.
Post 8vo. Price 2*s.* 6*d.* cloth.

Travels in Assam.

By Major John Butler.
One vol. 8vo, with Plates. 12*s.* cloth.

BIOGRAPHY.

Life of Sir Robert Peel.

By Thomas Doubleday.
Two vols. 8vo. Price 18*s.* cloth.

Women of Christianity

Exemplary for Piety and Charity.
By Julia Kavanagh.
Post 8vo, with Portraits. Price 5*s.* in embossed cloth.

Woman in France.

By Julia Kavanagh.
Two vols. post 8vo, with Portraits.
Price 12*s.* cloth.

The Novitiate;

Or, the Jesuit in Training.
By Andrew Steinmetz.
Third Edition, post 8vo. 2*s.* 6*d.* cloth.

RELIGIOUS.

Historic Notes

On the Old and New Testament.
By Samuel Sharpe.
3rd and Revised Edition.   8vo. 7*s.* cl.

Sermons.

By the Rev. C. B. Taylor.
Author of "Records of a Good Man's
Life."
12mo.   Price 1*s.* 6*d.*

Signs of the Times;

Or, The Dangers to Religious Liberty
in the Present Day.
By Chevalier Bunsen.
Translated by Miss S. WINKWORTH.
One vol. 8vo.   Price 5*s.* cloth.

Sermons on the Church.

By the Rev. R. W. Evans.
8vo.   Price 10*s.* 6*d.*

Tauler's Life and Sermons.

*Translated by Miss Susanna
Winkworth.*
With Preface by Rev. C. KINGSLEY.
Small 4to, printed on Tinted Paper,
and bound in Antique Style, with
red edges, suitable for a Present.
Price 7*s.* 6*d.*

Testimony to the Truth of Christianity.

Fourth Edition, fcap 8vo.   3*s.* cloth.

MISCELLANEOUS.

The Life of J. Deacon Hume.

By the Rev. Charles Badham.
Post 8vo.   Price 9*s.* cloth.

"A masterly piece of biographical narrative.
To minute and conscientious industry in searching out facts, Mr. Badham conjoins the attractions of a graceful style and a sincere liking for
the task he has in hand. He has produced one of
the most useful and judicious biographies extant
in our literature, peculiarly full of beauties, and
peculiarly free from faults."—*Atlas.*

The Life of Mahomet.

And History of Islam to the Era of
the Hegira.
By W. Muir, Esq., Bengal C. S.
Vols. 1 and 2. 8vo.   Price 32*s.* cloth.

"The most perfect life of Mahomet in the
English language, or perhaps in any other. . . .
The work is at once learned and interesting, and
it cannot fail to be eagerly perused by all persons
having any pretensions to historical knowledge."
—*Observer.*

The Education of the Human Race.

*Now first Translated from the
German of Lessing.*
Fcap. 8vo, antique cloth.   Price 4*s.*

"This invaluable tract."—*Critic.*
"A little book on a great subject, and one which,
in its day, exerted no slight influence upon European thought."—*Inquirer.*
"An agreeable and flowing translation of one
of Lessing's finest Essays."—*National Review.*

William Burke the Author of Junius.

By Jelinger C. Symons.
Square. Price 3*s.* 6*d.* cl.

"A week's reflection, and a second reading of
Mr. Symons's book, have strengthened our conviction that he has proved his case."—*Spectator.*
"By diligently comparing the letters of Junius
with the private correspondence of Edmund
Burke, he has elicited certain parallel passages
of which it is impossible to evade the significance."—*Literary Gazette.*

The Oxford Museum.

*By H. W. Acland, M.D., and J.
Ruskin, A.M.*
Post 8vo, with Three Illustrations.
Price 2*s.* 6*d.* cloth.

"There is as much significance in the occasion
of this little volume as interest in the book itself."
—*Spectator.*
"Every one who cares for the advance of true
learning, and desires to note an onward step,
should buy and read this little volume."—*Morning Herald.*

Goethe's Conversations with Eckermann.

Translated by John Oxenford.
Two vols. post 8vo.   Price 5*s.* cloth.

True Law of Population.

By Thomas Doubleday.
Third Edition, 8vo.   Price 6*s.* cloth.

MISCELLANEOUS—*continued.*

Poetics:
An Essay on Poetry.
By E. S. Dallas.
Post 8vo. Price 2s. 6d. cloth.

Juvenile Delinquency.
The Prize Essays.
By M. Hill and C. F. Cornwallis.
Post 8vo. Price 6s. cloth.

The Endowed Schools of Ireland.
By Harriet Martineau.
8vo. Price 3s. 6d. cloth boards.
"The friends of education will do well to possess themselves of this book."—*Spectator.*

European Revolutions of 1848.
By E. S. Cayley, Esq.
Crown 8vo. Price 6s. cloth.
"Mr. Cayley has evidently studied his subject thoroughly, he has consequently produced an interesting and philosophical, though unpretending history of an important epoch."—*New Quarterly.*
"Two instructive volumes."—*Observer.*

The Court of Henry VIII.:
Being a Selection of the Despatches of Sebastian Giustinian, Venetian Ambassador, 1515-1519.
Translated by Rawdon Brown.
Two vols. crown 8vo. Price 21s. cloth.

Principles of Agriculture;
Especially Tropical.
By B. Lovell Phillips, M.D.
Demy 8vo. Price 7s. 6d. cloth.

The Bombay Quarterly Review.
Nos. 1 to 9 at 5s.; 10 to 14, 6s. each.

Hints for Investing Money.
By Francis Playford.
Second Edition, post 8vo. 2s. 6d. cloth.

Men, Women, and Books.
By Leigh Hunt.
Two vols. Price 10s. cloth.

Table Talk. *By Leigh Hunt.*
Price 3s. 6d. cloth.

Austria. *By Thompson.*
Post 8vo. Price 12s.

Social Evils.
By the Rev. C. B. Tayler.
In Parts, each complete. 1s. each, cloth.
I.—THE MECHANIC.
II.—THE LADY AND THE LADY'S MAID.
III.—THE PASTOR OF DRONFELLS.
V.—THE COUNTRY TOWN.
VI.—LIVE AND LET LIVE; OR, THE MANCHESTER WEAVERS.
VII.—THE LEASIDE FARM.

ORIENTAL AND COLONIAL.

Suggestions towards the Government of India.
By Harriet Martineau.
Second Edition, demy 8vo. 5s. cloth.

Lectures on New Zealand.
By William Swainson, Esq.
Crown 8vo. Price 2s. 6d. cloth.

Victoria,
And the Australian Gold Mines in 1857.
By William Westgarth.
Post 8vo, with Maps. 10s. 6d. cloth.

Australian Facts and Prospects;
With the Author's Australian Autobiography.
By R. H. Horne,
Author of "Orion," "The Dreamer and the Worker," &c.
Small post 8vo. Price 5s. cloth.

New Zealand and its Colonization.
By William Swainson, Esq.
Demy 8vo. Price 14s. cloth.

ORIENTAL AND COLONIAL—*continued.*

The Commerce of India with Europe,
And its Political Effects.
By B. A. Irving, Esq.
Post 8vo. Price 7s. 6d. cloth.

The Cauvery, Kistnah, and Godavery:
Being a Report on the Works constructed on those Rivers, for the Irrigation of Provinces in the Presidency of Madras.
By R. Baird Smith, F.G.S.,
Lieut.-Col. Bengal Engineers, &c. &c.
Demy 8vo, with 19 Plans. 28s. cloth.

The Bhilsa Topes;
Or, Buddhist Monuments of Central India.
By Major Cunningham.
One vol. 8vo, with Thirty-three Plates.
Price 30s. cloth.

The Chinese and their Rebellions.
By Thomas Taylor Meadows.
One thick volume, 8vo, with Maps.
Price 18s. cloth.

Traits and Stories of Anglo-Indian Life.
By Captain Addison.
With Eight Illustrations. 2s. 6d. cloth.

Infanticide in India.
By Dr. John Wilson.
Demy 8vo. Price 12s.

Grammar and Dictionary of the Malay Language.
By John Crawfurd, Esq.
Two vols. 8vo. Price 36s. cloth.

WORKS OF DR. FORBES ROYLE.

Culture and Commerce of Cotton in India.
8vo. Price 18s. cloth.

Fibrous Plants of India.
Fitted for Cordage, Clothing, and Paper.
8vo. Price 12s. cloth.

The Resources of India.
Super-royal 8vo. Price 14s. cloth.

Review of the Measures
Adopted in India for the Improved Culture of Cotton.
8vo. Price 2s. 6d. cloth.

Rangoon.
By Lieut. W. F. B. Laurie.
Post 8vo, with Plates. 2s. 6d. cloth.

Pegu.
By Lieut. W. F. B. Laurie.
Post 8vo. Price 14s. cloth.

The Theory of Caste.
By B. A. Irving, Esq.
8vo. Price 5s. cloth.

Indian Exchange Tables.
By J. H. Roberts.
8vo. Second Edition, enlarged.
Price 10s. 6d. cloth.

The Turkish Interpreter:
A Grammar of the Turkish Language.
By Major Boyd.
8vo. Price 12s.

Indian Commercial Tables.
By James Bridgnell.
Royal 8vo. Price 21s., half-bound.

NAVAL AND MILITARY.

Gunnery in 1858:

A Treatise on Rifles, Cannon, and Sporting Arms.

By William Greener,
Author of "The Gun."

Demy 8vo, with Illustrations.
Price 14s. cloth.

"A very comprehensive work. Those who peruse it will know almost all, if not all, that books can teach them of guns and gunnery."—*Naval and Military Gazette.*

"The most interesting work of the kind that has come under our notice."—*Saturday Review.*

"We can confidently recommend this book of Gunnery, not only to the professional student, but also to the sportsman."—*Naval and Military Herald.*

"Mr. Greener's treatise is suggestive, ample, and elaborate, and deals with the entire subject systematically."—*Athenæum.*

"A work of great practical value, which bids fair to stand, for many years to come, the chief practical authority on the subject."—*Military Spectator.*

"An acceptable contribution to professional literature, written in a popular style."—*United Service Magazine.*

Russo-Turkish Campaigns of 1828–9.

By Colonel Chesney,
R.A., D.C.L., F.R.S.

Third Edition. Post 8vo, with Maps.
Price 12s. cloth.

"The only work on the subject suited to the military reader."—*United Service Gazette.*

"In a strategic point of view this work is very valuable."—*New Quarterly.*

The Native Army of India.

By Brigadier-General Jacob, C.B.
8vo. Price 2s. 6d.

The Militiaman.

With Two Etchings, by JOHN LEECH.
Post 8vo. Price 9s. cloth.

"Very amusing, and conveying an impression of faithfulness."—*National Review.*

"A very lively, entertaining companion."—*Critic.*

"The author is humorous without being wilfully smart, sarcastic without bitterness, and shrewd without parading his knowledge and power of observation."—*Express.*

"Quietly, but humorously, written."—*Athenæum.*

Military Forces and Institutions of Great Britain.

By H. Byerly Thompson.
8vo. Price 5s. cloth.

"A well-arranged and carefully digested compilation, giving a clear insight into the economy of the army, and the working of our military system."—*Spectator.*

Sea Officer's Manual.

By Captain Alfred Parish.
Second Edition. Small post 8vo.
Price 5s. cloth.

"A very lucid and compendious manual. We would recommend youths intent upon a seafaring life to study it."—*Athenæum.*

"A little book that ought to be in great request among young seamen."—*Examiner.*

LEGAL.

Handbook of British Maritime Law.
By Morice.
8vo. Price 5s. cloth.

Commercial Law of the World.
By Leone Levi.
Two vols. royal 4to. Price 6l. cloth.

Land Tax of India.
According to the Moohummudan Law.
By N. B. E. Baillie, Esq.
8vo. Price 6s. cloth.

Moohummudan Law of Sale.

By N. B. E. Baillie, Esq.
8vo. Price 14s. cloth.

Moohummudan Law of Inheritance.

By N. B. E. Baillie, Esq.
8vo. Price 8s. cloth.

ILLUSTRATED SCIENTIFIC WORKS.

Results of Astronomical Observations
Made at the Cape of Good Hope.
By Sir John Herschel.
4to, with Plates. Price 4*l.* 4*s.* cloth.

Geological Observations
On Coral Reefs, Volcanic Islands, and on South America.
By Charles Darwin, Esq.
With Maps, Plates and Woodcuts.
Price 10*s.* 6*d.* cloth.

Zoology of South Africa.
By Dr. Andrew Smith.
Royal 4to, cloth, with Coloured Plates.

MAMMALIA	£8
AVES	7
REPTILIA	5
PISCES	£2
INVERTEBRATÆ	1

THE Botany of the Himalaya.
By Dr. Forbes Royle.
Two vols. roy. 4to, cloth, with Coloured Plates. Reduced to 5*l.* 5*s.*

MEDICAL.

The Vital Statistics
Of the European and Native Armies in India.
By Joseph Ewart, M.D
Bengal Medical Service.
Demy 8vo. Price 9*s.* cloth.

"A valuable work, in which Dr. Ewart, with equal industry and skill, has compressed the essence and import of an immense mass of details."—*Spectator.*

"One main object of this most valuable volume is to point out the causes which render the Indian climate so fatal to European troops."—*Critic.*

On Disorders of the Blood.
Translated by Chunder Coomal Dey.
8vo. Price 7*s.* 6*d.* cloth.

On the Treatment of the Insane.
By John Conolly, M.D.
Demy 8vo. Price 14*s.* cloth.

"Dr. Conolly has embodied in this work his experiences of the new system of treating patients at Hanwell Asylum."—*Economist.*

"We most earnestly commend Dr. Conolly's treatise to all who are interested in the subject."—*Westminster Review.*

On Abscess in the Liver.
By E. J. Waring, M.D.
8vo. Price 3*s.* 6*d.*

Manual of Therapeutics.
By E. J. Waring, M.D.
Fcap 8vo. Price 12*s.* 6*d.* cloth.

FICTION.

Cousin Stella ;
Or, Conflict.
By the Author of " Violet Bank."
Three volumes.

"An excellent novel, written with great care; the interest is well sustained to the end, and the characters are all life-like. It is an extremely well-written and well-conceived story, with quiet power and precision of touch, with freshness of interest and great merit."—*Athenæum.*

"'Cousin Stella' has the merit, now becoming rarer and rarer, of a comparative novelty in its subject; the interest of which will secure for this novel a fair share of popularity."—*Saturday Review.*

Confidences.
By the Author of " Rita."

"This new novel, by the author of 'Rita,' displays the same combination of ease and power in the delineation of character, the same life-like dialogue, and the same faculty of constructing an interesting story."—*Spectator.*

"Decidedly both good and interesting. The book has a fresh and pleasant air about it: it is written in an excellent tone, and there are touches of pathos here and there which we must rank with a higher style of composition than that usually attained in works of this class."—*New Quarterly Review.*

FICTION—*continued.*

Phantastes:
A Faerie Romance for Men and Women.
By George Macdonald.
Post 8vo. Price 10s. 6d. cloth.

The Cousins' Courtship.
By John R. Wise.
Two vols.

"The 'Cousins' Courtship' is a kind of prose idyll, in which an earnest, pure, simple love is developed without any hysterical romance. To a decided talent for satirical illustration and comment, Mr. Wise unites a nice observation, delicate reflections, and a sympathy for what is beautiful. Its cleverness, its genial tone, its playful satire, its scholarly yet perfectly easy and natural language, with its vivid portraiture of scenery, entitle the 'Cousins' Courtship' to a grateful recognition."—*Spectator.*

"We are well pleased with Mr. Wise's novel. Those who begin to read the 'Cousin's Courtship' will finish it. We rarely meet with one possessed of so many good qualities."—*Morning Post.*

"A very clever novel: it possesses some excellent qualities. The merits of the book are great. It is thoroughly true: we take it, indeed, that it is a collection of personal experiences. Mr. Wise can fairly lay claim to the merit of vivid and powerful description of what he has seen."—*Morning Herald.*

The Fool of Quality.
By Henry Brooke.
New and Revised Edition, with Biographical Preface by the Rev. CHAS. KINGSLEY, Rector of Eversley.
Two vols., post 8vo, with Portrait of the Author, price 21s.

"If the 'Fool of Quality' be perused with reference to the period at which it was written, as well as from its author's point of view, and if it be considered as the earnest, heartfelt production of an accomplished gentleman and a sincere philanthropist, whose life was devoted to efforts to do good, its excellences, which are many, will be admitted."—*Illustrated London News.*

Trust for Trust.
By A. J. Barrowcliffe,
Author of "Amberhill."
Three volumes.

"It is seldom we find, even in this great age of novel writing, so much that is pleasant and so little to object to as in 'Trust for Trust.' It contains much original thought and fresh humour."—*Leader.*

Ellen Raymond;
Or, Ups and Downs.
By Mrs. Vidal,
Author of "Tales for the Bush," &c.
Three volumes.

"The characters are good, the style pure, correct, brisk, and easy."—*Press.*
"This novel will find a great many admirers."—*Leader.*

THE
Dennes of Daundelyonn.
By Mrs. Charles J. Proby.
Three volumes.

"This is a novel of more than average merit. There is considerable knowledge of character, power of description, and quiet social satire, exhibited in its pages."—*Press.*

"'The Dennes of Daundelyonn' is a very readable book, and will be immensely popular. . . . It has many beauties which deservedly recommend it to the novel reader."—*Critic.*

The Two Homes.
By the Author of "The Heir of Vallis."
Three volumes.

"There is a great deal that is very good in this book—a great deal of good feeling and excellent design. . . . There are some good pictures of Madeira, and of life and society there; and there are evidences of much painstaking and talent."—*Athenæum.*

"'The Two Homes' is a very clever novel. . . . Madeira furnishes Mr. Mathews with a fertile theme for his descriptive powers. The dialogue is good: the characters all speak and act consistently with their natures."—*Leader.*

The Moors and the Fens.
By F. G. Trafford.
Three volumes.

"This novel stands out much in the same way that 'Jane Eyre' did. . . . The characters are drawn by a mind which can realize fictitious characters with minute intensity."—*Saturday Review.*

"It is seldom that a first fiction is entitled to such applause as is 'The Moors and the Fens,' and we shall look anxiously for the writer's next essay."—*Critic.*

Lost and Won.
By Georgiana M. Craik,
Author of "Riverston."
One volume. Second Edition.

"Nothing superior to this novel has appeared during the present season."—*Leader.*

"Miss Craik's new story is a good one and in point of ability above the average of ladies' novels."—*Daily News.*

"The language is good, the narrative spirited, the characters are fairly delineated, and the dialogue has considerable dramatic force."—*Saturday Review.*

"This is an improvement on Miss Craik's first work. The story is more compact and more interesting."—*Athenæum.*

An Old Debt.
By Florence Dawson.
Two volumes.

"A powerfully written novel; one of the best which has recently proceeded from a female hand. . . . The dialogue is vigorous and spirited."—*Morning Post.*

"There is an energy and vitality about this work which distinguish it from the common head of novels. Its terse vigour sometimes recals Miss Brontë, but in some respects Miss Florence Dawson is decidedly superior to the author of 'Jane Eyre.'"—*Saturday Review.*

FICTION—*continued.*

My Lady.
A Tale of Modern Life.
Two volumes.

"'My Lady' is a fine specimen of an English matron, exhibiting that union of strength and gentleness, of common sense and romance, of energy and grace, which nearly approaches our ideal of womanhood."—*Press.*

"'My Lady' evinces charming feeling and delicacy of touch. It is a novel that will be read with interest."—*Athenæum.*

"The story is told throughout with great strength of feeling, is well written, and has a plot which is by no means common-place."—*Examiner.*

"There is some force and a good deal of freshness in 'My Lady.' The characters are distinctly drawn, and often wear an appearance of individuality, or almost personality. The execution is fresh and powerful."—*Spectator.*

"It is not in every novel we can light upon a style so vigorously graceful—upon an intelligence so refined without littleness, so tenderly truthful, which has sensibility rather than poetry; but which is also most subtly and searchingly powerful."—*Dublin University Magazine.*

Gaston Bligh.
By L. S. Lavenu,
Author of "Erlesmere."
Two volumes.

"The story is told with great power; the whole book sparkles with *esprit;* and the characters talk like gentlemen and ladies. It is very enjoyable reading."—*Press.*

"'Gaston Bligh' is a good story, admirably told, full of stirring incident, sustaining to the close the interest of a very ingenious plot, and abounding in clever sketches of character. It sparkles with wit, and will reward perusal."—*Critic.*

Sylvan Holt's Daughter.
By Holme Lee,
Author of "Kathie Brande," &c.
Second Edition. 3 vols.

"The well-established reputation of Holme Lee, as a novel writer, will receive an additional glory from the publication of 'Sylvan Holt's Daughter.' It is a charming tale of country life and character."—*Globe.*

"There is much that is attractive in 'Sylvan Holt's Daughter,' much that is graceful and refined, much that is fresh, healthy, and natural."—*Press.*

"The conception of the story has a good deal of originality, and the characters avoid commonplace types, without being unnatural or improbable. The heroine herself is charming. It is a novel in which there is much to interest and please."—*New Quarterly Review.*

"A novel that is well worth reading, and which possesses the cardinal virtue of being extremely interesting."—*Athenæum.*

"A really sound, good book, highly finished, true to nature, vigorous, passionate, honest, and sincere."—*Dublin University Magazine.*

Eva Desmond;
Or, Mutation.
Three volumes.

"A more beautiful creation than Eva it would be difficult to imagine. The novel is undoubtedly full of interest."—*Morning Post.*

"There is power, pathos, and originality in conception and catastrophe."—*Leader.*

The Professor.
By Currer Bell.
Two volumes.

"We think the author's friends have shown sound judgment in publishing the 'Professor,' now that she is gone. . . . It shows the first germs of conception, which afterwards expanded and ripened into the great creations of her imagination. At the same time her advisers were equally right when they counselled her not to publish it in her lifetime. . . . But it abounds in merits."—*Saturday Review.*

"Anything which throws light upon the growth and composition of such a mind cannot be otherwise than interesting. In the 'Professor' we may discover the germs of many trains of thinking, which afterwards came to be enlarged and illustrated in subsequent and more perfect works."—*Critic.*

Below the Surface.
Three volumes.

"The book is unquestionably clever and entertaining. The writer develops from first to last his double view of human life, as coloured by the manners of our age. . . . It is a tale superior to ordinary novels, in its practical application to the phases of actual life."—*Athenæum.*

"There is a great deal of cleverness in this story; a much greater knowledge of country life and character in its various aspects and conditions than is possessed by nine-tenths of the novelists who undertake to describe it."—*Spectator.*

The Three Chances.
By the Author of "The Fair Carew."
Three volumes.

"Some of the characters and romantic situations are strongly marked and peculiarly original. . . . It is the great merit of the authoress that the personages of her tale are human and real."—*Leader.*

"This novel is of a more solid texture than most of its contemporaries. It is full of good sense, good thought, and good writing."—*Statesman.*

The Cruellest Wrong of All.
By the Author of "Margaret; or, Prejudice at Home."
One volume.

"The author has a pathetic vein, and there is a tender sweetness in the tone of her narration."—*Leader.*

"It has the first requisite of a work meant to amuse: it is amusing."—*Globe.*

Kathie Brande.
A Fireside History of a Quiet Life.
By Holme Lee.
Two volumes.

"'Kathie Brande' is not merely a very interesting novel—it is a very wholesome one, for it teaches virtue by example."—*Critic.*

"Throughout 'Kathie Brande' there is much sweetness, and considerable power of description."—*Saturday Review.*

"'Kathie Brande' is intended to illustrate the paramount excellence of duty as a moving principle. It is full of beauties."—*Daily News.*

FICTION—*continued.*

The Noble Traytour:
A Chronicle.
Three volumes.

"The story is told with a graphic and graceful pen, and the chronicler has produced a romance not only of great value in a historical point of view, but possessing many claims upon the attention of the scholar, the antiquary, and the general reader."—*Post.*

"An Elizabethan masquerade. Shakespeare, the Queen, Essex, Raleigh, and a hundred nobles, ladies and knights of the land, appear on the stage. The author has imbued himself with the spirit of the times."—*Leader.*

Riverston.
By *Georgiana M. Craik.*
Three volumes.

"Miss Craik is a very lively writer: she has wit, and she has sense, and she has made in the beautiful young governess, with her strong will, saucy independence, and promptness of repartee, an interesting picture."—*Press.*

Perversion;
Or, the Causes and Consequences of Infidelity.
By the late Rev. *W. J. Conybeare.*
Three volumes.

"This story has a touching interest, which lingers with the reader after he has closed the book."—*Athenæum.*

Maud Skillicorne's Penance.
By *Mary C. Jackson,*
Author of "The Story of my Wardship."
Two volumes.

"The style is natural, and displays considerable dramatic power."—*Critic.*

"It is a well concocted tale, and will be very palatable to novel readers."—*Morning Post.*

The Roua Pass.
By *Erick Mackenzie.*
Three volumes.

"It is seldom that we have to notice so good a novel as the 'Roua Pass.' The story is well contrived and well told; the incidents are natural and varied; several of the characters are skilfully drawn, and that of the heroine is fresh, powerful, and original. The Highland scenery, in which the plot is laid, is described with truth and feeling —with a command of language which leaves a vivid impression."—*Saturday Review.*

The White House by the Sea:
A Love Story.
By *M. Betham-Edwards.*
Two volumes.

"A tale of English domestic life. The writing is very good, graceful, and unaffected; it pleases without startling. In the dialogue, people do not harangue, but talk, and talk naturally."—*Critic.*

Extremes.
By *Miss E. W. Atkinson,*
Author of "Memoirs of the Queens of Prussia."
Two volumes.

"A nervous and vigorous style, an elaborate delineation of character under many varieties, spirited and well-sustained dialogue, and a carefully-constructed plot; if these have any charms for our readers, they will not forget the swiftly gliding hours passed in perusing 'Extremes.'"—*Morning Post.*

Farina:
A Legend of Cologne.
By *George Meredith.*
One volume.

"A masque of ravishers in steel, of robber knights, of water-women, more ravishing than lovely. It has also a brave and tender deliverer, and a heroine proper for a romance of Cologne. Those who love a real, lively, audacious piece of extravagance, by way of a change, will enjoy 'Farina.'"—*Athenæum.*

Friends of Bohemia;
Or, Phases of London Life.
By *E. M. Whitty,*
Author of "The Governing Classes."
Two volumes.

"Mr. Whitty is a genuine satirist, employing satire for a genuine purpose. You laugh with him very much; but the laughter is fruity and ripe in thought. His style is serious, and his cast of mind severe. The author has a merriment akin to that of Jaques and that of Timon."—*Athenæum.*

The Eve of St. Mark.
A Romance of Venice.
By *Thomas Doubleday.*
Two volumes.

"'The Eve of St. Mark' is not only well written, but adroitly constructed, and interesting. Its tone is perhaps too gorgeous; its movement is too much that of a masquerade; but a mystery is created, and a very loveable heroine is pourtrayed."—*Athenæum.*

Stories and Sketches.
By *James Payn.*
Post 8vo. Price 2s. 6d. cloth.

"Mr. Payn is gay, spirited, observant, and shows no little knowledge of men and books."—*Leader.*

Undine.
From the German of "De La Motte Fouqué."
Price 1s. 6d.

The Rectory of Valehead.
By the Rev. *R. W. Evans.*
Fcap, cloth. Price 3s.

Cheap Series of Popular Works.

Life of Charlotte Brontë
(Currer Bell),
Author of "Jane Eyre," &c.
By Mrs. Gaskell.
Price 2s. 6d.

"We regard this record as a monument of courage and endurance, of suffering and triumph . . . . . All the secrets of the literary workmanship of the authoress of 'Jane Eyre' are unfolded in the course of this extraordinary narrative."—*Times.*

"Mrs. Gaskell has done her work well. Her narrative is simple, direct, intelligible, unaffected. She dwells on her friend's character with womanly tact, thorough understanding, and delicate sisterly tenderness. Many parts of the book cannot be read without deep, even painful emotion; still it is a life always womanly."—*Fraser's Magazine.*

Lectures on the English Humourists
Of the Eighteenth Century.
By W. M. Thackeray,
Author of "Vanity Fair," "Esmond," "The Virginians," &c.
Price 2s. 6d. cloth.

"What fine things these lectures contain; what eloquent and subtle sayings; what wise and earnest writing; how delightful are their turns of humour; with what a touching effect in the graver passages the genuine feeling of the man comes out, and how vividly the thoughts are *painted*, as it were, in graphic and characteristic words."—*Examiner.*

"This is to us by far the most acceptable of Mr. Thackeray's writings. His graphic style, his philosophical spirit, his analytical powers, his large heartedness, his shrewdness, and his gentleness, have all room to exhibit themselves."—*Economist.*

British India.
By Harriet Martineau.
Price 2s. 6d. cloth.

"Lucid, glowing, and instructive essays."—*Economist.*

"A good compendium of a great subject."—*National Review.*

"As a handbook to the history of India it is the best that has yet appeared."—*Morning Herald.*

The Town.
By Leigh Hunt.
With Forty-five Engravings.
Price 2s. 6d. cloth.

"We will allow no higher enjoyment for a rational Englishman than to stroll leisurely through this marvellous town, arm in arm with Mr. Leigh Hunt. The charm of Mr. Hunt's book is, that he gives us the outpourings of a mind enriched with the most agreeable knowledge: there is not one page which does not glow with interest. It is a series of pictures from the life, representing scenes in which every inhabitant of the metropolis has an interest."—*Times.*

Jane Eyre.
By Currer Bell.
Price 2s. 6d. cloth.

"'Jane Eyre' is a remarkable production. Freshness and originality, truth and passion, singular felicity in the description of natural scenery and in the analyzation of human thought, enable this tale to stand boldly out from the mass, and to assume its own place in the bright field of romantic literature."—*Times.*

"'Jane Eyre' is a book of decided power. The thoughts are true, sound, and original; and the style is resolute, straightforward, and to the purpose. The object and moral of the work are excellent."—*Examiner.*

Shirley.
By Currer Bell.
Price 2s. 6d. cloth.

"'Shirley' is the anatomy of the female heart. It is a book which indicates exquisite feeling, and very great power of mind in the writer. The women are all divine."—*Daily News.*

"'Shirley' is very clever. It could not be otherwise. The faculty of graphic description, strong imagination, fervid and masculine diction, analytic skill, all are visible. . . . Gems of rare thought and glorious passion shine here and there."—*Times.*

Villette.
By Currer Bell.
Price 2s. 6d. cloth.

"'Villette' is a most remarkable work—a production altogether *sui generis*. Fulness and vigour of thought mark almost every sentence, and there is a sort of easy power pervading the whole narrative such as we have rarely met."—*Edinburgh Review.*

"The tale is one of the affections, and remarkable as a picture of manners. A burning heart glows throughout it, and one brilliantly distinct character keeps it alive."—*Athenæum.*

Political Economy of Art.
By John Ruskin, M.A.
Price 2s. 6d. cloth.

"A most able, eloquent, and well-timed work. We hail it with satisfaction, thinking it calculated to do much practical good, and we cordially recommend it to our readers."—*Witness.*

"Mr. Ruskin's chief purpose is to treat the artist's power, and the art itself, as items of the world's wealth, and to show how these may be best evolved, produced, accumulated, and distributed."—*Athenæum.*

Italian Campaigns of General Bonaparte.
By George Hooper.
With a Map. Price 2s. 6d. cloth.

"The story of Bonaparte's campaigns in Italy is told at once firmly, lightly, and pleasantly. The latest and best authorities, the Bonaparte correspondence in particular, appear to have been carefully and intelligently consulted. The result is a very readable and useful volume."—*Athenæum.*

Cheap Series—*continued.*

Wuthering Heights and Agnes Grey.
By Ellis and Acton Bell.
With Memoir by CURRER BELL.
Price 2*s.* 6*d.* cloth.

"There are passages in this book of 'Wuthering Heights' of which any novelist, past or present, might be proud. It has been said of Shakespeare that he drew cases which the physician might study; Ellis Bell has done no less."—*Palladium.*

"There is, at all events, keeping in the book the groups of figures and the scenery are in harmony with each other. There is a touch of Salvator Rosa in all."—*Atlas.*

A Lost Love.
By Ashford Owen.
Price 2*s.* cloth.

"'A Lost Love' is a story full of grace and genius. No outline of the story would give any idea of its beauty."—*Athenæum.*

"A tale at once moving and winning, natural and romantic, and certain to raise all the finer sympathies of the reader's nature."—*Press.*

Deerbrook.
By Harriet Martineau.
Price 2*s.* 6*d.* cloth.

"This popular fiction presents a true and animated picture of country life among the upper middle classes of English residents, and is remarkable for its interest, arising from the influence of various characters upon each other, and the effect of ordinary circumstances upon them. The descriptions of rural scenery, and the daily pursuits in village hours, are among the most charming of the author's writings; but the way in which exciting incidents gradually arise out of the most ordinary phases of life, and the skill with which natural and every-day characters are brought out in dramatic situations, attest the power of the author's genius."

Tales of the Colonies.
By Charles Rowcroft.
Price 2*s.* 6*d.* cloth.

"'Tales of the Colonies' is an able and interesting book. The author has the first great requisite in fiction—a knowledge of the life he undertakes to describe; and his matter is solid and real."—*Spectator.*

"It combines the fidelity of truth with the spirit of a romance, and has altogether much of De Foe in its character and composition."—*Literary Gazette.*

Romantic Tales
(Including "Avillion")
By the Author of "John Halifax, Gentleman."
A New Edition.   Price 2*s.* 6*d.* cloth.

"'Avillion' is a beautiful and fanciful story, and the rest make very agreeable reading. There is not one of them unquickened by true feeling, exquisite taste, and a pure and vivid imagination."—*Examiner.*

"In a nice knowledge of the refinements of the female heart, and in a happy power of depicting emotion, the authoress is excelled by very few story tellers of the day."—*Globe.*

Domestic Stories.
By the Author of "John Halifax, Gentleman."
Price 2*s.* 6*d.* cloth.

"In a nice knowledge of the refinements of the female heart and in a happy power of depicting emotion, the authoress is excelled by very few story-tellers of the day."—*Globe.*

"There is not one of them unquickened by true feeling, exquisite taste, and a pure and vivid imagination."—*Examiner.*

After Dark.
By Wilkie Collins.
Price 2*s.* 6*d.* cloth.

"Mr. Wilkie Collins stands in the foremost rank of our younger writers of fiction. He tells a story well and forcibly, his style is eloquent and picturesque; he has considerable powers of pathos; understands the art of construction; is never wearisome or wordy, and has a keen insight into character."—*Daily News.*

"'After Dark' abounds with genuine touches of nature."—*British Quarterly.*

Paul Ferroll.
Fourth Edition.   Price 2*s.* cloth.

"We have seldom read so wonderful a romance. We can find no fault in it as a work of art. It leaves us in admiration, almost in awe, of the powers of its author."—*New Quarterly.*

"The art displayed in presenting Paul Ferroll throughout the story is beyond all praise."—*Examiner.*

School for Fathers.
By Talbot Gwynne.
Price 2*s.* cloth.

"'The School for Fathers' is one of the cleverest, most brilliant, genial, and instructive stories that we have read since the publication of 'Jane Eyre.'"—*Eclectic Review.*

"The pleasantest tale we have read for many a day. It is a story of the *Tatler* and *Spectator* days, and is very fitly associated with that time of good English literature by its manly feeling, direct, unaffected manner of writing, and nicely-managed, well-turned narrative. The descriptions are excellent; some of the country painting is as fresh as a landscape by Alfred Constable, or an idyl by Tennyson."—*Examiner.*

The Tenant of Wildfell Hall.
By Acton Bell.

Just ready,
Kathie Brande:
The Fireside History of a Quiet Life.
By Holme Lee,
Author of "Sylvan Holt's Daughter."

Below the Surface.
By Sir A. H. Elton, Bart., M.P.

Juvenile and Educational.

NEW BOOKS FOR YOUNG READERS.

The Parents' Cabinet

Of Amusement and Instruction for Young Persons.

New Edition, carefully revised, in Twelve Shilling Volumes, each complete in itself, and containing a full page Illustration in Oil Colours, with Wood Engravings, in ornamented boards.

CONTENTS.

AMUSING STORIES, all tending to the development of good qualities, and the avoidance of faults.
BIOGRAPHICAL ACCOUNTS OF REMARKABLE CHARACTERS, interesting to Young People.
SIMPLE NARRATIVES OF HISTORICAL EVENTS, suited to the capacity of children.
ELUCIDATIONS OF NATURAL HISTORY, adapted to encourage habits of observation.
FAMILIAR EXPLANATIONS OF NOTABLE SCIENTIFIC DISCOVERIES AND MECHANICAL INVENTIONS.
LIVELY ACCOUNTS OF THE GEOGRAPHY, INHABITANTS, AND PRODUCTIONS OF DIFFERENT COUNTRIES.

MISS EDGEWORTH'S *Opinion of the* PARENTS' CABINET:—

"I almost feel afraid of praising it as much as I think it deserves. . . . There is so much variety in the book that it cannot tire. It alternately excites and relieves attention, and does not lead to the bad habit of frittering away the mind by requiring no exertion from the reader. . . . Whoever your scientific associate is, he understands his business and children's capabilities right well. . . . Without lecturing, or prosing, you keep the right and the wrong clearly marked, and hence all the sympathy of the young people is always enlisted on the right side."

*** The work is now complete in 4 vols. extra cloth, gilt edges, at 3s. 6d. each; or in 6 vols. extra cloth, gilt edges, 2s. 6d. each.

By the Author of "Round the Fire," &c.

Unica:

A Story for a Sunday Afternoon.

With Four Illustrations. 2s. 6d. cloth.
"This tale, like its author's former ones, will find favour in the nursery."—*Athenæum.*
"The character of Unica is charmingly conceived, and the story pleasantly told."—*Spectator.*

II.

Old Gingerbread and the Schoolboys.

With Four Coloured Plates. 2s. 6d. cl.
"'Old Gingerbread and the School-boys' is delightful, and the drawing and colouring of the pictorial part done with spirit and correctness."—*Press.*
"This tale is very good, the descriptions being natural, with a feeling of country freshness."—*Spectator.*

III.

Willie's Birthday:

Showing how a Little Boy did what he Liked, and how he Enjoyed it.

With Four Illustrations. 2s. cloth.

IV.

Willie's Rest:

A Sunday Story.

With Four Illustrations. 2s. cloth.
"Extremely well written story books, amusing and moral, and got up in a very handsome style."—*Morning Herald.*

V.

Uncle Jack, the Fault Killer.

With Four Illustrations. 2s. 6d. cloth.

VI.

Round the Fire:

Six Stories for Young Readers.

Square 16mo, with Four Illustrations. Price 2s. 6d. cloth.
"Simple and very interesting."—*National Review.*
"True children's stories."—*Athenæum.*

The King of the Golden River;

Or, the Black Brothers.

By *John Ruskin, M.A.*

Third Edition, with 22 Illustrations by Richard Doyle. Price 2s. 6d.
"This little fancy tale is by a master-hand. The story has a charming moral."—*Examiner.*

Investigation;

Or, Travels in the Boudoir.

By *Miss Halsted.*

Fcap cloth. Price 3s. 6d.

Rhymes for Little Ones.

With 16 Illustrations. 1s. 6d. cloth.

Juvenile and Educational—*continued*.

Stories from the Parlour Printing Press.

By the Authors of the "Parent's Cabinet."

Fcap 8vo. Price 2s. cloth.

Religion in Common Life.

By William Ellis.

Post 8vo. **Price 7s. 6d.** cloth.

"A book addressed to young people of the upper ten thousand upon social duties."—*Examiner*.

"Lessons in Political Economy for young people by a skilful hand."—*Economist*.

Books for the Blind.

Printed in raised Roman letters, at the Glasgow Asylum.

A List of the books, with their prices, may be had on application.

Little Derwent's Breakfast.

Price 2s. cloth.

Juvenile Miscellany.

Six Engravings. Price 2s. 6d. cloth.

Elementary Works on Social Economy.

By William Ellis.

Uniform in foolscap 8vo, half-bound.

I.—OUTLINES OF SOCIAL ECONOMY. 1s. 6d.
II.—PROGRESSIVE LESSONS IN SOCIAL SCIENCE.
III.—INTRODUCTION TO THE SOCIAL SCIENCES. 2s.
IV.—OUTLINES OF THE UNDERSTANDING. 2s.
V.—WHAT AM I? WHERE AM I? WHAT OUGHT I TO DO? &c. 1s. sewed.

. These works are recommended by the Committee of Council on Education.

Poetry.

Homely Ballads

For the Working Man's Fireside.

By Mary Sewell.

Ninth Thousand. Post 8vo, cloth, 1s.

"Very good verses conveying very useful lessons."—*Literary Gazette*.

"Simple poems, well suited to the taste of the classes for whom they are written."—*Globe*.

"There is a real homely flavour about them, and they contain sound and wholesome lessons."—*Critic*.

Wit and Humour.

By Leigh Hunt.

Price 5s. cloth.

Jar of Honey from Hybla.

By Leigh Hunt.

Price 5s. cloth.

Sketches from Dover Castle, and other Poems.

By Lieut.-Col. William Read.

Crown 8vo. Price 7s. 6d. cloth.

"Elegant and graceful, and distinguished by a tone of sentiment, which renders Colonel Read's volume very pleasant reading for a leisure hour."—*Daily News*.

"It is not often that the heroic couplet is in these days so gracefully written. Colonel Read is to be congratulated on his success in bending this Ulyssean bow. His little volume contains some very fine lyrics."—*Leader*.

Ionica.

Fcap 8vo. Price 4s. cloth.

"The themes, mostly classical, are grappled with boldness, and toned with a lively imagination. The style is rich and firm, and cannot be said to be an imitation of any known author. We cordially recommend it to **our** readers as a book of real poetry."—*Critic*.

The Six Legends of King Goldenstar.

By the late Anna Bradstreet.

Fcap 8vo. Price 5s.

"The author evinces more than ordinary power, a vivid imagination, guided by a mind of lofty aim."—*Globe*.

"The poetry is tasteful, and above the average."—*National Review*.

"This is a posthumous poem by an unknown authoress, of higher scope and more finish than the crowd of poems which come before us. The fancy throughout the poem is quick and light, and musical."—*Athenæum*.

National Songs and Legends of Roumania.

Translated by E. C. Grenville Murray, Esq.

With Music, crown 8vo. Price 2s. 6d.

Poems of Past Years.

By Sir A. H. Elton, Bart., M.P.

Fcap 8vo. Price 3s. cloth.

"A refined, scholarly, and gentlemanly mind is apparent all through this volume."—*Leader*.

Poetry—continued.

A Man's Heart: a Poem.

By Dr. Charles Mackay.
Author of "Life and Liberty in
America."
Post 8vo.   Price 5s. cloth.

Magdalene: a Poem.

Fcap 8vo.   Price 1s.

"Rarely have we been more deeply touched than in reading this wonderful little book. There is nothing more sweet, more touching in the English language than this exquisite poem."—*Morning Herald.*

Poems.

By Ada Trevanion.
Price 5s. cloth.

"There really is a value in such poems as those of Ada Trevanion. Perhaps nowhere can we point to a more satisfactory fruit of Christian civilization than in a volume like this."—*Saturday Review.*

Poems.

By Henry Cecil.
Price 5s. cloth.

"If Mr. Cecil does not make his name famous, it is not that he does not deserve to do so."—*Critic.*
"There is an unmistakeable stamp of genuine poetry in most of these pages."—*Economist.*

England in Time of War.

By Sydney Dobell,
Author of "Balder," "The Roman," &c.
Crown 8vo.   Price 5s. cloth.

"That Mr. Dobell is a poet, 'England in time of War' bears witness."—*Athenæum.*

The Cruel Sister,

And other Poems.
Fcap 8vo.   Price 4s. cloth.

"There are traces of power, and the versification displays freedom and skill."—*Guardian.*

Balder.

By Sydney Dobell.
Crown 8vo.   Price 7s. 6d. cloth.

Poems.

By Mary Maynard

Stilicho: a Tragedy.

By George Mallam.
Fcap 8vo.

Poems.

By Mrs. Frank P. Fellows.
Fcap 8vo.   Price 3s. cloth.

"There is easy simplicity in the diction, and elegant naturalness in the thought."—*Spectator.*

Poetry from Life.

By C. M. K.
Fcap 8vo, cloth gilt.   Price 5s.

"Elegant verses. The author has a pleasing fancy and a refined mind."—*Economist.*

Poems.

By Walter R. Cassels.
Fcap 8vo.   Price 3s. 6d. cloth.

"Mr. Cassels has deep poetical feeling, and gives promise of real excellence. His poems are written sometimes with a strength of expression by no means common."—*Guardian.*

Garlands of Verse.

By Thomas Leigh.
Price 5s. cloth.

"One of the best things in the 'Garlands of Verse' is an Ode to Toil. There, as elsewhere, there is excellent feeling."—*Examiner.*

Poems.

By Currer, Ellis, and Acton Bell.
Price 4s. cloth.

Select Odes of Horace.

In English Lyrics.
By J. T. Black.
Fcap 8vo.   Price 4s. cloth.

"Rendered into English Lyrics with a vigour and heartiness rarely, if ever, surpassed."—*Critic.*

Rhymes and Recollections

Of a Hand-Loom Weaver.
By William Thom.
With a Memoir.   Post 8vo, cloth, 3s.